I0713299

WALTER'S WONDERFUL WANDERINGS

Written by Ans Stausebach

Dedication

To all animals, large and small..

And to the people who love and help them all.

Ans Stausebach

Chapter I

The night cannot hold on much longer. Already some light is breaking in the eastern sky. Walter sits near the river, his back against an old willow tree.

He has been here for more than an hour, waiting, wanting the new day to begin. He is excited and also, scared about what he has done. Slipping away so early this morning, from the farm where he grew up. This farm, where nobody cared for him, ever! Never a kind word and not enough food to eat. Working more than twelve hours a day. Sleeping in the barn with the animals, his only friends.

They comforted him when he was sad, and they were happy when he was. Nobody understood him better. Being always so close together, Walter understands them too. He does not even know that this is something very special. Something other people can't do. For him, it is the most natural thing in the world. It was very hard to say farewell to his friends, but it had to be done. He could not stay at the farm anymore. At fourteen years of age, his time to start a new life has come. If only he would not feel so alone now. Walter sighs a bit sadly. He reaches for his flute, knowing that the music will console him. It always does. How kind of Silas, the shepherd, to give this flute to him? They knew each other for a long time. Silas, a very silent man, talked through his music, bringing joy to everyone who heard him. Walter spent every free moment he could find around Silas. He saw him making flutes from the river reeds and tried to do the same. Only then did Silas start to pay attention to him. He corrected Walter where he went wrong and later even began teaching him to play. He got more and more involved when noticing how fast Walter learned.

"You do have a good feeling for music," Silas said. "Soon you will play better than I ever could."

His words prove true. Within a year, Walter was playing far better than his teacher.

Then Silas told him, "You have a very rare talent Walter, use it. One day, it may give you the chance to make a different life for yourself."

Those words set Walter thinking, and from then on, his plans to escape began. Later, Silas left to live with his brother in another

town. But before doing so, he gave Walter one of his own
beautifully made flutes. It is this flute that Walter now holds in his
hands. Bringing it to his mouth, he starts playing. How lovely
those first notes sound in the early morning air. Just then, the sun
peeps out from over the horizon. It is as if she wants to see who's
making such sweet music. Walter's mouth glides over the reeds of
the pan flute. First, the melody is a bit sad, for the friends he left
behind. For all the times they shared together and the knowing
that they may never meet again, From there, the flute begins to tell
the story of his life as an orphan. Dumped by strangers on a lonely
farm, brought up by a cruel farmer and his family, in terrible
poverty. But then, a new sound can be heard. A feeling of joy, of
being free and strong and the hope for a better future. Suddenly, a
most charming sound melts together with his.

"How wonderful," Walter thinks. Looking up, he sees a small
bird on a nearby tree branch, singing its heart out. "Can this be
true?" he asks himself, but he plays on, and together they make the
most beautiful music. Tune after tune Walter plays. The little bird
follows him in perfect harmony. Even the wind seems to sing
along with them, rustling through the reeds at the riverside. Silvery
shining fishes jump up from the water, to hear better. They appear
to be dancing for joy. Finally, Walter stops and so does the bird.
The two of them look at each other, filled with contentment.

"This was good," Walter remarks.

"Very good," the bird replies. Then she says, "I am Rita, the red
robin. What is your name?"

"I am Walter," he answers. Smiling at her, he asks, "Wouldn't it
be nice if we could always make music together?"

"Yes indeed," Rita chirps. "Let's do that."

"Oh, but I can't stay here," Walter says. "I am going to leave now."

"Can I come too?" the little bird asks.

"That would be great," Walter laughs. "But tell me," he goes on. "Don't you have a family? Surely, you can't just go without saying goodbye?"

"I am all on my own," Rita answers. "That is why I would love to come with you. Then I will never be lonely again."

"You must be an orphan like me," Walter says. "Well," he continues, "If that is so, let's waste no more time, let's just go." He flings the stick that holds his few belongings bundled onto it, over his shoulder, and they are on their way. A fourteen-year-old boy, with long curly black hair and a red robin, flying in front of him. They keep near the river's edge. That is where most of the trees grow, making it even more pleasant to be out and about. Such a nice day it has become. Sunny and warm, but not too warm. Just pleasant. Rita is enjoying it, as much as Walter does. She flies here, then there. Sometimes in circles overhead, or she sits and waits for Walter on a low-hanging tree branch. Now and again, she lands herself on one of his shoulders, chirping happily. Towards midday, they reach a little village. It lies at the bend of the river. 'A very quiet, little village,' Walter thinks. 'No people anywhere.' "Strange, is it not?" he remarks to Rita. "One would expect some people. Shall we go and look around a bit?"

"Yes," Rita answers. "Let's do that." The streets are empty. Nobody to be seen. Until they arrive at the village square. The whole square is filled with people. They all seem very worried. "What is the matter? What is going on?" Walter asks.

"Look for yourself," an old man answers him, pointing to the middle of the crowd.

"My, my," Walter utters in amazement. He sees an enormous man sitting there. "It is a giant," he says.

"He must be," Rita replies.

"Yes, he is," the old man confirms. "It is Barto. He lives on the one side of the mountain, over there. His brother Marto lives on the other."

"They are not bad guys really," somebody else chips in. "It is just, well, his boots are stolen and now, he is very cross."

"My, my," Walter says again. Yes, he can see, the giant is cross. His face looks angry. Even his feet look angry. The giant keeps staring at them. They are bare and huge and look sore, too. What strikes Walter as stranger still is the thick rope the giant holds in his hands. Or rather, who is on the end of that rope? It must be the Mayor of the village! One can see he is the Mayor, because of the heavy gold chain he wears around his neck. He looks cross as well and also totally embarrassed. To sit here, in front of all the village people. Really, it is an outrage. But, he is scared too. Everybody is. They shudder when the giant jerks the rope.

"My boots," his voice thunders over the square. "I want my boots."

"I don't understand it," Walter says. "How could his boots have been stolen and by who?"

"Nobody knows," the old man answers him. "Fact is, they are gone, and he wants them back. I must tell you," he adds, "That Marto and Barto visit each other every month. This month, it is Barto's turn to go and now, he can't. He walked barefoot from this side of the mountain, up to here. He hurt his feet doing so and now, he has taken our mayor prisoner out of revenge. He says he won't let him go. Not unless he gets his boots back."

"What colour are they?" Rita asks. As only Walter can understand her, he has to repeat the question. "They are red," comes the answer back. "Bright red and big, very big."

"I saw something red, lying in a deep hollow, near the river," Rita says. "What do you think, Walter? Could that be them?"

"Maybe," Walter answers. "Let's go and take a look." To the bystanders, he shouts. "My friend Rita, the red robin, might have seen the boots. Shall we go and find out?"

"Yes, yes," lots of people , want to. At once, things have changed. A let's-have-some-fun feeling takes hold over young and old, as they follow Walter a Rita, away from the square.

"My boots," Barto roars again. He jerks the rope so that the unhappy mayor on the other end nearly falls flat on his back.

"We will go and find your boots, Barto," some of the children cry out. "You will see."

"Good, good," the mayor mutters. "The sooner this is over, the better."

Barto says nothing anymore. He just stares at his sore feet again. Rita flies overhead, leading the way. Now and then, she comes and sits on Walter's shoulder. They talk together as one can plainly see, but nobody seems to find this strange. In a land with giants, many things are possible. They do not have all that far to go. Soon, the deep hollow, Rita noticed, is reached. And yes, a pair of colossal red boots lie there. Although they are covered with some bushes, one can still see them quite well. Some of the youngsters run down the sandy banks. In no time at all, the boots are recovered and carried up and away towards the village.

Such a happy mood, everybody is in now. The whole way back, there is laughter to be heard, along with singing and jokes about the size of those boots. Turns are made in carrying them, because they are very heavy. Of course, Walter and Rita are praised from all sides as the procession makes its way back towards the village.

"It was you, Rita," Walter compliments the little bird on his shoulder.

"Oh, it was nothing, I was just lucky to spot them," Rita chirps happily.

"No, you are a very alert little bird," Walter laughs. "Still, I wonder who took them," he adds after a while. Rita has no answer to this. But, there are some dwarfs living in the mountain holes. They know Barto and his brother Marto well. They are scared of them. Those monthly visits of the two brothers, when the one goes to see the other. It is a nightmare for them. Every time their big boots stride over the mountains, the earth shakes. The holes in which the dwarfs live get filled with sand and sometimes totally ruined. That is why the plan was made to take Barto's boots away. They would do it during the night, when he was asleep. Not that it had been easy, to carry the boots out of Barto's large cave. It took more than twelve dwarfs to move each one. Luckily, Barto was fast asleep when they came. Also, he snored terribly loud. He never even knew the dwarfs were in his cave, nor that they took a long time to remove the boots. First, they had to carry them away from where they were standing next to him. Then, down the moonlit mountain, they went. Towards the deep hollow, where no one would see them. Surely, no one could ever find them now. No, no one but Rita, that is. She is indeed a very clever and alert little bird, as Walter has noticed. Even now, flying to and fro, nothing escapes her sharp eyes. It is she who sees the little people hiding behind some rocks. Then she knows.

"It were the dwarfs," she cries out. "They did it."

"The dwarfs hid Barto's boots?" Walter asks.

"Yes," Rita answers. "I can see them. They are watching us from those rocks over there."

"What?" the people around them ask. "You think it were dwarfs?"

"But yes, of course," everybody agrees at once. "It must be them. Such little trouble makers. Can you believe it?" These and other remarks fly around.

"How could you?" one man shouts, waving a fist towards the rocks. "How could you cause so much trouble for our people?"

"Yeah," somebody else shouts, "Don't you ever do that again. It might become very unpleasant for you. Very unpleasant indeed!" The dwarfs hear them and become even more scared.

"No, no. We don't want more unpleasant things happening to us," they whisper among themselves.

"Maybe we should move away from here altogether," one says. The others agree. Discussing where to go, they slowly leave their hiding places. Walter and the villagers take no further notice of them, certain as they are, the dwarfs will heed their warnings. Soon the happy mood returns. Some children start singing again and the others fall in. Even though the heavy boots slow down their pace, the journey back seems shorter. Soon, the village comes into sight.

It does not take long either, before they hear Barto shouting. "My boots. I want my boots!"

The children start running. "We are going to tell him that they are found," they laugh. "He will be so pleased!"

"Yes, and the mayor will be too," Walter chuckles. "Thanks to you, Rita," he adds.

"Ooh, it was nothing," Rita utters. She flies away from him, following the children. "I will see you later," he hears her call out.

"Yes, that's fine," Walter replies with a wave of his hand. He is at the forefront of the group as they reach the village square. Barto is standing upright now, waiting. His enormous figure towering over everyone. In particular, over that of the unhappy mayor, who is still tied to the rope in Barto's hands. However, as soon as Barto spots his footwear, he lets go of the rope. With outstretched hands, he grabs the two colossal red boots. Seeing they are still in good order, it doesn't take long before they are on his feet. Then, without a word, the giant walks away. Past the silent crowd he goes. One huge step after the other. In no time at all, he is gone. No doubt, off to visit his brother. While everybody is still looking after him, the mayor quickly hurries back to his chambers. Glad to be alive. Glad that this whole shameful affair is over. Safely back in his office, he at one frees himself from the rope. Utterly exhausted, he sinks into his chair, thankful to be alone.

On the square, the people start wandering around. Happy everything is back to normal. They do not want to go to their houses just yet. Not with this festive mood, they're still in. Walter is happy too. That is why he takes out his flute and starts playing one of his happy songs. Rita, who is back on his shoulder, falls in with glee.

"How lovely," someone remarks. "How truly lovely."

The crowd gathers around them. After the first song , they beg for more. Walter, nor Rita, need much begging. Gladly, they play and sing. Tune after tune. More artists join in. The sound of a barrel organ can be heard on the other side of the square. A man with a violin comes and stands next to Walter. They smile at each other and from then on, make wonderful music together. From somewhere, a small wooden bowl appears in front of them. People start throwing money in it. A second bowl is placed right in front of Walter, and the money keeps trickling in. The villagers know that without Rita and Walter, bad things could have happened today.

That is why Walter's bowl is soon filled to the brim. The crowd is cheering and singing along with the music. There are even some people dancing on the cobblestones of the square. The partying goes on till late. But, at long last, people start getting tired and leave for home. Walter and the other artists find themselves with a lot of money. It has been a wonderful evening for all of them. They part the best of friends, wishing each other luck. Who knows, they might meet again some day, somewhere. In a haystack, on a farm just outside the village, Walter sleeps that night. Rita has found a safe place for herself, in between the rafters above his head.

Early the next morning, they are on their way again. Eager for more adventures. Before midday, they reach quite a big town. The streets are full of people. Colourful flags, gaily blowing in the wind, are everywhere. There is music in the air mixed with the sound of laughter.

Children are running in front of the adults' feet, but nobody seems to mind. They all go in the same direction.

"This is great," Rita remarks. "I like this."

"Yes, so do I," Walter replies. By following the crowd, they arrive at an open area. Open, that is, there are no houses, but tents and stalls fill every nook. A big fair is taking place. The stalls have so many articles for sale, one doesn't know where to look first. And the food, it all smells so good. The fish they are frying here, the doughnuts, dripping with oil and sugar, there. It makes Walter very hungry. 'What shall I buy?' he wonders.

"What would you like Rita,?" he asks.

"Me?" Rita chirps. "No, I am not hungry, Walter. I found some nice seeds this morning while we were on our way over here."

"Ooh, well, I will buy some doughnuts," Walter decides. "I think we can afford it. After all, we made so much money yesterday. You know, I still can't believe it."

"Yes, it was very good," Rita agrees.

"Indeed, you can say that again," Walter laughs. Proudly, he pays for his food. 'Silas was right,' he thinks. 'I can make a different life for myself.' The doughnuts taste delicious and so does the milk he buys from another stall. "Aaah, this is great," he sighs. "So much better than the dry bread I took with me when leaving the farm."

"I am happy you enjoy this so much," Rita says. "I wonder," she goes on, "do you always need money to get food?"

"Mostly," Walter answers.

"If you want food or other articles, yes, you need money to buy that. But," he adds, "money cannot buy you everything. It cannot buy you friends, for instance. Not real friends, anyway."

"Yes, yes, I see what you mean," Rita replies. How well they understand each other, this young man and the little red robin.

"Now, what else can we buy, I wonder?" Walter says after a while. He has seated himself on a low wall, next to one of the stalls. From there, he watches all the passersby. Rita, on his shoulder, does the same. Suddenly, they both catch sight of an old man who walks alongside a huge bear. The bear, on his hind legs, has a chain dangling from his neck. The old man holds the other end of the chain. Although they keep at a safe distance, lots of people follow them. Walter's heart goes out to the odd couple. The bear, who also looks old, has put one arm around the shoulders of the man and so they both shuffle on. Not far from Walter and Rita, they stop. The bear starts to do some dance steps, but one can see his heart is not in it. Walter decides to address the man. "Good day sir," he begins, "have you travelled far?"

"What?" the old man asks. Looking up, he sees Walter smiling at him. "Aah," he sighs, "good day to you too. And yes, yes, we have. We are tired. It is such a problem nowadays," he adds. "It seems people do not like us anymore. We are getting too old. It is time to go home."

"Well," Walter urges him on, "why don't you?"

"I can't," the old man answers. "As for myself, I can go back to the village I come from, but I am afraid they would not want Bruno, my old bear there."

"That is a pity," Walter remarks.

"Yes," the old man and the bear both nod their heads in agreement.

"A great pity," Rita joins in. She looks from one to the other, her head a bit aside, as she often does. "Can't Bruno come with us, Walter?" she then asks.

"Uh, uhum," Walter utters, taken by surprise.

"What uhum?" Rita wants to know. "We can take him, can't we?"

"That would be great," the old man cheering up, says. "I won't ask much for him and Bruno really is a great friend!"

"Yes, I am," the bear confirms, nodding again. Letting go of the old man's shoulder, he grabs Walter's hand. Shaking it as only a bear can.

Walter nearly falls down to the ground. "All right, all right," he says while freeing himself. "If all of you believe we should do this, then we will."

By now, a large crowd has gathered around them and upon hearing Walter's words, they begin to clap hands.

"Yes, people do like a happy ending, it seems," Walter mutters to himself. He starts emptying his pockets. "Here," he says to the old man. "This is all the money we have. Is it enough?"

"O yes," the man answers, looking at the money Walter holds out to him. His eyes get a greedy shine as he grabs it all. Quickly, he empties it into his own purse. "Well, that is it then," he says, handing Walter Bruno's chain and the metal money box. "He is all yours now. Farewell my friend," he addresses the bear, giving him a hug. "I hope you will be very happy with your new owners."

Giving him a bear hug in return, Bruno repeats his nodding. "Yes, for sure I will," he says, and everyone understands him.

After greeting both Walter and Rita, the old man, without looking back, disappears into the crowd.

"Well, well," Rita chirps. "Now we did what you said we could not do. We bought ourselves a friend!"

"You are so right," Walter admits with a smile. Then he adds, "and such a big friend at that!"

Bruno does not know what to make of it. He looks from Walter to Rita and back to Walter. "Thank you for taking me," he utters at last.

"You are very welcome," Walter assures him.

"We love having you with us," Rita chirps.

Walter is still a bit dazed, though. "My, my," he mumbles, "from a small robin to a big bear. I wonder how we are going to feed him? I suppose you eat a lot," he asks Bruno.

"I don't know," Bruno, a bit taken aback, answers truthfully. "I never did get a lot to eat really. Most of the time, I go hungry." Rubbing his belly, he adds, "honey is nice, I think. I could eat a lot of honey."

The people still standing around start laughing. They enjoy what they have seen so far. Walter laughs too, while doing a bit of quick thinking at the same time.

"Good, good," he echoes Bruno. "I hear what you are saying. You like honey, but honey costs a lot of money. Don't you agree?" he asks the crowd. "Yes, yes," comes the answer from all sides.

"Right," Walter continues, "and money must be earned, is it not so?"

"It is so," his listeners shout back.

"Right," Walter says again. "Sooo, that is what we will do!" He reaches for his flute and, bringing it to his lips, starts to play. So sweet is the melody he produces. It seems to bewitch the crowd. They just stand there and stare at the three of them. Then Rita's lovely voice mingles with Walter's tune. Bruno begins to dance, because he feels it is the right thing to do now. And such fun too. The music makes all the difference. The bystanders are enjoying themselves hugely. No wonder the money box Walter placed in front of him, gets fuller and fuller. The children in the crowd start to dance as well and there is cheering after every tune played. At long last, Walter stops. The flute gets back in his pocket and, with a grateful bow to his public, he empties the money box into his pockets as well. Followed by much hand clapping and cheering again, they move away.

"My, my, this was excellent," Walter says after a while.

"Yes, wasn't it just?" Bruno booms. "And we made a lot of money," he adds. Making money has always been very important in his life. Even more so for the people who owned him. It meant travelling from town to town and for him, Bruno, it meant dancing and travelling all his life. In rain and snow, going hungry most of the time. More often than not, it also meant being treated unkindly by a harsh master. A great many masters there were. The last one, being the best one. But there was never anyone like Walter. A young man who understands animals, who understands him, Bruno. When Walter smiles at him and says, "with this money we can buy a lot of honey," Bruno knows Walter is the best one of all!

At that moment, Rita flies away from them, high up into the sky. They both stare after her.

"Rita does not care much about money," Walter remarks. "She does not need any. Not for food or clothes, nor for something to drink. Her fine feathers are all the clothes she could ever want. Her food comes from the finest seeds and the water she drinks from everywhere around us. She knows where to find it and moreover, it is all for free."

"I wish it was the same for me," Bruno sighs.

"It could be," Walter answers him. "After all, you can live from seeds as well. You could catch fish, and honey can be found where the bees hide it."

"I know, I know," Bruno whines. "But I am too old now and I was never brought up that way. All I can remember is walking and working. Dancing for a dry slice of bread, mostly."

"Well," Walter says softly, "from now on, you don't have to do that anymore. Not if I can help it. But, let's talk about that later. First, let's get some honey."

While talking and slowly walking on, they have arrived at a quiet area of town. The streets are lined with lots of trees and here and there, a small shop can be seen. Strolling over to one of them, Walter goes in, while Bruno rests in the shadow of a nearby tree. It isn't long before Walter comes back. His arms can hardly hold all the goodies he bought. There is bread and butter, some plates and spoons, as well as a new knife to cut the bread with. But Bruno has eyes only for the large pot of honey that Walter puts in front of him. "Goody, goody," he says, licking his lips. "Thank you Walter. This is great!"

"It's my pleasure," Walter smiles. He sits down next to Bruno and helps him to open the honey-pot. After also handing him a spoon, he leans back against the tree, just as Bruno has been doing all the time. It gladdens his heart to watch Bruno for a while. To see how much he enjoys his treat. He messes a bit and spills some of the honey, but is all done with such delight that it makes Walter hungry too. Quickly, he slices the bread and spreads lots of butter on. After that, he piles some cheese on top. The bread is still warm and everything tastes great. Rita sits on a tree-branch, looking at them. She chirps a happy song. All is peace in this street where no people are to be seen because everyone is still at the fair.

"Aaahhh," Bruno says at last, after finishing half of the honey. "I suppose that is enough for now. I must keep some for later, too."

"Good," Walter comments. "I am also finished." It was lovely with all this good food. "Don't you want to try some of it, Rita?" he asks, looking up at her. But Rita does not want.

Bruno, rubbing his back against the tree-trunk while at the same time rubbing his tummy, declares; "I am so happy. To be here with you is fabulous. I have not been so happy for a long, long time!"

"That is good," Walter smiles at him. "That is just what Rita and I want you to be. And another thing," he adds. "We want you to know you are free to go wherever you want to go. If you choose to live somewhere in a forest, that is fine with us. On the other hand, if you want to stay with Rita and me, you are more than welcome to do so. It is your choice." The next moment, before Bruno even knows what is going on, he releases the chain from the large bear's collar. "There," he says. "How does that feel?"

Bruno looks a bit dazed. "It feels strange," he answers. "I cannot believe this is happening to me." He shakes his head. "Strange," he says again. Then he adds, "but nice!"

"Fine," Walter comments.

Rita flies down and settles herself on Bruno's shoulder. "Is it not wonderful to be free?" she asks. "You can now go anywhere you like."

Bruno's face drops. "I do not want to go anywhere," he wails. "What must I do on my own? I cannot even look after myself. No, I like to be with you two. You are my friends, are you not?"

"But of course we are," they both assure him. "We are very happy that you do not want to go away from us."

"Oh, oh well, that is good then," Bruno sighs. Feeling a bit embarrassed, he continues, "I, ee, I think I could do with some sleep."

"That is a good idea," Walter agrees, glad to talk about something else.

"Let's go to the forest first," Rita says. "It is not far from here. There, you both can sleep as long as you like while I find myself some nice seeds."

"Right, let's do that then," Walter replies. He quickly tidies up around them. Thereafter, they start walking towards the forest. Rita flies than here, then there. From Walter to Bruno and back again. Sometimes she just flies up and up into the air, diving and tumbling for joy. The forest is a bit further than it looked to be and Bruno cannot walk very fast. Still, they reach the first trees well before darkness falls. A bit further, Walter finds a nice sheltered place for them underneath an enormous tree.

Bruno is very pleased. "Aaah, this is it," he utters. Without further ado, he eases himself into his favourite position, his back against the tree. His eyes close. Bruno is asleep.

"He looks so happy," Rita chirps softly.

"Yes, he does," Walter agrees. Both he and Rita are glad Bruno is here with them in the forest. They want things to be good for him. They want him to have a better life from now on. Walter lies down next to Bruno. He is sleepy too. "How nice," he murmurs before dozing off. "How great to be here with these two good friends. Already my life has become so very much better than before." He dreams about all the things that have happened since leaving the farm. About giants and dwarfs and large red boots. Of people on market squares and stalls packed with lovely food. But then, something wakes him up. Someone is picking and pecking at him. Still sleepy, he tries to focus on who is doing this. Does he see a face or a beak or both? All of a sudden, he knows. It is a peacock! There he stands in all his glory. His tail feathers spread out in gold and blue shiny patterns. It is looking down at him, a bit haughty, a bit bored even.

"Now," Walter exclaims. "Was it you who pecked me? Who are you? Where do you come from and what do you want?" By this time, Walter has hauled himself into a sitting position. Leaning against the tree, he eyes his visitor with guarded curiosity. Who knows, he might start picking at him again. He doesn't though. Looking straight back at Walter, he says, "Well, to tell you the truth, I do not have a clue! And yes, it was me who touched you." He waits a moment and then goes on, "but please, you rather tell me where you come from. Who are you and where are you going?"

"My, my," Walter starts to answer and then begins to laugh. "You know how to turn the tables on someone," he declares. "I really think that's funny, don't you?"

The peacock clearly thinks it is not. He still seems bored.

"Oh well," Walter sighs, "let's try again now that I am fully awake. My name is Walter and I am in no hurry to go anywhere.

Me and my friends, Rita the robin and Bruno the bear, are just having a good time travelling the country. I play the flute, Rita sings and Bruno dances. People are giving us money for that and that is great. Is there anything else you want to know?"

"Yes, where do you come from?" the peacock asks again. He keeps staring at Walter, who starts feeling a bit uneasy now.

"Well, if you must know, I ran away from the farm," he tells his newfound companion. "It was very unpleasant there," he adds.

"Ran away?" the peacock chuckles suddenly. "That is what I did too!"

"Really?" Walter asks. "And why did you run away?"

"Oh, I don't know," the big bird mutters. "I suppose I got bored," he adds slowly.

Walter thinks about this a bit, then he asks, "Don't you want to go back?"

"Oh, I don't know," comes the reply.

"Well, what is your name then?" Walter asks. "And don't tell me that you don't know!"

The bird looks a bit taken aback. He pauses a moment and then says coldly, "My name is Max and I also come from a farm of sorts. I liked it there, but then I felt I should see something of the world before becoming too old. Can I come with you? Maybe just for a while?" he asks, for the first time sounding a bit unsure of himself. "I would like to find out what I want to do with my life. So, if we maybe just see how things go?"

"It is all right with me," Walter answers. "Let's hear how Rita and Bruno feel about it."

"It is all right with me too," Rita sings from the treetop above. She goes on, "I have been here all the time, listening to you. All I want to say is; welcome Max."

"Yes, yes," Bruno, who has woken up, joins in. "You are very welcome, Max."

"Fine, fine," Max responds, a bit emotionally. "It is very kind of you and decent, yes, you're a decent lot the three of you."

"Good," Walter replies cheerfully. "That's that then. Now, let's see what comes next?"

"Food," Bruno bellows. "I am hungry again."

"Well, that is not a problem," Walter says. "We have enough food to last us for quite some time. Do you want bread with honey or honey with bread?"

"You can give me both," Bruno answers. "I am very hungry!"

"Right," Walter laughs, "you shall have them." Opening one of the food bags bought earlier, he asks, "Rita, what about you? Maybe you like some bread now?"

"No thank you," Rita chirps back. "I found and ate so much fine food here in the forest. So I am not hungry."

"I have some, if you don't mind," Max the peacock utters.

"Not at all," Walter answers him. "You are welcome to eat with us." He cuts some of the bread, butters it and ladles lots of honey on top. He then divides it onto three plates. One he puts in front of Max and gives another to Bruno.

"Thank you, thank you," Bruno beams. He starts eating with total contentment and lots of 'mmmm, mmmm,' sounds. Walter smiles. It makes him feel good to see Bruno eating so happily. However, the smile fades from his face when, turning around, he notices two empty plates. Max not only emptied his own, but that of Walter as well.

"Why did you eat my food, too?" he asks, not over-friendly.

"I was hungry," Max shrugs. "Is there some more?"

Walter does not like Max's behaviour and decides to tell him so. "I will give you some more," he says, "but then you must behave yourself. It is bad manners to gobble down your food so, and it is very bad manners indeed to empty somebody else's plate as well."

"Oooh, don't fuss so much," Max replies. Then he adds, "I would like some more food, please!"

"Gee," is all Walter can find to say. 'Such cheek,' he thinks, but he cuts some more bread and prepares it the same way as before. This done, he again makes up three portions. Bruno gets some more, Max gets his and this time Walter manages to eat his own food before Max can get hold of it. He sees Max's beady eyes follow his every move. "If you're still hungry after this, you better find your own food," he remarks, stashing everything into the big bags again. Max just looks away. "I know what you are thinking," Walter declares, "but don't you dare! You are not to touch this food when I am not looking or when I sleep. It is not yours and although I do not mind giving you some, you have no right to it. Rita, Bruno and me. We earned it."

"That is so," Bruno says, smacking his lips. "We earned it!" Then he adds, "yes well, I think I go back to sleep." Slipping into his old position, he at once falls asleep again.

Max does not say anything. He just smirks a bit, rakes the ground with his feet and is all of a sudden very busy looking for food from some nearby bushes. Walter, although still a bit upset, begins to understand. Max is Max. It won't help to get cross with him. He will always be himself. Bored with everything but food. Searching for and gorging on it, wherever it is to be found.

Rita comes over and sits on his shoulder. "It is all right though, is it not?" she chirps, "We have enough food and some money to buy more if we need to?"

"Of course," Walter laughs with relief. "Actually, it is not really a problem is it?" he sighs, "It was just, I became a bit …"

"I know, I know," Rita says. "Come on," she suggests, "let's make some music."

"Yes, yes," Walter exclaims. It will make him feel better as always. He takes the flute out of his pocket. The first notes come softly. Rita falls in and follows easily. It sounds so cheerful and lovely. Max the peacock is very taken by it. He comes prancing out of the bushes and even tries some dance steps.

Bruno, who is suddenly wide awake, sees this and calls out, "that's great Max. Wait, I'll join you." He gleefully, though a bit slowly, gets himself into an upright position. It is with great gusto that he and Max dance together. Walter and Rita can hardly control their amusement. It is such a funny sight, these two performing their dance-steps in the forest.

"Never to be forgotten," Walter breathes in between a few notes, to Rita.

"No, never," Rita agrees, with a nod of her little head. It is late when at long last they go to sleep. This, because of all the music-making and dancing and having such a good time together.

CHAPTER 11

They spend the following days lazing around, enjoying each other's company. Bruno sleeps a lot. It is his favourite pastime now. Max keeps himself busy, feeding throughout the day. It is a never-ending process. Walter now and then walks around a bit, more often than not, with Rita on his shoulder. There is no hurry to go anywhere. Things are fine, just as they are.

They even find a small stream winding itself through the forest.

"Great," Walter gushes. "Let's set up camp near the water. We can wash up here, clean here, and even take a bath."

"Yes," Rita chirps, "let's do that." And so they move over to the little stream. Bruno loves it. As the days are still warm and sunny, he many times just wades in and sits there, waist deep in the water, splashing it all around him. Max mostly watches from a distance. He is not all that keen to get wet, but Walter and Rita often join Bruno, bathing and playing while having a whale of a good time. It is something they will try to repeat, seeking for water to bathe in and wash up wherever they go. It is also at this lovely place that Rita starts teaching Bruno about the different plants and bushes here in the forest. She shows him the bushes that have berries on.

"Some of them, one can eat, others are harmful," she tells him. "You have to learn the difference."

"I can do that," Bruno declares.

"Good," Rita chirps. "I will also show you which trees have lovely nuts and seeds."

Walter watches the two of them from a distance, Rita hovering over Bruno, who willingly follows her from plant to plant and from bushes to trees. "How endearing these friends of mine are," he ponders, smiling inwardly. Then he notices Max trailing Bruno and Rita. Wondering why this is, Walter decides to fall into line as well. None of the three in front detect him. They are much too busy with their own actions. Coming nearer, Walter can hear Max cry out to Rita, "Why is it that Bruno does not know these things? That is more than silly. Me, on the other hand, I know everything! All the plants, the seeds, the bushes. I did not have to learn this from a bird."

"That is because you were never on a chain, going from market place to market place to dance and make money for your master,"

Rita, coming up for Bruno at once, replies. "Now were you?" she asks.

"No," Max a bit sheepishly admits.

"Well then," Rita berates him, "better think before you speak. This is good advice, my friend, I promise you!"

Max, without saying another word, turns around, nearly bumping into Walter.

"My, my," Walter chuckles, "Such wise words, from such a small bird. We all should listen to her, don't you think?" But Max does not want to hear anymore. He hastily scuttles away. Bruno does not seem to have taken much notice of Max's words, nor Rita's. He is too excited over all the new things he learned.

"Hi Walter," he proudly declares, "I can now look after myself. I can find my own food here in the forest. Berries and nuts, so many things. Here, try these sweet berries. I took them from that bush over there. They taste great!"

"Hmm, indeed," Walter agrees, while putting a few into his mouth." You are a great teacher, Rita. Pity you did not tell me all you know about these things. I might have grown healthier by the day."

"I thought you knew," Rita twitters. "But you are very healthy anyway,"

"All right, all right, I hear you," Walter laughs; adding, "Come, let's go back to our camping place. Max will be there already. Maybe he does feel a bit bad about the things he said. I do not want him to be unhappy." But once back at their resting place near the river, they see Max pick-picking for his food amongst the bushes as usual - very much his old self again. Clearly, he is not greatly disturbed at all. "Good," Walter sighs, "That is very good then,"

The days after this one are spent in harmony with each other. Bruno, when not splashing about in the little stream, eagerly searches for food in the forest; the juicy berries, the tasty nuts, many times bringing some for Walter as well. Rita never tires of showing them both all the nice food one can find to eat in the forest. They are days of bliss; days that Walter and Rita will always remember. To see how Bruno improves and recovers from years and years of neglect is just so wonderful, however, as more days pass by Walter sees some of their supplies need restocking.

Bruno also starts noticing that the honey is nearly finished. "And the other food as well," he complains.

"Yeah, it seems we do not want to live from berries and nuts alone." Walter laughs. "Maybe we are a bit spoiled. So, let's think about getting some other things again then. I suppose it is shopping time all over! We can go to the same shop we visited before, because I know they have stacks of honey there. Rita, do you like to come with me? As for you, Bruno and Max, it is better that you stay here!"

"Fine," Bruno yawns.

"No problem," Max replies. "I really do not want to go shopping!"

"Good," Walter answers. "That is how we are going to do it. Are you coming, Rita?"

"Oh yes, I am ready," Rita chirps. Nestling herself on Walter's shoulder, she urges, "Let's be off."

After saying their goodbyes to Bruno and Max, they soon are on their way. It is a pleasant walk and both of them are in a happy mood. Rita sings during the whole journey with many other birds along the way, joining in. After reaching the shop, Rita flies into the nearby standing tree again. She will wait here while Walter does the shopping.

The first thing Walter buys is again a large pot of honey for Bruno. Then he buys bread, butter and cheese. Also, some eggs as well as some fruit. Apples, pears and peaches. Rita watches Walter through the window, perched on a branch of the tree that gives her a look into the charming little shop. There is an old man behind the counter. He seems very friendly and wears a striped apron. There are racks and racks with pots and bottles and urns. All are filled with colourful goodies. Bags with flour and a great assortment of dried beans stand half opened on the floor. Walter himself holds quite a few bags as he leaves the shop again. In a jiffy, Rita is back on his shoulder and so, they journey back to the forest to meet up with their newfound friends. They are still some way off when they notice Max running towards them. Clearly he is in a hurry, feathers flying, his legs working overtime.

"Come," they hear him calling out. "Come quickly!" Rita flies over to him.

"Why? What is going on?" Walter wants to know.

"Is something wrong?" Rita asks Max. "You seem so upset. It is not … there is nothing wrong with Bruno, I hope?"

"NO, no, it is not that," Max screeches. He is out of breath as he reaches Walter. "It is, e, the thing is, we found a dog!" he manages to gasp out.

"A dog," Walter echoes. "Ooh, and where is this dog, then?"

"That's the problem," Max answers. Walter and Rita both see he is very worried. "You must quickly come and see if you can help." Max adds. "This poor dog is nearly starving. He fell into a deep hole and cannot get out. He has been there a long time already, for he can't even bark anymore. He just whines the whole time. Maybe you can do something."

"I certainly hope so," Walter replies while starting to run alongside Max, who has turned around and is now leading the way. "Just show me where it is," he mutters. Rita flies in front of them. As soon as they reach the forest, Walter places his parcels under one of the first trees. "We'll come back to them later," he says. Max is still running and Walter has to double his speed to catch up with him.

"It is quite a bit further," Max informs them. Max now has time to catch his breath because Walter's tempo, even without all the groceries, is slow for a peacock such as himself. He becomes more and more talkative as they go on. "Bruno and I, we were walking around a bit when we heard him," he says. "The whining from the dog, I mean. It was very soft, though. Still, we heard it and went to look and find out where it came from. At last we found him. I saw the dog first. I think it is near dead, poor thing. Bruno is staying with him while I went to look for you both."

"Very good," Walter praises the peacock, still running as fast as he is able to. After some time, he becomes aware of a deep voice, humming. Humming one of the melodies Walter often plays.

"I suppose Bruno wants the dog to know he is not alone," Rita remarks. She flies off, chirping all the while. Max follows in a flurry, leaving Walter to find his own way.

Bruno's humming helps. Soon, Walter reaches them. "Hi Bruno," he greets. "I hear there is a dog down there."

"Ooohh, hi yes," Bruno greets back, adding, "I hope we can save him?"

Walter puts his head over the opening of the hole. Not only is it deep, but very narrow and dark as well. He can barely see the dog. It is lying very still. The whining has stopped too. Even Rita's chirping near it fails to get any reaction. "My, my," Walter sighs, as he often does when something bothers him. "I wonder what we can do about this situation," he adds. "Hey doggy," he calls down. "Don't you worry though, we make a plan to get you out there!" A soft whimper from below is his answer.

"We still have Bruno's chain, haven't we?" Rita asks. She has flown away from the dog again onto Walter's shoulder.

"Yes, we have," Walter replies. "I was thinking about that, too. The only thing is, it might not be long enough. Still, let's go and see. We might be able to do something with it. We are just going to fetch your old chain, Bruno," he informs the still-humming bear. "We will be back shortly. Are you staying here, Max?" he asks the peacock.

"Yes, yes, fine, no problem," Max answers. "I will keep Bruno company. Do you hear Dog?" he shouts down the hole. "Walter and Rita will be back soon."

"Yes," Bruno bellows, "We will have you out just now.!" Once again a soft whimpering can be heard. "Good." Bruno replies. "I will sing for you some more." He starts humming anew while Walter and Rita make their way back to where they camped out the last couple of days. Rita watches as Walter picks up the chain.

"Just as I thought," he utters. "It is too short." He grabs the bundle in which he keeps his meagre belongings. Opening it, he remarks, "There must be a piece of rope in here, I am sure. Yes, yes. There it is." Gleefully, he holds it up.

"Will it be strong enough?" Rita asks.

"It is very strong," Walter declares. "So strong, we can even split it into two if we have to." Quickly they return to where Bruno and Max still keep watch at the deep hole. Both of them are glad to see them again.

"Aah, there you are," Bruno exclaims.

"And is the chain long enough?" Max asks.

"We'll make a plan," is Walter's answer. "The chain is too short, but this piece of rope that I always carry around with me will help too."

"How?" Max cackles as Walter holds the rope out to him. "This is not long enough either, as far as I can see."

"Then we are going to split it," Walter explains. "Here," he says, handing Bruno one end of the rope. "You hold this while I start splitting from the other end."

"Right," Bruno agrees. The others watch as the rope quite easily divides into two. It is a bit awkward handling it, though. As soon as one end comes loose, it starts to curl up again. Rita and Max solve the problem by taking turns in untwining it. Rita dives under and around, holding a piece into her beak, while Max now and then takes over and runs away with it. That helps. Everyone is happy when at long last the two pieces of rope are joined together by Walter.

Fastening it onto the chain, Walter states, "It should be long enough now. At least, I think so. The best way to find out is by trying. So, let's go and do it." One end of the rope he secures to a tree which stands near the hole. "Bruno, can you hold the rope and lower me slowly down the hole?" he asks the big bear.

"Of course I can, I am very strong," Bruno booms.

"Fine, well here we go then," Walter utters while slipping slowly over the edge of the hole. "Careful," he shouts when Bruno releases the rope a bit too quickly. "Don't let it go too fast now!"

"NO, no," Bruno calls back "I won't," and he doesn't.

Walter lands safely at the bottom of the hole, the rope being long enough, after all. The dog moves slightly as Walter bends over him. "How are you?" he asks. "Are you all right? Nothing broken?" His only answer is a soft moan. The dog's ribs are sticking out horribly. It looks as if he is not far from dying. "I'll take you away from here," Walter promises. "We'll soon fix you up, my friend. You'll see." The dog looks up at him. His eyes full of sadness. "You will see," Walter says again. Rita has followed Walter down into the hole. She is looking and listening to everything Walter says and does. Max and Bruno are peering down at them, eager to see what is going on.

"How is he?" Bruno wants to know.

"He is still alive," Walter calls back. "You can start pulling us up now, Bruno." He has taken the dog in his arms. The animal lies very still. It is in a totally exhausted and weak state. Bruno gently starts pulling. Up and up they go. The rope holds, and Bruno is indeed very strong. Rita has already flown away and waits for them as Bruno, apparently without too much effort, brings them safely to the top.

First, Walter pushes the dog over the edge. After that, he hoists himself over it before lying down next to the animal. "Gee, thanks Bruno, that was good work!" he gasps a bit out of breath.

"Yeah, it was not too bad, I think," Bruno replies proudly.

"No," Max chips in. "Not at all!" He runs over to Walter, who is now gently stroking the dog. His eyes open, he follows the movements of everyone around him. Rita sitting on Walter's shoulder, Max peering over him. Bruno coming nearer to have a closer look.

"Will he live?" Bruno asks.

Walter unties the rope from his body. "Yes, I think so," he answers. "We must get him something to drink, though. That is very important. I will carry him to the stream that is running here as well. I know, because I can hear the murmuring of the water."

"Yes, of course," Bruno says. "I heard it too."

"And me," Max adds.

"I flew over it," Rita twitters. "It is nearby!"

"All right, all right," Walter quietens his excited friends, "We all go."

With the dog in his arms and Rita leading the way, they trot off. Max runs directly under Rita, then comes Bruno, who carries the rope and chain with him. It does not take them long to reach the little stream trickling its way through the forest. Walter kneels down, while placing the dog in front of him, its head a few inches from the water. He forms his hands into a cup, scoops water in it and then holds it out to the animal. The dog starts licking at once, emptying Walter's hands. It is very thirsty. Again and again the water is brought to him in this way until at last he stops drinking. After that, he seems to be looking a bit better already. There is some movement in his body, and his tail appears to be moving a bit as well. They are all watching him intently.

"Well," Walter remarks, "The next thing needed is some food." His friends agree. Especially Bruno and Max.

"Ha, yes," Max utters. "Food, I like some food!"

"And me," Bruno announces with gusto. "I could do with some honey. Did you buy a pot of honey, Walter?"

"Yes, I did," Walter grins, "Although, I was actually thinking about some food for the dog."

"Yes, yes," Max agrees, "But surely we can all go and eat something?"

"Right then, let's go," Walter answers. "There is enough for all of us." Thus, they march off, in the same order as before. Walter carrying the dog again, who is without doubt, now trying to wag its tail.

"The idea of getting some food must sound very good to you," Walter smiles. The dog tries to lick his hand, as if to answer 'yes it does!'

Once back at their camping site, Walter puts the dog down under one of the big surrounding trees. Then, he goes back to where he left his shopping.

No sooner has he returned and piled the bags under another tree, Max has his head already inside one of them. "There are only two pots of honey in here," he declares. "Where is the other food?"

As he moves over to the next bag, Bruno yells, "Honey, that is for me!" He shuffles forward as fast as he can.

"Calm now, calm now," Walter urges. "First, we must feed our new friend. Max, stop whatever you are doing. Please, Max," he repeats a bit louder, but Max doesn't hear. Pieces of paper, as well as bread, fly around. Max picks here, and he picks there. "Oh, no, no," Walter cries, while grabbing the bag away from Max. "That is not the way we do things here, you understand? You must wait your turn. And that goes for you too, Bruno," he continues. "Your honey can wait."

Max, looking a bit dishevelled, scurries off without saying anything, and starts pecking for insects nearby, all the while though he keeps a beady eye on what is going to happen next.

Bruno, a bit shamefaced, gets himself seated against the tree. From there he mutters, "Oh well, then I wait a bit."

Walter, in the meantime, is busy slicing the bread he saved from Max's beak. He spreads butter on it and some soft cheese. Breaking it into small pieces, he offers it to the dog. "Here he says, try eating this. It will make you feel a lot better." The dog has been watching Walter's preparations. He takes one of the pieces of bread and starts chewing. After that, he takes another and another, until everything is finished.

"Good," Walter sitting next to the dog, exclaims, "That is very good. Now tell me, what is your name and what is your story?"

The dog starts wagging its tail again. It is a good sign, showing that he is slowly recovering. "My name is Bones," he says, speaking for the first time. "Thank you all so much." He speaks softly and with some difficulty. One can see he is still very weak.

"You are very welcome, Bones," Walter assures him. "It was lucky, though, that Max and Bruno found you, otherwise you surely would have died there."

Max has come nearer and casually picks up a few crumbs that have escaped Bones' attention. "I heard you first," he remarks.

"And me," Bruno grumbles. "I heard you too!"

"Indeed," Bones replies, "And I will never forget what you did for me."

"I went to fetch Walter," Max says.

"Yes, and I sang for you," Bruno blurts out. "Did you hear that I sang for you?" he wants to know.

"Yes, I did hear you," Bones replies. "It was so very nice."

"Good, good," Bruno beams. "Can I now have some honey, Walter?" he asks.

"Of course," Walter answers, standing up. "Let's all get something to eat." He places the food he bought neatly in front of him. Bruno gets a large portion of his beloved honey, Max some bread and cheese, of which Walter takes some for himself as well. Rita picks on a few crumbs, while the dog contently watches.

"Right," Walter says after they have all eaten. "Please tell us your story now, Bones."

"Yes, well," Bones replies, "let me start by saying, I am a fox hound. I grew up in a kennel together with lots of other dogs of the same breed."

"Yes, I can see you are a beautiful young dog," Walter remarks. "Wait till we have fattened you up a bit. You will become very handsome indeed."

"Thank you," Bones says gratefully. "Anyway," he goes on, "In those kennels we were trained for the hunt. Every now and then our master would let us out as a pack, to go hunting. I was very good at it and my master more and more singled me out. I became the top hunter of the pack. The only thing was, after a while, I got a bit fed up with that. You see, I wanted to go where I wanted, and to do what I wanted to do. Being in those kennels was very depressing. I longed to be free!"

"Oh yes," Walter laughs. "I know the feeling. Rita, Bruno, Max, we all do! You really are one of us, it seems."

Bones gazes up at him then he continues, "Well, I sometimes forgot to lead the pack and wandered off on my own. After I had done so a few times too often, my master gave me to a farmer. He exchanged me for some geese." Here Bones pauses a bit. One can see he is getting very tired again.

"Would you rather stop now?" Walter asks. "After all, we have lots of time. You can tell us the rest of your story later."

"No, no," Bones replies. "Let me rather go on. I just needed to get my breath back. Where was I? Ooh yes, I was at this farm, which was not bad because there I did not get locked up in a kennel anymore. Only, this farmer had a terrible temper. Every time he became cross for some reason or another, he started hitting me. The pity was, he got cross so many times. So I got hit and kicked a great deal. For me, it was lucky that another farmer visited one day. He liked me and asked if he could exchange me for a few piglets. My master happened to be in a good mood that day 'You are my friend,' he said. 'I will give the dog to you. I just have to warn you though, he is a very free spirited animal that likes to go its own way.'

Later that day, with my new owner, we set out for his farm in his old creaky wagon. It had become quite dark by that time and my new master mumbled something about his place being a long way off. I went to sleep in the middle of the wagon, only to be awoken by a horrific noise. The wagon's axle had broken. We were stuck in this forest. There was nothing for it, than to go and look for help. It was a pitch dark night, with no moon, and we were far away from everything. To tell you the truth, I think my master got lost. We walked for hours and hours. Then a thunder-storm came up, which made things even worse. At a given moment, while trailing a bit behind, I suddenly slipped and fell in this hole where you found me. I yelped and yelped, but it did not help, for the wind howled even louder than I did. It started to rain as well and what can I say? Maybe nobody ever bothered to look for me. In any case, I was never found. For how long my stay in that hole was, who knows, but here I am now and this is my story." By now Bones is whispering. He can hardly keep his eyes open anymore. They have all listened in silence.

Then it is Walter who says, "that was a very interesting tale you told us. Sad yes, but then Bruno and I could also tell some very sad tales. I suppose Rita and Max could too. Not today though," he continues. "Today we are just happy to be together and enjoy each other's company. You can stay with us for as long as you like Bones. If you decide later on to go your own way, you are free to do so."

"No, no, I will never go away from you," Bones answers. "Never for as long as I live. His eyes are open again and full of adoration as he gazes up at Walter. 'I trust you,' those eyes say. 'You are my friend and new master. For ever and ever.'

Walter understands. He is very moved. "That is fine then," he says after a short pause.

Rita flies from his shoulder over to Bones. "We like having you with us," she says. "We will have good times together."

Bruno, while scratching his back against the tree, booms; "Nice to have you here, Bones!" Then he sleeps; something that comes very easily to Bruno.

Max trots over and stands in front of the dog. "You are very welcome with us, Bones," he says. "Very welcome!"

"Thank you," Bones answers. Then he too falls asleep.

Walter yawns and also dozes off after a while. Rita settles herself on a tree branch above their heads. Only Max goes on, picking for food all the time. Eating anything he can find.

CHAPTER III

They stay in the same place for a few more days. Now it is mainly to give Bones the dog time to recover. And it is amazing to see how rapidly he does just that. Every day he is a bit more perky, staying at Walter's side mostly. After the second day, he starts playing with Bruno, who patiently endures his antics. Even when Bones pretends to attack him, Bruno just sits or lies very still. His eyes watch every movement though. Now and then he waves one of his big paws into the air, as if he wants to slap Bones. For Bones, this is even more fun. He barks and moves in a circle around Bruno, very much aware that if Bruno wanted to, these paws could harm him a great deal. But, they have a good understanding and the two of them become the best of friends. Walter and Rita enjoy watching them. Max, on the other hand, does not want any of it. He makes it very clear Bones must stay out of his way and gets grumpier by the day. His pick-picking for insects and the like becomes more and more frantic.

"Something is the matter with Max," Walter decides. He has to find out what it is. He follows Max when he sees him wandering off a bit. Bruno and Bones are sleeping, curled up, close to each other. Rita, as usual, sits on Walter's shoulder.

"Max," Walter begins, coming a bit nearer, "What is it that worries you so?"

"Oh, it's nothing," Max grumbles.

"That's not true," Walter replies. "Something is bothering you. Are you not happy being with us anymore? Is that it? Do you want to go back to where you came from?"

"Oh, I don't know," Max answers, adding, "Maybe."

"That is it then," Walter says. "I am sure you long for your own kind. And I am sure that you long for the farm that you were born at, as well. Is it not so? Come, tell me. Out with the truth, Max." When Max still doesn't say anything, Walter pleads, "Come on now, Max. We have become friends, is it not?" Max nods. "Well then," Walter, seeing this, continues. "Friends can tell each other things. Who knows, maybe Rita and I can help you if there is a problem." This time it is Rita who nods in agreement.

"Nobody can help me," Max utters.

"Ooh nonsense," is Walter's reply. "You never know until you try. Come," he sits down on the grass, "Tell us about it."

"Yes, tell us," Rita chirps.

It is a long story," Max hesitates.

"That does not matter," Walter assures him. "We have lots of time."

"Yes, lots," again Rita joins in.

"Oh well," Max uneasily scrapes the ground with one of his feet, scattering leaves and earth in all directions.

"Let me help you," Walter suggests. "Firstly, you were not really bored with your life back at the farm, isn't it? There was another reason for you to run away. Something happened back there. What was it?"

"It was, it was unfair," Max practically shouts. "That was what it was."

"What?" Rita asks, before Walter can say anything.

"Everything." Max answers. "You see, the farm where I come from belongs to Judge Martins. He is nice enough, but being always very busy judging in town, he needs a foreman to run the place for him. Me and my family, we were always perfectly happy with the way things were at the farm. We had our own large house with shelter for the night and in the daytime we could do as we pleased and walk all over the place. It was a good life. Yes, very fine indeed," Max remembers fondly. There is a deep sadness in his voice as he goes on, "We couldn't ask for more. A beautiful place, a gentle master. But things changed when a new foreman was taken on. The old gardener, who also acted as foreman, became ill. In his place came Hector, but he made life miserable for everyone. He was a horrible man, always shouting at us; always grumbling. In particular, about me and my voice, which he did not like." Max pauses to catch his breath, giving Walter a chance to speak.

"Oh yes, that voice of yours," he remarks. "Well, I must admit, when you raise that voice of yours, maybe not everybody cares for it. Though I believe this might be beside the point. Anyway, come to think of it, you do not shout out aloud all that much."

"There is nothing to shout about these days," Max answers. He is even more upset now by learning Walter does not like the sound he makes either.

Walter, sensing this, hastens to add, "But you are so beautiful, Max. The one thing balances the other. Surely one can't have everything and no one is perfect."

"No, I suppose not," Max says rather sharply, although he cannot help being flattered by Walter's remark that he is so beautiful. Spreading out his feathers in full splendour to show them off again, he continues, "Well, coming back to this man, Hector, he made our lives unbearable. Often he would throw stones at us but when our master, the judge, came to look how things went, Hector always pretended to be a nice, kind-hearted person, making the judge believe he really cared for us. If judge Martin had only known," Max says bitterly, "The worst thing, however, was the incident with the golden candlesticks. I know about it because I am always watching things, just so, to stay out of trouble."

"Tell us about it?" Walter, who wholeheartedly agrees with this statement, urges.

44

"Oh yes, please do," Rita chirps.

"Well, yeah," Max sombrely goes on. "They were stolen!"

"Stolen?" Walter and Rita echo after him.

"They were!" Max repeats, adding, "And I know who did it."

"Tell us then," Rita twitters full of curiosity, for this is such an interesting story.

"It was Hector," Max replies. "It was him, but the silly thing is, he did not even know they were made of gold. That only came out later. No, he just stole them. I don't know why. It was a foolish thing to do. Afterwards he sold them to a young gypsy, who just happened to pass by. He did not get much money for them either. I know about it, because I saw it with my own eyes." After a moment or so, Max goes on, "I would have liked to tell my master what happened, but unlike you, Walter, he cannot understand what I am saying."

"Yes, it is a pity that so few people can," Walter agrees. "But tell us what happened after that? Were the candlesticks ever found?"

"Oh yes," Max responds. "They were indeed. The judge missed them soon afterwards. The commotion following this was unbelievable. The candlesticks were very valuable, made of real gold and very, very old. They were for ages in the family, the judge told everybody. Also, everybody was asked, over and over again, if they had seen them. And where could they be? It put a lot of pressure on the people who were near or in the house when the candlesticks were stolen. Because of the warm weather, the large doors leading into the garden had been left open, people could easily have walked in. That is what Hector did. When leaving with

the candlesticks, he saw me trying to hide behind a bush. He knew
I had seen him, and thereafter he made sure the candlesticks were
found. They arrested the young gypsy boy and send him to jail. He
tried to tell his side of the story, but nobody believed him. As far
as I know, he is still in jail," Max ends his tale.

"That is unfair," Walter declares and Rita agrees.

"Can't something be done?" she asks.

"Ooh, I don't know." Max falls into his old routine of looking
and sounding bored again. "Well, nobody understands a thing of
what has been going on, anyway," he continues after a short pause.
"But after this incident, Hector made my life even more
unbearable than before. That is why I had to leave, eventually. It is
sad, but that is how it is." His voice trails off and slowly he starts
pick picking the ground again.

"I wish we could help," Walter says. "I will think about it, but
not right now. Let's first go back to Bruno and Bones to see if they
are still sleeping." They walk back to where Bruno and Bones are
and find them indeed, still lost to the world. Bruno snoring to his
heart's content and Bones curled up next to him.

"This is so good for Bones," Walter remarks. "It helps him to
get strong again soon. Then we can go on with our journey. We
don't want to stay here forever."

Chapter IV

They don't. Within a week, they start moving again. All along the forest, which seems to stretch for miles and miles. Bones is eager to go. He looks and feels so much better. One can see, he is a very handsome dog. Grey-white, with tan spots above his eyes. Standing high on legs that promise speed. Also, he has a fine, intelligent face.

Bruno is happy to go wherever Walter leads them. Max, since becoming so restless nowadays, seems to stride in great haste. Rita, cheery as always, flies sometimes over and around them, until she comes to rest on Walter's shoulder again.

Walter decides to stay away from the villages and its people for a while. "Only when we need money for food, shall we go to the built-up areas to play and sing," he announces.

His friends have no objections. "Can I also take part, then?" Bones asks.

"Of course," Walter responds. "While we play, sing or dance, you can collect the money."

"What is money?" Bones wants to know.

Walter laughs, before explaining, "With money you can buy food and things."

"Ooh, that's fine. I collect the money then," Bones says.

"And me?" Max asks "What can I do?"

"Well Max, to tell the truth, I think it might be better if you do not come with us when we are going to perform," Walter answers him.

"Why not?" Max wants to know, sounding upset at once. "Is it because you do not like the sound of my voice? But what then if I keep quiet? And I can dance. Let me show you how nice I can dance," he declares, while at the same time displaying his stunning feathers in their full splendour. He also slowly begins to hop around. It truly is a magnificent sight. No use in denying that. They all stand in awe. As Max stops his act, he hopefully looks at them. "What do you think?" he asks. "Can I come too?"

"I wish you could," Walter tells him. "You dance really well, but you are simply too beautiful. I am afraid people will try and grab you and you might get hurt. I don't want that to happen. Surely you don't want that either?" As always, Walter has chosen just the right words.

Max is very flattered and no, he does not like to be grabbed and hurt by people. "Well, all right then," he says, "but what must I do while you are all out there?"

"The best thing for you is to stay here in the forest," Walter tells him. "You just wait. We will find you again."

"I hope so," Max mutters, still a bit upset. Although he will not say so, he very much likes the company of his new friends. It is much better than stalking the forest on one's own, as he did before.

After a few days of travelling slowly along the edge of the forest, they notice some houses and a church tower in the distance.

"Well," Walter declares, "that's it, partners, I think it is time to get our act together. Our provisions are very low, so tomorrow might be a good day for trying to earn some money to buy food."

All of them are excited. Bruno, at once, starts shuffling through a few of his dance paces.

Bones feels a bit envious as he sees his heavy friend strut around on his hind legs. "How do you do that?" he asks.

"Ooh, it's easy," Bruno answers, pleased by the approval in Bones' eyes.

"Can you teach me how to do it?" Bones wants to know.

"Yes, of course I can," Bruno mumbles. "Here, I show you." Coming down, he grabs Bones by his front legs up to a standing position. While holding him and facing each other, they start shuffling around. It is a delight to watch. Bruno towering above Bones who is looking up to him, his expression one of wonder. Quickly, Walter takes his flute and starts playing. Rita promptly flies onto his shoulder and joins in with sweet and cheerful tones. Max just stands there, looking from the one to the other, following the whole exercise eagerly. Walter can almost hear him think how he, too, would love to be part of all this. But then, he seems to lose interest and strolls off, only to start pick picking again in his endless search for food.

The following morning, with Max staying behind, they undertake the journey to the nearby village. It is bigger than Walter thought at first. Busy too. People are everywhere. Walter and his friends attract a lot of attention. Children begin trailing after them. They love it when Bruno starts to walk on his hind legs and make a few dance steps.

Before meeting or encountering people, Walter has tied Bruno on his chain again and holds the chain in his hands. This way everybody is happy. They now move along with the mainstream of people, towards the centre of the village. What a sight to see, and smells to smell. Colour and noise abound. There is a festive feeling in the air. Flags are fluttering in the wind. Jugglers are juggling all sorts of objects, high, high up, and catch them again. Men on stilts wriggle their way through the crowd. On the sides of the road, many stalls sell a mixture of items, from food to household goods, but mostly food. Clowns run around in green and red jester clothes. On their heads are pointed caps with a bell on top clinge linging with every step they make. Bones is confused, and a bit scared, too. He walks as close as possible to Bruno and Walter.

Walter, noticing this, fastens the other end of Bruno's chain onto Bones' collar. "So," he says, "I'll hold the chain in the middle and now none of us can get lost. Is that not a good plan?" Bruno and Bones agree.

Rita chirps on Walter's shoulder, "I never get lost. I never get lost."

"I know, Rita," Walter replies, "but for us, who cannot fly like you, it is a different matter. I wonder," he goes on, "seeing so many happy people here all around, do you think they are celebrating something?"

"Wonder no more, my friend," a voice booms next to him. "Yes, there is celebrating going on. It is the king's birthday and we have a very good king! That is why the people are so happy."

Walter sees a friendly face beaming towards him. It is the man from one of the stalls they are passing. He sells small copies of the yellow and red flags one sees everywhere. In his hands he holds about five or six, which he waves about.

"Here," he says, handing one to Walter. "And for you too," he adds with a smile, putting one into Bruno's big paws. "Have a good day."

"Thank you sir," Walter responds. "Thank you very much."

"It's a pleasure," the man answers. "I am happy. I want you to be happy, too."

"Ooh, but we are," Walter laughs. "And we will be even happier if we can find some space to perform our music and dance show."

"Well, well, of course," the man reacts, "I should have known that you are artists. Here," he continues, "stand here by me. I have enough extra space. Furthermore, this is an ideal place! Nice and busy, as you can see, and we could make a lot of money today."

"Thank you!" Walter says again. "This is very kind."

"Not at all, not at all," the man smiles. He goes on, "let me introduce myself. My name is Antonius. What is yours?"

"I am Walter, and the bird on my shoulder is Rita, the red robin, who can sing very well," Walter answers. He proceeds, "my other companions are Bruno the bear, who dances very well and Bones, the dog who has been with us for only a short time yet."

"Good, good," Antonius grins. "Well, let's hear and see then what the four of you can do!"

"Right," Walter agrees, "let's do that!"

There is indeed space enough for all of them. Walter shows Bones to sit next to him with the tin to collect money in between them. He takes his flute and begins to play. Immediately Rita joins in and Bruno starts his dancing routine. All of a sudden and as if by magic, they are surrounded by lots of people. What is more, they all are silent, listening to the lovely music Walter and Rita bring forth. They watch Bruno's imposing figure dancing in tune with the golden tones from a small robin's throat and a flute made of reeds.

When the threesome stops for a while to catch their breath, there is loud applause. Money starts tinkling into the money box over which Bones keeps watch. People also start buying lots of small flags. Antonius was right to offer Walter and his friends a place to play. It means good business for all of them. After some time, Walter and Rita start playing and singing again while Bruno dances. The big bear slowly moves backwards and forwards, waving his big paws with the little flag still in one of them. Now and then, he daintily touches one of the children standing in front. They love it, none of them are scared. They see his chain fastened to Bones and also Walter's foot firmly resting on it, where it lies loosely between him and the animals. No, everybody understands there is nothing to be scared of here. The children clap their hands when Bruno walks over to Bones and raises him up on his front legs. The two of them dance together as if they did so for years. Bruno, the old trooper that he is, makes the whole exercise such fun. He performs and carries on, helping Bones, who looks a bit bewildered, to keep in pace with him. The crowd cheers and claps their hands. They enjoy themselves tremendously, and the money keeps rolling in.

Then suddenly, there is a great upheaval. Something is happening. 'What can it be?'

People start whispering, "It is the king. The king is coming." The rumour spreads like fire. "It's the king and his daughter, the Princess Elina!"

Walter and Rita fall silent. Bruno and Bones stop their dancing. The mass of people begin moving towards the main street. There, they will be able to see the carriage with their king and his daughter when they come along.

With a deft movement, Walter picks up the money tin. It is nearly overflowing. "Good work." He smiles. "Come, my friends, let's go. We have earned more than enough for today." He adds, "I would love to see the royal carriage."

"Yes, me too," Rita chirps. "Shall we move together with the crowd in that direction, then?" she asks.

"Fine," Walter replies, "we'll do that. Goodbye Antonius," he calls out. "Thank you for letting us share your space."

"Goodbye Walter," Antonius calls back. "It was a pleasure having you here with me. We both did well because of it. I wish you lots of luck for the future, my friend!"

"Thank you and for you too, Antonius," Walter answers, while emptying the contents of the money box into his pockets. With Bruno and Bones still on their chain and him holding onto it, they are swept away with the stream of people. Most of them waving flags as they run forward. "Just as well Max isn't here," Walter mutters. "He certainly would have got hurt or lost in this crowd."

The royal procession must be coming nearer. Already the sounds of trumpets can be heard. Coming into sight are the heralds, splendid in their blue and gold uniforms, riding on white horses. The horses have blue plumes fastened onto their heads. With every step, the plumes move up and down, up and down. And then there is the golden carriage, glowing and glittering in the sunshine. It is pulled by eight, dapple-grey horses who almost dance in front. The coachman, elegant in blue and gold as well, cracks his whip high above the horses' heads. The foot men, four on each side of the carriage, are in white uniforms. They walk with solemn faces. After all it is a serious business, guarding their king and princess.

Suddenly, Walter sees them, the king strikingly dressed in red and gold, smiling and waving to the people. And the princess. Oooh, she is a dream in white and blue, with golden hair streaming alongside her face. Such a lovely face it is, so sweet Walter instantly loses his heart to her. How gracious she waves and smiles. And can it be true? Yes, it must be. She is smiling directly at him and his friends.

Walter waves his flag at her, with Bruno following his example. Bones barks a greeting at the lovely princess, and truly, there they see it again. The princess smiles and waves at them. Rita, cheeky little thing that she is, flies towards the carriage. She circles around it, diving up and down, singing all the while. The king and princess seem to enjoy her antics and so do the watching crowd. Rita ends her showing off with one last dive, then heads back to Walter, landing on his shoulder as usual. A last wave before the princess is out of sight.

"But, my dream princess," Walter sighs, "You will be forever in my heart. For always and ever!" Suddenly, he feels very lonely, even in the midst of all these people and his friends on his side. And why is it that the day seems less glorious than before?

Bruno touches his arm. "Shall we go, Walter?" he asks. "We still must do some shopping. We're almost out of honey, you know."

Walter smiles into Bruno's troubled face. "I know," he replies. "Don't worry, we'll get your honey." Thankfully, Bruno's urgent voice has brought him back to the here and now. They buy all the things that are needed in a shop, at their way back. Walter even purchases a neat pouch he sees on a shelf there. It comes in handy for safe-keeping the money they earn. The more so, since it has a cord to tie around the waist, making it safer still! Once outside, he shifts the money they made this morning over to the new pouch. "So, this is much better," he says contently. "Much less bulky, too. Also, I keep it under my shirt, so no one can see it."

"Good, can we go and eat now?" Bruno wants to know. He is getting hungry and longs for his portion of honey.

"Can't you wait until we are back in the forest?" Rita chirps. She is thinking of Max, who is alone and waiting for their return.

"Yes, I suppose so," Bruno grumbles.

"I am sure you can," Walter declares. "It is not such a long way off, you'll see."

Max already spots them from afar. He has been on the look-out for most of the morning, a bit edgy and agitated, pick-picking for food, a bit here and a bit there, looking up all the time, staring into the direction his friends will come from. And now, at last, there they are! He runs towards them. "Did you bring food?" is his first question, after they have greeted each other.

"Yes, we did," Walter answers. "And how was your day?" he asks, but such remarks are lost on Max. He is so full of himself, the thought of asking how or what his friends experiences where, does not even enter his head. Instead, he complains.

"You surely took your time. It's been a very long day."

"Yeah," Bruno agrees, "but what a day it was."

"Yes," Bones joins in.

"We were at the market and we made a lot of money." Rita chirps, "and we saw the king and the princess in their golden carriage."

"What king? What princess," Max asks. Surly.

"Ooh, a very nice king and the most lovely princess," Walter says dreamily.

"I wanted to see them too," Max wails. "I told you I wanted to come with."

"You know that was not possible, Max," Walter replies. "But look here," he adds, "I brought you this." He hands Max an enormous bread roll full of raisins and with seeds on top, from one of the bags he carries.

Max is delighted. "This is great," he exclaims. "Just what I like." Hastily he starts devouring the delicious treat, all else is forgotten, just as Walter thought it would be.

That evening, they have a lovely meal together. There is a good feeling all around. Everything is so peaceful and harmonious, it fills their hearts with joy. Later, they watch the moon come up like a huge golden ball, spreading a warm glow over them and their surroundings. It gives them a cosy feeling as well as making them sleepy. Bruno, of course, is the first to doze off. Even his snoring sounds very content. Bones snuggles up to him. It is nice and warm next to Bruno. Soon he sleeps too. The others follow not long afterwards.

That night, Walter dreams of the beautiful princess with the golden hair and the friendly smile.

Chapter V

They continue their journey the next day and the next, travelling at a slow pace. There is no hurry, really. They find it very pleasant to wander from one place to the other. To enjoy the landscapes, changing from riversides to villages and hills, or fields of corn. The sun that shines their evenings together. Then, one afternoon, they meet up with the gypsies. They spot their wagons, painted in bright colours, at the fringe of the forest. Ten or twelve of them are gathered in a circle. People are moving about, dogs can be heard barking. Coming nearer, they see children playing, laughing and shouting to each other.

Max has become very excited. "These could be the gypsies I told you about," He says to Walter.

"Mm, they could be," Walter answers.

"They must be," Max ponders. "After all, I don't think there are many gypsies travelling around the country."

"Well, maybe you are right," Walter admits. "I suppose we can go and ask them."

Bruno is not happy with this idea. "I do not want to go there," he declares. "Those dogs might be a problem. What if they attack us?"

"Yes, well," Walter thinks aloud, "maybe it is best then that Rita and I go. We should be able to find out if it is really the same group Max is talking about."

After discussing this a bit more, the decision is made. Although Bones would love to come, as did Max, Walter eventually leaves with Rita only.

Before reaching the gypsy's camp, they cross a little stream and there, far apart from the others, stands a lonely wagon, all by itself. A young girl, carrying a bucket of water, walks towards them. Rita quickly flies over to her, chirping in sweet tones while circling above her head. The girl laughs, wiping away the long black tresses, the wind is blowing in her face. Now she can have a good look at the little bird.

By this time, Walter also has arrived. "Good day to you," he greets gaily. "Please let me carry this bucket for you."

The girl is startled, but Walter looks so young and friendly, she trusts him at once. "Good day to you too," she smiles. She hands the bucket over to him and they start walking towards the wagon. "Is this your bird?" the girl asks, pointing to Rita, who now lands on her shoulder.

"Well, that is to say," Walter answers, "Rita is a free bird, but she is a very good friend and we are travelling together. Rita, meet,?" he stops. Looking with a question on his face at the gypsy girl.

"My name is Rosa," comes the reply. Her smile is for them both.

"Good," Walter smiles back. "Nice meeting you Rosa, my name is Walter."

They have reached the wagon by this time, and Walter puts the bucket down.

"Thank you very much," Rosa says. She seats herself on some grass in front of the wagon. "Won't you sit and rest for a bit as well?" she asks, looking up at Walter.

He notices she has sad eyes. "Fine," Walter agrees, taking place next to her.

"Tell me about yourself, Walter?" she says. "Where do you come from?"

"It is a long story," Walter answers.

"I like long stories," Rosa laughs.

"Good," Walter responds, and he begins, telling her about himself and the group of friends he travels with. When he describes Max and the tale that goes with it, he sees how tense Rosa becomes.

"What is this?" she wants to know. "You mean to say you have a peacock in your party who speaks to you and mentions things like a pair of golden candlesticks that were stolen?"

"Exactly," Walter replies. "Do you know about this too?"

"Of course I do," Rosa responds, her dark eyes filling with tears. "My husband is in prison because of them. I assure you, though, he is not guilty. He bought those candlesticks, but nobody believes this. His life is ruined and so is mine. I do not know when I will see him again. I am all alone. Even the other gypsies do not want anything to do with me anymore. They say it is because of people like my husband Marik, who go around stealing things, that gypsies are scorned everywhere."

"Ooh, so that is why you are standing so far apart from the other wagons," Walter remarks. "I was wondering about that."

"Yes, it is true," Rosa sniffs. "Not even my own family believes me when I say Marik is not guilty."

"I believe you," Walter says.

"You?" Rosa asks through her tears. "How can that be?"

"That is because I know your husband is not guilty," Walter replies. "Max the peacock told me the true story. It was the gardener who took them. Afterwards, and, maybe because there was such a huge uproar about it, he sold them to your husband, who did not know they were stolen."

"That is it," Rosa cries. "That is exactly what Marik told me. Oh, I am so glad you came along to tell me this. Thank you, thank you," she sobs, taking Walter's hand and squeezing it. "Now they have to let him go, isn't it?" she asks. "They can't keep him in that awful prison anymore? Is that not so? Oh please, please tell me he will be set free?"

"Of course," Walter assures her. "I am confident they will let him go."

"When?" Rosa wants to know, her eyes full of hope now.

"Well, let's see," Walter replies. "Firstly, I think we must get a message to this judge, the master of Max. We must explain why Max ran away and what really happened."

"How can we do that?" Rosa asks eagerly.

Walter looks at the gypsy wagon with its bright red, green and yellow colours. "Do you have horses?" he asks.

Rosa, following his eyes, understands at once. "Yes," she exclaims. "I have two good horses. They are grazing with the others, a bit further down. I will get them, then we can go."

"Only if you are willing to take the others in my group as well," Walter remarks.

"Of course, of course," Rosa answers, already up and on her way.

"Let me remind you who they are," Walter tries to stop her.

"It does not matter," Rosa calls back over her shoulder. "Anyone can come if we can get Marik free."

Before long she is back with the horses and in the shortest possible time they are in front of the wagon, rearing to go. Walter takes his place next to Rosa on the front seat of the wagon. Rita is circling overhead. As Walter tells Rosa who her other passengers will be, she starts to laugh.

"You already told me about them," she says. "So, it is the bear and the dog and Max the peacock. Right? Well, that's fine with me." She cracks the air with her whip and the horses gallop away.

'A real gypsy she is,' Walter can't help thinking. 'Daring and brave and a bit wild.'

Rosa's long hair flies in the wind as she sweeps up her horses even more. Soon they arrive at the place where the others are waiting. Max is the first to hop on the wagon. He does not even wait until it comes to a full stop.

"What, what,?" he cries out. "What is going on, Walter? Are we going where I think we are going?"

"Rosa," Walter says, "This is Max the peacock as you can see. Because of him, you husband soon could be free!"

"Fantastic," Rosa exclaims. "Welcome Max, I am very grateful to you. And yes, indeed, we will be hurrying off to the town where you came from."

"That is great!" Max shouts. "Come, let's go! Let's put things right."

"We certainly are going to try and sort things out, Max," Walter tells the nervous peacock. "Bruno, what are you waiting for?" he calls out. "Come on board, my friend." Bones joyfully jumps into Walter's arms, but Bruno has to make use of the short stepladder that Rosa puts up for him.

"Welcome," she exclaims. "Welcome, all of you. Walter has told me you are his friends. Now I hope that you will be my friends too." Rosa the gypsy is in high spirits and the others feel the same kind of joy. And yes, they agree all of them will be friends forever.

Then their journey begins. Bruno is content sitting in the back, resting against some pillows. It does not take long before he sleeps again. Bones, like Max, sits in front, together with Walter, Rosa and Rita. They love their ride, going very fast, hour after hour. The horses all along keep up a good pace. For them too, it is a pleasure to be out and about, back on the road again. Evening time finds them still at the edge of the forest, but already well on their way. What otherwise would have been a few days travelling by foot, now done on one stretch. It is time for a rest, so a stop is made next to a small creek. Everyone, including the horses, can drink as much water as they want.

Later, Rosa cooks a lovely meal over the fire made by Walter. Here, they camp over for the night. The long evening is spent with much talking between Rosa and Walter while the others laze nearby. Come bedtime, Rosa sleeps in the wagon and Walter makes himself comfortable next to the fire. Bones and Rita were at his side, with Bruno snoring close to the fire as well. Max can be seen hip hopping here, then there, in and out of the shadows, more jumpy and restless than ever.

CHAPTER VI

They continue their journey the following morning, all in the same
order of position as the previous day. Luckily, the weather is in
their favour as well. Warm summer days with now and then a
trickle of rain, just enough to keep the sun from becoming too hot.
Bruno sleeps most of the time, while Bones sometimes jumps off,
running alongside the wagon or in front with Rita keeping him
company, now and then circling high above into the sky and then
again standing on Bones back. Bones keeping steady no matter
how fast he runs.

It keeps them all amused. That is to say, except Max. He has become very still. He just sits, staring in the distance. Often shifting from one leg to the other, as if ready to run off. Knowing full well, this would not be very wise, he doesn't. He just waits and watches, as Walter observes, getting more and more impatient to be back at his own place and family.

As they travel on, Rosa tells Walter about herself and her people, the gypsies. How they go from place to place, trying to find work wherever they go. Nobody really wants them around or trusts them.

"Gypsy girls often marry very young," she says, adding, "Marik and I were very lucky. We did get quite a bit of money at our wedding from our parents and friends. Also, Marik is a hard worker. That is why we could afford to buy our own wagon and horses."

They ride far that day, stopping only to rest the horses while having some food and water for all of them. In the evening, they find another quiet spot to camp out. By putting all their food together, Rosa is able to once again prepare a lovely meal. Walter helps Rosa to clean up by rinsing their plates in the stream next to their camping site. When all the clutter is cleared away, they start talking again. Walter describes the story of what happened to him thus far, and Rosa listens with great interest and understanding.

"You could have been one of us," she smiles. "We also travel the world and many of us earn a living by singing, dancing and making music. My father plays the violin and my mother was a stunning dancer. Yes, we gypsies are famous for our beautiful music."

"I know," Walter answers. "I have heard people talking about that."

"Yes," Rita chirps, "and I have seen and heard this."

"You?" Walter addresses the little bird on his shoulder who has been listening quietly to all the talk going on so far.

"Yes, me." Rita chirps, "I once was at a real gypsy party. You know," she goes on, "It might have been in the village where Max comes from. Maybe it was your people, Rosa. Yes, the more I think about it, the more I think it must have been so! I suppose it was before the commotion of the missing candle sticks. Anyway, it was a lovely party, full of music and dancing. I was hiding in one of the trees there and enjoyed myself hugely. I loved the whole evening."

Walter quickly explains to Rosa what the little bird on his shoulder tells him.

"Right," Rosa cries out. "I remember that night and it was indeed just before those awful things happened to us. Marik and I were so happy. We danced and sang and ate the wonderful food our mothers prepared for the feast."

"I know, I know," Rita sings. "Just a pity I can't recall seeing you there."

Again Walter translates. Rosa laughs, "O well, we must have been looking all more or less the same to you," she says, "What with our colourful dresses and shawls fluttering in the wind. From high above in a tree, it must have been difficult to see who is who!"

"Yes, that is so," Rita agrees.

"My, my," Walter grins.

"Isn't it a small world? And you, Rita, not telling me anything about this? Actually," he goes on, "You never told me much how your life was before we met. It seemed to me you never wanted to. But tonight, seeing that we all recall the stories of our lives, don't you want to do the same?"

"Ooh, I don't really mind doing so," Rita answers. "It is just, it is very painful to remember those things that happened to me. You see," she goes on, "I was brought up with my sisters and brothers by our parents who were very good to us. We had plenty to eat and enjoyed each other's company. But then something terrible happened. There was this bird. I believe it is called a cuckoo who came into our lives. When my parents were out to search for food, she came and laid her egg in our nest. My parents were amazed when they came back and found it there. They were even more amazed when, soon afterwards, this egg broke open. Out came a far bigger chick than us. It was hungry all the time and ate much more every day. My parents could not keep up feeding it and this chick pushed us aside when we also wanted something to eat. It even started pushing my sisters and brothers out of the nest. Not me though. I dug myself in under some twigs and refused to give way. It was a long and hard struggle but I survived, as you can see," Rita sighs. They all have listened to her story. Even Bruno, sleepy as ever, somehow managed to stay awake, nodding his head in sympathy over and over again.

Walter breaks the silence. "That is quite a tale indeed."

Rosa is the only one who does not know what happened to Rita. "What did she say?" she asks, "What happened to her?"

Walter then tells her the whole sad story of Rita's sufferings and Rosa, like the others, takes pity on her.

"How did it go from there?" Bones wants to know.

"Ooh, I left when I was big enough to do so," Rita replies. "Although this cuckoo bird tried to get me out of the way all the time, I still managed to get some food now and then. I even managed to learn to fly. But this cuckoo bird drove me dilly, I tell you. It kept on calling, 'cuckoo, cuckoo,' every day, the whole day. At long last, I had enough of this. It was time to go. I said goodbye to my parents, who were in such a frantic state by the horror of it all they did not even try to keep me from going. They understood. Yes, well, from then on I looked after myself. I also found out I could sing; I believe that came naturally because I am a Robin and we are born with very good voices." Rita just states this fact without giving herself any airs. She goes on. "So time went by and not too long afterwards, I met you, Walter," Rita ends her story.

"Indeed," Walter responds. "That was a happy day indeed." He gently smiles at Rita and tells Rosa the rest of the story. How the two of them met and how things went from there.

They go to sleep very late that evening in the same order as before. Rosa sleeps in the wagon while Walter and his friends camp out in the open air as they are used to do. Max again hardly sleeps, he keeps fretting about, restless as only he can be.

"We should reach your village by tomorrow," Walter assures his friend. "Then you will see your family again."

"That is good," Max exclaims. "That is very good."

Chapter VII

They leave early the next day and indeed, that afternoon, the village where Max used to live, is reached. Max can hardly contain his excitement. "We're here," he keeps shouting over and over. "We're here!"

They attract a lot of attention while driving through the main street. Max keeps giving directions, wriggling all the time, folding and unfolding his magnificent feathers, hardly able to stay on the wagon. But he does and so, at long last, they arrive at the judge's house. There Max makes them stop. He can't wait to get off. They watch him running away, hopping through the front garden, past the house to the back. Rita, curious as ever, flies after him.

"Bones, I think you should stay here," Walter declares. "And you too Bruno. I know it is hard, but it is better this way." Placing the step-ladder in position and holding out his hand, he asks, "Are you coming Rosa?"

"Ooh yes," Rosa answers, taking his hand while climbing down onto the street. "Let's get this matter cleared up now!"

Together, they walk through the open gate to the front door of the house. That door is already being opened by a rounded figure of a man. He seems a bit alarmed. "What is going on?" he asks. "What is all this commotion?"

"Good day, sir," Walter greets politely. "My name is Walter, and this is Rosa. We suppose you are the judge Max told us about?"

"Max?" comes the amazed reply. "Yes, yes," he then adds, "I am Judge Martins." He shakes hands with both of them. Asking, while doing so, "but tell me what is this? Did you bring Max back? I thought I saw him running past our window." Without waiting for an answer, the judge starts moving towards the back of the house, looking for Max.

"You are correct, sir," Walter answers, following him with Rosa on his heels. He adds, "We did indeed bring him back to you."

"That is very nice," Judge Martins says. "I missed him. I can't tell you how pleased I am. I can't wait to see him again."

As Walter and Rosa catch up with him, Walter feels he must begin to explain the situation. "Sir," he says. "I have to tell you that I am a person who understands animals and birds."

"What do you mean?" the judge asks. "I also love animals and think I understand them."

"No, sir, not like me," Walter insists. "You see," he goes on, "I understand their language, the things they are saying."

"Truly?" the judge stops in his tracks. "That is incredible," he reacts. "Tell me then, what did Max say? Why did he run away?"

"That is what we want to discuss with you, sir," Walter answers. "That is why we came." At that moment they see Max coming, running towards them, feathers flying, a trail of other peacocks following close behind. It is a whole family, making a lot of exited noises together.

"Quiet, quiet please," Judge Martins calls out. His tone of voice changes as Max nearly tumbles over him. "My goodness, it is so nice to see you again, Max," he utters. "We all have missed you terribly."

Max bows his head in a greeting and Judge Martins fondly strokes the beautiful feathers of this proud and gorgeous bird. The whole peacock family gathers around them in one happy reunion.

"Come, let us people sit down on the bench underneath that tree over there," the judge suggests after a while. "I would like you to tell me everything you know. Everything that I should know."

Max and his family tag behind them as the judge and his visitors walk over to the nearby tree. Once they are all seated, Walter begins to unfold the tale that brought them here. Max is standing right beside his master, listening, watching, as Walter explains the things that happened. He tells Judge Martins how unpleasant his foreman Hector had been to all the animals. How he in particular singled Max out as his victim. He also reveals that Max saw Hector take the golden candlesticks out of the house and that he later saw Hector selling them. Selling them to Marik, the gypsy, who just happened to pass by.

"Is this true?" Judge Martins asks.

Max nods his head. "Yes, yes, it is true," he says. Now, for the first time, the judge really understands him.

"Well, this is outrageous," he fumes. "And you, my dear?" he addresses Rosa. "How do you fit in with all this? Are you Marik's sister?"

"Rosa is Marik's wife," Walter answers in her place.

"Ooh, oh," is all the judge replies. For a moment or so everyone is quiet, then Judge Martins stands up. "We must rectify things at once," he declares. "Your husband, dear Rosa, must be set free immediately. As for you, Max," he adds, "you do not have anything from this man to fear anymore. As your family may already have told you, he no longer works here! I let him go soon after you left. I did not actually like or trust him. I heard he is now working somewhere else not too far away. We'll find him later, but first things first. We urgently must visit the prison at once. This matter needs to be attended to now! As it happens, my wife is out of town for a few days so we can leave forthwith without me having to go back to the house."

"We can all fit into my wagon," Rosa proposes.

It takes a few seconds before Judge Martins answers … Walter can almost hear him think, 'odd, it will look very odd. Imagine me, the judge, riding through the streets in this multi-coloured gypsy wagon.' Then slowly, a smile lit up his face. "Fine," he agrees. "That will be just fine. Thank you Rosa, it is a good idea. Now people will realize something special is going to happen. Let them all come to witness that though an error has taken place, it shall now be made undone. An innocent man shall be set free!" He hurries to the front of the house where Bruno and Bones still guard the wagon. Noticing them, the judge seems to be taken aback a bit.

"Don't worry." Walter, who has been trailing the judge along with the others, calls out. Bruno and Bones mean no harm. They are very friendly.

"Yes, yes," Bruno grumbles. "Friendly, are we." He nevertheless decides to move to the back of the wagon again. After all, Walter has returned now, and he loves the comfort there, with the softness of the cushions that give him the chance to sleep as much as he likes. Bones is wagging his tail to show his good intentions as Walter first helps Rosa, then Judge Martins up onto the wagon. Only then does he climb on himself. Rita, who has been watching from a distance, flies back on Walter's shoulder.

A lot of children, along with some adults, including members of the judges' household, are gathered around. They are curious to find out what is going on.

Judge Martins makes the most of the situation by waving to all of them. "I'll be back soon," he declares. "I am just going to give a man his freedom! Justice must be done!"

Max, who with his family, is standing a bit on one side, can not endure this anymore, "I must go too," he says and with a few leaps, lands safely near the others, on to the front of the wagon. "I will be back soon," he echoes the judge, while Rosa cracks the whip and the horses, cheered on by the crowd, start galloping away.

All along their route, people wave and smile at them. Judge Martins enjoys every moment of the ride and, together with the others, smiles and waves back.

"This is great," he remarks. "Such an unusual event this is!"

Rosa follows his directions on how to arrive at the prison. It does not take all that long to get there. The rumour has already spread; it seems. A large crowd is waiting for them. "They're coming, they're coming," people shout.

Judge Martins, smiling broadly, keeps waving to everybody, and so do Rosa and Walter. Bones, not wanting to be left out of all this, starts barking. Bruno, woken up from the noise, is now leaning out of the back, showing his sleepy face and flapping his big paws about. Max, seeing this is his chance to be also part of a show for once, hops up and down in the front while displaying his magnificent feathers. Rita has taken to the air again, hovering very low over the whole area.

The crowd loves it. As soon as the horses come to a halt, a man in uniform steps forward to greet them. It is the head warden of the prison. Judge Martins stands up and begins to speak. At once everybody is quiet, for all of them know the judge and love and respect him.

"Dear citizens," are his first words. "I am glad to see so many of you here today. For today, an innocent man will walk away from this prison, free!"

His listeners call back. "Yes, yes, innocent people should not be in prison. Who is he? Who is he?."

The judge, helped by Walter, who has put the step-ladder out, climbs down.

"It is Marik the gypsy," he answers. "And this is his wife, Rosa," he adds, taking Rosa's hand as she climbs down as well. He lifts her hand, still in his, high up into the air and the crowd cheers them both. "Thank you." Judge Martins beams. "But that is not all," he continues, taking Walter's hand too. "This young man here he understands the language of animals and birds. It is to him that my beautiful peacock Max, who, as you can see, is also here, told the true story. It is all about those golden candle sticks who were stolen from my house. You all know the tale by now but what you do not know is that Hector, my foreman and gardener took them.!"

A gasp of disbelieve goes up from the gathering around them.

"But that is wicked," someone shouts.

"Indeed," the judge agrees. "It truly is. We will get him though," he goes on. "However, first things first."

The crowd watches as he shakes hands with the head-warden, as do Rosa and Walter. Moments later, the prison doors swing open and the four of them enter. Bruno and Bones remain on the wagon as before, and so does Max. Once inside the prison, they are taken to a large office, where lots of papers have to be sorted out and signed. It all takes time and Rosa gets impatient.

"When will Marik come?" she asks.

"Presently, my dear, presently," the judge answers.

At long last, another warden is summoned to fetch Marik from his cell. It is a great reunion. Rosa and Marik are so happy to be together again. With faces full of joy, they hold each other.

"Good," judge Martin declares. "I am very glad for both of you. I hope you will forgive us Marik," he adds. "It was terrible what happened to you, but luckily, everything is cleared up now. The real thief will soon be arrested, of that you can be sure. In the meantime, you can thank this young man, Walter, with his gift to understand animals and birds. Because of him and my peacock Max, who told him the true story, you are now a free man!"

Marik is very grateful. With tears in his eyes, he thanks first Walter and then asks for Max.

"Let's go outside," the judge says. "You will find him in your wagon."

The people start cheering as soon as they notice Marik and Rosa walking hand in hand towards their wagon, along with Judge Martins and Walter. Everybody is waving and clapping hands. Marik and Rosa wave back, smiling happily.

Marik calls out to the peacock. "Thank you, Max, thank you for getting me free!" He leaps up the steps, pulling Rosa with him. They both try to embrace Max, who loves the attention, but hugely dislikes embraces. He struggles to get out of it.

For the watching crowd, it is amusing to see. A roar of laughter arises. Every one enjoys the show.

Judge Martins is speaking to the head warden, who has followed them outside. "Word must be sent to the police," the judge says. "They must apprehend Hector. I want this man arrested and expect him to be our new prisoner by tonight."

"Very well," the head warden answers. "We have an empty cell waiting for him."

At last, after the usual parting greetings have taken place, the judge mounts the steps onto the wagon again, followed by Walter. In a matter of seconds, Walter has heaved the steps up, hanging them in their fixed place alongside the wagon. By this time Marik, who now holds the reins, just wants to leave.

Under loud whip-cracking the horses pull off, first slowly, then faster and faster they go. Farewells are waved to the crowd. Children for a while, try to run beside the wagon, but they soon are left behind. Back at the judge's house, the horses never grow tired of galloping at a steady pace. They like their outing and being part of such a happy occasion. People greet them everywhere.

Once the judge's place is reached, he invites his fellow travellers to come in. Walter likes the idea, but Marik and Rosa feel differently. They like nothing better than to drive off, back to their own people.

"Yes, well, I can understand that," Judge Martins declares. "You have great news to tell them." The happy couple again and again thank Judge Martins and Walter, as well as Max, before taking their leave from all of them. Marik gives the horses the go-ahead and away they speed. For a short while, Rita keeps them company. She charms them with a song as she settles on Rosa's shoulder. But then she takes off again, performing a few goodbye dives before flying back and landing on Walter's shoulder. He, together with the judge and the other onlookers, keeps following the wagon with their eyes, until they're out of sight. Walter's arm feels limp from all the waving after them. He is happy with Rosa's return. That this little bird still chooses him as her best friend is something to be grateful for, 'very grateful,' he ponders.

Judge Martins smiles at him. "I am glad about the good ending," he says.

"Yes, so am I," Walter replies.

"Well," the judge goes on, "I have been thinking and this might come as bit of a surprise now, but I would like to offer you the position of foreman here Walter. I tried to take care of things here on my own since letting Hector go, but am not very successful. In a few months, I shall be retiring. Only then will I be able to look properly after my animals and birds and all that needs to be looked after. In the meantime, I am looking for someone who can help me out. You seem just the right person for this. What do you say? Would that suit you?"

"Ooh, yes, that would suit me just fine," Walter manages to utter. He really is surprised about the judge's offer, but at the same time, very pleased. To settle down for a while here with Judge Martins, who is such a nice man, appeals to him. Max, who amidst his family, is listening nearby, seems pleased too.

"What do you say guys?" Walter asks Bruno and Bones. Bruno likes the idea of staying at this place as well. "I am all for it," he beams, thinking of how nice it will be to just spend lots of time sleeping.

"It's fine with me," Bones says.

"Rita?" Walter calls out. From above their heads comes her answer.

"Yes Walter, let's stay, I say."

So it is decided. Walter and his friends become part of the judges' household. There is a little cottage in the garden, where Walter, Rita and Bones move in. Bruno senses winter is coming, which for him means time to hibernate. Yes, a winter sleep. So he happily makes himself at home in the small wooden cabin next to the cottage. Max and his family have their own living quarters a bit further away. It is a perfect arrangement. Walter is very content doing what he does; looking after the animals and the birds overseeing the garden. Also, when needed, he does other chores as well. Cleaning and polishing Judge Martin's carriage is one of those. Sometimes he even acts as coachman when Dieter, the regular driver, has a day off. Judge Martins and his wife are very friendly. They both take a kind interest in him, treating him almost as a family member. The judge's wife and Walter liked each other from the moment they met. Short and a bit plump, like her husband, Mrs. Martins has a ready smile and twinkling eyes. Her whole person radiates warmth, and this gives Walter, as well as everybody else around her, a sense of wellbeing. For Walter, this is a whole new and pleasant experience. Never before has he been with such wonderful people. On top of that, he also is paid a nice wage, of which he saves every penny. The judge keeps him informed about Hector, the previous foreman. Hector has indeed been arrested. His confession that it was he who stole the golden candle-sticks will keep him quite some time in prison.

Chapter VIII

The weeks slowly go by, bringing autumn. Bringing lovely golden days with trees everywhere wearing rust brown and yellow leaves. Softly, surely, winter will follow. Bruno, instead of spending most of the time together with his friends, now feels like withdrawing from them for a while. Walter understands. He brings some extra blankets from the stables to Bruno's wooden cabin.

"You want to go into your winter sleep," he states. "Feel free to do so, my friend. You have earned a good rest."

"Thank you," Bruno answers with a yawn he cannot keep back. "Thank you for everything, Walter. For the food, for the honey, for all the things to eat, you have put on the shelves here. There never was a friend like you are."

"Ooh, nonsense," Walter laughs, adding, "and what about Rita and Bones here?"

"You all are," Bruno replies, yawning again. He really is overcome by sleep and hardly hears Walter's promise anymore, that the three of them will come often to see if everything is well.

"So, that's that then," Walter sighs. "Bruno is asleep for months to come."

"Gee, I will miss him," Bones says.

"And I," Rita chirps.

"Yes," Walter remarks. "But what can we do? It is as it is and those months will also pass. Let's just be happy for Bruno that now at least he can have a real winter sleep. That's how it should be. I don't think he ever had one before."

"No," Bones agrees, "he told me as much."

"I know," Rita falls in, "I heard him saying, he had to work, work, every season of the year."

"Right." Walter says, "well, let's go back to our cabin. It is getting chilly already."

Wintertime is a quiet time. There is not much to do in the garden and many evenings are spent with Walter playing the flute. Rita, instead of resting , usually joins in.

"You are not like other birds I know," Walter tells her. "Normally, birds are silent after the sun has gone down. They go to sleep then."

"Not me," Rita chirps. "No, not me!"

"Well, you must be the odd one out," Walter declares. He adds, "I am glad, though, for I like your company. Also, now we can even make music together during the evenings."

And that is what they do. Bones usually is lying near Walter's feet, his head resting on his paws. Often, he falls asleep. Sometimes he dreams of the good life he enjoys with his friends here. Bruno, though, is unaware of the things that go on around him. He does not know how carefully his friends watch over him, looking in everyday to see if he is safe and secure.

Meanwhile, Judge Martins and his wife are very pleased with the good order Walter has brought to their estate. They take a warm interest in all he does and praise him many times. The music he and Rita make also gets noticed. Max and his family often hear them play, as do Dieter, the coachman and his wife who live in the dwelling near the main house. They sometimes come over to listen and enjoy the beautiful sound of flute and birdsong melting together. Soon, Mr. and Mrs. Martins come to hear of it too. They promptly invite them over to their house to come and make music for them as well. Because he is such a gentle, good behaving dog, Bones is also allowed to come inside. Near the open fire is his favourite place to lie down. Many a pleasant evening is spent thus. Evenings filled with music and lively talk about a wide variety of subjects. Sometimes the judge tells stories from books he has read. Interesting tales that made Walter wish he could read also. But he can't. He cannot even write his own name. This fills him with sadness but, as always, tries to find a solution to this problem. He is longing to ask if Judge Martins can help, but decides to wait for the right moment.

Then, one morning on Harold's day off, he again drives the judge to the courtroom. As it happens, Judge Martins seems to have a notion about the things that keep Walter's mind so occupied. Is it a sixth sense, or has he been pondering over this as well? So, to Walter's surprise, the judge starts telling him how important it is, to be able to read and write. How, with that skill, one can study further to gain knowledge and wisdom.

"Yes, yes," Walter responds, "but I can do neither. I have been wanting to talk about it, but never dared to. I would so love to have an education. Is there nothing that can be done?"

"Indeed," the judge smiles. "Of course, something can be done. Trust me, I will see to it." And see to it, he does. Arrangements were made for Walter to follow evening classes in the small church hall nearby. Walter is a keen learner and soon becomes one of father Tobias' best students.

"This young man is so hungry for knowledge, he soaks it up, like a sponge soaks up water," he tells Judge Martins.

"That is what my wife, and I hoped for," the judge answers, adding, "we have grown very fond of him and believe he has a great future."

It is indeed true that Walter has become very dear to the elderly couple. He is a hard worker and willing to take on any task that comes along. This, together with his good natured behaviour, makes him well liked by everyone at the judge's place.

When not studying, Walter, Rita and Bones spend many more hours in the comfort and warmth of Judge Martin's cosy living room. Rita usually sits on one of the bookshelves that fills a whole wall there. Bones, of course, lies near the fire.

Judge Martins and Walter love to go through many interesting maps of the world. There is tea and cake, which Mrs. Martins provides, while her husband tries to provide answers to the many questions Walter asks. Walter wants to know about the stars and the sky and the moon."

"How is it that the sun shines over the earth by day and the moon by night? How did the earth begin and what is it all about?"

Although Judge Martins does not have answers to everything, he does the best he can. Father Tobias, of course, is also a good source of information, and is always willing to assist. He is a welcome guest, and many evenings come over to take the debates even further.

It is an amazing period in Walter's life. A period he will always remember with intense gratefulness. And so, the seasons pass.

Spring sees Bruno waking up from his winter sleep. He cheerfully joins his friends again and life goes on as before. Utterly pleasant days of working and studying for Walter. Lazy days for Bruno with enough food, especially honey, to keep him more than happy. Rita and Bones have no complaints either. They are with Walter most of the time, but also visit Max and his family often. They are friends with everyone in the judge's household, from the stable boy to the coachman and his wife and their children. Yes, with all the people in and around the estate, as is Walter, it is one big happy family now.

However, things seldom stay the same forever. Judge Martins is soon to retire and Walter starts feeling restless. One day, after finishing early with his work, he decides to go for a walk. He and his friends set out for the woodlands behind Judge Martin's place. The sun shines and already some bushes start flowering. Something special seems to be in the air.

Under an enormous evergreen tree, Walter sits down. Rita is on his shoulder. Bones stretches out next to him, as does Bruno. As always, Walter carries his flute in the inner pocket of his jacket. His flute with the golden sound that gladdens his heart. Before long, a mellow tune drifts through the air. Rita joins in, enhancing the loveliness.

Then suddenly, there is a stirring high up in the density of the tree. Squeaky noises. What is going on? Rita stops her singing, Walter rests his flute, they all look up.

"I'll go up and see what it is," Rita says. She flies into the tree, and at once, starts chirping away.

"Well, who is there?" Walter calls out. Bones begins to bark. "No," Walter reprimands him. "Don't Bones, you must not scare whoever is up there in the tree."

"Ooh," Bones responds, a bit sheepish. "I won't then."

"You never guess who I found here," Rita calls out to them.

"Well, please tell us," Walter calls back.

"Its two little monkeys," Rita almost shouts.

"Get them down. We also want to see them," Walter replies.

"They don't want to come," Rita hollers.

Bones is standing directly under the tree trunk now, gazing up, but obeying Walter's orders, he keeps quiet. Walter and Bruno join him there. Looking up into the density of the tree , they see nothing.

"I can climb up," Bruno remarks, adding, "I can climb trees, you know."

"Yes, I believe you," Walter says. "Still, I think it might be better if I go."

This is easy enough for the tree has many branches. To get onto the first one, though, is a bit of a problem.

"Come," Bruno utters. Standing underneath the tree, he cups his forepaws together

"Aah, thank you," Walter replies. "It makes things so much easier, my friend." He steps into Bruno's paws and then on to the first low-hanging branch. From there, it takes him only a short while to reach the monkeys. They sit, hugging each other, looking scared, although Rita has told them Walter is a friend.

"Hi, hello, you two," Walter greets them, sitting down, close by. "My, my, this really is a surprise," he goes on. "Tell me, how did you get here?" The monkeys just keep on clutching each other, their eyes afraid and helpless.

"They're too scared to talk," Rita chirps.

"Yes, I can see that," Walter replies. "Strange," he goes on, "finding them here. I wonder where they come from? I suppose it must be from some faraway place. They should not be in this country, I think."

"You are right," Rita says. "Although they are scared of people, they did talk to me. It seems that a wicked person stole them; snatched them from out of their forest. After that, they were taken on a ship, away from their parents, brothers and sisters and all the others they used to know."

"That's awful," Walter reacts. "Who would do something like that? Taking such young ones away from their families. They're still very young now, even."

"Yes, they are," Rita agrees.

"Won't you tell me your names?" Walter asks gently.

"Youtoo," one of the monkeys blurts out. "We are called, Youtoo."

Walter shakes his head. "That is odd," he says. "I have never heard of such a name. Let me think, the person who gave you this name, I suppose, he always said that?"

"Always," the other monkey replies.

"Yes, that is what I thought," Walter remarks. "You see," he goes on, "this man did not give you both a name, he just called to you, 'You two!'. I also said that just now, remember? Do you understand? No?" He helplessly shakes his head again as does Rita and the monkeys do the same. "Well, anyway," Walter laughs, "I am pleased to see you are no longer so scared of me. I am sure we will all become very good friends. But," he continues, "we should start by giving you proper names. What about Mona and Rona?"

"That sounds nice," Rita chirps. "Rona can be the one with the reddish colour hair and Mona, the other. It is easy to remember then, don't you think?"

"Fine," Walter responds. "Rona and Mona, it is. Do you like it, my dears?" he asks the monkeys. "Are you happy with it?" The monkeys nod their heads. "Good," Walter says. He looks down to see if Bruno and Bones are still underneath the tree. "Everything is so quiet," he calls to them. "Are you guys there?"

"Oh, yes," Bruno booms. "We are here."

"We are watching and waiting," Bones answers.

"Fine," is Walters' response. "I am afraid you have to watch and wait a bit longer, my friends. We have to find out a bit more about these two monkeys. I hope we can get them to leave this tree!"

"No problem," Bruno replies. "We are in no hurry, Walter. Bones and I can do with a little snooze, anyway."

"Now then," Walter says to Mona and Rona, "tell me. Have you been here a long time? And how did you come to be here?"

"We ran away," Mona answers.

"Yes," Rona confirms, "we did and then we found this tree."

"Nobody can see us here," it is Mona speaking again. "The squirrel looks after us," she goes on.

"Yes," Rona chatters, "his name is Theo, and he gives us lots of food."

"Aah, I understand," Walter says. "So this squirrel has taken pity on you and shares the food he gathered for the winter with you. He must be a very nice squirrel, for sure. Anyway, this is all very well, but what happens next? You can not stay here forever, or what do you say?"

The monkeys look at him with dazed eyes. They don't know.

"Well, let me think," Walter mutters, "let me just think for a moment. I could, of course, take you to a real forest," he ponders.

"There you would be free to roam and wander about as much as you like. Luckily, the winters here are not all that cold. I am sure you will be able to survive them quite easily. Shall we do that?" he asks the two little monkeys who are still clinging to each other. Their eyes move from Walter to Rita and back again.

"They don't know," Rita says. "I think they are afraid to go away from here."

"Yes," the monkeys agree. "We do not want to go away from this tree," Rona declares. "We are safe here," Mona adds.

"Fine, fine," is Walters' reply.

"Can I also say something?" a shrilly voice asks.

"This must be Theo the squirrel," Rita remarks.

"Yes," the voice comes again and Walter, looking up, sees a large squirrel glaring at him. He must have been there all the time, listening and watching.

"Indeed," the squirrel declares. "I have heard all you had to say. I just want to tell you. Leave them be. Good day and goodbye!"

"And good day to you as well," Walter answers. "Nice to know you, Theo."

Rita, always the one to try and help things along, chirps, "This is Walter, Theo, and my name is Rita."

"Yeaah, yeaah," Theo reacts, not very friendly. "Why don't you leave the monkeys alone?" he says. "They are safe here and I look after them well."

"That is very good of you," Walter answers soothingly. "You must agree though," he goes on, "they cannot hide in this tree forever."

Theo sniffs. "What exactly do you have in mind then?" he asks.

"I heard you talking about bringing them to the forest so that they can be free, but I don't think that is a good idea. They are too young to be free just yet!"

"Of course, you are right," Walter says. He goes on. "I do not really want to set them free in the forest, Theo. I was actually thinking more about taking them with me. After all, one can't expect you to look after them forever. You may want to start your own family,"

"That might be true," Theo admits. "But that does not mean I cannot at the same time look after these monkeys. I have become very attached to them, you know."

"I would think so; and they to you," Walter answers him. "But, in the end, the whole situation might become a bit of a problem. You are aware of that, aren't you?"

"Yes, it could be," Theo answers half-heartedly.

"That is why I think it might be better if they come with me," Walter says. "We will look after them very well, me and my friends, I can assure you. What do you say, Rita?" he asks the robin who is now on his shoulder.

She has been listening quietly to the whole conversation, but now she gives her full support to Walter. "We will indeed," she chirps. "They will be well looked after by all of us."

Theo is not fully convinced yet, so he decides to ask the monkeys themselves. "What would you like to do?" he wants to know from them.

Mona and Rona look at him, then at each other, and lastly, to Rita and Walter. "We are very thankful for all you have done for us, Theo," Mona utters, "But I think it would be fun to go away from here with Walter and Rita."

Rona blurts out. "Yeaah, there is not much to do here in this tree."

Mona utters. "It does get a bit boring, you know."

"It could be, yes," Theo has to admit. Then, turning to Walter, he says, "It seems to me you are the one person they trust. And you are right, it might become a bit of a problem for me to always look after them. I will miss them but seeing they want to go, then that is what they should do. Are you planning to take them with you now?" he asks Walter.

"No, not right away," Walter answers. "That would not be very thoughtful, would it? No, it might be better to take them in a few weeks' time. Let's all get used to the idea first, shall we?"

One can see Theo is pleased that the monkeys will be staying with him for a while longer. The monkeys themselves have no objection, either. After all, Theo has been so good to them. They feel somewhat guilty about their eagerness to leave him and go away with Walter and Rita the robin. Now at least they can make up for this by staying a little longer.

"Yes, well," Theo remarks, "it is not so bad here either, is it?" he asks Rona and Mona.

"No, no, it isn't," they assure him in choir. "We love being here with you. Only, it is as Walter says, we cannot stay here forever." Now the two monkeys take turns in speaking. It is quite funny really. When the one finishes, the other takes over. They do not want Theo to feel bad. They also do not want to appear ungrateful for all he has done for them, but both of them long to get away and Walter gives them the change to do just that. Their excited chatter brings a smile to Walter's face. They are such a cute pair. Seeing him smile, the monkeys all of a sudden let go of each other and start clinging onto Walter. It seems they have totally taken to him, just like most anyone else does too.

Walter embraces them, saying, "My, my, how lucky we are to have found each other. First, it was Theo who found you here, and you were so lucky that he looked after you both this long winter. It was more than kind of him, don't you agree?"

"Yes, yes," Rona and Mona answer him. "Thank you Theo," they both call out to the squirrel, who is still sitting on the tree branch above them.

"Ooh well," Theo utters, a bit overwhelmed by all this praise. "There is more where that came from. It was a season of plenty this year. I stored so much food away, there is enough for all of us. It will see us through spring as well. And yes, I understand that these two little friends of ours can not stay here." He addresses Walter. "It is a pity, but they will be better off with you," he ends his prattle.

"Well, I hope so," Walter answers. "It will at least give them the chance to widen their horizons. I'll try to give them a good future. Of that you can be sure. And as for you. Theo," he adds, "you won't be lonely for long. Come summer and you find yourself a sweet she squirrel to be your friend. There must be lots of squirrels around here somewhere."

"Ooh yes there are," Theo replies. "Don't worry about me Walter, everything will turn out just fine."

"Good," Walter smiles, rising to go. "We have to leave now, but we come and visit you often. I promise," he adds, after seeing the faces of Mona and Rona drop.

"Ooh good," Mona sighs.

"And you will tell us when we can come and go with you?" Rona asks.

"Of course I will," Walter replies, "but for now, it is goodbye to you all," he says while putting the two monkeys on the tree branch next to him.

"Bye, bye," Mona and Rona call back, clutching each other for comfort again.

Rita is still on Walter's shoulder as he climbs down. Theo the squirrel follows them. Keeping a safe distance from Bruno and

Bones, he settles himself on a far outer branch where no one can see him. From there he looks on, as first Bones and then Bruno welcome Walter and Rita back. He hears how the two of them tell of their encounter with the two small monkeys and with him, Theo. Also about the promise they made to take them away and look after them.

"Great," Bruno hollers. "That is just great. I like little monkeys. I know little monkeys. One of my masters had two of them as well. I looked after them and we became great friends."

"Well, if you like them, I am sure I will like them too," Bones joins in.

"Wonderful," Walter exclaims. "I can't wait to have them with us," he says. Then he goes on, "My friends, it might be time to think about leaving. No, not only this place … well, that too … but maybe we should restart our journey. Remember? We were travelling all over the land and enjoying it."

"Yes, yes, I remember." Bruno cries.

"And I do too," Bones, as usual, falls in with his friend.

"I am all for it," Rita chirps. "When shall we go?"

"Soon," Walter answers. "We should leave soon."

Theo is content with what he has seen and heard. He knows know it is a truly great group of friends who will look well after the two monkeys that are still in his care. When the time comes for them to leave, he can let them go with a happy heart.

"Goodbye," he calls after them while climbing down onto another tree branch from where they are all able to see him.

"Goodbye Theo," Walter calls back. "We will see you soon again."

"Goodbye Theo," Ria greets him.

Bruno waves one of his big paws towards him. "Goodbye Theo," he booms and Bones barks a friendly farewell as well.

After this outing, Walter becomes more and more restless. He longs to be free again and go where ever he wants to go. Not least because there is also the thought of a beautiful princess somewhere in his mind. He knows he will never be able to forget her. In spite of all his efforts, he could not find out much about her. Father Tobias' answers to his questions always seemed vague.

'Yes, there is the king and his daughter Princess Elina. And yes, he is a good king,' is all the response he did get. Even Judge Martins could not provide much information. He did tell Walter, though, 'King Frederik is a good king and the people love him and his daughter.' He also mentioned some strange rumours. Rumours of a kingdom split in two.

'Split in two?' Walter wanted to know. 'How can that be?'

'Nobody knows exactly what the truth is here,' was judge Martin's answer. 'It is all kept very hush-hush. So rather forget about it, Walter. If the king in his wisdom does not want this matter revealed, so be it.'

'Well, maybe,' Walter cannot help thinking. 'It is all very puzzling, though.' He can't help wondering if there is any truth in those rumours, and really would like to find out more.

Judge Martins seems to sense the unrest in Walter. One morning, he confronts him. "Only a few weeks from now, Walter," he says. "Then I retire and you can be on your way. Or would you rather stay here? You can, you know," he adds. "My wife and I have become very fond of you, and you are a good worker. We would like you to stay with us."

Walter shakes his head. "Thank you sir," he says. "but no, I don't think so. It was nice to be here. I have learned a lot and I thank you for it. You and your wife gave me so much, I can never repay you for that. I can now read and write. I can find my way anywhere and feel it is time for me to move on."

Judge Martins sighs. "As you wish, Walter," he says, "But remember, you will always be welcome here."

Walter can only thank the judge again and watches him walk towards his carriage. Climbing on, he remarks, "I'll better go to the courtroom now. I am not retired yet!"

Harold the coachman spurs on the horses and away they go. Judge Martins and Harold both wave at him and Walter waves back. Soon they disappear from sight. Walter returns to his work, pondering all the while where he will go from here.

During the next few weeks, he is kept pretty busy. Spring cleaning the garden and the quarters of Max and his family, as well as those of the others. Even so, he makes time to visit Rona and Mona the monkeys, now and then, bringing them some fruit, nuts and other titbits.

Rita is always eager to go and so are Bruno and Bones. It makes for an enjoyable outing. The monkeys are always very glad to see them all. They are not afraid of Bruno nor of Bones, strangely enough. They find them great play mates and move from the one to the other while making charming little noises of contentment. Theo usually is also there and the whole group of them have a pleasant time together. But the monkeys are getting restless too.

"Are we going soon?" is what they want to know.

"Yes, soon," is Walter's answer then. Even Theo the squirrel is getting a bit fidgety. It seems spring stirs everyone up a bit. Walter, noticing this change in behaviour, asks him: "Have you befriended some other squirrels yet, Theo?"

"Yes, I have," Theo replies. "They asked me to join them and I think I will." He jumps from tree branch to tree branch now, as if to make it clear he is ready to leave.

"Well," Walter says, "as I told Rona and Mona just now, it won't be long before we come to fetch them. It might even be this month still. Is that all right with you?"

"Yes, of course it is," Theo answers. "After all, I can visit the other squirrels every day. They are not too far from here. So take your time. I will look after these two little monkeys some more. It is not a problem."

"Fine, thank you," Walter replies and with that, takes his leave. A lot of waving and goodbyes follow as he and Rita, as well as Bruno and Bones, make their way back. There is still a lot of work to be done at judge Martin's place, but every day Walter can see he is making progress. Soon, he will have everything in order so that Judge Martins can easily take over.

CHAPTER IX

One morning, as he is busy in the garden, Max, with his family in tow, walks by. "Hi guys," he greets, "what is happening here?"

Rita, who sits on Walter's head this time, chirps. "I am not a guy, I am Rita, the red robin!"

"Yes, yes," Max utters. "I know! Good morning Rita," he grumbles.

"Good morning," Rita sings. She flies away on to a nearby tree branch to watch and listen from there. She listens to Max's family as they greet Walter as well. She also hears how he returns their greetings and kindly speaks to them. Max seems to have a sense that things are going to change soon. He has heard some talk going around and wants to find out more.

"Is it true you are leaving soon?" he wants to know.

"Yes, I think it is time for us to move on," Walter answers him. "Are you coming with us?" he asks. He is sure about what Max will say to this and indeed, Max shakes his head.

"Noo, no," he responds. "You can all go, but here is where I belong!"

"We understand that, Max," Walter assures him. "We know you are happiest with your family."

"When are you leaving?" Max asks.

"Ooh, not yet," Walter replies, "but don't worry, we will come to say goodbye before we go."

"Good, that is all right then," Max declares. He starts pick-picking again, the old Max Walter knows so well. Always looking for food. His family, busily, does the same. Walter can't help smiling. He is happy for Max. Happy, he is together with all his loved ones just as before.

Bruno and Bones, enjoying the warm spring day, are lying underneath the same tree where Rita has nestled herself. Then Walter sits down between the big bear and the dog, his four-legged friends. They all ponder over the coming journey.

After a while, Walter remarks. "Tomorrow is my day off. That gives me a chance to do some shopping. I need new clothes before we leave. A few shirts, shoes, socks. It might be best if you all stay here."

"Me too?" Rita asks.

"Yes, you too," is the answer she gets.

"No problem," Bruno yawns. "It is nice here in the sun."

"I keep you company," Bones offers.

"Ooh, well, then I will go and visit Rona and Mona," Rita says. "I am sure they will be happy to see me. I shall show them the tree I found. It is not far from where they are and has lovely berries which they can eat. Actually," she adds, "it might be a good idea if you came also, Bruno. I can show you some bushes with very nice fruit that you could eat. You really will love it."

"Fruit to eat?" Bruno pricks his ears. Eating always sounds good to him. "You say it is nice?" he wants to hear this again.

"Very much so," Rita assures him.

"Hmm, Yeaah, if you say so," Bruno mumbles. He goes on, "I'll think about it then. Maybe I will come."

"Right," Walter declares. "So you all find something to do tomorrow while I am going to spend some of the money I earned here."

Spending money is easy, he finds out the next day. The shops are full of many fine things. There is one particular shop he likes the best. They dress him from top to toe. Shirts, jacket, trousers, socks and shoes. Staring in a mirror, he cannot believe the image looking back at him. What a difference the new outfit makes.

"Now you are a truly handsome young man," the shop owner tells him.

And yes, the man is correct in saying so. Walter can see it. Feeling very pleased with himself, he pays what is owned for all the new finery. Leaving the shop, he walks in the street with his head held up high. How nice it was to spend money this way. The money earned by working hard for a long time at Judge Martin's place. And there is even a bit left over.

Suddenly, by rounding a corner of the street, he comes face to face with an elephant. And another one. There are several of them. On the back of each one sits a small boy, wearing colourful clothes. The elephants themselves have red head bands adorned with bells which look very striking. They step gingerly, slowly, making the bells clink softly as they go. They're not in a hurry at all. A whole procession of gaily painted carriages follow them. Men on horseback tred in between. They wear wide-brimmed hats and crack long whips into the air. A cart with a large wire cage on top also drives by. In the cage are two large striped animals.

"Tigers," Walter hears people standing near to him say. "Very dangerous too."

There are other horses with beautiful ladies riding them. They wave to the people, smiling all the while.

Children are calling out, "The circus. The circus has come!"

Clowns in bizarre outfits and oversized shoes tumble around amidst the crowd. Music seems to come from everywhere. How exciting to hear, see and watch this grand display.

Walter is spellbound by it all. "How wonderful it must be to belong to the circus," he thinks. "How fascinating. That is what I would like to do. To be with the circus! Travel around with them. It must be absolutely fabulous to be part of their world. And why not?" The thought does not want to go away. His mind is brooding over it. How can he make it come true? He decides to follow the procession. A plan will come to him. He just wills it.

Walking among the circus people, he imagines himself to be part of their lives. But, for that to happen, one must have something to offer. An act of some sort. People must like it, they must be wanting to come and see it. In his mind he invents and creates all sorts of scenes. Bruno dancing with Bones, while he, Walter, plays the flute and Rita sings. Yes, he knows that will work, although he feels something else is needed as well. 'The monkeys' it comes to him. 'Yes, yes, this will make a very good act.' He just knows it. His brain works at full speed. What else can be useful for his plans? The old doll's pram he saw in the shed. It must have been there for a long time already. "Surely, Mr. And Mrs. Martins won't mind giving it to me," he ponders. He can see it taking shape; this act that will enable them to join the circus. The pram can be done up with some paint. Mona and Rona can sit in it, and Bones can push them. "Yes," he nods his head. "It really could work."

"Aaha, and what might you be thinking about then?" a voice calls out to him. Walter looks up. His eyes meet those of a tall man walking next to him. A black and red cape dances over his shoulders. His top hat is tilted to one side. The long thin whip in his hand touches Walter's shoulder very lightly as he says; "I have been watching you. You keep on mumbling to yourself and nodding your head." He could have added that he noticed Walter because of his appearance. The strong and open face combined with dark curly hair. A strikingly good looking young man.

"Oooh," Walter smiles, "I was just trying to think up plans that might get me into the circus."

"You would like that? Would you?" the man asks.

"Yes indeed I would," Walter answers, adding, "One must have an act, of course. A show of some kind. The sort of thing people must like watching."

"Correct," the man agrees. He has a friendly face, Walter observes. His eyes twinkle when he asks, "I wonder, do you have such an act or show?"

"I think so," Walter replies earnestly. "I really think so."

"Won't you tell me about it?" the stranger prods.

"Yes, why not?" Walter responds. He then goes on, telling the man walking next to him about himself and his friends. How first he and Rita, the red robin, set out on their travels together and how the other animals just happened to come along. How they earned money by making music and how nicely Bruno and Bones can dance. All this time, they keep moving with the parade. Walter finds it so easy talking to this man beside him. He does not notice how people make way for them. How careful the horses are made to step around them. Walter is unaware of the fact that the stranger he tells his story to is Mr. Landini, the owner of the circus.

Mister Landini enjoys walking in between the rows of wagons, animals and people, when his circus parades through the streets. It gives him the chance to make contact with the townspeople and oversee the goings on.

When Walter begins to speak of the act he wants to invent with Rona and Mona, Mr. Landini stops him. "What is your name?" he asks.

"Eh, uuhm, me? My name is Walter," comes the answer, a bit startled. Again, the whip lightly touches his shoulder.

"Good, I remember that," the man says. Then he hurls himself aboard the open wagon in front of them. Once seated, he brings his hand in a sort of salute to his head. "Come and see me," he calls out to Walter. "The name is Landini, from the Landini circus!"

In disbelief, Walter stares at the smiling face in front of him. The other people in the circus carriage burst out laughing. They watch his total amazement with glee. Walter steps aside, letting the rest of the parade pass him by. "It cannot be true," he repeats over and over to himself. "How can it be true? Nothing comes that easy, does it? Aah, well, maybe once in a while it does," he ponders, while slowly making his way back to Judge Martin's place.

He finds Max and his family there, along with his other friends. They are all gathered under the big tree in the back garden. Rita is on his shoulder at once. After the first greetings, Walter's new clothes are admired and then he has to tell them everything about his journey into town. They want to know what he has seen and what he has done there. When Walter tells them the circus is in town, he first has to explain what is a circus. His friends get very excited by hearing that there are lots of animals at the circus. They are amazed when he tells them he saw elephants and tigers. When Walter comes to the story of how he met Mr. Landini, the circus owner, they are very impressed. That he is invited to come and see him, stirs them even more.

"Can we come too?" Bones wants to know.

"Yes, of course," Walter answers. "We have to present ourselves as an act!" This needs some further explaining.

After understanding what an act is, Rita wants to know if the monkeys can come too. "We have been to see them," she declares and they want to be with us now!"

"Good," Walter answers. "We can fetch them tomorrow. They will be great for our show."

"Ooh Walter," Bruno chips in. "Walter, Rita showed me this morning the shrubs with the nice berries on. I have eaten lots of them. I know now where to find them. I know the shrubs that have the tastiest berries."

"That is wonderful, Bruno," Walter answers. "Really wonderful. I am so glad for you. And our Rita, although so small, Rita, you are the greatest."

"I am?" Rita chirps.

"Yes, you are," Bruno also tells her.

Rita looks pleased. She fluffs her feathers a bit and flies off over their heads, circling around them before settling herself on Walter's shoulder again. It is her way of dealing with all this praise. "Come Walter," she utters, "let's go on. You were telling us about the circus. What is it that we can do?"

"Oh, lots and lots," Walter laughs. He then starts to describe all he has thought up. The show they can put together. The things they can do. Totally taken in by this, they don't even notice how Max, along with his family, slowly moves away from them. Max looking a bit unhappy, because for him there is no part in all these plans.

The appearance of Judge Martins startles Walter and his friends. They did not hear or see him coming.

"Good afternoon, and what sort of meeting is this?" the judge asks. "You must be discussing your coming journey, I suppose? I see you have already bought some new clothes, Walter, and I must say, you are looking extremely smart in them."

"Thank you, sir," Walter answers him, glad that his attire has the judge's approval. "Yes, it is true sir," he goes on. "We are planning to join the circus."

"The circus eh?" Judge Martins grins. "Well, well, please tell me, how is that coming about?" He sits down on the bench underneath the tree, gesturing Walter to do the same.

Taking place next to the judge, Walter again relates the story of all the things that happened to him this morning. He also tells the judge about the two monkeys, Rona and Mona. "I think they will fit perfectly in my circus show plan," he concludes.

The judge nods his head by hearing Walter likes to use the old doll's pram for the monkeys to sit in. "Yes, you can have it," he smiles, adding; "those plans of yours sound very good to me, Walter. It will be great to see you all in action. What do you think, can Mrs. Martins and I come and watch the performance?"

"Of course you can," Walter laughs. He goes on, "we love to have you there. That is to say, if Mr. Landini takes us on! Do you believe we stand a chance?"

"Yes, I certainly think so," Judge Martins answers. "Otherwise, Mr. Landini would not have invited you to come and see him. Something else," he adds, "when is all this going to happen?"

"As soon as possible, sir," Walter responds. "Can I paint the pram today?"

"Yes, indeed you can." Judge Martins says. "There are lots of half full tins of paint in the shed. Also, some brushes and other things you may need. Have a look, see what you can use, but better put some old clothes on first."

"Yes sir, I will," Walter responds. "And, thank you sir," he says. "Thank you so much."

"It is nothing," the judge waves Walter's utterances away.

Walter continues to think out loud. "If I fetch Rona and Mona tomorrow morning, then in the afternoon we can go and see Mr. Landini."

"You do that," Judge Martins smiles. "But now if you'll excuse me, I still have some work to do. I must go!" Embracing them all with his smile, he walks away, allowing Walter and his group to go on with their preparations.

After Walter has changed into some work clothes, his friends come along as he fetches the old pram from the shed. The half empty paint tins Judge Martins spoke of are there as well, standing on some shelves. And so are the brushes and thinners. A dusty wooden box in a corner holds a nice surprise. "Doll's clothes," Walter says smugly, holding them up for all to see. "My, my," he declares, "everything we need is here, so let's start working."

Before long, the old pram has taken on a new look. Red and yellow, as well as blue, are the main colours it is painted in, with dots and zigzag patterns all around. The end result is quite spectacular. As for the doll's dresses, they are still in a good condition. There are two. One blue, the other one red.

"Perfect," Walter exclaims. "I am sure they will fit our two monkeys beautifully," Bruno and Bones think so, too.

Rita has been watching them all being so busy from one of the wall shelves. "I think you did very good," she praises them. "And yes, I am sure those dresses are just the right size and they will look lovely on Rona and Mona."

That night they go to sleep with lots of expectations for the following day. Rona and Mona are very glad to see them early the next morning. Only Walter, Rita and Bones have come because Bruno likes to sleep late.

Theo the squirrel is very emotional, as Rona and Mona say their goodbyes. "Please take very good care of them," he pleads.

"We will," Walter assures him.

Rona and Mona fondly hug Theo a last time, then they're off, waving to Theo until they're out of sight. Rita flies in front, with Bones running closely behind. Walter carries the monkeys each in one arm, but after a while, they decide to sit on his shoulders. This gives them more freedom to look around because they want to see where they are going.

Then Walter tells them what his plans are. He speaks about the circus and how pleasant it will be to travel along with it. Explaining the role he has worked out for them comes next.

Rona and Mona listen intently to all Walter says. Riding around in a pram and getting dressed up sounds interesting. Although they don't really know what Walter is talking about, he makes it sound exciting. Surely, it will be much better than hanging around in the same tree, all day. Once at judge Martin's place, it is Bruno they see first.

"Hello," the monkeys greet him a bit shyly at first.

"Good day," Bruno booms. "It is so nice to see you here at long last. Welcome, welcome you two."

Upon hearing his friendly tone of voice, the monkeys run up to him and jump into his outstretched arms. They at once feel very much at ease with him. Max and his family are staring at the newcomers from a bit of a distance. They seem to find the monkeys weird and the youngest peacocks make all sorts of disturbed noises.

Walter waves at them, saying, "Don't be upset. No one is going to harm you." He then leads the way towards the pram. It stands in full colour, dry and ready, in front of Bruno's hut. The monkeys push each other aside in their haste to climb aboard.

Proud and with a broad grin on his face, Walter looks at the scene in front of him. "Perfect," he says after a while. "Much better even than I expected."

Rona and Mona love the pram. They rock in it and pull funny faces.

Mrs. Martins, who saw Walter and his friends come through the gate, has followed them. Her husband has given her all the details of Walter's plans. Now she wants to find out if she can be of any help. Noticing the playful mood everyone is in, she asks, "Can I join in the fun?"

Pleasantly surprised, they all turn around, "Please do, Mrs. Martins," Walter answers, after greeting her. Pointing at the pram, he asks; "You don't mind me having the pram and painting it?"

"No, not at all, I am glad it can be of use to you," Mrs. Martins replies. "I must say," she goes on, "it is quite an improvement, all these gay colours."

"Whose pram was it, actually?" Walter asks.

"Ooh," Mrs. Martins laughs. "My little niece stayed with us for a while. That was years ago. My husband happened to be at an auction and saw the pram there. He thought it would make a nice present for her, so he bought it. I made a nice doll to go with the pram. The only thing is, she, being a bit of a tomboy, was not really interested in dolls and dolls prams. That is why she not even took it back home. So the pram has been standing here for years and years. The doll and its clothes also were left behind. I kept them, though. Now the clothes have been washed, and I brought them with me. The cushions that belong in the pram are here as well. Look," she goes on, showing them the items she has draped over one arm. "Let me put the cushions inside. You will see they fit very nicely."

As she nears the pram, Rona and Mona quickly seek shelter in Walter's arms. "Tut, tut," Mrs. Martins says softly. "I won't hurt you. See? I just put the cushions here inside. They are very soft and nice to sit on. They give quite a bit of height as well. Now you can see much better what is going on around you. And see these dresses, aren't they lovely?"

Rona and Mona are both very interested and Mrs. Martins makes use of this. She steps over to Walter and quickly slides the red dress over Rona's small head. "Isn't it pretty?" she asks, and everyone has to agree. Rona, indeed, looks adorable in the frilly dress that fits her perfectly. There are "oohs and aaahhs," all round, with Rona proudly dancing up and down in Walter's arms. Now Mona also wants some of the attention. She even bends forward to Mrs. Martins, who in an instant has her dolled-up in the blue dress. This gives off another round of "ooohh's and aaahh's" with the monkeys enjoying every minute. They hop back into the pram and start shaking it to and fro, while their dresses twirl around them. It is an amusing scene, delightful to watch.

"Well, I am sure the circus will be much enhanced by having all of you in their midst," Mrs. Martins laughs.

"I hope so," Walter's answer sounds somewhat uncertain.

"I know so," Mrs. Martins insists. "What with you looking so handsome in your new clothes. My husband and I can not wait to see you perform. I am sure we are going to be there."

"That will be so nice," Walter smiles. "You are not cross that we are leaving?" he asks.

"No, of course not," Mrs. Martins assures him. "We understand and are just glad you spend some time with us. It was a blessed time and as we have no children, it felt as if you were sent to us. It is a pity you want to go, but we would never hold that against you! After all, children are known to leave. If their future lies somewhere else, one just has to accept those things. So, no hard feelings, my dear. Just please keep us informed somehow. We'd love to hear from you now and then."

"Ooh, but for sure. That is what I will do," Walter answers her.

"Good," Mrs. Martins smiles. "And as for people helping out here, don't worry about that. We'll find someone and very soon my husband will be able to take over. We want you to take this chance, Walter." With that and after greeting them all, she walks back to the house while Walter and his little group call their goodbyes after her.

After taking a deep breath, Walter says, "Come, my friends, let's do it then. Up to the circus, I'd say."

Happily, they all fall in with this, and so they're on their way. Walter, with Rita on his shoulder, pushes the pram holding Rona and Mona. Bruno's chain is fastened onto the pram; Bones runs next to it. They attract a lot of attention. It is not every day one sees a huge bear walking next to a red and yellow pram with two monkeys in it.

"Of course, they must belong to the circus that is in town," someone says."

"Yes, yes, that must be it!" Others agree.

It is not long before Walter and his friends have a group of mostly children following them. Rona and Mona are a bit scared at first, but Walter soon puts them at ease. "Nothing is going to happen to you. Nobody means any harm. They all love to look at you because you are so cute. Just sit still, that is all."

"Yes, that is all," Bruno repeats after Walter. "You can wave to everybody though," he encourages them. "See?" he prattles on while waving his big paws around. Mona and Rona bravely follow his example. First a bit unsure, then becoming aware of so many friendly laughing faces, a bit more daringly.

Walter is delighted. "This is fun," he remarks. "Don't you think so?"

"Yes, yes," Rona and Mona answer him. "It is!" They keep on waving to everyone and everyone waves back at them. Bones, every so often, takes over from Walter, pushing the pram. He does this walking on his hind legs, which makes for even more amusement among the crowd. They also watch the little bird on Walter's shoulder who now and then takes off to fly in circles, high above their heads. Yes, everybody loves this free entertainment. And so the merry procession moves along to an open field, where the circus is. The children more or less lead the way. They are sure now Walter and his group belong there. Walter can only hope Mr. Landini will be of the same opinion after he has seen and heard them perform. From far, they already see the gigantic circus tent in the middle of an open area. A colourful flag flies gaily from its top. Lots of wagons are standing nearby. Here, Walter's escort comes to a halt, not daring to go further than this. They rather keep staring from a distance at what is going on here. People are busy with their daily chores, chatting and laughing with each other; washing and hanging clothes on makeshift washing lines. Children are running around. A troupe of elephants is standing a bit further away. And there, unmistakably, in the shadow of a tree, sits Mr. Landini. Although now, without the black and red cape and his top hat, Walter knows at once it is him.

The same holds true for Mr. Landini. He has noticed the procession with Walter in front and waves a hand into the air as his small group comes nearer. "Welcome, welcome to circus Landini," he greets them with a broad smile. His friendly manner make even Rona and Mona feel at ease. Bruno, still upright, waves one of his paws at him and Bones wags his tail, while Rita chirps sweetly from Walter's shoulder.

"Thank you, sir," is Walter's response. He is very pleased with the way they are received.

"Well, well, so these are your artists, I take it?" Mr. Landini remarks.

"Indeed, sir," Walter replies. "We have come to perform for you."

"But of course," Mr. Landini answers. Some of the other circus people are coming closer, curious to hear and see what Walter and his group can do. They all watch as Walter takes out his flute. The first notes of a lively melody soon fill the air. Rita's pure voice follows in perfect harmony. It sounds heart-warming and happy. Bruno starts dancing in tune with the music, while Bones, also on his hind legs, pushes the pram with Mona and Rona around. The monkeys, in their frilly dresses, bounce up and down, frolicking with each other in a most charming way.

Everyone, including Mr. Landini, is laughing. Suddenly, Pico, the circus clown, still in his oversized shoes and even larger silly trousers, from the midday show, joins in the fun. He does handstands in front of the pram and then dances along with Bruno.

The onlookers are thrilled. They applaud loudly when Walter and Rita end their first tune.

Bones drops back on all fours, Bruno stops dancing and Pico comes to a standstill as well. Rona and Mona sit unmoving in their pram. They all look up at Mr. Landini. Seeing the broad smile on this gentleman's face, Walter realizes the act is a success.

"Very good,' is Mr. Landini's comment. "Really, I am impressed." There is more applause and the circus people gather round Walter and his group, praising him and the others. It seems, they are accepted.

Walter is on top of the world. He proudly looks at Rita and his other artists. "You did well," he says, making them all feel very good.

"Please come with me," Mr. Landini invites Walter. "I do like you to become part of my circus. Let's sign the papers to make it official."

"Thank you," is Walter's eager reply. "Thank you for taking us on."

The other circus people smile in encouragement as Walter and his group walk off with Mr. Landini. Walter, still with Rita on his shoulder, follows Mr. Landini into the wagon he uses as an office. The pram, with Rona and Mona in it, stays outside; Bruno and Bones keep watch over them. This is a day full of surprises for Walter and his party. Not only are they offered a nice wage, they also get the use of a wagon for themselves. Thanks to the lessons of Father Tobias, the signing of the papers presents no problem. Walter does so with a happy heart.

"Fine," Mr. Landini says, "I am glad that is done. Welcome in our midst, young man, and that goes for all of you."

"We are very grateful, sir," Walter answers. "Thank you again."

"It is my pleasure," Mr. Landini replies smilingly. "Now," he goes on, "I advise you to first go and see our Madame Emma. She is the lady in charge of costumes. Just tell her what each of you does and she will find you something nice to wear for the show."

"Ooh, great," Walter beams. "And when will our first show be, sir?" he asks hopefully.

"Well," Mr. Landini laughs, "that can be tonight if you wish. We do have an opening. One of the 'Deodora's', our juggling group, is ill. They have gone back to their home country."

All Walter really hears is they can already perform this evening. "We will be here tonight for our first show, sir," he says, full of glee and delight.

"Good, that is how it shall be then," Mr. Landini declares. He adds, "after you have been to see Madame Emma, talk to Pico the clown as well. He will be able to tell you exactly when to go on. I think it might be best after the elephants act. Tell him that. And, it won't be a bad idea for Pico to perform with you, as he did just now. That was excellent. People will love it."

"Yes, I liked it too," Walter answers.

"Agreed then," is Mr. Landini's comment. "We'll see you tonight." Rising from his chair, he hands Walter two tickets from a pile on his desk. "Maybe you have some people you like to give these to," he says.

Walter is overjoyed. "Thank you, sir," he utters, standing up as well. Shaking Mr. Landini's hand, he says, "I know just the people, sir."

"Fine," Mr. Landini smiles. "I hope they will enjoy being with us." He is standing at the door as Walter and his friends walk away. Madame Emma's wagon is soon found. Through her open door she is visible, sitting behind a table packed with a glittering collection of materials. Obviously Madame Emma is hard at work making artists' outfits.

"Yes, young man," she calls out to Walter. "Can I help you with something?"

Walter eases himself up the steps in front of her wagon. "Good afternoon," he responds politely, adding; "Mr. Landini send me here. You see," he goes on, "me and my group here have just been taken on by Mr. Landini, to perform in the circus. Tonight will be our first show. Mr. Landini told us to go to you. He said you would find us something nice to wear for the show."

Madame Emma is a very skinny and friendly woman. She likes her work. She likes Walter's manners too. "Tonight eeh,?" comes her smile. "Well, then it is urgent." With that, she tosses her work aside. "Let me see," she muses, looking past him at Bruno, Bones and the pram with the monkeys. "Ooh," she laughs, "This is not a problem, really." Glancing at Rita, who as usual is on Walter's shoulder, she remarks; "this red robin is fine as she is. More than fine, I dare say." Rita bows her head in a silent 'thank you.'

"As for the monkeys," Madame Emma continues, "they look splendid as well in those dresses. Although, come to think of it, maybe two small bonnets could do even more for them." She rumbles through an open drawer and comes up with two very tiny hats. "Try these," she says, handing them to Walter. "I am sure they will fit. So," she goes on, "then it is only you, the bear and the dog that have to be taken care of."

"I suppose so," Walter answers meekly, a bit overwhelmed by this energetic lady who seems to take everything in her stride. Nothing, not even Walter and his unique mix of friends, distract her. "She must have seen many unusual things," Walter ponders by himself. "Well, working for a circus, one gets used to that, I would think."

Madame Emma, meanwhile, is rummaging through the materials on her table. "Here," she says after some time, handing Walter two rolls of gold and red sash. "This will be perfect. Just cut them to size. For you, a sash around the waist will look good together with those nice clothes you are wearing. The bear can have a sash hanging over his shoulder and for the dog, you can use the same material. Tie it in a large ribbon around his neck. It is going to look splendid. I assure you."

"Yeaaah," Walter responds, a bit uncertain. "It might be festive."

"Indeed," Madame Emma replies. "For the time being and at such short notice, you can't ask for better." She waves him on, saying, "you must go now please, I still have lots of work to do."

"Thank you Madame, we then bid you farewell," Walter reacts formally, winking at her at the same time.

This makes her laugh. "And goodbye to you too," she answers back. Once outside again, Walter deposits the two tiny hats along with the rolls of sash into the pram. "The hats are for you, my lovelies," he tells Rona and Mona.

This gives for great delight. The monkeys have seen people wearing hats so now they try them on straight away. It is amusing to see. After they have placed them a bit topsy-turvy on their heads, the rolls of sash get their attention. All this happens while Walter and the others are on their way in search of Pico. Of course, knowing Rona and Mona, the rolls of sash soon unwind and gaily billow over the pram. Walter can just grab them before to much harm is done.

"I'll keep it for you," Bruno offers.

"Thank you," Walter sighs, rewinding the rolls as best as he can before handing them over to the large bear. He knows Bruno will take good care of them. They find Pico where they left him. Most of the other circus people have gone back to whatever they were doing before Walter and his group came along. Pico is chatting with two men who also wear clown outfits. Seeing Walter and his friends coming nearer, he waves at them. "Hi," he jovially calls out, "You are looking for me, I guess?"

"Yes, good afternoon," Walter greets, including them all in his smile.

"These are my friends, Arno and Carlos," Pico says, introducing his companions. The three of us have our own show here in the circus. You must come and see us. We are rather good, you know."

"I am sure you are," Walter replies, "and yes, I will come and watch you, but first things first. Mr. Landini said I must ask you when we have to come up for our show tonight. He thought maybe just after the elephants act?"

"You mean you are performing tonight already?" is Pico's amazed response.

"Yes, we love to," Walter replies.

"Ooh well, in that case," Pico says, "Yes, then I would say, indeed, after the elephant's act would be best. They usually are finished by eight, so be sure you are on time."

"We will be," Walter assures him. Then he adds, "Mr. Landini thought it a good idea for you to perform with us!"

Pico laughs. "Yes, that was quite good, wasn't it? If Mr. Landini liked it, then indeed, we better keep it in!"

"Thank you, I am glad," Walter answers. "With you helping us, things will go smoothly, I am sure."

"Yes," Pico comforts him. "Don't worry, everything will be just fine." The other two clowns nod their heads in agreement. "Yes, just fine," they utter. "Don't you worry."

"Have you visited our Madame Emma?" Pico goes on, pointing to the rolls of shiny sash Bruno is holding.

"Yes," Walter replies, "Mr. Landini told me to. Do you think this will be nice and the right thing for us to put on? Madame

Emma says it should be tied into a bow around the neck of Bones. Bruno should have a sash hanging from his shoulder and I must use some for a waistband."

"It will do for now," Pico answers him. "Madame Emma can make a nice costume for you at a later stage."

"Ooh, that would be great," Walter brings out. By this time, his friends are all becoming a bit restless. "Right," Walter calms them, "We'll go now. By the way," he adds, "I haven't introduced my friends to you people, as yet. This is Rita," he says, touching the little bird on his shoulder. Pointing to the big bear on his side, he goes on; "this is Bruno and then we have Bones, our faithful dog, next to him. Rona and Mona are our lovely monkeys in the pram here with me."

"Very good," is Pico's reply. "Now we all know each other." He gives one of his big smiles away to them while the other two clowns smile as well. The animals with Walter greet back in their own manner. Rita sings a few notes, sounding perfectly sweet. Bruno waves his paws, Bones wags his tail and Rona and Mona clap their tiny hands together. These two are quickly learning their role in being part of a circus act. After this, they take their leave. "See you tonight at eight then, don't forget," Pico urges.

"We won't," Walter promises. While walking away, he notices how warmly the other circus people greet them. 'All these artists are our friends now,' he thinks out aloud. "We are going to lead a totally different life from here on. It really is wonderful and you, my friends, are wonderful too. Also, you are excellent performers." Walter's happiness and praise spreads a festive mood around.

"Let's go and tell Max about it," Bruno suggests. "He must be wondering how it all went."

"Yes," Rita chirps in, "and Judge Martins and Mrs. Martins."

Bones starts racing round the pram, yap, yapping to Rona and Mona, but they are no longer scared of him. They know by now he means them no harm. It just gets them worked up. Making excited noises, both are starting their jumping up and down again.

"Quiet, quiet, please," Walter pleads, adding; "of course we will go back to judge Martin's place first. How else? I'll have these tickets here that Mr. Landini gave me. Now Mr. and Mrs. Martins can come to see our show for free."

Again, walking the town's streets, they attract a lot of attention.

Judge Martin and his wife are sitting on the veranda in front of their house, as if waiting for their return. "Well, helloo," is the warm greeting Walter and his friends receive. "How did it go?"

"Good afternoon sir, Mrs. Martins," Walter gushes. "It went well. Mr. Landini took us on! We belong to the circus now!"

"Good for you," Judge Martins responds. "Congratulations to all of you."

"And from me," Mrs. Martins joins in. "I hope you all will be very happy there."

"Yes, and so do I," Judge Martins exclaims.

"Thank you," Walter smiles broadly. Reaching for the tickets in his pocket, he says gleefully; "These are for you. Mr. Landini gave them to me. You said you wanted to come to see us in the circus?"

"My, that is great, Walter, thank you," Judge Martins replies while taking the tickets from him.

"We are impressed, dear," Mrs. Martins tells Walter. "And yes, we very much like to come and watch you all perform."

Their reaction is as pleasing to Walter as it is to his friends. Bruno makes a few dance steps because of this. This greatly amuses the onlookers, who are still lingering in front of the gate. They start cheering him on, but Walter unlocks the chain on Bruno's neck and the big bear slips away to the back of the garden.

Max is there, as is his family. "And?" he asks.

"Ooh, I don't know," Bruno teases.

"You don't know?" Max doesn't get it.

"Ooh well then," Bruno bellows. "We only have been taken on by the circus!!!"

"Really?" Max brings out. Although staying with his family is still his first choice, he can't help feeling a little bit envious now. By this time Bones is also with them. He leaps and jumps around, having Max's family scatter in all directions, which does not go without loud protests.

Then Rita flies into all this din, tweetering, "Sush, sush, how noisy can it get here?"

Even in front of the house, one can hear the rumour. Walter excuses himself and hastens to the back as well. Once there, he can't help laughing as he sees feathers flying off little peacocks who run in all directions, with Bones barking after them. They all know very well Bones won't hurt them. It's a game they often play, only now it is a bit more boisterous and loud. Bones is all fired-up because of this circus event. Walter calls out his name only once. Bones hears the urgency in his voice and promptly races back. The peacocks come to a standstill; they watch Bones retreat for a few moments and then start pick-picking for food again as if nothing has happened.

Max, meanwhile, is walking up to Walter. "Is it true then?" he asks. "You are going with the circus? You could have stayed here, you know."

"I know, I know," Walter agrees, "but," he continues, "we decided not to. So here we are to say goodbye, Max. Are you not going to wish us well?"

"Indeed," Max grunts, shifting from one leg to the other. "Yes, I wish you all the best, Walter, and that goes for all of you," he adds.

Walter hugs Max close to him. "Goodbye, my dear friend," he says. "It was so good knowing you. I will never forget the times we had together." He politely greets Max's family as well, who by now has slowly come nearer again. Rita, Bruno and Bones also say their farewells to Max and his clan. Then they are off to collect Walter's belongings, some odds and ends, some clothing.

Rona and Mona have left their pram and are rummaging in the cupboards. "Can we eat this?" Rona asks Walter, showing him some grapes they found there.

"Yes, yes, of course you can," Walter answers. Then he says; "Ooh my goodness, I forgot to feed you, didn't I? You must all be very hungry! Let's first eat then. I did not even think of food with all this circus business. Come, let's see what we can find around here. I know we have some apples, some pears as well, I am sure. You can have those Bruno. The fruit trees in Judge Martin's garden gave such a good crop. There is an abundance of everything. We can even take some with us to the circus. We have permission to take as much as we want, Mr. Martins said. So that is

128

what we shall do. And here we have some bread and butter and that nice jam Mrs. Martins gave us. I shall eat some of that now." Walter talks and talks on and on while preparing and handing out food to his friends. He is in such an upbeat mood that he actually can hardly eat at all.

Bones, on the other hand, heartily eats the food that Mrs. Martins prepares for him every day. Every evening without fail, it is there, standing in a corner in a big bowl. "I will miss that," he thinks to himself, "But never mind. I suppose while at the circus, I won't go hungry either. Walter will see to that, I am sure."

Rona and Mona are nibbling from this, that and the other things Walter prepares for them. Pieces of fruit, bread with jam. Bruno also eats to his heart's content, even emptying the last honey from the honey pot he found in one of the cupboards.

Rita only picks a few breadcrumbs. "A small bird like me does not need much food," she tells Rona and Mona, who can't eat all that much either.

Walter quickly cleans up afterwards, and then it is time to go. They greet Dieter and his wife, as well as the other people who work at Judge Martin's place. That done, they again join Mr. And Mrs. Martins in the front garden. On such a lovely late afternoon they spend most of their time together here, drinking tea on the veranda, reading and talking, enjoying each others company.

Walter is restless. He thanks Judge Martins and his wife again for all their caring and kindness, then he declares; "I think we better go now. We must be early for tonight's performance."

"Right," Judge Martins agrees. "We'll see you all after the show, I take it?"

"Of course," Walter replies. "We look forward to that." He and his friends greet the Judge and his wife, who walk them to the garden gate. From there, they wave them along as they stroll away. Rona and Mona are in the pram again, Walter and the others around them - an endearing little group trailed as before by the now already familiar crowd. They reach the circus in good time.

"Pico, the clown is in the big tent," somebody tells them. And that is where they find him, busy making sure everything is in order for this evening's show.

"Oh, there you are," he greets them. "I was just wondering if you were going to make it on time."

"Always," Walter answers.

"Good," Pico laughs. "That is very good."

They stand looking at each other. Each of them feels as if they are old friends already. This feeling enfolds all of them and after the greetings from everyone are over, they regard themselves now as being part of one big family. This is because Pico has the remarkable gift of setting everybody at ease.

"Well," Pico remarks, "we have still plenty of time before the show starts, so let me show you your wagon. I hope you like it."

"I am sure we will," is Walter's reply. "And thank you. It is very nice of you to take us there."

Without his clown's outfit, Pico looks very different, but his eyes are the same; friendly and gentle, and so is his broad smile. "Mr. Landini told me you can have the wagon that was used by the 'Deodora's,'" Pico says.

Walter and his friends follow Pico outside to the half circle of wagons, a bit further on. The one he leads them to is freshly painted and cleaned. They love it at once. It will make a perfect home. Everything inside is neat as a pin as well. There are small cubboards with drawers on one side, and lots of shelves above them. A longish table stands in the middle of the wagon. Two beds, one placed above the other, are on the other wall. They look very inviting, especially to Rona and Mona. They at once clamber from bottom to top, top to bottom.

Bruno, ignoring their antics, instantly spreads himself out on the lower one while Rita settles herself down on a shelf. Bones chooses a rug to lie on.

"And you?" Pico laughs, looking at Walter.

"Oh, I take the bed at the top," Walter smiles. "From there, I can oversee everything. That will be great. And really, Pico, I must say, everything is just so perfect here. I am sure we will all be very happy at circus Landini."

"Good, that is very good," Pico grins.

"Yes it is," Walter grins back. He goes on, "What is also good is that extra space there in the corner. It is an excellent spot to put the pram, so Rona and Mona can sleep in there."

"Good," Pico responds again, adding, "well you are all comfy then, and remember, if there is anything I can help you with, just let me know!"

"There is," Walter replies, his voice sounding a bit unsure. "I wonder if you can help us with the sashes we have to put on?"

"Is that all?" Pico grins. "Yes, I am the handyman around here," he goes on. "I am certain I can put on sashes too! Where are those rolls of sashes Madame Emma gave you?"

Walter quickly takes them from the bag he carries over his shoulder. "Here they are," he says, putting them on the narrow table in front of him. "I have no idea how these things are done in the circus," he adds.

"Ooh, you will learn soon enough," Pico smiles at him. Then he says; "Scissors, we need scissors. There should be some in one of the drawers here. Circus artists always have scissors somewhere!" Rumbling through the drawers, he comes up with candles. "Right," he mumbles. "This should come in handy too if your oil lamp runs dry." He goes on with his search and soon finds what he is looking for. "See." He smiles gleefully. "Got them! Now," he continues, holding a length of sash in front of Walter, "this should do it." After cutting the sash, he hangs it over Walter's shoulder. "It is perfect," he declares. "The gold colour looks very good on you, Walter. The red I think will be nice for your friends. Bruno's sash can be done the same way as yours, Walter," he says. "All you have to do now is to sew it together. Can you do that?"

"Yes, I can," Walter replies. "I have always mended my own clothes. Needles and thread are here in the same drawer as the scissors, I see, so let me start."

"Good," Pico beams. "Bones, you are next," he utters. "Now, let me see what we can do for you." Taking the roll of red sash, he measures it against Bones, allowing for quite a bit extra. Then, after cutting it, he deftly ties the broad ribbon into a beautiful rosette around his neck. Bones proudly trots through the wagon, cheered on by his friends. They all dole out compliments, which makes him feel extra special.

"So, the monkeys and me get nothing?" Rita chirps.

"You're already stealing most of the attention anyway," Walter laughs, making them feel good again, like Walter always manages to do.

"All right then," Pico says. "I hope you'll excuse me. I still have some work waiting for me. See you all then, just before eight o'clock," he states, already on his way out.

"Absolutely," Walter answers.

Pico, once outside, pokes his head back in. "Ooh, I forgot," he says. "If you're hungry, old Pedro keeps some foodstuff in his wagon, which he sells. Do you have money?"

"I have," Walter assures him, adding, "thank you, yes, we will get something there."

"Fine," Pico replies. "I might as well tell you," he continues, "Pedro is a cripple. He fell from the trapeze years ago. Now he is making a living by keeping a small store. He also helps me out sometimes. There are always so many things that need to be done in a circus. Anyway, just ask the folks around here. They will tell you which one is Pedro's wagon."

"Don't worry, we'll find him," Walter says, but Pico is already gone. "Well, it might be a good idea to buy some food now, for tomorrow morning," Walter tells his friends.

"Yes, smart thinking," Bruno agrees at once. Rita and Bones have no objections. They are curious to see the rest of their new surroundings.

"All right then," Walter decides. "Let's go. Rona and Mona, come on, we will have you in your pram, please!" The monkeys pull faces at him and Rona throws a pillow in his direction, just missing some glasses. "Ooh, I think I will call you the terrible twins from now on," Walter sighs, grabbing them each by one arm. Stepping outside, where the pram is still standing, he deftly deposits them inside. They shriek with indignation, but Walter is firm with them. "No girls," he warns, "you must not be naughty now. You will see, I get you some nice things to eat from old Pedro. Maybe, he sells bananas or other fruit. I am sure you want to go and have a look?"

"Yes, yes," Rona and Mona answer. They are very fond of bananas and decide to behave now.

"Good," Walter praises them, "here we go then." With the others in tow and Rita flying up front, they're off. Pedro's place is soon found. Walter has only to ask one of the children playing around and some walk along to show the way. They like Bones with his beautiful ribbon still around his neck. Bruno also gets a lot of attention. As does Rita, who flies over and above everyone, to get noticed. But they like Rona and Mona best of all, because they are so cute and full of beans. There is no end to their antics.

"It must be the jolly circus mood that has come over them," Rita utters as she takes her place on Walter's shoulder again.

"It must be," Walter agrees. He goes on, "I see now though, they like children. Do you notice how they play up to them?"

"Oh yes, that is so," Rita replies.

"And another thing," Walter remarks. "I also noticed how clean and neat they are. I wonder where they learned that."

"Aah, I can tell you where they learned this from," Bruno says. "It was Rita who gave them some lessons. That was when you went to town and we went to see Rona and Mona. I remember it well because I also learned a thing or two that morning."

"Ooh yes, and what was that again then?" Rita chirps back.

"Well, you taught me from which bushes I could eat the fruit and so on," Bruno says.

"Yes, and a very good idea that was too," Walter grins. "Yeah, I told you before, and I tell you again, Rita, you are a star!"

The two monkeys meanwhile go on, pulling funny faces at the children, while romping about in the pram. They are so amusing one can't help but laugh. Who has the most fun is easy to see. They all have!

There is a large side opening in Pedro's wagon. This is because a big piece of wall was cut loose and then fastened with heavy bolts. The loose piece is turned outside. Supported by wooden poles underneath, it makes a perfect display counter. Lots of fruit, sweets, eggs and many other things are neatly arranged there. Pedro, sitting on a low chair behind all his wares, watches as Walter and his friends come nearer. "Good evening," he calls out to them. "You must be the new group they told me about."

"Indeed," Walter smiles. "It seems to me news travels fast in the circus world."

"Ooh yes," Pedro replies. "We know everything about each other. I even know your name is Walter."

"Aahaa, and I know yours is Pedro," Walter answers. They both are laughing now. Good friends at first sight.

"What can I sell you?" Pedro asks, shaking hands with Rona and Mona, who, after having left the pram, climb all over him.

"I think a bread for tomorrow morning would be nice, plus six eggs and butter. Six bananas, one for each of us. You will have some banana, Rita?" he asks the little bird on his shoulder.

"Yes, bananas are nice," Rita chirps.

"Good," Walter goes on, "and honey, if you have, for our friend Bruno here."

Bruno, tall on his hind legs, waves a paw into Pedro's face. "Yes, honey," he drawls. "I do hope you have?"

"Of course, my friend," Pedro replies. He places a huge jar full of that good stuff on the counter next to the other items Walter asked for.

"Fine," Walter goes on. "And then I would also like something nice for our friend Bones here, please." Bones looks up hopefully, and yes, even this, Pedro manages to pull off. A large, meaty bone appears from somewhere underneath the counter.

"Marvellous." Walter exclaims. "I must say, you are a most useful shopkeeper."

"Yes, I do agree with you," Pedro laughs. He takes a few pieces of candy from a glass bottle next to him. "One for you," he says, "and one for you," giving Mona and Rona each a colourful sugar ball.

"And me? And me?" the children around them start chanting.

"Ooh wait," Walter remarks. "I have had such a good day, let me pay for some sweets for the kids." Taking out his purse, he hands Pedro a few coins.

"Aah, for this I can give each child one of those same sweets. Shall I do that then?" Pedro asks.

"Yes," Walter agrees, nodding his head. "Let's do that."

Pedro duly doles out the pink and red sugary sweets. How the children love it. They thank Walter with beaming faces. "Now you have completely won them over," Pedro chuckles.

"That's good," Walter smiles, adding, "the more friends, the better, don't you think?"

"True, true." Pedro answers while packing Walter's purchases in two large paper bags. Bruno takes one, the other goes into the pram. Promptly, Rona and Mona are there too.

"No, no, don't touch you two," Walter warns them. "We will take the bag out just now once we arrive at our own wagon. Are you going to be at the show tonight?" he asks Pedro.

"Yes, but first I will be selling tickets," Pedro replies. He goes on, "I am always around to see if I can help with one thing or another. My days of performing are over, but I can still make myself useful."

"Of course," Walter responds. "You and your shop must be a tremendous asset for the circus as well." He pays for his food and, after they have all said their goodbyes, toddles off. Many of the children follow.

"See you tonight then," a broadly smiling Pedro calls out after them. He is very pleased with Walter's remarks. 'Such a nice young man,' he ponders while closing up. 'Talented too, I hear. Yes, leave it to Mr. Landini, he knows how to choose them.'

Meanwhile, the day is fading fast. Already the sun is setting behind some trees. "We better hurry," Walter urges his team.

"Yes," Bruno mumbles. "We must be on time on our first night."

"And always," Walter says. "We should never, ever be late!"

"No, never, never," Rona and Mona shout, making all of them laugh again.

Chapter X

Once back in their own wagon, Walter lights the oil lamp. "Aah, but it does look cosy in here," he declares. "A bit small for all of us perhaps, but still, it will be fine. We must just keep everything neat and tidy."

"Yes, well," Bruno utters, "but what about all this food you bought from Pedro. I mean that big jar full of honey you're unpacking now–can I have some of that, please?"

"Ooh Bruno, you remind me of Max. Always on the lookout for something to eat," Walter laughs. "But no, my friend," he adds while arranging all the food items neatly in front of him. "We had a good meal this afternoon before we came here. You cannot be all that hungry. I would say let's wait till after the show. I think that might be better." He stores the food in the cupboards that fill almost one whole wall of the wagon. "Very good," he remarks. "It is excellent to have all this storage space. Now, as I said, we must just keep our home tidy and clean. For this is our home now," he adds, meeting his friend's eyes. "So everyone of us must do their bit."

"I don't have to do anything," Rita says. "I don't make a mess. I don't even eat here!"

"Ooh yes you do," Walter reprimands her. "You sometimes eat bread crumbs which can be messy."

"Not really," Rita answers.

"It can," Walter insists.

"Oooh, nonsense," Rita replies, a bit irritated. "Isn't it time to go yet?" she asks, wanting to get away from the argument.

"Actually, yeah, that might be a good idea," Walter agrees. "Come on girls," he says to Mona and Rona, "we have to go to the show!" They don't complain as he carries them to their pram outside. "Rita, my dear, are you coming too?" he asks, smiling his nicest smile at her. Rita flies on top of his head and then starts ruffling his curls with her beak. "Don't Rita, please," he begs. "We must perform for lots of people just now, remember?"

"Tweet, tweet," Rita chirps. Bruno waves one of his paws at her, which she does not like very much. Bones, full of energy, is already running outside. Walter trying to smooth his hair back with one hand while pushing the pram, follows him. Now Rita is settled on his shoulder, Bruno trails behind. They do not see many people but from the big tent comes the sound of an orchestra, playing lively music. Walter hastens in that direction.

"The show must already have started," he mutters.

"The artist's entrance is at the back on your left," he hears someone shout. Walter nods gratefully in the direction of the caller, then he and his small group quickly make their way towards the opening at the back of the big tent. It looks like chaos inside. Figures in all sorts of colourful costumes seem to be running around in what seems like total confusion. It is very difficult to make any sense of what is going on here, but there is Pico coming towards them, grinning and waving.

"Nicely on time," he praises.

"Good," Walter answers, after greeting back. "And what do we do now?" he wants to know, very relieved to hear they are not really late.

"Wait," Pico replies. "I will tell you when to go up. First Mrs. Landini will perform. She is the lady who does the act with the horses. After that, we have the elephants and then it is your turn. You can have a peep at what is going on in the ring from here. If you gave your friends their tickets, they should be sitting in the front row over there!" Pico points out the place to him by opening the canvas, shielding them from the arena. It is just a tiny opening but big enough to see through.

"Yes," Walter nods happily, "I see them."

The others take a peep as well. "Yes," they whisper; "they have come. We see them sitting there. Mr. and Mrs. Martins, they are both here. See?"

"We see them, we see them," Rona and Mona almost sing. But Walter scarcely hears, for now he watches Mrs. Landini as she enters the arena with some beautiful horses. She herself is beautiful too. Tall and dark-haired, with enormous brown eyes. She wears a long dress in the colour of the evening sky. It is adorned with golden stars that shine and twinkle with every movement she makes. Her eyes sparkle as she whispers to the horses who circle around her with elegant steps, their heads held high. It is a magnificent sight, and people already start applauding their appearance and presentation. It is only now that Walter becomes aware of how many people have come to watch the performance tonight. It really makes him feel a bit overwhelmed. Looking at Mrs. Landini, he observes how wonderfully she handles the horses, letting them do whatever she wants with barely a whisper. They gallop, trot, and canter, stand on their hind legs or step with their legs up high, slowly, slowly, around the arena. This under the long whip Mrs. Landini dramatically swishes above their heads but which never touches any of them. There are cheers and hand-clapping, over and over again. Walter is entranced. This is all new to him. He knows horses, but not these kind. So proud and faultless, the horses even bow elegantly as a finale to their performance. A curtsy and a lovely smile from Mrs. Landini supplements this. They leave the arena under thunderous applause.

After that, the elephants come up. They are introduced by the ringmaster, who is none other than Mr. Landini. Dashing and elegant again in his black cloak with red lining. Smart, with his top hat and the long whip in his hand. Slowly and with much grandeur, the elephants walk in. Their heads bob up and down, up and down. They are bedecked with fringed rugs in gay colours. Sitting on their backs are lovely girls in short white dresses. Anew, the applause rumbles through the big tent. Walter sees that small round stools have been placed in the arena now. The girls are helped off the elephants backs by circus assistants. They then stand aside and Walter watches in amazement as the large elephants each sit down on one of these stools. Their bodies sway along with the melody that the orchestra plays. After a while, they stand in a circle touching one another with their long trunks. Thereafter, the girls are helped up those huge backs again and skipping ropes are handed out to them. They light-footed, start skipping away while the elephants slowly walk a few rounds around the arena. Mr. Landini cracks his whip into the air and praises their performance, this, under loud applauding from the spectators. Then, slowly, they walk out of the arena.

Walter knows now it is time for him and his group to come up. They are ready. He neatly straightens his sash and then Bruno's. The rosette around Bones neck still looks fine. 'And yes,' he ponders, 'Madame Emma was right, it does look good and festive.'

Suddenly, Pico is standing next to them. "Now," he says, "You have to go up now!"

Walter quickly fastens Bruno's chain on to his belt. Bones pushes the pram with Rona and Mona in it.

"Here we go," Rita chirps from his shoulder.

"Yes, this is it!" Walter declares and smiles encouragingly at his little group. They listen as Mr. Landini announces them.

"Ladies and gentlemen, tonight we like to introduce to you a completely new act. It is very different from all you might have seen before. We found a young man who can understand and speak the language of animals and birds. He speaks with them, he plays with them. Ladies and gentlemen, please welcome 'The Walteras', our new group of artists."

The orchestra starts up. The drums bang dramatically through the big tent.

"And there they are," Mr Landini's voice is jubilant.

Loud applause follows for Walter and his animals, who are now standing before them. The people like what they see. Walter is so handsome, the monkeys adorable in their frilly dresses, hopping about in their pram. Bones on his hind legs holds on to the handrail with his forepaws. Bruno is prancing around them while Rita, the small red bird, flies in circles above their heads.

"We have a grand name now," she twitters, "We are called 'The Walteras', Did you hear Walter?"

"Yes, yes I did," Walter answers her. He then bows for the many people applauding them and smiles his most dazzling smile. He stretches out his arm to Rita, who promptly comes and sits on it. She fluffs her feathers where-after she moves up to his shoulder again.

Then there is silence in the big tent. Everybody is waiting in expectation. Walter takes the flute from his inner pocket, puts it to his lips, and starts playing. Joyfully, cheerfully, a happy melody. After a few moments, Rita joins in. The crystal clear tones she brings forth gently weave in and out, along with Walter's music. The crowd listens intently, everyone from children to grown-ups, enthralled by the beauty of this moment. So amazingly powerful in sound and perfect it all is.

Then Bruno starts dancing close to the people in the front row and this brings a smile to everybody's lips. More so even when he is followed by the pram pushing Bones. The children giggle with excitement as Rona and Mona start tumbling in and out of the pram. Sometimes they even quickly allow one of the children to touch them and then sprinting away as fast as they can. And all this time Rita and Walter play on. Beautiful, cheerful songs which gladden the hearts of all who are gathered here this evening.

Suddenly Pico the clown, all dressed up in his utterly absurd outfit of ballooning purple trousers and grotesque, oversized shoes, is also there. It looks as if he is almost sailing through the air in handstand after handstand, bringing extra sparkle to the performance of the 'Walteras'.

The hand-clapping is overwhelming when Walter and Rita stop the music. Bruno and Bones also come to a stand-still. Rona and Mona jump back in their pram and Pico, together with Walter, bow gratefully to the audience.

At that moment, totally unexpected, a loud noise is rumbling through the big tent. A screeching, grinding sound. Then, from out of the tent's roof, a large bird flies straight onto Walter's only other available shoulder. It is an enormous parrot with feathers in brilliant colours of red, blue and yellow.

"What is going on? What is happening now?" people are asking.

"It is Lorenzo, Mr. Landini's parrot," Pico exclaims. "He has been missing for days."

Lorenzo proudly looks around. "Caramba!" he screams. "Caramba." The public finds this highly amusing, and so does Walter.

"Good evening," he says in a very formal tone of voice. "May I ask what brings you here?"

"Yes, yes," the parrot shrieks. "You may well ask."

"Well?" Walter insists. "What is your answer, then?"

"What answer?" the parrot wants to know. "What do you want?"

By now, most people are starting to laugh out loud. All the goings on here sound and look so funny.

Walter is aware of this and decides to make the most of the situation. "All right, all right, let me start again," he says. Walter's friends silently group around him, wondering what will happen next. Walter carefully and softly starts stroking Lorenzo's feathers. "Where do you come from?" he asks.

"From up there," Lorenzo yells, looking up to the roof of the tent. Laughter fills the air again. It shows how the crowd enjoys the to-and-fro bantering of words between this young man and the parrot.

"Whose bird are you then?" is Walter's next question.

"I belong to Mr. Landini, Landini," the parrot shouts.

"But why did you go missing?" Walter wants to know.

"Because, because, that's why," Lorenzo answers. Then he screeches again; "Caramba, Caramba."

"Why do you shout Caramba, Caramba, all the time?" Walter asks.

"He always does that," Pico, now very much into this act as well, answers for the bird. "Ever since Mr. Landini bought him from a sailor some months ago, he keeps saying it."

"Aahaa," Walter smiles, "So you come from the sailor and the sea."

"Yes, yes," Lorenzo agrees, a bit snappy.

"Did you like the sea?" Walter, ignoring this, asks further.

"Yes, yes," the bird begins, but then changes his mind. "No, no," he shrieks. "I do not like the sea." More laughter goes up.

"All right," Walter sighs, still playing up to the public. "What do you like then?"

The parrot, to everyone's delight, answers by yelling, "I like, I like, I like you!"

"Ooh, that is nice," Walter grins. "Very nice, but," he goes on, "If you don't mind, we are busy with a performance here. Can we finish, please?"

"Yes, yes," the parrot snaps again, dribbling from one foot to the other. "You go on. I just sit here on your shoulder."

"Good, well, fine," Walter agrees. And so it happens that Walter ends his show with one artist more than he expected. 'Actually, it went even better because of Lorenzo,' he admits to himself.

They get a standing ovation, and Walter is overjoyed. His faithful friends are just as happy as he is. They frolic around during the applause and Pico, smiling from ear to ear, shares in the fun. The orchestra starts up again. Ta, ta, ra, ta.

"Time to go," Pico signals. "It is interval time."

Thus, with a last bow to the audience, they're off, finding themselves face to face with Mr. Landini.

"Your show was a great success," he tells them with a big smile.

"Thank you, sir, thank you very much," Walter smiles back. He adds, "I must say, Pico, and Lorenzo the parrot also, were a great help, sir."

"That might be so," Mr. Landini responds, "but Lorenzo should not even have been there! What is the matter with you?" he asks the parrot. "I thought you were my friend."

"Yes, yes," Lorenzo yaps, "you are my friend."

"Ooh, and why do you hide away in the roof of the tent? Getting us all worried?" Mr. Landini wants to know.

"Because I wanted to," Lorenzo howls back.

"Hmmm, I see!" Mr. Landini answers. "And what do you want to do now then?" he asks.

"I want to be with Walter," is Lorenzo's reply.

Mr. Landini stays very calm. "Right," he says. "If that is what you want, so be it. Walter, do you like having Lorenzo with you?"

"It's fine with me as long as you don't mind, sir," Walter responds.

"That's decided then," Mr. Landini declares. "I must admit, I do mind," he goes on, "but Lorenzo's appearance indeed did something extra for your show. It would be foolish to deny that."

"I don't," Walter grins.

"Well," Mr. Landini continues, "if only you can keep him coming back for each performance."

"Indeed," Walter agrees. "I hope he will."

"I will. I will keep coming back," Lorenzo calls out.

"I must say, you are a very unusual bird," Walter smiles, adding, "it would be great if I could count on you!"

"But you can," Lorenzo shrieks, flapping his wings.

Mona and Rona are getting restless. All this talk, talk, it takes too long.

Pico, who has many other things he needs to do, feels the same. He asks to be excused, and after greeting everyone, leaves hurriedly. By this time, after jumping high and low in their pram, Rona yanks Mona's hat away from her, throwing it as far as she can–which is not very far–so Rita quickly picks it up.

"I leave you and your friends now," Mr. Landini says. "I know the monkeys must be tired. We'll see you tomorrow at the next show." With that, he turns around and makes his way to the arena again.

"Thank you, sir," Walter calls after him. Mr. Landini waves a hand over his shoulder before vanishing from sight. Mona and Rona both start wailing softly. They really are tired.

Walter bends over to the pram and takes both of them in his arms. "Shush, shush," he says. "Don't cry, my little ones. Come, we are going home to our wagon. There you can sleep and rest." Bruno and Bones are already on their way out. Walter follows close behind, pushing the pram in front of him. This with two monkeys in one arm and Rita on the one shoulder while Lorenzo stays put on the other. "Good night everybody," Walter calls out. Most of the circus people smile as they greet back. Walter is just so unique with these animals and birds wanting to be near him. One can't help becoming aware of him being a very special person, one who has the gift of attracting and spreading a feeling of well-being to all around him.

Outside, a full moon helps them to find their way back to their wagon. Once there, Walter heaves the pram with the monkeys inside. He then lights the oil lamp again. "So," he says, "now we can see what we are doing." He places the pram in the empty corner while declaring, "it is small monkeys sleep time now. You both have been so very good today. It really was wonderful the way you acted your part, and yes, that goes for all of you," he goes on, including the others as well.

"Yes," Bruno nods. "I think I was excellent!"

"And me," Bones joins in. Bruno lies down on his bed, ready to go to sleep. Bones folds himself on the floor next to Bruno. Rona and Mona make happy gurgling noises and very soon doze off. Lorenzo, by now, has parked himself outside on one of the wagon railings from where he can still look inside. Rita flies onto a shelf which is quite near to him so she can have a good look at this large parrot.

"Does Lorenzo make you feel a bit uneasy?" Walter asks.

Rita shrugs her feathers as an answer. "Yeah, I suppose so."

Walter says. "I must admit, he comes over a bit strong, but I am sure he means well."

"I am your friend," Lorenzo shouts, "and I do mean well."

"See?" Walter laughs.

"Yes I see," Rita chirps. She continues, "Oh, I will get used to him in time, I think."

"Of course," Walter responds warmly. "We will all be the best of friends."

He bends down to pick up the sashes of Bruno and Bones. "Look at that," he says, "they just shook them off onto the floor. You guys must learn to put away your things neatly. I remember telling you so." Bones only wags his tail in reply. Bruno is already snoring softly. "Oh well, let's hope you will all learn this then in your own good time," Walter sighs, "I don't think it helps to go on about it so." He folds his own sash along with the others and puts them in a drawer. "Right," he says, "I want to go and find out if Mr. And Mrs. Martins enjoyed their evening at the circus."

"I'll come with you," Rita says.

"And me," Bones instantly at attention, now joins in.

"Yes, of course you can come." Walter assures his friends.

"I am not going," Lorenzo shrieks from outside. "I will keep watch over the monkeys and that old snoring bear over there on the bed."

"That is very kind of you, Lorenzo," Walter responds. "Thank you."

After turning the oil lamp down, he blows out the flame, then goes outside. The full moon hangs bright and golden in the sky. The light it spreads into the wagon enables Lorenzo to watch every possible movement there. Walter trusts him. Somehow he knows a better caretaker than this, his new friend the parrot, will be hard to find. Walking up to the big tent, they hear the orchestra playing. The circus performance is not over yet. Walter decides to wait at the front entrance. Standing a bit to one side, they should be able to notice Mr. and Mrs. Martins as they make their way out, along with the other people. Bones lies down at Walter's feet while Rita, on his shoulder, snuggles up very close to him. Walter knows she is still a bit troubled by Lorenzo's sudden intrusion into their lives. He tenderly strokes her little head. "You are very dear to me, Rita," he whispers. "Don't ever forget that, please."

"I won't," Rita murmurs. "I won't."

Bones, with a question in his eyes, is looking up to them. "But of course, you too," Walter laughs. "Maybe you don't know this, Bones, but the saying goes, "a dog is a man's best friend, so what more can you ask for?"

Bones wags his tail with enthusiasm. "That's nice," he reacts. "And Bruno?" he probes.

"Bruno is very special too," Walter answers. He adds, "Bruno is a very wise old bear. He knows many things. He knows that when a new friend like Lorenzo the parrot comes along, we will have even more good times to share." They hear applause coming from inside the tent. The orchestra plays another fanfare, ta, ta, ra, ta, Then they hear Mr. Landini, the ringmaster, announce the end of the evening's performance.

"Ladies and gentlemen, thank you for being with us tonight. We hope you all have enjoyed our show and our time together. From our talented artists and me, comes the wish to see you again soon.".

Once more, the orchestra plays a few loud pulsating beats and there is more applause. After that, the first people are starting to stream outside smiling and talking to each other about all the wonderful things they have seen and heard. Judge Martins and his wife are also smiling as they step out into the evening air. Spotting Walter and his friends, their smiles widen even more and they quickly walk up to them.

Mrs. Martins places her arms around Walter in a warm hug. "It was great," she praises. "We enjoyed your show so much."

"And that's the truth," Judge Martins joins in. "It was a splendid performance." He shakes Walter's hand.

"Thank you, thank you," is Walter's response. He feels quite overwhelmed by their flattering words.

"Your friends too," Mrs. Martins goes on. "They were terrific."

"And the parrot?" the judge asks. "Did he really appear just by chance? We certainly never saw him before."

"Neither did I," Walter laughs. "And yes, his arrival was totally unexpected. It was great fun though, don't you think?"

"Indeed," Judge Martins agrees. "All the people loved it and so did we."

"And the clown?" Mrs. Martins asks.

"That was Mr. Landini's idea," Walter replies.

"Well, he also added some extra sparkle to your show, I must say," Mrs. Martin's remarks.

"Absolutely," Walter admits. "Pico is a very talented man," he adds. "You did see him with those other two clowns doing a comedy act after the interval?"

"Yes, yes, it was very funny," both Mr. And Mrs. Martins tell him.

"I thought it would be," Walter muses. He continues, "and besides that, Pico also sees to it that everything concerning the circus runs smoothly. He is Mr. Landini's right hand. That is how I see it, anyway."

"It is all very interesting," Judge Martins responds. "And you?" he asks. "Have you settled in yet?"

"Oh yes we have," Walter tells him. "We did get a very nice wagon for our own use, as I might have told you already. Also, the circus people are very friendly and I am sure we will be happy working and travelling around with them."

"Good," Judge Martins says, "that is just what we want to hear."

Along with the other people, they slowly are moving away from the big tent. Bones follows close behind while Rita never stirs from Walter's shoulder.

"Well," the judge remarks, "it is getting late. I suppose we have to say goodbye to each other now." His voice trembles a bit and Walter is very touched by this. He also finds it hard to speak.

It is Mrs. Martins who says, "Think of us now and then, will you? Yes, you too, Rita," she goes on, stroking the little bird. Then she pats Bones, murmuring, "please greet the others from us as well? We will miss you all."

"True," Judge Martins confirms. "It is very true, but we hope to hear from you every now and again? After all, you can write letters now and when the circus comes back, we will see you for sure." He shakes Walter's hand while putting an arm around his shoulder. Then it is Mrs. Martins' turn to hug him again. They are emotional moments. Walter has tears in his eyes. His words come haltingly as he over and over, thanks to these two people that have become so dear to him and his friends. And, 'yes,' he promises to write and, of course, they will see each other again. Indeed; what with the circus travelling back and forth, they are bound to meet up again in the not to distant future. So they part, but not before Mr. Martins says his good byes to Bones and Rita as well. Then he and his wife walk away towards their carriage, where Dieter, the coachman, was waiting to drive them back home.

After they have gone, Walter, without haste, saunters behind Bones, who is eager to return to their wagon. "Right," he says, "I can see you want to be with Bruno and the others. Well, they are all asleep and I think we should do the same. It has been a long day."

All the days in the circus are long, they soon find out. Early morning is training and exercise time for people and animals. The various acts have to be practiced over and over to perfection. At ten o'clock the first show starts then there is an afternoon one with in the evening a last performance. There are also fitting sessions in between at Madame Emma's, who is making some really fine outfits for them. Walter looks more than handsome in the frilled large white shirts he receives. With them goes a deep red-coloured jacket as well as a plumed beret from the same material. The gold braiding on both makes it look even more outstanding. The black trousers are tight fitting and shiny black boots complete the costume. Bruno and Bones are now the proud owners of a military type jacket. They are in the same deep red colour as Walter's. Here also, gold trimmings give a rich and very impressive effect. Mona and Rona are not forgotten either. Madame Emma has made some pink and white dream dresses with tulle and silks for them. They look enchanting in them. Even Mr. Landini, on seeing all this, mutters, "Good, very good." And that is high praise indeed.

The circus never stays in one place for long. When moving, everyone has to lend a hand. The big tent is taken apart and, along with the heavy poles holding everything up, loaded onto transport wagons. It is an enormous task that has to be tackled every time. They travel from town to town, from village to village. Still, Walter and his group find it exciting and enjoy it very much. Travelling and working together with all these people, they make many friends and learn a lot. Walter even gets the promise of riding lessons from Mrs. Landini, who performs with the horses. On the farm, he learnt to ride fairly well, but this outspoken woman tells him it is not good enough.

"A young man with such talents as yours must also be a good horseman," she declares. "It will stand you in good stead, believe me." True words, which Walter fondly remembers sometime later in his life.

Meanwhile, Lorenzo turns out to be a wonderful companion. He loves looking after Rona and Mona and tries to be pleasant to everybody. He sticks close to Walter, and surprisingly, to the promise he made as well. At each show, he makes his appearance. Screeching and shouting from out of the tent's roof, the big parrot sails onto Walter's shoulder. From there he starts yelling, "Caramba, Caramba!" just as he did the first time he showed up. It always brings a feeling of wonder and amazement to the audience.

On one such show, Lorenzo at long last tells why he likes to hide himself in the roof's tent. "I hide so I can watch you all," he shouts. "That is great fun, you know."

"Right, and now we can watch you," Walter responds. "That is even more fun, you know!"

"Yes, yes, Caramba. But of course it is." Lorenzo shrieks back, much to the delight of the crowd. They hang onto his every word and never get enough of his antics. As time goes on, Walter and his group become more and more used to the circus life. The training, the shows and, most importantly, the contact with their public. The applause they receive over and over always makes them very thankful and happy. They learn a lot and Pico is always there with a helping hand. Walter gets to know the circus people very well and makes friends with all of them. The young girls who do the act with elephants turn out to be Mr. and Mrs. Landini daughters. They are twins, with the names Leila and Lena. The parents of the other two girls who perform with them work in the circus as well. Then there are the four acrobat brothers who have a very good show together with their little sister, Ingrid. She is a wispy girl with the face of an elfin, but clever and sharp as can be.

Sometimes at the morning training sessions, Walter goes there to watch their exercises. It is amazing to see what these acrobats are able to do with their bodies. It is almost like dancing, the way they move, rolling over and with one hand at the back, the other one on the floor; turning around and around as if it is the easiest thing to do. Then the manner in which they handle their little sister, as if she were a large elastic doll, throwing her high into the air from the one to the other.

"Are you not afraid of falling?" Walter asks her at one of those mornings in between a rest pause.

"Afraid?" she asks. "Why should I be? They are my brothers. They know what they are doing and they never ever let me slip out of their hands!"

"And that is trust for you," someone quips. It is Pico, who, as always, is there to oversee the goings on and if everything is running in good order.

"Indeed," Walter smiles. "It is."

He spends many hours with all these people, getting to know and respect them. But it is mostly with the younger ones he uses the little spare time he has. Nice times, and Rita and Bones are always by his side. They also enjoy the company of these talented people. Ingrid and her brothers, Leila and Lena the twins, and Mitzi and Jana of the elephants act, these four who perform together. There are many other young people as well. They are good fun to be with and all have the same love for their work at the circus.

Mr. and Mrs. Landini take a lively interest in all their artists, being almost like a father and mother to everyone. And not only do they care for the people of the circus, the animals also have a warm place in their hearts. There is a strict rule—every animal has to be protected and looked after with the greatest consideration.

This pleases Walter very much. Mrs. Landini especially wins a soft spot in his heart. She herself makes the rounds each day to make sure things are as they should be. And if not, she sees to it that is put right. This goes for the artists as well as for the animals they maintain for their acts. Even Lorenzo, who does not easily show affection, is often found sitting on her shoulder. Stroking her cheek with his sharp beak he tells her now and then; 'I love you, I love you!' Mrs. Landini in turn, and with a lovely smile, assures him of the same!

Walter finds it a great honour when one day she fulfils her promise of giving him riding lessons. Being able to mount those beautiful horses Mrs. Landini does her circus acts with is something he secretly longs for. It happens on one of those morning training sessions he so often comes to watch. Bruno takes care of Rona and Mona, seeing to it that they keep safe in their pram. Rita has flown on to the roof of the tent where she keeps

Lorenzo company. From there, both of them watch what is going on in the arena underneath. Bones lies near Bruno and the pram as Walter goes to choose which horse he would like to ride. They are all so supreme, so he just walks up to them, whispering his admiration, then, mounting the nearest one to him, he has no difficulty holding on to it. Riding on the farm was never like this– on a horse like this! There is really no comparison!

Mrs. Landini leads the way, showing him what to do, and how to follow her example. Leila and Lena clap their hands as Walter deftly leads the horse in gallop and trot, gallop and trot.

"You are a born horseman," Mr. Landini, who is watching the exercise, compliments Walter, when he at last dismounts.

"Thank you sir," is Walter's reply. "And thank you Mrs. Landini," are his next words.

She smiles a charming smile in answer. "You're very welcome, Walter," is her reply.

Leila and Lena find Walter attractive beyond words. Mrs. Landini, now standing next to her husband, is very well aware of this. "You have stolen their hearts," she tells Walter, "And not only theirs. The other young girls here also think you are great!"

Walter blushes. He does not know what to say.

"Pity Walter already lost his heart," is the next thing they hear. The words come from Ingrid who, together with the others, has been watching Walter for a while.

"Oh? And who is this lucky girl?" Leila wants to know.

"Yes, please do tell," Lena's voice comes eagerly.

But Walter turns to Ingrid, asking, "My, my, and where do you get this wisdom from?"

"Oh, I can see it in your eyes," Ingrid answers. "You get the same faraway look in them as my brother Olaf when he thinks about his girlfriend in Sweden. And another thing," she goes on, "I also have a feeling you won't be staying here with us in the circus." There is an uneasy silence as she stops speaking.

Walter does not really know how to react. He looks at Ingrid's small face with the short, very blond hair encircling it; the enormous blue eyes staring straight back into his, then he decides to just shrug his shoulders. "I do not know what you are talking about, Ingrid," is his answer.

"Enough," Mr. Landini says. "It seems to me some people here are running around with strange ideas, but I just want to say that we hope to have Walter and his group with us for a long time to come."

"Indeed," Mrs. Landini adds in a light-hearted tone. Staying with that, she adds, "and tomorrow morning we can do some more exercises with the horses, Walter. So, will we see you then?"

"Oh yes, yes, thank you Mrs. Landini. I love to have some more lessons," Walter utters. Then he says, "And really, I have no plans to leave the circus. We love it here, my friends and I."

"Good," Olaf, one of Ingrid's brother's remarks. "That is very good. We love having you here!" He is a bit upset with Ingrid, putting Walter in such a spot. Ingrid, though, while stepping over to Walter's side, looks at her brother without saying anything further.

"Thank you Olaf," Walter smiles. "That is just what I needed to hear."

"You're very welcome," Olaf answers and, with that, the conversation comes to an end.

Mr. Landini puts his arm around his daughter's shoulders. "Come," he says, "let's go to our wagon so we all can rest for a while." Addressing his wife he asks, "You are coming too?"

"Yes, yes, of course," Mrs. Landini answers him as she hands her beloved horses over to the waiting grooms. Now everyone starts moving back to their own wagon.

Meanwhile, Walter has some very urgent questions he would like answered. "What is it that you know and others don't?" he asks Ingrid, who is still beside him.

"I knew you were going to ask me," Ingrid answers.

Bruno now starts pushing the pram with Rona and Mona, fast asleep inside. Rita, having left Lorenzo at his favourite roof spot, is settled on Walter's shoulder again while Bones runs in front of them.

"I am sorry, Walter, if I made you feel uneasy," Ingrid apologizes. "You see," she goes on, "I am always observing people and it seems I do have a sort of sixth sense as well. Moreover, I also have the irritating habit of blurting out what I sense about them. With you, I just know you have lost your heart to someone very special. You do not even want to admit this to yourself, but still, you are longing for her. Am I right or not?" Without waiting for an answer, she adds. "Today I maybe spoke up because I do not want anyone to get hurt or get false hopes of winning your heart. You must know that all of us girls are trying to do just that.

Not only Leila and Lena but also Mitzi and Jana and I know of a few other girls as well," Ingrid concludes.

"Aah and can I count you with them?" Walter asks with a chuckle in his voice while smiling at her. "I am not taking all you are telling me as the truth, you know," he adds. "All this nonsense about so many girls losing their hearts to me. Please give it a rest, Ingrid!"

"Think what you will," Ingrid responds. "And to answer your question, yes, you can include me also as one of those." She teasingly grins at him. "Anyway, I hope you are not cross with me? Can we still be friends?" she asks.

"Yes, of course, we will always be friends, you and I," Walter assures her.

"Oh I am glad," Ingrid sighs. "Very glad." She puts a hand on his shoulder and, before Walter can say anything more, moves away from him to join her brothers.

Walter has mixed feelings over the whole episode. He does not want to leave the circus. Neither does he want anybody else to think he wants to. No, doing what he and his group are doing here, performing at circus Landini, suits them all just fine. 'Who could wish for anything else?' he asks himself as he enters their wagon. So comfortable they all have made themselves here in these past months. "No, really," he mutters again. Bones is already there and Rita, without uttering a sound, flies up to her usual place on the bookshelf. Bruno ushers the pram into the wagon. The sleepy Rona and Mona are still inside and clinging to each other, they just doze on.

"Now, what was Ingrid talking about?" Bruno asks.

"Ah, it was all just silly prattle," Walter replies.

"Well, that is why I am asking," Bruno says, "We are not going to leave again, I hope? I really don't want to, you know. I like it here and Pedro always keeps the nicest honey for me."

"Yeaah, I also like to stay," Bones remarks from where he lies totally content on the soft blanket specially put there for him.

"And me," Rita chips in. "I do not see why we should leave from here."

"And neither do I," Walter hastens to assure them all. "Believe me, we are going nowhere," he adds. Still, he knows Ingrid spoke the truth when she said that he loves a very special person. Only, she does not really know how special. 'And so way above my reach as well,' he ponders broodingly. That is why it is best to just try to forget this dream. And what better place is there to do so than here at circus Landini with all its hustle and bustle? So many new people, so many places to visit. Always something else crops up while life goes on, day by day.

Walter has more riding lessons from Mrs. Landini and becomes a perfect master in the art. A few times he even stands in for Mrs. Landini. Once when she comes down with the flu, another time she has to attend to family matters somewhere. He and the horses have become the best of friends. They listen to his every word faultlessly performing all he asks of them. And again the public loves it. Watching him with his own group, seeing him with the horses, the applause always comes rumbling afterwards.

Now and then Walter writes a letter to Mr. And Mrs. Martins telling them of the day-to-day happenings at the circus. When there is a mail coach going their way, Walter sees to it that this letter goes with it. He also receives news back from them.

Everything is fine at the estate and Max and family are fine as well. Everybody is sending their best wishes. 'Missing you though!' Mr. Martins usually adds. And Walter's letters also sometimes echo the same feeling, but there is never much time for that.

'A good thing too,' he often thinks to himself. A good thing because mostly it keeps him from letting this vision enter into his mind again–the vision of a lovely princess with long golden hair and a friendly smile to whom he has lost his heart.

"If I only could look at her. To see that lovely face again will be enough," he tells himself many times. Meanwhile, Rona and Mona, when not sleeping or performing, have a great time with both Bones and Bruno. They often ride on Bones back, and play to their heart's content with Bruno, that old cuddly bear with the big heart. They are all over him, pulling his ears, dancing on his big tummy when he tries to sleep, and that, he often tries. Although protesting and grumbling, Bruno enjoys their frolicking on and around him.

Lorenzo, as always, is then here, then there, going his own way but still spending a lot of time together with Walter and the others. And so time goes on, travelling with the circus from one place to another.

CHAPTER XI

Then one day they come to a charming little town. It lies at the foot of a wooded hill. Halfway between the treetops, a few towers can be seen. "It must be a palace," Walter mutters to himself. He has been looking at them since they came into sight.

"It is a palace," Rita tells him. She knows because she had already flown over there without Walter being aware of it.

"Who's palace can it be, then?" Walter asks out loud. The lion tamer, passing by on his wagon, overhears him.

"It is the king's palace," he answers Walter's question. "He lives there with his daughter, Princess Elina."

Walter can hardly believe his ears. And yet somehow it is as if he has known all along that someday this would happen. Of course, he has been waiting and hoping for this, he suddenly understands. And to tell the truth, deep in his heart, he knows this was one of the many reasons for him wanting to join the circus. So that maybe they might travel to the place where Princess Elina lives.

They drive through the streets in their usual procession. The elephants first, Mrs. Landini with the horses. The lion tamer with his animals. The acrobats and the clowns, Arno and Carlos, with Pico in the lead. Mr. Landini is there as always, striking in his black and red cape, the high hat and carrying the long whip. All the others belonging to the circus follow close behind.

Having spent a long time in their company now, Walter knows these people. They're mostly kind and helpful. He knows the animals too. They are not unhappy with their lives in the circus. Their trainers treat them well, with good food and good care. The older animals, though, can't help wondering what will happen to them when they get too old to perform. They have talked to him about it and sometimes ask, "What then?" But he has no answer for them, which he finds very upsetting. And now he even feels rather distressed by the thought of leaving them all. For leave, he will. When the circus leaves this town again, he will not. He wants to stay near where Princess Elina stays. In this lovely place where he at least has a change of seeing her again. Yes, Ingrid's words were really truthful when she told everyone he would not stay with the circus. Strangely enough, this comes about even sooner than expected.

Shortly before the evening performance, Mr. Landini receives some surprising news. A messenger from the palace has come over to announce that the king and his daughter Princess Elina will visit the circus this same evening. The news spreads in no time at all. People come running with it from everywhere.

Walter and his group are just more or less ready to leave their wagon when Pedro knocks. "Have you heard?" he asks, sticking his head through the open door.

"No, I haven't," Walter replies. "What can you tell me?"

"Well, I can tell you the king is coming tonight to watch the show. Princess Elina also comes."

Walter is stunned. He cannot even answer.

"Did you hear me?" Pedro wants to know.

"Yes, yes, I hear you, but I can hardly believe it," Walter utters. "Rita, Bruno, Bones, Princess Elina is coming," he calls out.

"And the king," Pedro repeats.

"Ooh my." Rita replies. "I suppose we better leave now, then. Maybe we will see them arrive."

"Yes, let's quickly go," Bones joins in.

"Not so quick," Bruno mutters. "I am not so quick."

"Anyway, I have to hurry," Pedro declares. "See you all just now."

"Yes, we'll see you," Walter answers. "We are ready. Bruno, let me look at you. Yes, you look fine. Rona and Mona, you look fine too. Yes, well, let's be off then. Lorenzo will be waiting for us in the tent, so we'll see him there." Nervously, he picks Rona and

Mona up in his arms. "You are both so good today," he says, while stepping outside and putting them in the pram, which Bruno has already taken outside. "Tell me, are you looking forward to see Princess Elina?" he asks.

"Is she nice?" Mona asks.

"Very nice," Walter answers.

"It is you who is looking forward to this the most," Rita tweeters.

"Oh, let's just go," Bones barks. He starts running around them.

"Please stop," Walter begs of him and Bruno waves one of his big paws as a warning to Bones. At least that makes him stop. They move along to the big tent. A whole gathering of circus people move in the same direction, grouping together at the entrance. Pico and Pedro, with other helpers as well, are busy rolling out a red carpet.

A very excited Mr. Landini marches up and down between them. His wide cloak swirls around him as he gives all sorts of instructions. "Let's make rows," he suggests. "One row of artists on each side of the carpet."

No sooner is it said than done. In no time at all, two neat rows of colourfully clad artists line the red carpet in front of the tent. It so happens that Walter and his group are placed at the front of one row, Mr. Landini and his family on the other. Bones sits quietly behind Walter, but Bruno, wisely, has moved some distance away with the pram. So as not to give Rona and Mona any chance of troublemaking, he holds them securely in his arms. Rita is staying on Walter's shoulder. They all wait, but not for long. Very soon, the sound of trumpets fills the air. The heralds, all splendidly dressed and seated on their white horses, first come into sight. It is the same as Walter remembers it from the first time he saw the royal procession. The heralds, the footmen around the carriage; the carriage itself, glittering gold in the last rays of sunlight. Then, in the carriage, the king, smiling broadly. Opposite him, the beautiful Princes Elina.

The coach comes to a halt and after one of the footmen opens the door, the king and his daughter step onto the red carpet. Mr. Landini comes forward, followed by his wife and the twins, Leila and Lena. Formal greetings and the shaking of hands, as well as bows and curtsies, follow. Walter can't help but stare, as the others do, at so much imposing and lustrous majesty. And the princess is so sublime; her sparkling smile takes his breath away. Along with her father, the king, she glides past him as Mr. Landini and his family usher them towards the tent. The king now and then stops to speak a few words with one or another of the circus artists. Of course, each of them feels greatly honoured by this.

Once the royals have entered the big tent, the artists, one by one, disperse to the back entrance. For sure, the evening performance will be very special tonight! Mr. Landini takes his quests to the reserved area for important visitors.

Walter and his group join the other artists at the back. There they jostle to get a look through the small curtain holes. Everyone wants to see some more of the king and the princess. There is not much time, though. The first townspeople, who have come to watch the show, are already arriving. Nobody has to tell them anything for the king's carriage. Standing a bit to the side now, is there for all to see, as are the footmen watching over it, and the heralds waiting next to their splendid horses. Everybody knows then that king Frederik, and most likely his daughter too, must be here for tonight's performance.

Such a festive effect this has. People's faces light up with expecting smiles. "Surely, this will be a show to remember for all times!"

Even the animals sense something very special is taking place. They all behave extremely well; Bruno and Bones at Walter's side, the monkeys in their pram and Rita still perched on Walter's shoulder. All the others are just as good while waiting for their turn to come up.

There is a hush, mixed with excitement going around. The orchestra plays with immense enthusiasm. The opening fanfare sounds extra joyful and the big tent is filling up fast.

Exactly at seven o'clock, Mr. Landini strides into the arena. "Ladies and gentlemen," he begins, "I have a wonderful announcement to make. As you can see, King Frederick and Princess Elina are honouring us with their presence tonight. Let's give them a warm welcome!" Loud applause soars through the big tent. The crowd cheers and waves. No doubt here, they love their royals.

From their private enclosure, the king and princess wave back, smilingly. The orchestra starts playing the national anthem. The royal visitors, standing now like everyone else, listen respectfully.

After this, Mr. Landini, being the ringmaster and master of ceremonies all in one, starts to speak again. "Dear king and princess, ladies and gentlemen," he calls out. "We are very honoured to have our beloved king and his daughter, the princess Elina, here with us tonight. I hope and wish that all of us shall have a wonderful evening. And now, let the show begin!" There is more applause while Mr. Landini takes his seat next to the king again.

Under a loud fanfare of music, the first artists come running into the arena. It is Ingrid and her four brothers. They start by throwing rings into the air and catching them while swift as the wind they climb on each other's shoulders. It is amazing to see; how alert they are, and how light on their feet. They keep throwing those rings and catching them every time; Ingrid, a lovely figure in a short multi coloured dress, bows every time her brothers pause for a while. Then it is her turn. As lightly as they threw the rings to each other, now the four brothers almost do the same with their sister. High above their heads she goes from the one brother to the other. The orchestra plays together with the rhythm of what is almost a ballet performed in the air. It is a dazzling show, full of energy and enthusiasm, which deserves the thundering applause they receive at the end of their performance.

And the show goes on, one act followed by the next. Mrs. Landini and her horses also make an enormous impression with their act full of beauty and grace.

Soon it is Walter's turn to appear with his group. Although very nervous at first, his music calms him down again. This evening he plays his flute for Princess Elina only. He does it with such tenderness it brings tears to her eyes. Rita gives it her all too, melting in with Walter's performance in a most enchanting way. After the first melody is played, Rona and Mona are taking over, melting many hearts with their playful pram cavorting while Bruno and Bones have them laughing out loud. They both act so droll, prancing around the pram in a very absurd manner. Of course, they are intensely aware of the royal visitors and play up to them as well.

So does Pico, who has joined them by now and amuses everyone with his antics.

And then, there is Lorenzo. His timing is perfect. Just at the right moment, he comes down, shrieking and yelling, making as much noise as possible. Walter tries to pacify him, but Lorenzo does not want any of this. Not tonight. Tonight he is staging a special presentation for very special people. First, he dribbles from one foot to the other, then he hops onto the side of the pram, much to the delight of Rona and Mona. They at once start plucking his feathers. This Lorenzo does not like. Next he is on Bruno's head, but now it is Bruno who does not like that and shows it too. Bones begins to bark because he sees Bruno struggling with Lorenzo. Rita, by this time, is also getting upset, and takes off from Walter's shoulder, flying in circles around them all.

"What a commotion," Pico wails, annoyed and alarmed at the same time. After all, it is he who is responsible that everything concerning the show goes smoothly. But tonight of all nights, it does not! "What can we do?" he wants to know from Walter while trying to catch Lorenzo. But Lorenzo is far too fast for him.

Walter does not even try. He just stands there, waiting, with one of his arms outstretched. "Leave him," he tells Pico. "It will be all right, you'll see. If only you can get me a table from somewhere."

"Yes, yes, I can," Pico answers. "One table please," he calls out. He nearly trips over his own far to large shoes as he runs towards a handler who hurriedly brings a round table from the back.

The people are beginning to laugh. They find the whole situation confusing, but amusing too, believing it is all part of the show. They watch as Pico places the table in front of Walter.

Lorenzo watches as well. He flies away from Bruno, straight onto Walter's arm. "Why do you need a table?" he asks.

"For you," Walter answers.

"Why?" Lorenzo wants to know.

"Because," Walter replies, "You have seen how nice Bruno and Bones dance and how our royal visitors enjoyed that." He bows into the direction of the royal box with the king and the princess, then goes on, "Now I think you also want to do something special. Correct me if I am wrong, but I have a feeling that you would like to dance as well. Yes?"

"Yes," Lorenzo agrees, nodding his head briskly.

"So," Walter continues, "here is your chance. This table should do fine."

Lorenzo, holding his head to one side now, nods again, this time more slowly.
"Yes," he says. "It will do!" He flies over to the table and starts walking on it. Up and down, up and down.

Bones and Bruno, Bruno with Rona and Mona in his arms, gather around Walter. Rita is on Walter's shoulder again. Unhurriedly, Walter brings the flute to his mouth and starts playing one of his happy tunes. Merrily Rita joins in. All eyes are on Lorenzo. He no longer walks, but instead, with the first notes from Walter's flute, turns around and around, while making some awkward steps. He seems to believe this is dancing–but dancing it is not! He only makes himself dizzy, and it shows.

'This does not work out,' Walter thinks, looking at the pathetic scene before him. He stops playing, and Rita falls silent too. But

Lorenzo wobbles on. Nobody knows what to make of it; neither the king, the Princess Elina, nor the other people.

Walter has had enough. Stepping forward, he grabs Lorenzo from the table. Holding him tight to his chest, he bows to the audience. "Thank you for letting us perform for you," he says. Still clutching a dazed Lorenzo, he walks away. The others of his group follow closely. However, they all have to come back. There is such a loud and spontaneous applause, they simply have to. Walter does not quite know what to make of it. Surely with Lorenzo out of control, their act ended a bit shakily? Still, the audience seems to have loved it.

"Well, very good then," he says. "If we are liked, even with this odd show, so much the better."

"Yes, let's give it to them, my friends," Pico agrees, so back they all go and bow over and over again, to the king, the princess, Mr. Landini and family, and to the whole cheering crowd. But during all this time Walter never loses his grip on Lorenzo, who does not even utter a sound. At long last they are off, back to where the other artists are gathering. The orchestra, having given fanfare after fanfare to Walter's group, is playing some lively music again.

Pico, now standing in for Mr. Landini, announces the next attraction. Quick as ever, he has changed into a brown, tight fitting pair of trousers and vest. The wide cloak over this is brown horizontal yellow stripes.

"He looks like a bee," Walter notes with amusement. "But then, it suits Pico very well, him being so busy always," he smiles to himself. It is the magician with the lady helping him who are being introduced by Pico. After entering the arena, this wizard does many bewildering tricks and even saws his lovely assistant in half. Luckily, she appears a few moments later as one person again, smiling and thanking the public for their applause over this trick.

Meanwhile, Walter and his artists are praised from all sides.

"You handled the situation very well," Pedro remarks. "People thought everything that happened was part of the show. But really Lorenzo," he addresses the big parrot, "how silly can you get?"

Lorenzo, for once, has no reply. He feels very bad for behaving so foolishly.

"I am sure it won't happen again," Walter says. "It was just because things were so exciting tonight. What with the king and princess being here and the princess so beautiful. I can understand it."

"Yes, and you always seem to understand everything," Pedro responds with a smile. They leave it at that.

Soon afterwards, Walter takes his companions with him out of the tent. On arrival at their wagon, he puts Lorenzo at his usual place on the railing in front of the wagon's entrance. "Are you feeling better now?" he asks.

Lorenzo starts to dribble around and flap his wings. "Yes," he snaps, becoming his old self again. "I am fine."

"Good," is Walter's answer, "then you can keep watch over Rona and Mona because I want to go back to the big tent."

"Oooh,? That must be because of the princess," Rita chuckles. She likes teasing Walter every now and then.

"Yes," Walter replies, not at all upset by her remark. "I would indeed love to see her again. "Are you coming with me?"

"Always," Rita chirps. She nudges his curls with her small beak while nestling on his shoulder.

"You can tease me as much as you like," Walter laughs, "but this evening cannot be spoilt anymore. To see my beloved princess, ah, who could ask for more?"

However, there is going to be a lot more, although Walter does not know this yet.

Bones, wagging his tail, announces, "I am coming too."

"And you, Bruno?" Walter asks, while trying to calm Mona and Rona. "You two must go to sleep now," he sighs.

"Leave them," Bruno yawns. "They will fall asleep just now. Lorenzo and I will both keep an eye on them." He yawns again and wobbles onto the bottom bed. There, he lazily stretches himself out. Rona and Mona are watching him. It only takes them a few leaps to land on Bruno's tummy.

"Yes, yes, and what are you doing? You can sleep in your own pram, you know," Bruno utters.

Ignoring his words, they cuddle up to him in utter contentment. Walter can't help but smile. So often this happens. Bruno is the one they turn to for some extra comfort. Whenever Walter tells them something they don't like, such as that they must go to sleep, they seek solace with Bruno. And Bruno loves it. Even if he sometimes grumbles at first, his arms are always welcoming them. Then, from this place of safety, they look around with innocent but gleeful little faces. Faces that say, "See who really cares for us." It helps, of course, that Bruno himself loves to sleep often. So mostly the three of them happily sail off to dreamland together.

On his return to the big tent, Walter, along with the other circus people, wait for the end of the evening's show. They are all hoping to catch a glimpse of the royals again. A rumour is also going around. Some say the Princess Elina is going to give a children's party tomorrow. They claim that a few circus artists will be invited to perform. Walter hopes the rumour is true. Who knows, maybe his act might even be chosen. Maybe? Could it be? Everyone is guessing. The air is filled with expectation. At long last, the orchestra plays the closing fanfare. They all know it by heart. The performance is over. Soon afterwards, people start streaming outside. Instead of going home, they gather around, waiting for the king and princess. Already the royal carriage is brought nearer. A loud 'hurray' goes up when, soon after this, the king and princess make their appearance.

The smiling king and his daughter wave as they are assisted back inside the coach. Amidst much cheer, they drive away. Soon, the crowds disappear too. It is late; people want to get back to their homes.

It is Mr. Landini who confirms the rumour that is going around, "Yes, it is true, a children's party will be held at the palace tomorrow. It will be a garden party. And yes, among those invited to perform are also Walter and his group." Mr. Landini smiles when he sees how absolutely delighted Walter is. "You earn it," he says. "You did well tonight. The king and his daughter enjoyed your show very much. They thought Lorenzo was very funny. Still, I must have a few words with him. He went a bit too far tonight. Anyway, that can wait until tomorrow. And speaking about tomorrow, I think we should get the arrangements in order now. Not all of our artists are going, so let's work out how many wagons we need. I think two or three should do it. And something else. Let's forget about our usual shows tomorrow and concentrate on our palace performance. Those who are not taking part have the day off!"

This announcement gets much approval. Everybody likes having a day for themselves. Days off really do not happen too often at the circus. Soon Mr. Landini is busy talking things over with Pico and Pedro while the other artists are giving their opinions as well. There is an excited babbling going on.

Only Walter does not take part in this. He is to overcome with joy. 'How wonderful,' is all he can think. "How marvellous," he sighs happily.

Rita chirps her agreement with that and Bones just wants to run off to tell the others the great news. Walter holds him back. "No, no," he says. "You better stay with us. Tomorrow we tell them. It will be such a surprise!"

That night, Walter can hardly sleep. 'What a day it will be tomorrow', he keeps thinking. 'What a day it will be!'

And so it is. A day full of excitement and laughter. It starts early with Mona and Rona waking everyone up, as always playing, romping about and shrieking to each other. When Walter tells the great news, there is no end to the merriment. Bruno promptly wants to wear his uniform jacket, but Walter informs him it is far too early for that.

"No matter," Bruno declares, "let's go!"

"Ooh, and what about food?" Walter asks.

"Yes, yes, food is good," Bruno beams. So they first have breakfast. Lorenzo prefers not to come inside. Walter later takes him some fruit and nuts at his post in front of the wagon.

"I don't think I will go to the party today," Lorenzo mumbles. He pecks busily, all the time avoiding Walter's eyes.

"Nonsense," Walter replies. "Of course you go to the party. The children love you, you know they do."

"But I made a spectacle of myself last night," Lorenzo answers.

"All of us do, one time or another," Walter tells him. "It is not the end of the world, you know. Please remember that."

"Ooh, if you think so," Lorenzo mutters, looking up at Walter now. "You are not cross with me?" he asks.

"I was never cross with you," Walter says.

"Really? So that is all right then," Lorenzo reacts.

It does not take much for Lorenzo to be his perky old self again. Rita, who is taking a bath in a half empty bowl of water, playfully splashes water all over him.

Every morning Walter sets the bowl out for her, nearby Lorenzo. The two birds have become very good friends, so Lorenzo takes no offence, but just fluffs his multi coloured feathers, causing a myriad of water drops to sparkle in the morning sun.

"No more spinning on the table," Rita teases.

"No, no, I won't do that anymore," Lorenzo bawls.

"I am glad to hear it," Walter declares.

Rona and Mona suddenly come running towards Walter and jump into his arms. Just as well, these arms are always ready to catch them. Bones and Bruno also join Walter and the others outside. Here, Walter tells them that Mr. Landini has given the day off for all the artists not performing at the palace.

"Oh, that is great," Bruno reacts. "With no morning show to do, can't we go and visit the elephants? They are such a nice crowd."

"Yes, we can. There is plenty of time," Walter replies. "The performance at the palace is only at midday."

"Hurray," Rona and Mona shout, "we are going to visit the elephants." They bounce away from Walter again, leaping over each other in their enthusiasm.

"I won't go," Lorenzo states. "I am not feeling all that well."

"It is no problem," Walter assures him. "You can wait for us here if you like."

Lorenzo puts his head in between his feathers. He is not ready to meet any of the other animals yet, and Walter understands.

"We'll be seeing you then," he says, toddling off with the others to the small watercourse where the elephants are. The whole troupe welcome their visit. Jumbo, the oldest, declares, "Well, how very nice to see you all. Such a fine day it is too, with us having the day off. We hear you, with some of the others, are going to the palace?"

"Yes indeed," Walter answers. "Isn't it great?"

"For sure," Jumbo replies. He goes on, "I have also heard some other great news. Do you know there is a zoo at the back of the palace gardens?"

"No, I don't know anything about that," Walter admits.

"Ooh but it is true," Jumbo says, "ask Julia the stork. She has been there!"

Walter follows Jumbo to where Julia the stork stands on one leg at the water's edge.

"I have just flown in from that zoo this morning," she tells Walter after all of them have been introduced. "They took care of me thereafter. I had an accident," she explains. "My one wing was hurt in a storm and I fell down in somebody's garden. Luckily, the people living in the house there found me and brought me to the king's zoo. They gave me the best of care, as you can see, because now I am better again."

"I am glad to hear it," Walter responds.

Rona and Mona have dashed off into the stream where they merrily splash each other with mud. The noise they make while doing so is deafening. Bruno has waded in as well, trying to catch them, but they are far too fast for him. Bones is not much help either. The only thing he does is run around the monkeys in obvious delight, barking and sloshing water in all directions. It all seems like huge fun.

Only, Julia the stork plainly does not think so. "These animals chase all the fish away," she wails, moving further away. Jumbo and Walter follow her. Rita has flown into a tree near the hustle and the bustle of the happy water party. Clearly, she enjoys watching the whole hilarious racket.

"There is more to tell," Jumbo persists. "Wait until you hear the rest of Julia's story."

"I will, I will," Walter assures him. They meet up with Julia a bit further down the stream. Here again, on one leg, she stands very still. It seems she does not even want to look at them anymore as she keeps staring down into the water.

"Please forgive the disruption," Walter addresses her. "My friend Jumbo tells me you have some more information about this zoo?"

Slowly, Julia turns around. "Oh very well," she utters, "I told Jumbo there is a care centre for old animals at the king's zoo, as well."

"My, my," Walter exclaims, "that is good news indeed. See Jumbo," he goes on, "now you don't have to worry anymore about what might happen after you have become old."

"Yes, that is what I make of it too," Jumbo agrees. He nuzzles his trunk against Walter's face. Walter smiles. "You want me to find out more about it, don't you?" he asks.

"Well," Jumbo responds. "If you are going there anyway...."

"Fine, fine, I'll do it!" Walter says. "I report back to you, I promise."

"Good," Jumbo replies, letting go of Walter's face. "I keep you to that!" They say goodbye to Julia, who scarcely notices them anymore.

Walking back to the others, Jumbo asks, "how much longer will you be staying at the circus, Walter?"

"Why?" Walter wants to know.

"Ooh," Jumbo answers, "there is something about you. How can I say, something faraway? As if you already have taken leave from all of us? I sense you prefer to stay on here in this village?

And if so, why? Does it have something to do with Princess Elina?"

"My, my," Walter says. "So many questions you have, Jumbo. But," he smiles, "You may be right. I am thinking of staying behind. Perhaps one can read this on my face?"

"Perhaps," Jumbo answers.

"Well let's see how things go from here," Walter says. By this time, they have reached the others where the fun and games are far from over yet. Jumbo, in high spirits, joins in by filling his trunk full of water, whereafter he sprays it over himself and over everyone who is nearby. The monkeys are delighted.

"This is nice," they decide, and Jumbo's back looks so inviting. Within seconds, they have installed themselves there and get showered as well. A lot of shrieks and shouts go along with this, of course. Bruno and Bones just stand there, taking it all in.

Walter laughs out loud. "This is priceless", he says to Rita, who has flown back on his shoulder.

"Yes it is," Rita answers. She is enjoying it as much as he does.

The other elephants decide to join in the fun too. Soon, there is loud trumpeting to be heard and water splashes everywhere. It goes on for quite some time. There is a feeling of togetherness which makes each moment very special.

Bruno, who is still standing in the stream, decides to sit down now in a shallow spot. Bones, as always nearby, does the same. The two of them look a bit silly as they stare open-mouthed at the tumultuous scene in front of them. But then the whole situation might be a bit silly, although most hilarious.

Walter can't resist it. He wades in too. The water is nice and refreshing at his bare feet. He sloshes around Bruno and Bones and then up to the elephants, taking good care, not to come to close. Seeing Rona and Mona are perfectly happy and safe, he slowly toddles back again. "Don't you want to take a bath here?" he asks Rita, who is still sitting on his shoulder.

"No thank you, not with this commotion going on," Rita answers. "If you don't mind, I'll take a bath some other time. Which reminds me," she adds; "looking at sun's position, is it not time for us to go yet? It must be past midmorning by now."

"Yes, you are right," Walter agrees, looking up at the sun as well. "I think we better make a move. Come Bruno, Bones," he calls out, "we have to go."

Hearing Walter's words, Bones is already up and running towards them, but for Bruno, this is not so easy. He seems to have a problem getting up. Walter quickly walks over to him. "Give me your paw," he says. "I'll help you." Bones is at Walter's side, panting, his mouth open in a wide grin. Bruno truly looks very comical. Even Walter cannot hide his amusement. Luckily, Bruno does not mind. He has a good sense of humour. "Fine," he utters, after standing on two hind legs at last, "I am up and coming."

"It would have been wiser of you to just switch on all fours," Rita comments.

"Yes, yes, indeed," Bruno says. "Well, I keep that in mind for next time, then!"

"Yeaah, you big bouncy bear, I hear you," Rita twitters. She is sitting on his head by this time, picking on some tufts of hair there. While Bruno is protesting loudly, Walter fetches Rona and Mona from Jumbo's back. "Come on girls," he says. "We are expected at the palace, remember?"

"Yes, yes, that will be nice too," the monkeys cry. They clamber into Walter's arms while saying goodbye to their elephant friends. "I'll be seeing you later then," Walter tells Jumbo.

"Right," Jumbo answers, moving his trunk up and down and sideways in greeting. They all greet back and then walk off together, still well in time for the afternoon's events. Lorenzo though, does not seem to think so. He meets them in a very alarmed state. "Why did you stay away for so long?" he shrieks, while wildly flapping his wings. "I have been waiting for ages. We still have to go to the palace you know!"

"I know and we will," Walter assures him. "Don't worry."

"Why do you say, don't worry?" Lorenzo asks. "Of course I worry. Somebody has to. You just go off and leave me all alone."

"Ooh Lorenzo, please," Walter laughs. "You know very well, we did not do that. Besides, you knew we were with the elephants and could have flown over there if we stayed away too long for your liking."

"Right," Rita chirps in, adding; "and another besides, you did not want to come with us, remember?"

Lorenzo does not answer. Instead, he flies up into the air.

Walter knows the big parrot is still edgy and very upset because of what happened the previous night. On top of that, he still has to face Mr. Landini, which does not help to calm him either. "Don't let it get you down," he calls out after him. "Everything will turn out all right Lorenzo, you'll see!"

Rona and Mona choose this moment to struggle free from Walter's arms. They bounce, leap and jump into the wagon. Bones, wanting to be part of the fun, jumps inside, along with them. Bruno yawns, all he longs for is a nice long sleep. It is not to be.

Walter makes them all freshen up, have a bite to eat, then they're off to the big tent. That's the place where everyone who is going to the palace, has to meet. Two open carriages will take them. It is decided. Walter and his group will go with Mr. Landini. Pedro takes the rest of the artists in the other. As they all board the carriages, Lorenzo is still nowhere to be seen. "Where can he be?" Mr. Landini asks. "The princess wants him to be there as well. She expressly asked,"

"Ooh, I would not worry too much about it," Walter replies. "I know Lorenzo is still feeling very bad over what happened last night, but I also know he wouldn't want to miss this show for the world."

"Yes," Rita chirps. "Lorenzo was even upset with us for not getting ready sooner." After Walter has translated Rita's words, Mr. Landini seems calmer. "Well, I hope you are right," he declares. He goes on; "Anyway, Lorenzo knows I can never be cross with him for long. But with him, one always has to expect the unexpected!"

"Shall I go and look for him?" Bones asks.

"No Bones, you stay here please," Walter answers. "You won't be able to find him and we don't need any other problems right now, thank you." Bones knows, when Walter speaks in this tone of voice, it is better to obey. He snuggles up to Bruno, who, all dressed up in his favourite army jacket, has once again happily dozed off in the back.

Rona and Mona clamber all over Mr. Landini. Usually he has a lot of time for them, but today, he is nervous. For today, everything has to be just right, and now Lorenzo is missing. He picks up Rona first, then Mona, handing them to Walter. "You take care of them," he says. "My mind is on other things."

Walter hugs the monkeys, who now cling to him for comfort. Mr. Landini cracks the whip and the horses start pulling the carriage. They like Mr. Landini, they also like Walter and his group. All of them have become very good friends. And so the journey to the palace begins.

It is not a very long distance they have to travel. The main street forks and from there the road begins to wind uphill, climbing towards the palace, which keeps on hiding behind the trees. So, well within an hour, the gates are reached. Guards, in red and black uniforms, let them get through at once. Clearly, they are expected. The horses' hoofs clatter contently over the cobblestone path. They're nearly there.

The white palace, surrounded by flowers in a profusion of colours, suddenly becomes visible. A man in a similar uniform as the gate guards walks up to them. After a friendly greeting, he asks Mr. Landini to keep following the curved road round the palace. "It leads towards the zoo. But first you will come to an open space with an arena next to it. That is where the party will take place," he informs them. After Mr. Landini has thanked him, they are off again, Mr. Landini still in front, the other carriage, driven by Pedro, following close behind. Soon, a festive sight unfolds before their eyes. On a soft green lawn, encircled by large trees, red and white sun shades stand over white tables and chairs. On the chairs, children in bright clothing fill the air with their laughter. The sound of soft music completes the idyllic scene.

"How lovely," Rita chirps.

"This is fantastic," Mr. Landini exclaims. "And," he goes on, "they are all waiting for us, I suppose."

"Of course," Walter laughs. "Well, it seems they are enjoying themselves in the meantime," he adds.

Bones is already gone. Full of excitement, he leaps towards the children. Walter calls him back. "No, no, Bones," he says, "you better stay with us. No Mona, no Rona, you are not to go either. We've come here to perform, remember?"

Bruno has woken up by now and, still half dazed, is looking around to see what is happening." Ooh, aha," he mumbles; "this seems to be a very nice party. Good food too, I would think." He is soon up and ready to go, but is also ordered to stay by Walter. The artists from the other carriage are calling out; "where do we go from here?" Mr. Landini waves them on "To the left, I think," he says. "I see the king standing there!"

Walter is on the lookout for Princess Elina. "Where can she be?" he wonders. Rita seems to know what his thoughts are because she says, "I'll go and look, Walter," and then flies away. She is the only one allowed to go. The two wagons make their way towards the king. Before they reach him, though, two guards come forward. "This way," they say, pointing in a different direction. "Your wagons can be parked in the space next to the arena," It is, as they have been told and soon, the wagons come to a standstill in the shadow of some tree's there.

Now the artists stream out. The jugglers, the acrobats, the magician, Pico with Arno and Carlos, the other two clowns. Mr. Landini, Walter and his group and they all are wondering what will happen next. They don't have to wait long. Suddenly, from behind the trees, Princess Elina appears. Wearing a long lilac dress with little yellow flowers, she looks like a flower herself. Settled on her shoulder is a very smug-looking Rita.

Walter can just hold on to Rona and Mona. They are jealous of Rita and also want to be with the princess,

"Thank you for coming," Princess Elina greets them with a smile. "The children will love your performance, of that you can be sure." They all respectfully bow before her. Again the princess gives them all a friendly smile, as do the ladies-in-waiting, who gather around her.

"Thank you for your kind words Princess," Mr. Landini says while turning his hat around and around in his hands.

Mr. Landini is nervous, Walter notices. He watches as Mr. Landini peers up into the sky. 'I think this is because of Lorenzo. Where can this big bird of ours be?' he wonders. He himself is now getting a bit upset too. Yes, although the princess seems not to have noticed it, Lorenzo is not at the party as yet!

"Well," the princess goes on, "the children are having lunch at the moment and this shall be followed by a puppet show. There after they will come to see your performance. In the meantime," she continues; "please have some refreshments yourself. Don't worry about your horses, they will be taken good care of."

As if by magic, some stable boys appear who unyoke the horses and lead them away and suddenly, servants in red and gold uniforms, are appearing as well. Some put wooden tables in place, others unfold embroidered table cloths over them. Still others carry on, baskets of food and crockery. In no time at all, the tables are set, inviting and pleasing, in an attractive U formation. Fruit juices are added and tumblers to drink from. Benches have been carried on and placed alongside the tables.

Bruno, wise old bear that he is, sees Walter, who is still carrying Rona and Mona, becomes a bit uneasy. Gently and without saying a word, he one by one, takes them in his own strong arms.

"Thank you, Bruno," Walter whispers gratefully. He watches as Bruno and the two monkeys, who are amazingly quiet, move to a nearby tree. Bruno sits down there and Bones promptly joins them.

"So good they are," Mr. Landini remarks. "Yes," all the artists nod and smile in agreement.

Princess Elina invites everybody to sit down and enjoy the tables fare. To his great surprise, Walter finds himself next to Princess Elina with Mr. Landini on her other side. He is overjoyed and can hardly believe his luck. After Mr. Landini has introduced him to the princess, his happiness is complete. Rita is happy too. She hops from Princess Elina's shoulder onto Walter's and then on to the table again. Fluttering her wings, singing merrily, cheered on by the smiling faces around her.

Princess Elina is delighted. "So sweet," she murmurs. "So very sweet this little bird is." Turning to her ladies-in-waiting who are sitting nearby, she asks. "Would it not be great if we could keep this little songbird here with us?"

"Oh, yes, yes, absolutely," comes the answer in unison from that end of the table. Walter tries to say something, but the princess wags a finger at him. "Oh no," she declares with a twinkle in her eyes. "I know what you are going to say. You think it is a very bad idea, because this little bird needs to be free to come and go where she wants. Not so?"

"Indeed, Princess," Walter manages to bring out, Rita quickly hops back on his shoulder.

Clearly, the princess has something more to say about this? And yes, she has. "I would never want to hold this lovely red robin captive," she says. "Never!" Adding; "but, I know something you do not know, Walter. It is a secret still. You just have to wait a bit longer to find out what it is!"

Everybody has been listening to her words and now the princess has them wondering what this secret can be. Most of all, Walter and Rita. As the princess plainly does not want to say anything more, the artists again start chatting to each other, and the episode is laid to rest.

Although Walter notices Mr. Landini has an earnest conversation with the princess, he is not able to hear all they are saying, but understands it has to do with the "Walteras".

In the meantime, old Bruno, with Rona and Mona still in his arms, has fallen asleep against the tree. The two monkeys so unusually quiet up to now, have been waiting for this! The lovely goodies displayed on the nearby tables are just too much to ignore. Before Bones, who is on watch, can stop them, they dash off and on to those tables. With enormous gusto, they lay into the food. Gobbling here, then there, great consternation and hilarity erupts as everyone tries to save what can be saved.

Walter is struggling to catch the two misbehaving monkeys. Then Mr. Landini deftly catches Rona by her tail and scoops her up into his arms. Mona is soon caught as well, where after both of them are handed over to Walter. He, totally embarrassed, starts mumbling excuses.

Princess Elina, however, waves them away. "No matter," she smiles.

"I suppose this is what could be called monkey business, is it not?" Walter tries to smile back, wishing meanwhile he could hide somewhere. No such luck, though. All he can do is to ask for permission to leave with the two wrong-doers.

After this is granted, he hastily departs, carrying the unruly monkeys in his arms. While so doing, he catches a glimpse of Ingrid's concerned face where she is sitting with her brothers.

"How could you do this?" Walter asks his small friends. "Why?"

"We were hungry," Mona wails, "And thirsty," Rona joins in.

"You could have waited a bit," Walter argues. He halts at where Bruno and Bones still sit in the shadow of the nearby tree. Bruno, wide awake now and Bones next to him, is feeling very guilty over what happened. Having not dared to go to the scene playing out before them, for fear of making things even worse, they just watched.

Meanwhile, some other servants have placed another table, laden with food and fruit, in front of them. Hardly even noticing this, they avoid looking Walter into his eyes. "Big help," is all they hear from him. "Really, such a big help I could do without!"

Rona and Mona, always alert, have spotted the other food now. "Hungry, hungry," they start crying. "Can we have this food then, Walter?"

"Oh, well, yes," Walter agrees. "As long as you two behave yourselves and don't come running up to the other tables again! Promise?"

"Yes, yes," they both utter as Walter releases them from his arms. They love the fruit and nuts, as well as the other goodies that have been put on the tables now in front of them. With much delight, both of them start munching at once. "Have some," they invite Bruno and Bones in between bites. "It's very, very, good!"

"Yes, have some," Walter urges them too. "Actually, I am not all that angry with the two of you," he tells Bruno and Bones. "I don't think you could have stopped our fast footed monkeys from escaping. I should have known that. So come on, no hard feelings. Eat something and enjoy it, Yes.?"

"Yes, ooh yes," Bruno responds, "We are all good friends and we are going to eat from all this nice food, which is good, goody good indeed!" They all have to grin about Bruno's words who immediately after this, starts eating. Then Bones also joins in, while Walter watches. "You will stay here now with Bruno and Bones?" he repeats his previous question to Rona and Mona. "Yes, yes, we will," they both assure him again. "We will be goody good, Walter," Mona says sweetly. This time Walter has to laugh out loud before walking back. Still, it is with a heavy heart that he returns to his table. Order has been restored there, he notices and to his relief, Princess Elina, as well as her ladies-in-waiting, are nowhere to be seen.

"Too bad, too bad," Mr. Landini cries dramatically, while waving his arms about, "I am sorry," Walter tells him. "I said so already."

"I heard, I heard," Mr. Landini snaps. "Not as if that has helped any. Princess Elina has left after all this uproar. Lorenzo is still missing. I don't see the king anymore over there. What next?"

"Don't be so hard on him, Mr. Landini." It is Pico, coming to Walter's aid. "The king would have joined us shortly, as Princess Elina told you, but he was called away. And the princess, when she excused herself from the table, also told you she had to go with her father. Surely you remember?"

"Yes, I know, even so," Mr. Landini admits grudgingly.

"Well then," Pico goes on. "I am sure they will be back just now, as the Princess said, they would."

Here, Pico stops for a moment.

'Ai,' Walter thinks to himself. 'Leave it to Pico. He knows exactly how to calm our Mr. Landini when he is upset.'

He is even more impressed when Pico, with a big smile, announces, "And as for Lorenzo, if you look up into that big tree over there. Yes, there where Walter's friends are sitting. You will see him at once, watching us!" All eyes follow Pico's directions.

"Can you believe this?" Mr. Landini cries out. "Here I am, worrying myself sick over this bird and there he sits, indeed, watching us."

"Maybe you were more worried if Lorenzo would turn up for our performance here, than anything else?" Pico remarks with a dry smile. Everybody knows it is only Pico who can get away with speaking to Mr. Landini like that. They have worked together for ages and besides, Pico, being his right-hand man, they are also the best of friends. Mr. Landini clearly thinks it better to ignore Pico's words. Instead, he walks up to the big tree. "Hallo Lorenzo," he calls out. "Are you going to perform this afternoon?"

"Hallo," Lorenzo calls back "Yes, I will." Suddenly he flies down, past Mr. Landini, straight onto Walter's shoulder. Rita, on the other one, decides to change places with the big bird and so she disappears into the big tree. Now Lorenzo is playing up again. "Hallo, Walter," he gurgles. "Did you have a good day so far?"

"Ha, Lorenzo," Walter laughs. "Yes, well, now that I see you, it is much improved. Thank you."

"Good, good," Lorenzo answers. "Remember, my friend, it is as you told me. We all have our day!"

"I remember," Walter replies. "I remember."

"And so do we," someone shouts from one of the tables.

"Yes, yes," others join in. Pedro starts cheering and tapping his hands on the table. More artists follow his example. In an instant, the jovial mood of before has returned. There is merriment and good humour again. The team of artists from circus Landini, are looking forward to their show. To be the guests of the king and his daughter, is very exciting. They enjoy the time here on the palace grounds. The food and refreshments are delicious and there even has been some amusement. This is thanks to Lorenzo, who delights in being the centre of attention. Also, the scene with the monkeys, Rona and Mona, was actually quite comical. But now, they want to do the entertaining.

And that is exactly how things turn out, for there is Princess Elina again. She is surrounded by children with happy little faces. Soon, the whole arena is filled with them. Long cushions for seating, in red and white stripes, are everywhere. Princess Elina and her maidens take place among the children. Rita, having left the big tree, quickly settles herself on the royal shoulder.

Then, all of a sudden, silence falls over the gathering of children. They are waiting, waiting for the show to begin. And so it does. First, the acrobats come up. Their slaloms take them high into the air.

The children love every moment of it. They cry out in alarm as the four brothers throw Ingrid around as if she were a stuffed doll, but no harm comes to her. Smiling sweetly after landing on the ground again, she makes a little bow and thereafter teases her brothers to repeat the act. This they do and anew, get a heartfelt applause. The jugglers too. It is amazing, breathtaking, what they can do with bottles that weave into the air. Six, seven, all together, swirling to and fro. Then it is the magicians' turn. He keeps the children spellbound with his tricks. Little white doves appear from nowhere and white rabbits hop out from under his hat. Not to mention the long long streamers in green, red and yellow colours that keep coming from his mouth and ears.

'A hard act to follow,' Walter thinks. More so, because Rita seems no longer to be his companion, but instead chooses to be with Princess Elina. Or does she? Of course, he knows very well that Rita, just as Lorenzo, does not belong to anyone, really. They can come and go as it pleases them. Sometimes choosing a friend from among people, other times flying away into the wide open sky. That is as it should be.

Still, at this moment, with their show coming up, he finds it a bit awkward. He looks at Bruno and Bones standing at the ready. Bones on his hind legs, holding on to the pram with Rona and Mona in it. Bruno and Bones, both, are still watching the monkeys every movement, so as not to let them get away with any mischief again. 'Friends,' Walter thinks. "Such good friends you are," he tells them. "I say this because it is right for you to know how much you mean to me," Bones looks up at him, wagging his tail and with love shining from his eyes. Bruno smiles his widest smile, while at the same time wrapping a large fore-paw around Walter's shoulders. 'Fine,' this implies, 'but you are telling us nothing new!'

Only four musicians from circus Landini are present today, though now, as they are blowing their trumpets, it sounds as if there are far more than that. This gives Walter a good feeling as he and his small group make their way on to the arena's stage. And see there, who comes flying over and nestles on his shoulder? Yes, it is Rita, of course. "Aah, well, this is great," Walter tells her, "So, now we are ready to make our own kind of magic, or what do you think?"

"Oh yes, definitely, we will," this little bird chirps back. And they do! As always, there is the wonder of Rita's singing and Walter's flute playing. Rona and Mona really try to make up for not behaving earlier on. They are, in one word, adorable! Pico, playing the dumb clown, brings much laughter, also with his antics. And Lorenzo? Yes, he comes down, shrieking and screeching, "Caramba! Caramba!" promptly on time. Prancing around while arguing with Walter.

The children scream with delight over such an outrageous bird. The king, in the meantime, has entered the arena as well. Waving to everybody around, he takes a seat next to Mr. Landini. The king seems to enjoy this show just as much as the one of the previous evening. He laughs out loud with every comical situation, which spurs the artists on even more. For they, in turn, are watching the reaction of their audience. The laughter and cheering of the children and also those of the grown-ups. It makes them act even better with every show. And so, the performance goes on. Act after act, the whole afternoon becomes an unforgettable experience. They get a standing ovation when, at last, the musicians play the finale. It is a long ovation and afterwards the king invites all present to come along with him.

"I would like you to see my zoo," are his words. "It is not an ordinary zoo. Here we care for old and sick animals and birds. They can stay here because we love them. They are all very dear to us!" As the king leaves the arena, Mr. Landini is still at his side. Princess Elina and her ladies follow. The artists and children trail after them.

Walter, while pushing the pram with Rona and Mona, notices how earnestly the king is talking to Mr. Landini. "Is it about me?" he wonders, seeing they glance in his direction, now and then. He forgets about it for a while, when Bruno tugs on his sleeve. "Do you think there will be bears in this zoo too?" he asks.

"And monkeys?" Rona and Mona, now again settled in their pram, want to know. "Yes, yes, there are," Lorenzo shouts. "Bears and monkeys too."

"My, my, so you were there already," Walter declares.

"Of course," Lorenzo replies. "I always want to find out everything."

"I know," Walter laughs. "Did you see any elephants, Lorenzo?" he asks. "I wonder if there are any at this zoo?"

"Yes, I saw two elephants," Lorenzo answers. He goes on. "It seems to me they look after all sorts of animals here. There are stables with some very old horses and in the fields nearby, I saw some horses grazing together with eland and other buck."

"Yes, I saw that too," Rita backs Lorenzo. "There are also birds who, after being hurt, are getting healed here, they told me."

"So, you had a look there as well, then?" Walter remarks.

"Yes, I did," Rita answers him. The two birds each sit on one of Walter's shoulders, something they often do and Walter loves it. He is very grateful. Rita is still with him. "I thought that maybe you prefer to stay with Princess Elina now," he addresses the little bird. "The princess made it very clear. She wanted you to."

"Stop troubling yourself about it, Walter," Rita almost sings. "You should know by now, I will never leave you! Although," she continues teasingly; "I must say, it is fantastic to be with Princess Elina. She is so charming."

"I know, I know," Walter sighs. "It is just a pity that when I am near the princess, I become nervous and scared I might say or do something silly."

"Just like me," Lorenzo utters. "Yes, indeed," he goes on; "but what can we do?"

"Nothing," Walter sighs again, adding; "I just hope the princess does not think all that bad of us."

"Oh, no, she doesn't," Rita chirps. "She actually likes you both. I heard her say so to one of the ladies who is around her all the time."

"That is great!" Lorenzo shouts.

"Did she really?" Walter asks unbelievingly.

"Yes, really," Rita answers.

By this time they have reached the first zoo-cages. The king stops at one of them. "In this cage we keep all sorts of different birds," he says. "We put them here after they have been healed from a sickness or injury. There is no roof over it, as you can see.

They are free to fly away, but many of them stay here or come to feed when they are hungry."

Bones, at once, is in front of the cage, wagging his tail. 'How exciting it would be to charge in among them,' Walter can almost hear him think. There is no chance for that, though. The king moves on, again with everybody else trailing him.

The zoo is very well laid out. The two elephants Lorenzo mentioned have an enormous enclosure and so have the other large animals. Walter can't get over it. "This is good news for Jumbo and his family," he says. "Very good indeed!" Looking around him, he becomes aware that only Bones is still at his side. Somehow, Rona and Mona have once again escaped. The Pram he is pushing is empty. He sees them soon enough, though. Monkeys as they are, he notices them climbing down into the cages of some newfound friends. They noisily greet each other and talk monkey talk. And Bruno? He has found other bears. They seem to be old buddies, guessing from the way they greet each other. Walter is very happy for him.

Lorenzo and Rita are getting ready to fly away as well. Both flap their wings. "If you don't mind, Walter, I like to go back to Princess Elina for a while," Rita declares. "Well, yes, and I like to speak to some of my own kind here in those cages," Lorenzo says. "We did talk already this morning," he adds; "but there is lots more to chat about."

"Fine, fine," Walter replies as they both fly off. "So Bones, now it is just you and me," he says."

"No matter," Bones tells him, "I can live with that!" So, they move on, following the king's tour. And very interesting it is. From cage to cage, enclosure to enclosure. Each one has a tale of the animals or birds in there. The king even tells a few of them but after a while, he says, "Maybe it is now time to have some refreshments again. For sure, the children will love to have some."

"Yes, Yes," the children shout. "We do love to, your Majesty,"

"So, they all walk back to the arena and are soon seated on a small terrace, overlooking it, King Frederik and Princess Elina with her ladies, as well as Mr. Landini have taken place on a small platform while the artists spread themselves on one of the arena's top benches, From there they have a good oversight of their surroundings, The children have found their places under the sun shades at the colourful tables again. Soft music from the orchestra, mingling with their excited laughs and voices, makes the whole scene even more festive. Walter is sitting a bit away from the other artists because not everyone likes to be up close to his ever present animal friends, Although at this moment, Mona and Rona are nowhere to be seen and neither is Bruno, But Bones, is as always, on his side, Servants walk to and fro, seeing to it that everyone gets served. They bring appetizing snacks and fresh fruit juices, of which Walter and Bones each get their fair share. Bones enjoys himself hugely, while happily munching along with Walter.

Sometime later, Walter catches Mr. Landini's eyes and sees him beckoning to come nearer. 'Right,' Walter nods and mimics; 'I am coming.'

"Will you stay here, Bones?" he asks; "Or would you rather go and look for the others?"

"Yes, I will see if I can find Bruno first," Bones answers, already on his way in the direction of the zoo.

"Good," Walter smiles, "then I see you all, later." He walks over to where Mr. Landini is sitting next to King Frederik and

Princess Elina. Bowing respectfully, Walter waits, wondering, as do all the circus artists, why he has been singled out to appear before them. Could it have something to do with the serious discussion the king and Mr. Landini seemed to be having earlier? Was the feeling they were talking about him correct, then?

Indeed, it turns out to be just so.

"Walter," Mr. Landini begins; "The king and I had a long talk about you and as a result, I believe the king wants to ask you something."

"Yes, your Majesty?" Walter bows again, his manner courteous and attentive. 'What can it be that a king would want to ask him?' he ponders. The answer is soon forthcoming.

"Well, Walter," the king addresses him. "We have a position of zoo keeper here that needs to be filled. We have been told you are able to understand both animals and birds. With that in mind, we would like you to take up this position. Are you willing to do so?"

For a moment, Walter is speechless. Him? Zoo keeper, here, at the court of King Frederik and his daughter? It is too good to be true! "Your Majesty," he utters. "Yes, yes, of course. Thank you, thank you." Then his thoughts turn to the circus. Although planning to stay behind anyway, he now wonders; 'can it be so easy?' Apparently, it is.

"Don't look so worried now, Walter," Mr. Landini chuckles. "You have my blessing. With the start of the new season, there are many artists applying for work at the circus. More than I can take on, actually," he goes on. "Besides that, I expect the "Deodoras," to be back soon as well!"

"Ooh good," Walter sighs with relief. "You don't object then that I take up this offer?"

"No, I don't object," Mr. Landini assures him.

All the circus artists have been listening intently and now it is Pico, who starts clapping his hands, soon followed by the others. They shout and cheer while walking towards Walter, shaking his hands and congratulating him. "What did I tell you?" Ingrid says. "Remember my words?"

"I do, I do," Walter declares. "You told me I would not be staying at the circus and you were right." He goes on; "But I will miss all of you and shall never forget the good times we had together!"

The king and his entourage, as well as Mr. Landini, look on smilingly. "Well," the king declares after some time. "We are glad to welcome you in our midst, young man. Furthermore, we expect you here tomorrow morning early." Standing up, he greets everyone with a nod of his head, then invites Mr. Landini to accompany him. Together, they walk away.

The princess and her ladies follow and ooh, wonder, the princess, with Rita still perched on her shoulder, smiles at Walter. Then, standing in front of him and placing Rita on the open palm of her hand, she says; "My wish that this sweet little bird should stay here with us at the palace has indeed come true. Isn't that amazing?" Her tinkling laughter, as well as those of her court ladies, fill the air as they also walk away.

In the midst of that, he hears Rita singing, "Never fear, Walter, I always come back to you!"

"My, my, my," is all Walter can utter while thinking; 'So that was the secret the princess spoke off. She knew all along.'

Still overcome by this day's events, he looks on as the children are gathered into a group by their caretakers. It has been an exciting day for them. A fabulous day, but now it is time to go. They clamber back into the open carriages in which they came. So pretty these are decorated. Lots and lots of flowers in different colours hang everywhere. On the sides, by the seats, even the horses in front of the wagons have wreaths of flowers around their necks. It is a cheerful sight. Smiling and waving, the children's voices ring out in a merry song of; "Thank you, thank you dear Princess Elina. We had a wonderful day!"

The princess, all smiles, waves back as do her ladies-in-waiting. A bit further on, the king and Mr. Landini halt for a moment, doing the same as the children pass by. Then, of course, there are the artists, who, in their enthusiasm, run along the carriages for a short distance. Pico the clown and his friends, acting up and fooling around as always. The others laughing and cheering them on.

From a distance, Walter waves to the children as well. He is still a bit bewildered by his good fortune. 'How did I get so lucky?' he asks himself over and over, 'How marvellous this all is!'

The monkeys, with Bruno as their escort, have arrived back by now. It is Bones who tells them what has happened while they were visiting their friends. At first they find it hard to believe and cannot get over it. They have a mixture of feelings and are not quite sure how to react.

"Will it be fun?" Rona asks. "Are we going to stay with the other monkeys, then?" Mona wants to know.

"And me? Will I be together with the other bears here at the zoo?" Bruno utters. None of them have an idea of what to really expect. But they do understand, their time at the circus has suddenly come to an end. Without waiting for an answer from Walter, Bruno says, "I will miss the circus though," Sighing, he adds; "Well, it might be for the best, is it not so?" He clearly wants a positive answer to his question and Walter at once gives this to him. "Absolutely," he states with such confidence that they all feel much happier about it.

Walter goes on; "Our time at the circus was a fantastic experience. We learned a lot, but now I think we should move on. Who knows, we might find even more great and amazing adventures. And as for your questions about how it all will be, I haven't any answers to that as yet. Let's first see how it all turns out."

"Yes," his friends agree with him; "Let's see how it goes, then."

At this moment, Rita comes flying towards them. Fluttering her wings, she nestles herself on Walter's shoulder again.

"So, you have decided to come back?" Walter smiles a smile full of affection.

"Always," Rita chirps. "Always Walter," Turning to the others she asks; "Isn't it wonderful news that we are going to stay here at the palace?"

"You think so?" Bruno, still a bit in doubt, asks.

"But of course," Rita sings. "It will be great! We have lots and lots of friends at the zoo. The ones we met today and all the others as well. You shall see!" Rita's words at once make them feel so much better. They lift their spirits no end.

That Lorenzo is still absent from his group is barely noticed by Walter. He is full of contentment. On the way back, the joyful smile never leaves his face. The others tease him a bit, but he does not mind. He is the happiest young man in the world. This feeling flows over to his group as well. The thought of being with Walter at the palace becomes more and more attractive to them.

"I did meet some old friends at the zoo today," Bruno declares. "They are very happy there."

"Yes, and we already made many new friends," Rona and Mona announce, uttering, as they often do, the same words at the same time.

"It will be good," Bones says. What he actually hopes, is for more time alone with Walter. If Bruno and the monkeys are visiting their new friends and Rita often being with the princess, he and Walter will have even more time together. After all, a dog is man's best friend, as Walter himself has said.

There is a lively discussion in the wagon about the day's happenings. Everyone has something to say. The king was so friendly, the princess more than beautiful. The show went well, and the food was splendid. They tease and compliment Walter at the same time and, on the whole, enjoy a jolly good return journey together.

Remarking on Lorenzo's absence, Pedro says; "Well, with him still being at the zoo, he is the only one who does not know you are leaving us, Walter."

"My, my, yes, that is true," Walter reacts.

Mr. Landini, sitting in front again with Walter on his side, looks at Walter and Walter looks at him. Mr. Landini's eyes say; 'What is to be done?' Those of Walter ask, 'what must I tell him?'

Then, Mr. Landini smiles a bit sadly and understanding this, Walter's face lights up. "You mean?" he gasps. "Yes," Mr. Landini answers. "If Lorenzo wants, he can go with you. It must be his decision."

"Ooh, you are so good," Walter blurts out.

"Nonsense," is Mr. Landini's reply, "You heard what the princess said about birds having to be free and to go where they want to go. Apart from that, you also must have noticed Pico's remarks. He implied I was more worried about the show than the parrot. And maybe I was," he adds with a sigh.

"Pico is a good friend," Walter says, "But that is not to say he is always right. We all know you care very much about Lorenzo."

"Ooh and what else do you know?" Pico responds cheerfully.

Walter, with a chuckle, goes on. "Well, I know I deserved to be told off for not controlling Rona and Mona."

"Ah, yes, indeed and blaah blaah blaah," Pico laughs teasingly, and Rona and Mona, hearing their names mentioned, full of joy, leap into Pico's arms. It makes for all over hilarity.

Sometime later, back at their own base, everyone clambers down from the wagons. They receive a warm welcome from the others who did not take part in the palace performance.

"How did it go?" they ask. "How was the show? Did the children enjoy it? It must have been great to be at the palace?" After all the questions are answered, Mr. Landini announces the big news about Walters' appointment as head zoo keeper at the royal zoo! This causes great excitement and Walter is congratulated from all sides. "How marvellous," they say, "but are you not going to miss us and the circus?"

"Of course I will," Walter utters in an emotional voice. "You have all become such good friends. I will never, never forget you, nor the wonderful times we had together. Don't think though, you're not going to see me again. When circus Landini comes to this town, I promise I am going to visit."

"Good, that is very good," his friends respond under much shoulder and back clapping.

"Well, enough is enough," Mr. Landini finally says. "And remember, although I gave you all off for the day, for tonight, the show is still on! So let's all get ready, please!" It is good advice.

Slowly, the artists of circus Landini amble off to their wagons to prepare for the evening performance. As it is still early and Walter's act is somewhat later than most of the others, he still has a bit of time on his hands. This gives him the chance to report back to the elephants, as promised. Jumbo and his friends are glad to see him.

"And? Did you find out anything?" Jumbo asks almost at once, after they have greeted each other.

"Yes I did," Walter replies. "The king himself showed us around," he continues. "Every animal or bird is welcome at his zoo, he told us. Especially the old and sick ones."

"Aah, that is marvellous news," Jumbo reacts, And how does it look there?" is his next question.

"Fantastic," Walter answers. "It really is great. There are lots of trees, large enclosures and good food. I know," he goes on, "because I asked about it. I got the same answer from everyone. The food is good and they are all very happy at this zoo."

"Well, that is excellent," Jumbo says. "Excellent!!"

"I thought so too," Walter responds, glad that he can bring such fine news. By now, the elephants are forming a circle around Walter and his friends. They all want to hear what Walter is saying.

Rona and Mona, already seated on Jumbo's back, now jump from one elephant to the other. The two monkeys find this brilliant, only, nobody pays much attention to them. Not even the elephants themselves. They are too busy debating Walter's news.

"What about the horses?" one of the elephants wants to know. "Can they also go there?"

"Yes, they can," Walter tells them. "I saw stables there, with some older horses in them."

"Great, that is great," Jumbo declares. "Now we can let them also know. I am sure they will be very happy to hear this. They asked us about it, you know."

"Right," Walter responds, adding, "anyway, the horses who went to the palace with us will tell them as well. They know every last detail, because they went over to the horses in the stables and talked to them." By this time, Rona and Mona urgently want some attention. "We are going to stay at the palace," Mona shouts. "Yes, at the palace," Rona echoes. Now at last, they get some reaction.

"What are they talking about?" Jumbo asks, "Ooh yeah, I was coming to that," Walter replies. "It is e, well, the king offered me the position of zoo keeper and I have accepted. Tomorrow will be my first day there."

"Ooh, but that is splendid!" Jumbo exclaims. "Congratulations Walter. Things could not have worked out better than this. For you and for us."

"Yes, for us too," one of the other elephants joins in. "With you at the zoo, we, from the circus, can be certain to be allowed in, when necessary. It really is brilliant!"

"Gee, it is nice to see you all so happy and pleased," Walter laughs. He adds; "If not for my sake, then surely for yours?" There is all round merriment over his remark, increasing the good fun they have. "Right," Walter says at last, after they all have calmed down a bit. "I think we better go and get ready for our last performance. What do you say, Rita?" he asks the Robin on his shoulder.

"Yes, of course," is her reaction. Walter turns to Bruno and Bones, who are patiently waiting next to the pram. "Come on guys," he smiles. "What do you think?"

"Good, yes, let's go," Bruno answers, getting himself in an upright position. Bones eagerly jumps away. Rita chirps; "It is getting late, everyone!"

"Indeed," Jumbo agrees. "We must be getting ready too!"

"Good, then we see you again in the big tent," Walter replies. They greet and thereafter, Walter and his group wander off towards their wagon. Mona and Rona have leapt back into their pram and hop up and down and then all over Walter, who pushes the pram. They are now full of excitement about their going to stay at the palace. Walter keeps telling them to quieten down.

When that does not help, he puts on his 'no nonsense, now that we are going to perform,' face. Only then, they wisely decide to behave.

"Does everybody know now we are leaving?" Rita asks.

"I suppose so," Walter replies. "Otherwise, we must tell them tonight."

They don't have to. That evening, just before Walter and his friends start their act, the orchestra plays its usual loud fanfare, then, in the middle of the arena, stands Mr. Landini. Superb and splendid as always in his swaggering black cape with the red lining, his top hat and with the riding crop in one hand. "Ladies and gentlemen," he announces after the music subsides somewhat. "Tonight, we want to bring an outstanding young man to your attention. He and his group have been with us for some time. They have given wonderful shows for circus Landini. You'll see what I mean when they come up just now, for their last appearance here. You may ask; but why are they leaving us then? And my answer to that is, yes ladies and gentlemen, wait for it! It is the king, our very own king, who has chosen this person, who can understand and speak with animals and birds, as keeper of the royal zoo! We will sorely miss him and his artists, yes, but we have to let them go! And here then, dear listeners and spectators, I present to you, for the last time; The Walteras!"

Ta ta ta ra, sounds the fanfare again and there is Walter, bowing for the overwhelming applause, as do his friends, who are gathered around him. Their performance that evening is better than ever, and Lorenzo, this unpredictable large parrot, as ever, makes a grandiose entrance again.

The animals behave at their utmost best and the music Walter and Rita make is heavenly. After finishing their act, the audience does not want to let them go. Time and time again, they have to come back to more applause. It is an unforgettable evening. Afterwards, when the performance is over and people have left, there is a farewell party for Walter and his friends. Those who have not done so yet wish Walter and his group the very best for their future.

Ingrid puts her arms around him and whispers; "You won't forget me, will you?"

"Never ever will I forget you, Ingrid," Walter promises while gently freeing himself. "And me?" Leila wants to know. "Will you remember me?"

"I also want to be remembered," Lena sulks at his side.

"Ooh, you lovable, wonderful young ladies. How could I ever forget anyone of you?" Walter laughs. He is feeling a bit uneasy though, with all their attention.

It is Pedro who comes to his rescue by asking if Walter needs a ride the next day. "It will be no trouble for me, driving you to the palace grounds, because I have to do some shopping anyway," he says. "So, if you and your friends want to come along, you are most welcome!" Walter accepts gratefully. It will save them quite a walk.

Suddenly, Lorenzo flies onto his shoulder again, shoulder, "Can I come too?" the parrot asks in a casual manner. Walter's heart fills with gladness. He opens his mouth to answer, but before he can do so, Mr. Landini is with them and addresses Lorenzo first. "So, you know then that they are leaving?" he asks. He goes on; "Well, I suppose you have been watching and listening from a distance, as always, Lorenzo. And now, this is what you want to do? Going away from circus Landini? Without saying a word? Really, I am very upset with you, my friend. Furthermore, I am also still very upset about your sorry performance last night when Princess Elina and her father, the king, were here at the circus. Why did you just stay away and why did I not hear any excuses about this from you!?"

Lorenzo, taking small steps on Walter's shoulder while bobbing his head to and fro, looks very uncomfortable. "But I am very sorry, Mr. Landini," he cries out at last. "Yes, very sorry, that I behaved so badly." He continues; "And yes, I do like to go with Walter to the palace. Will you let me go?" He hops onto Mr. Landini's shoulder and, in a caressing way, starts nudging his beak all over this good man's face.

This, Mr. Landini cannot withstand. It softens his heart. Forgotten now are the feelings of being let down and the reprimands. "Yes," he answers. "Yes, I will let you go. On one condition though," he adds. "Don't forget, every time circus Landini comes to this town, we expect to see you too! Promise?"

"I promise," Lorenzo pledges.

"Good, that is settled then," Mr. Landini responds. Shaking Walter's hand, he wishes him and his friends all the best and then walks away.

With Lorenzo on his shoulder and Rita taking her place at the other available one, Walter now wants to look up all the circus people who they have not said goodbye to as yet. Only, Bruno does not feel like coming along. "It is late already", he says. "I am sleepy and Rona and Mona are also very tired. Can we be excused?"

"Of course," Walter answers. "I shall give your regards to everyone. They will understand, I am sure." He looks after them as Bruno, pushing the pram with the already sleeping monkeys, walks away.

Mrs. Landini is glad they remembered to come and greet her. She is sad also, because of their leaving. Taking Lorenzo tenderly away from Walter and placing him on her outstretched hand, she whispers; "We wish you lots of happiness, Lorenzo. We will see each other again now and then, because you are coming to see us when we perform here?"

"Right, right," Lorenzo answers. "Always, always," He flies onto her shoulder and then starts rubbing her cheek while uttering; "Lorenzo loves you, loves you!" Then he dashes into the air, circles around their heads a few times and flies away, while crying out, "Goodbye, goodbye, for now." Looking after him, Mrs. Landini remarks; "I so hope to see him again."

"Oh, but you will," Walter assures her. "And me and all of us!"

"Good," is the answer he gets to those words. "I'll keep you to that, Walter. I shall miss your flute playing, also, your sweet voice singing along with Rita," Mrs. Landini tells them. Then she adds, "And believe me, your beautiful dancing as well Bones."

"Thank you, Mrs. Landini," Rita sings, "Oh, my, thank you," a very flattered Bones comments. Before Walter can say anything, Mrs. Landini takes his hand and warmly wishes him a great future. Then only can Walter respond and tell her how grateful he is, for all she has done for him. For the riding lessons. For her kindness and all the good things he experienced at circus Landini.

"I am so glad you enjoyed your time with us, Walter," Mrs. Landini smiles. "But really, we loved to have all of you with us. Me, my husband, and everyone else here truly did."

When a visibly moved Walter at last takes his leave, he keeps looking back. He sees how Mrs. Landini puts one hand up into the air and, with twirling fingers, waves them on. Him, Rita and Bones, then, in spite of feeling a bit sad, he cannot help but smile. Still later that evening, after all the farewells are over, the three of them go back to the wagon, which from tomorrow on, they can no longer call theirs.

Bruno and the monkeys are in deep sleep when they arrive and exhausted, from a day so full of events, they quickly drift off to sleep as well.

Waking very early the next morning, it is packing in and packing up time. All the belongings gathered during their travels, Walter neatly piles together. At breakfast, he tells Mona and Rona. "It is very kind of Pedro to take us along, so we must be nice and at our best behaviour on this journey, don't you agree?"

"Yes, yes, of course," Rona and Mona promise, And so, after a while, they ride with Pedro. The sun has just come up and the streets they drive through are still very quiet. "It's a fine day today," Pedro remarks, and Walter agrees. They are all in a happy mood. Rita and Lorenzo are perched on one of the wagon beams near Walter. Bones is lying next to him, Bruno, together with Rona and Mona have found themselves a snug place inside the open wagon. The two monkeys become more and more excited as they travel along, but Bruno has them very well under control. The nearer they get to the palace, the more elated they all become. Having been there the previous day, they know it is not all that far. Fairly soon, the pathway leading up to the palace is reached. Then it is time to grab their belongings and say their thanks and goodbyes to Pedro. Their horse friends, pulling the wagon, are not forgotten either. Then, the wooded lane leading to the palace beckons them.

A last farewell wave to Pedro and they are on their way. Again, a whole new way of life is about to begin.

CHAPTER XII

"What will it bring?" Walter wonders as they move forward. First, they have to pass the gates.

Before arriving there, Walter secures Bruno and Bones together on Bruno's old chain. "We don't want any trouble with the guards," he explains. Holding on to them this way, they don't. In any case, it seems orders have already been given to let them pass, for as soon as they come nearer, the gates swing open. The guards greet very politely and they greet very politely in return.

Mona and Rona jump up and down, up and down in their pram, so much so that it nearly tumbles over. "No, no," Walter, who pushes the pram, while at the same time trying to not let go of the chain, reprimands them. "You must behave now, girls. No more jumping please. I want you to sit!" Luckily, his tone of voice makes them obey. "Right," Walter says after they have walked a bit further. "Let's go directly to the zoo. I suppose we will find someone there to tell us what to do next."

"Fine," Bruno answers.

"Good," Bones declares.

"Let's do that," both Rita and Lorenzo, who are perched on Walter's shoulders, agree.

They follow the curved road, past the white palace. Only a few gardeners, working amidst the flower beds, are to be seen. Coming nearer to the zoo, they hear a clanging of doors and animals bawling.

"What a noise," Bruno remarks.

"What is going on?" Bones asks.

Rona and Mona leap forward to go and see for themselves.

Walter can just grab both of them. "No, no, I want you to stay here," he says, putting them back in the pram. Rita and Lorenzo have already left Walter's shoulders. "Why can they go?" Rona whines. "Why can't we go?" Mona cries. "They are grown-up birds," Walter answers them. "You are still small. I want to keep an eye on you both. We don't want any unpleasant incidents again."

As they reach the first cages, an unnerving sight unfolds before their eyes.

"My, my," Walter exclaims. "What on earth is this?" Two enormous gorillas roll about on the lawn in front of their cages. Two zoo keepers in their dark green uniforms are inside! They bang on the closed door bars. Just what the gorillas sometimes are doing, I suppose, Walter can't help thinking.

"Let us out," the wardens shout, "Let us out!"

The whole zoo population also want out, it seems. Such an uproar of clattering cage-bars, combined with all sorts of screeches and screams, makes for total chaos.

'What a difference from yesterday,' Walter ponders. 'Everything was calm and pleasant then.'

Rona and Mona are delighted, though. They shriek and yell to their hearts' content, along with all the other animals and birds. Rita and Lorenzo are watching the spectacle from a nearby tree. Walter can hardly keep Bruno and Bones from running away with him. They would love to rush towards all this din.

"No, no," Walter urges them. "You better stay here!" Walking up to the tree in which Rita and Lorenzo are, he declares; "Bruno and Bones, I am sorry to do this to you, but believe me, it is for the best." With that, he hooks the chain on one of the tree's thick branches. "Just wait here please," he says. "As soon as everything is under control, I come back to you."

"Yes well, if you say so," Bruno mutters.

"This is not so nice," Bones splutters.

"It can't be helped," Walter declares, while picking up Rona and Mona from the pram. Placing them in Bruno's arms, he adds; "These two will keep you busy, so you won't get bored. Yes?" Smiling, he walks over to the two huge gorillas on the lawn. They have stopped their antics and watch in silence as Walter comes nearer. The clanging and banging has stopped, too. Instead, an uneasy silence has taken its place.

All and sunder want to find out what is going to happen now, for they know gorillas can be very dangerous. Walter knows this too, but he is not afraid. The gorillas sensing this, watch his every move. Walter shows them his outstretched hands. "I come as a friend," he says. "Tell me what is wrong. Maybe I can put it right."

When Walter is close to him, the male gorilla stands up. "My name is Gordon," he booms in a deep voice. His broad body towers over the human figure in front of him. "I have heard about you," Gordon goes on. "Your bird friends and also that big bear Bruno told us yesterday. They couldn't stop talking about what you are going to do here. You being the new zoo keeper and all. It is very good you speak our language. Everybody here hopes things will change for the better now!" Looking into Walter's eyes, he sees the caring there and the friendly smile. Who can resist it? Not Gordon the great gorilla. Gently, his colossal hands lift Walter up to his face. "I trust you," he says, "You will be my friend!"

All of a sudden, the concern, the tension over what could happen in this situation, is broken. Enthusiastic approval from the onlookers, breaks out.

"He did it!" Bruno cheers.

"He certainly did!" Bones says admiringly.

Rona and Mona are delighted. They want to run up to Walter and the gorillas, but Bruno has them well in hand. Rita and Lorenzo flap their wings while making joyous sounds. The whole atmosphere has changed into one of cheer. Walter, who by now is put back on his feet by Gordon, is again picked up by Wosa, the female gorilla. She gives him a tender hug.

It is all very moving, but very uncomfortable too for Walter. He, at long last, manages to wriggle himself out of her embrace and thankfully lands back on his feet, "Yes, well," he utters; "Can you tell me what it is that you are so unhappy about? "

"It is the food." Wosa answers.

"We did not get any food today," Gordon joins in. He adds; "and Leesam, the old man who looks after us, is not here either."

"And the wardens did not lock our door properly when they gave us fresh water," Wosa goes on.

"That is why we slipped out," Gordon beams.

"Then we caught the wardens and put them in our cage," Wosa grins.

Walter himself cannot prevent a smile either, by hearing the sheer delight in which these words are spoken. "Right," he says then, "Let's see now. Firstly, you must agree, the wardens cannot stay in that cage. We need to open the door and let them out! Do you have the key for me Gordon?"

Again, there is suspense in the air as Gordon hesitates. It is only after Walter asks him for the second time that Gordon gives in. From a hollow tree, standing a bit forlorn on the lawn, he fetches a whole bunch of keys. After a lot of swinging and dangling them about, he at last hands them over to Walter.

"Very good, Gordon," Walter praises the gorilla. "Well done, my friend!" Keys in hand, he walks over to the unhappy wardens, freeing them in no time at all. Keeping the doors open, Walter looks at Gordon and Wosa. "Please?" he asks. Without any protests, the two gorillas enter and, amid a stunned silence, let themselves be locked up again. The wardens can't believe what is happening. They are very grateful, though, thanking Walter over and over.

But Walter shrugs this off. "I want to know what is going on here", he says, adding; "my name is Walter. I am the new zoo keeper as you may have guessed. What are your names and where and who is Leesam? Things are a bit confusing here at the moment. I never expected to find a situation like this one at the king's zoo.

"Neither did we," the one warden answers, adding; "my name is Keenan, and this is Simon, my helper. We were told you were coming and we are very glad you did sir, especially now," he goes on. "Everything just went wrong today," he moans. At that moment, an elderly man comes huffing and puffing up the pathway. He is short, a bit heavy and has silvery hair. "Excuse me," he calls out, "Pardon, but you must be Walter the new zoo keeper?"

"Yes, that's me," Walter calls back. "Excellent," the man replies, sounding relieved. Coming closer, he says; "Good, something is going right at last," His voice sounds tired.

"It appears there are some difficulties here?" Walter remarks. A slow smile is building up at the corners of his mouth.

"Indeed," the man admits. "But please forgive my manners," he adds while grabbing Walter's hand and shaking it briskly. "I am

Roland, the royal house master," he introduces himself. With a deep sigh, he echoes Keenan the warden by saying; "Well, everything that can go wrong did go wrong today. Most of the staff did not turn up because everyone seems to have the flu. The king was called away on urgent and unexpected matters of state early this morning. Princess Elina went with him, as she usually does, but since then, we have one problem after the other. I hope things are all right here at the zoo?"

"Well, to tell you the truth, there are a few problems," Walter answers.

"Ooh, and what might they be?" master Roland wonders. "But perhaps I should ask Leesam. He is supposed to look after the food and keep everything in order. Where is he?"

"Could it be that Leesam also has the flu?" Walter asks. "Gordon and Wosa tell me they have not seen him this morning. They did not get any food either."

"You see?" master Roland throws his hands up in despair.

"Don't worry," Walter says. "I am sure we can bring things under control shortly. Turning to the wardens, he asks, "Shall we go and get the animal's food?"

"Yes, well, that's one of the other problems," Keenan replies meekly. "

"There were no deliveries this morning," Simon blurts out.

"Nor yesterday," Keenan adds.

"Oh, no, don't tell me that," master Roland cries out.

"My, my," is Walter's only comment. After a moment of silence, he goes on. "We must find some other solution, then. I think there should be lots of leftovers from yesterday's party, so will the royal kitchen not be able to help out?"

"Good idea," master Roland agrees. "Splendid thinking," he adds. He continues; "Wardens, Keenan and Simon, please go and find out what is available?"

The animals, hearing this, start making sounds of approval. Wosa and Gordon clap their hands as the two wardens hurry towards the palace. Rona and Mona, having been so good all this time, now notice how Bruno's attention is focused on what is happening over on Walter's side. Quickly, they make use of that and manage to wriggle free. Moments later, both of them triumphantly look around from Walter's shoulders.

"It is in order," Walter calms the little monkeys as well as Bruno, who seems very worried about their escape. "Things will come right now, you'll see!"

"Yes, I agree. We have the right man here now, precisely at the right time and place," master Roland addresses Walter. "Thank you,"

Walter smiles, then he says; "I like to make a beginning with the work here at hand, if you don't mind sir."

"No, no, not in the least," master Roland sighs with relief. "I am sure you will manage. As for me, there is so much work waiting at the palace. I must see to it at once. So, if you excuse me, I'll be off." With that, he huffs and puffs his way back to the palace.

As it turns out, the leftovers from the kitchen are indeed more than enough to feed all the animals and birds in the zoo. It is not exactly their usual fare, but no one is complaining. Rather the opposite, Gordon and Wosa are enjoying large slices of raisin loaf and even the elephants like this as well. Some cake does not go amiss either and Walter sees to it that none of the birds are forgotten. There are bananas and other fruit, nuts and breadcrumbs. No one goes hungry on this. Walter's first and rather unusual day. He does not mind spoiling everyone a bit, because a little bit of spoiling will hurt no one, in his opinion. And ooh, how the animals and birds agree. They love the way Walter treats and understands them.

Everything goes so smoothly with him around. Very different from the way old Leesam goes about things, because for Leesam, everything is a problem. So, Walter's first day is a pleasant one. He gets on very well with Keenan and Simon, his helpers. They are both very likeable and work hard, cleaning the cages, carrying the containers with food. Bruno and Bones, along with Walter's feathered friends, Rita and Lorenzo, like them too. Together with Walter, they follow the two wardens on their rounds. Every enclosure is visited while dishing out the food. This way they get introduced to all the animals and birds. It makes for a very pleasant experience and creates a good feeling among them.

That evening, Walter is satisfied with a day well spend. He is happy and so it seems, is everyone else. The food from yesterday's party has done wonders. There is enough for themselves as well. Bruno feasts on sweet cakes and fruit. Bones on nice sausages and naturally, Rona and Mona make sure they get something of every available food item. As for Lorenzo and Rita, those two choose only some tiny tit-bits. They never go hungry because seeds and fruit in abundance are everywhere.

Keenan and Simon, as well as Walter himself, do not go hungry either, for more and more food from the royal kitchen keeps arriving at the zoo.

"My, my, it looks as if they catered for a whole village," Walter comments to Keenan and Simon.

"Yes, indeed," they agree wholeheartedly. "Amazing, that's what it is." And even more whole heartedly is their tucking in into this feast of food. 'Clearly, master Roland experienced no delivery problems at the palace,' Walter ponders. 'But then, he might have ordered all the provisions for the children's party, far in advance already. Yes, of course, that is what must have happened,' he concludes.

Further surprises await as Keenan and Simon show them their lodgings. It is a lovely cottage in a private little garden, filled with flowers. It even has its own vegetable patch. Rona and Mona just love the fruit trees growing around the place. In no time at all, they climb into one after the other, finding peaches and plums aplenty, makes them happier still.

Rita and Lorenzo, after tasting some, agree with the two monkeys that this is the sweetest fruit one can wish for. There are also some berry bushes. That is great news for Bruno, because he loves berries now. This is thanks to Rita, who showed him which ones can be eaten. So, with great joy and straight away, he starts devouring them. Paws full of juicy berries vanish into his mouth, dripping reddish moisture all over him.

While Rona and Mona, along with Rita and Lorenzo, explore the garden, Walter decides to examine the wooden cabin standing next to the cottage. Bones follows close behind.

Bruno, noticing where they are heading, quickly leaves the berry bushes and totters after them. "Can I live in the cabin?" he asks, out of breath because of this unforeseen exercise. Walter can't help smiling at Bruno, who looks very comical, with so many berry stains on him.

"I thought you might like that," he replies with laughter in his voice. "That is why we are going there first. And yes, of course, if you want to, you can have the cabin."

"I love having my own place," Bruno says. "At Judge Martins, I did, and it was very nice."

"Good, then that is how it will be!" Walter declares.

"But I want to stay with you in the cottage," Bones utters.

"Fine, that will be nice too," Walter replies. "I come and visit you every day, Bruno," Bones promises.

"Ooh good, and if you don't, I will come and see you," Bruno answers.

As Keenan opens the door of the cabin, they peep inside and Bruno is very happy with what he sees. "A nice bench to sleep on, a table and chairs, a dresser. What more do I need?" he sighs happily. "Do you mind folks?" he asks in the same breath. "It's been a very busy day, I could do with a nap," Without further ado, he walks over to the sleeping bench and makes himself comfortable there, a big smile on his face.

Walter can't help smiling either. He knows Bruno needs his sleep.

"Let's leave him to it then," he says. "Meanwhile, we can go and inspect the cottage, Bones."

It is a wonderful place. They find all that needs to be there is there, and more. A lounge, a kitchen, a large bedroom with a washroom next to it. Fine furniture, flowered curtains and even vases with real flowers give a cosy feeling all round. It is a dream come true for Walter. He thanks Keenan and Simon, and soon these two are off to their own quarters, a bit further away.

The rest of the evening is spent in contentment for everyone. Bones at Walter's feet, Rita nestled nearby, with Lorenzo still outside, because he prefers to be on his own most of the time. Rona and Mona have come inside. They don't like the dark and Walter has managed to get them to sleep in their pram. He himself is sleepy too and so, fairly soon, there is silence in and around the charming cottage on the palace grounds.

The following day, things seem to be settling down. The food deliveries are made and together with Keenan and Simon, Walter sees to it that each animal and bird gets his or her share. Even old Leesam shows up. Still coughing and full of excuses for not being at work the previous day, He has come to see Walter at the cottage and these two like each other at once.

While making their way to the zoo, it is Leesam, doing most of the talking. Walter carries Rona and Mona in his arms, Bruno and Bones trot in front of them. Lorenzo and Rita had already disappeared shortly after breakfast. Walter is sure they won't come to any harm here on the palace grounds. He also knows they usually are somewhere nearby and come back regularly.

"Do you like the cottage?" Leesam wants to find out.

"Yes, it is great," Walter replies.

"Good," Leesam goes on. "My wife and I lived there for a long time, but we have moved to the village now. The king gave us a very nice place there where we can retire, so, actually, my time of working at the zoo is over. Now it is your turn. I think the king has many plans to enhance the zoo. I am too old now for these sorts of things. New ideas are needed and young hands to make it all happen. You could be just the sort of person to help the king with this."

"I would love to," Walter answers, adding, "I am so happy to be here. For me there is no better place than this." He speaks the truth, an almost impossible wish has been realised. To be near the Princess Elina. Working at this zoo. "No one can ask for anything better," he tells Leesam. His wish to see the princess again soon, he leaves unspoken.

'How long still before the king and his daughter shall return?' he asks himself every day. In the meantime, while waiting for this, his work at the zoo gives him no problems. Leesam helps and guides him every step of the way.

"I keep coming now and then," he assures Walter after the first two weeks, "But, you don't need much help. I can see that already."

Walter is grateful, both for Leesam's words, and for his promise of help, for some time to come. And so, the days go by, one by one. First thing every morning now, when doing his rounds at the zoo, Walter has a friendly chat with Gordon and Wosa. They enjoy having Walter with them. That goes for all the other residents, too. A lot of the animals are old circus artists, spending the last of their days here. They love being pampered and not having to work anymore.

'Yes, Jumbo, and Julia the stork were right about this zoo,' Walter ponders. 'One day, I will see them both here again, I am sure.'

The sick animals and birds are not forgotten by Walter and his helpers either. They are very well looked after indeed. Once a week the animal doctor from the villages visits them. He hands out instructions and medicines, with Walter watching and listening carefully. This way he learns more and more about many ailments. He gets to know about treatments too. How to heal and which food to give.

Mona and Rona always come along with Walter on his rounds. To sit on Bones back, while doing so, is what they like best. Sometimes they jump from cage to cage, clowning and pulling faces. The animals they visit mostly enjoy their antics. Bones, ever watchful, is constantly alert, that no harm comes to neither the monkeys or to his master. Not that anyone would want to. They all love and respect Walter, who cares so well for them. And Rona and Mona are actually quite fun to have around.

Bruno finds all this walking everywhere too tiring. He prefers to lean against one of the big trees in front of the zoo entrance. There he waits and dozes off, or thinks about the difficult years before meeting Walter. Thankful that things have changed so much for the better.

Rita and Lorenzo have become best friends. They spend a lot of time together, flying from tree to tree, with nice seeds to eat everywhere. Lorenzo feels free and happy, and so does Rita. They are never far away from Walter, though. Often, Rita sings one of her sweet songs, while following him from the one enclosure to the other. Walter finds this delightful, and he is not the only one. Everyone else enjoys it too. Lorenzo, on the other hand, sometimes frightens them a bit. He still has his own ideas about what entertainment means. There are days when he just falls out of the air, with an enormous speed. Then, after landing on some poor animal's head, he tumbles around and around it, before taking off again, more often than not, while screeching "Caramba! Caramba!" He always makes sure Walter hears and sees him doing this.

While Walter reprimands him about this, he can't help smiling now and then. Lorenzo knows that and cackles with pleasure afterwards but keeps at a safe distance, anyway. Still, Walter is happy that his friends become more and more comfortable in their new surroundings.

Bruno, when not sleeping, also likes to visit the other bears in the zoo. Rona and Mona spend lots of time there, having befriended so many monkeys. Thus, many weeks go by and still king Frederik and Princess Elina have not returned.

"When do you expect the king and his daughter back?" he asks master Roland.

"I really do not know when they will return," master Roland tells him. "So, let's just wait and see."

It is just as well. Walter's work at the zoo keeps him very busy. Having become close friends with Gordon and Wosa, he never gets tired of spending some time with them, making small talk, and asking how things are. The two gorillas are happy and tell Walter so.

Everything is going smoothly at the zoo now, with all the animals and birds remarking about it. A happy feeling is making itself felt. Being able to talk to Walter, to let him know what they think, makes all the difference. More so, because Walter really listens and does try to solve the problems anyone might have. In the evenings, Walter and his group are mostly together in the cosy cottage.

Sometimes, Bruno prefers to toddle off for an early night at his own place. Only after they have eaten of course, for food and sleep, in that order, will always be the things Bruno likes best. Not having to work anymore is also great! It suits him just fine.

As for Walter, these evenings give him the chance to read some of the books he finds on the bookshelves in the cottage. It is reading and studying at the same time, for there is much to learn from even the tiniest book, especially for someone like him, having never had access to so many books before. At other times, he writes letters. To Mr. Landini and his wife and daughters, knowing full well news from him, will reach everyone at the circus. Then, of course, he writes to Judge Martins and his wife also. Father Tobias is not forgotten either. He keeps everyone informed about his work and does so in an amusing way, covering the daily events with the animals and birds under his care. Luckily, the royal messenger sees to it. His mail reaches its destinations in good time.

Music, is as always, very important too. When Walter plays the flute and Rita sings, the whole cottage is filled with their sweet sounding music. While taking a short pause at one of those sessions, Walter remarks, "I must say, this is quite different from our performances in the circus."

"Very true," Rita answers him, adding; "I like it very much, though. It is like in the beginning, before we joined circus Landini."

"I agree," Walter tells her, "but," he goes on, "speaking about that, don't you miss the circus life? Wouldn't you rather go back there?"

"No, not at all," Rita replies. She goes on; "Now, at long last, I can go to sleep early, like most other birds do! And what about you?"

"For me, this is what I wanted more than anything," Walter says. "But I was not so sure about your feelings on this. And you Lorenzo?" he asks the big parrot who is sitting on the porch. He has his own perch there, enabling him to watch things inside the cottage, as well as out.

"I like it here, Walter," Lorenzo assures him. "Here I am free at last. This is what I also wanted more than anything."

"My, my," Walter brings out. "It gives me great pleasure to hear you say this, Lorenzo. We did the right thing, then?"

"Ooh, absolutely," Bruno joins in. He has been listening intently to the whole conversation.

"What do you say, Bones?" he asks.

"We could not have done better," Bones answers. "We are all very happy here, Walter!"

"What do you say, Rona and Mona?" Walter now wants to hear from the two monkeys.

"We like it here. We like it here," comes the reply from them at once.

"Good, good," Walter's smile reaches almost from ear to ear. "I am so glad we are all happy to be at this place. Thank you, my friends. Thank you. It is so good to know this!"

Rona and Mona break the mood of the moment by jumping over and up Bones and Bruno. From the one to the other. It is a game they often play. That is, until either Bones or Bruno strike out a paw at them. That is what happens now. They yell and yelp, running away in haste, while looking over their shoulders with disgusted little faces.

Walter, if he wants to or not, can't help but laugh with all this going on. But, this game is such fun, they keep coming back for more, so in the end, Walter picks the two up and carries them to the bedroom where their pram is standing in a corner. Not long after, they are fast asleep.

With peace returned, Walter and Rita resume their music making. The little cottage is filled with contentment. There is plenty of time to enjoy these evenings together. Walter has no need to worry about providing food anymore. Master Roland sees to it that meals from the royal kitchen are brought over every day. Lovely meals, enough for all of them and so varied, there is something for every taste. Meat and fruit and bread. No one goes hungry and Walter is very thankful for these good times they experience.

Most nights, when everyone has gone to sleep, he walks the pathway leading to the palace. As always, Bones is then with him. And always too, the wish, the hope, that maybe now, the king's carriage might appear, flickers in Walter's heart. Surely, the king and his daughter cannot stay away forever?

Then, one moonlight night, Bones points his ears. He hears something.

"Yes, Bones?" Walter asks eagerly. "Are they coming?"

"Yes, I think so," Bones answers. Then he utters, "Yes, I am sure there is a carriage coming this way."

"Yes, yes," they hear all of a sudden. It is Lorenzo flying towards them. "I have seen the king," he cries out. "The king and the Princess Elina are here!"

"My, my, this is great news," Walter exclaims. "Come, we must let the others know!" He runs towards master Roland's cottage, knocking at the door and then the windows. "Master Roland," he shouts; "They are here! Please wake up. The king and Princess Elina are on their way!"

"I am coming. I'll be there now," master Roland's voice comes back to him, but Walter and Bones can't wait. They are there as the royal carriage comes to a halt. The doors are opened and there they are!!! First the king, then the Princess Elina.

Master Roland's voice, somewhere from behind, utters all sorts of commands, but Walter does not hear. He can only stare at the vision of loveliness before him. Princess Elina, in a grey and white travelling suit, topped by a hat in the same colours, smiles at Walter and Bones. So does the king.

"Aah, it is good to see you, Walter," he says. "Very good. We regret not being here on your arrival. Urgent state affairs and an enormous land dispute, it all dragged on far too long. Anyway, everything has been sorted out and cleared up. So after all this time, we are back. We hope you have settled in well?"

"Yes, your Majesty, thank you we have," is Walter's reply. He adds; "Welcome home your Majesty, welcome home, Princess Elina." Making a deep bow after these words, he does not see how sweetly Princess Elina smiles. Even so, Walter is very happy. With Princess Elina so near to him, how can it be otherwise? It makes his heart sing.

Meanwhile, master Roland, a long night frock sticking out from under his robe, has reached them. Out of breath, he is muttering all sorts of apologies.

"Stop fretting," the king addresses him. "You did not know we were coming back tonight. Even we did not know, so, therefore, you are excused." To the ruffled servants following in master Roland's trail, he says; "Thank you all for coming. Just carry our travel bags inside and then go back to bed. We'll see you in the morning. As for you, master Roland, we would advise you to go back to sleep as well."

"Yes, your Majesty, thank you, your Majesty," come the sleepy answers, as one after the other, they shuffle away. Some servants stumbling along a bit with all the bags they are carrying.

"And then, there is you, Walter," the king continues, "I would like you to tell me all about your work at the zoo here. By the way, you are also excused, my dear," the king tells his daughter as he sees her shivering in the cool evening breeze.

With a graceful smile and greeting, the princess moves off to the palace. Its open doors and lights shining inside promise warmth and a good night's sleep.

While the king and Walter stay for a bit longer to watch the royal carriage and horses being led away, a second coach arrives. "Well, there is the rest of our entourage," the king declares. "They had a bit of trouble, with one of the wheels coming loose. Anyway, everything appears to be fine now. There is no need to wait for them. Instead, let us go over to the library. Never mind the late hour," he goes on. "We need no more than a few hours of sleep at night. Do you?"

"No, not at all, your Majesty," Walter replies. He still has to become used to this royal manner of speech, which uses the word 'we,' rather than 'I', or 'me'. It sounds rather strange to his ears. Although a bit bemused by it, he tells the king; "At the circus, we always had late nights, Your Majesty."

"Good, so you are used to it," the king says. Once inside the library, King Frederik sits down in one of the huge leather chairs there and invites Walter to do the same. For more than an hour, they talk. The king knows every animal by name and wants a report on all of them. After becoming certain, Walter cares deeply for the zoo and those that live in them, he asks; "Well, Walter, what do you think? Is the food supply what it should be? Can we improve on it and in your opinion, can we improve on the enclosures?"

"In time to come, I'd like some of them enlarged, your Majesty," Walter speaks up. "As for the food, I can't find any fault with it, sir."

"Very well," the king smiles, adding; "It is good we had this talk. Tomorrow, we shall come and see for ourselves what can be done to upgrade things even more." He stands up and Walter does the same. The interview has come to an end.

After taking his leave, Walter finds Bones and Lorenzo waiting for him outside. "Where were you?" Walter asks. "I didn't see you anymore."

"Ooh, I did not want to be a bother, so I watched from behind some trees," Bones answers.

"And I waited for you in the tree right above him," Lorenzo tells Walter.

"My, my, you two just seem to know when to show up and when not," Walter praises his friends. "It's amazing,"

"Nothing to it," Lorenzo declares smugly.

Bones, tail wagging, looks at Walter with devoted eyes, needing no words to reveal he likes the praise.

"I can tell you, the king is a kind and good man, my friends," Walter goes on.

"We know!" Bones answers. "

"Yes, we know," Lorenzo confirms Bones' words. "Who else would go and create a zoo for sick and old animals and birds?"

"Indeed," Walter agrees. "Who else would be so loving and kind?"

With the bright moon beaming down on them, they make their way back to the cottage. Like the others there, they too are soon fast asleep. The next morning, Walter is up very early.

'So sunny and glorious this day is,' he thinks to himself. Walking out into the garden, he decides to pick some flowers. 'Putting them in a vase on the breakfast table will brighten up this day even more,' is next thought. So he picks the nicest ones, which happen to be red roses, while humming a happy song.

Shortly afterwards, he has arranged them in a crystal vase. Displayed on a yellow tablecloth, it all looks very festive indeed. Soon, the fresh baked bread from the royal kitchen arrives promptly on time, as always. Walter gets busy making porridge while Mona and Rona, full of early morning bravado, jump up and down, then here, then there, before they sit down. They have their on own bench which is nearly table high. This enables them to eat their food at the table and eagerly watch what is happening there. The red roses have not escaped their attention, but Walter warns the two monkeys to behave and not touch them.

Before long, each has some porridge and fruit to eat. While doing this, everything else is forgotten. Bruno, although sleeping next door, still seems to smell the food. Food, as always, wakes him up. It is not long before his friendly head peeps around the kitchen door.

"Good morning," he greets, waddling inside.

"Good morning, Bruno," Walter responds with a smile. "Sit down and enjoy your breakfast."

Besides the crunchy bread and the porridge, there are boiled eggs, golden honey in a large pot standing next to the milk and cheese, as well as deep yellow butter. Bruno loves most of these things, but porridge with honey is his favourite. He hungrily starts eating from the generous portion Walter puts in front of him. Having taken his seat on his own very sturdy chair, his whole person oozes contentment. Walter also has some porridge. Bones just watches them all munching away. He only wants food once a day at dinner time. The others, while eating, include him, as always, in their chatter and jokes. Only Rita and Lorenzo are absent, unlike other mornings.

"Rita, Lorenzo," Walter calls out. "Where are you? I have some nice dishes with birdseed here."

"They are outside," Rona says.

Rita, having heard him calling, flies in, straight onto Walter's shoulder.

"I've just come back from the palace," she twitters. "Lorenzo told me the king and Princess Elina returned last night. And you did not even wake me, Walter," she utters. "O well, never mind now," she goes on; "Lorenzo and I went to the Palace this morning and yes, it is true. The Princess was walking outside and was very glad to see me. She also gave me some lovely seeds to eat. But Lorenzo just kept himself hidden in one of the trees near the palace. I think he still feels a bit uneasy about his performance in the circus some time ago. Anyway, the Princess says she hopes to see you today." Here, the little bird stops for a moment to catch her breath.

"My, my, Rita," Walter laughs. "I can understand you being all excited. I am too. It is great that the king and princess are back. I am sorry I did not wake you last night, but they came when Bones and I went for or our usual evening walk. It all happened so suddenly. Bones heard their carriage coming while Lorenzo spotted it. Shortly afterwards, the royal carriage arrived. It was wonderful! The king and princess were so friendly and I had a long talk with the king afterwards."

"My, my," Rita mimics Walter's words. This makes for great merriment all round the breakfast table.

"Now, as for Lorenzo," Walter continues after they all had a good laugh, "Yes, I think you are right, Rita. He is still a bit shy about what happened at the circus. Last night, he kept himself out of sight also. But did he not tell you he saw the royal carriage first?" he asks, adding; "He usually is not too shy to let everyone know about the things he sees and does."

Amidst the renewed chuckles these words cause, Rita answers; "Maybe he did, but I listened not all that well. I think I was too excited for that."

"No matter," Walter replies with a smile. "What matters is that the king and the Princess Elina are back now! The king promised to come and inspect the work I have done so far. And did I hear you say the princess hopes to see me soon? Hmmm, maybe she will also come to the zoo with her father, the king. That would be wonderful!"

"My, my," Bruno utters in turn. He has noticed how everyone started laughing when Rita used these words. That's why he decides to say them as well. Repeating them for a second time, he hopes to get the same reaction. "My, my," he booms; "Am I the last one to hear about all this?" It is just a pity his words get lost through Rona's whining.

"Why did no one tell us anything?" she cries out.

"Yes," Mona cries even louder, "Why didn't you, Walter? We were here all the time already. You gave us breakfast, and we were talking with each other, but you did not tell us that King Frederik and the princess came back!" After this unusually long speech, Mona looks at him with hurt in her eyes.

"I am so sorry," Walter replies. "I should have been much more thoughtful. Please forgive me and let's not be annoyed anymore? Let's just all be glad this fine morning of this fine day, shall we?"

"Good, good," Bones remarks. He has been very quiet so far, but is now getting impatient. "Let's all go to the zoo," he barks. "Let's go and do something!"

"Yes," Walter agrees. "You are right Bones, let us do something and do it quickly now. I want everything to be spick and span before the king arrives."

Luckily, there is no cleaning up to do at the cottage, because master Roland always sends someone over to tidy up in the mornings. So, very soon, they are on their way.

Keenan and Simon arrive together with them at the zoo. They too have heard the great news that the king and Princess Elina are back. Their 'good morning' greetings have a very cheerful tone, much more so than on other days, Walter notices. His mood matches theirs though, so he returns the well-wishing with a big smile and tells them, he hopes they have a good day too.

"Shall we do a big clean-up?" Keenan asks. "Maybe the king will come and see how things are going here?"

"Yes absolutely," Walter exclaims. "And yes," he goes on, "The king promised to come today to find out how things are here at the zoo."

Simon already is busy cleaning cages with lots of soap and water from a big bucket. Keenan lends a helping hand while Walter pays attention to the feeding of the animals and birds. He receives a warm welcome from them, as he does the food. Gordon and Wosa, being nearest to the entrance, have overheard the conversation about the king and Princess Elina.

"It is wonderful that they are back," Gordon tells Walter. "I like the king very much. He is a fine and good man."

"Yes, I like him too," Wosa joins in.

"You are both very right," Walter answers.

"And we like Princess Elina also," Wosa adds.

"That is great," Walter smiles. "I think she is the most lovely person on earth," he sighs. Gordon and Wosa just look at him with understanding in their eyes.

Soon, the whole zoo population knows the king is back, and that he is coming to visit them. Bruno has told his bear friends and Rona and Mona the other monkeys. Rita and Lorenzo have told the feathered colony about it, while Bones barks away the good news to each and everyone.

Walter goes from enclosure to enclosure, making sure everything is in order, while at the same time doling out the food. Luckily these days, the food is always promptly delivered, so every animal and bird gets his or her portion without fail.

Many of the old circus artists like chatting to Walter about old times. They know he and his friends were also circus performers. Being able to hear from him news of the ones they left behind is great. And the news about the king's return is just as great. They keep talking to Walter about it, so this morning, while doing the rounds, time seems to fly even faster than usual for everyone.

Before they know it, lunchtime has already come and gone. Some bread and milk, are among the food brought along from this morning's breakfast by Walter as well as by Keenan and Simon, have quickly stilled their hunger, but it does not still their longing for the king to come now. Surely he has not forgotten about them?

Indeed, the king has not. "Matters of state again," they hear him splutter when at long last he and the Princess Elina arrive by foot and alone. No ladies-in-waiting, none of the other usual followers trailing behind. Walter is glad. Now he and his helpers can have the king and princess all to themselves.

The happiness their appearance brings about makes everyone overlook the long wait. The whole zoo is humming with pleasure. Rita is on Walter's shoulder again, and Lorenzo, having returned a bit earlier, is sitting at a nearby tree branch. Bruno stands next to Walter, with Bones sitting on his other side. Mona and Rona are nowhere in sight, though.

"Where are those little rascals?" Walter says.

"Maybe they're still with the other monkeys," Bones answers.

"Yeah, maybe," Walter sighs. "Ooh well, in that case, leave them be then, for they can be a bit of a handful, as we all know."

The king shakes hands with Walter and then with the wardens, Keenan and Simon. When Princess Elina holds out her hand to Walter, he bows and blushes, while stammering how pleased he is to see her again.

"It is good to be here," the princess answers, smiling at him. She strokes Bones over his head, remembering him very well. With Bruno she shakes hands, making him very proud. Of course, Rita is on her shoulder by now, knowing full well she has a special place in Princess Elina's heart. Keenan and Simon also bow for the princess as she shakes their hands and talks with them for a bit. These two have been working a long time at the zoo already and know the princess quite well.

"Now, Walter," the king declares after the greeting formalities are over; "You lead the way, as we start with our inspection,"

"Only with pleasure, your Majesty," Walter replies. "Shall we go then?" are his next words and walking next to the king, with Princess Elina on the king's other side, they start their tour. As Gordon and Wosa are nearest, their enclosure is the first to receive the royals. Princess Elina stays in the background when Walter opens the door.

"Is this wise?" the king asks, unsure of what is going to happen next.

"If your Majesty will allow it?" Walter responds.

Before the king can answer, Gordon and Wosa both, are standing up and in front of him, their huge bodies towering over the king and all the others. It is a truly intimidating moment. Then, to the king's surprise, both gorilla's bow deeply.

"They want to thank your Majesty for all the good your Majesty has done here," Walter says. "For all the care they experience. They thank your Majesty not only for themselves, but for all the others as well here, be it animals or birds."

The king cannot help but smile upon hearing this and bravely shakes the gorilla's hands, reaching out to him. Princess Elina, seeing how amazingly gentle Gordon and Wosa behave towards her father, is a bit unsure. Then, overcoming her fear, she steps nearer and also gives each of them a handshake. The gorillas are very moved by this and so are the onlookers, going by the look on their faces.

After saying their goodbyes to Gordon and Wosa, Walter takes the king and his daughter further. They visit each enclosure and are met with joy everywhere. Walter tells the king all what is being said. It are only good things the king hears. And he can see, all the animals and birds are content and cheerful. They are more than happy with the food and the way they are being treated,

Lots of praise is heaped upon Walter. Finding this a bit embarrassing, he speaks in a matter-of-fact way about the changes he and his helpers have made so far.

The king, who now and then, likes to tease people a bit, now smiles and, with a twinkle in his eyes, he utters; "This is all good and well. I do detect a lot of cheer here, but what is this wailing then? Can you hear it? There must be some unhappiness somewhere!"

Yes, they all hear it now. It must come from a cage they haven't visited yet. Going by the noise it must be at the far end, Walter ponders.

Princess Elina is the first to move in that direction." Oooh," she cries out, "These are the little monkeys we saw at the circus. Why are they locked up here?"

"Yes, indeed, why?" the king, having come nearer, also wants to know.

Walter has no answer. He is just as amazed as the king and his daughter. "What happened?" he asks the whining monkeys, but they only keep on wailing.

"Someone must have locked them up," Bones barks.

"Yes indeed, someone must have, but who?" Walter utters while opening the cage door. It is very loosely bolted and slides open easily. For Rona and Mona, though, it proved to be hard to undo.

While Princess Elina and the king, together with the others, look on, the two at once jump into Walter's arms. Inspecting the surroundings and after that, in the sky above, Walter sees Lorenzo sitting on a tree branch.

"They can be a bit of a handful," he hears his own words repeated in a mocking voice. "It was you Lorenzo," he calls out to the big parrot. "Only you could be so cunning."

"How did he do it?" the king asks, not without some admiration.

"It was easy, your Majesty," Lorenzo replies, while flying straight onto Walter's shoulder. "I just called them away from the others and coaxed them into that closed-off cage. Closing the cage door was just as easy," he utters smugly.

"You terrible you," Walter reprimands his friend.

But Lorenzo does not want any of this. "You said so yourself," he splutters defensively. "They can be a bit of a handful you said. So I thought I get them out of your way for a while."

By now everyone is laughing about the whole affair, except Rona and Mona, who cling to Walter with perturbed little faces. Princess Elina, coming nearer, starts stroking them. This at once changes their mood to one of happiness. For Walter, it is bliss, having the princess standing so close to him. Lorenzo, glowing from all the attention his actions have given him, ruffles his feathers and looks very smug. He is sure of having redeemed himself now. What he did today, more than makes up for any past blunders, he reckons, Yes, Lorenzo is more than happy with himself.

Meanwhile, Rona and Mona are on the point of leaving Walter's arms to switch over to those of Princess Elina. It is Bruno who senses this first. He knows these two monkeys so well. Before they can implement those thoughts, his arms stretch out and catch them. Holding them close to his heart, his warmth enfolding them, they at once forget about any previous plans.

"Thank you Bruno," Walter mumbles. He too, has now grasped what Rona and Mona planned to do. The thought of this, makes him feel very uncomfortable. Imagine what trouble the two monkeys could have caused, had they indeed jumped over to Princess Elina, upsetting the princess and the king at the same time, of course.

"Thank you, Bruno," Walter says again, looking gratefully at his friend. And then, can this be? Yes, Bruno winks at him. Only, they did not consider Princess Elina's thoughts on this matter and are utterly taken aback when she says.

"I heard that. Really," she goes on; "There is no need that you all worry so much. I can handle two little monkeys anytime."

The king, having become aware of what is going on, now also joins the conversation. "We are perfectly sure of that dear," he tells his daughter, "But," he adds, "we soon have to leave and as you can see, the monkeys are happy where they are now. So, let it be, shall we?"

"Yes, father," the princess agrees with a smile. Noticing how uneasy Walter and the others have become, she says; "Don't be upset. It is just me. I always let people know what I think."

"And a good thing too," the king laughs. "Many are the times the princess told people what she thinks. In a nice way, of course. In matters of state, in disputes, in debates. Her observance and clear understanding of most situations has often led to the betterment of agreements and treaties. All for the good of our beloved country." Clearly, the king is very proud of his daughter and Walter now knows why. Where the king goes, the princess goes.

Since all the enclosures have been visited by now, the guided tour has come to an end. The king is satisfied with what he has seen. He is satisfied that Walter is just the right person to manage this zoo.

"It is good to have you here, Walter," he says. "Things go well. We can see that. Also, we are pleased to notice that you, Keenan and Simon work so well with our new man," Walter and the wardens beam from ear to ear. It is nice to hear the king is content with their work and their working together. That the king calls him; 'Our new man', gives Walter a good feeling as well.

"As for enlarging the enclosures, Walter," the king continues; "We must talk about that soon. However, as we have been away for such a long time, affairs of state need our foremost attention. It will have to wait. Such a terrific country," he sighs, "Such terrible problems. Maybe we will tell you about it one day. But, enough of this," he declares. "We will leave now, but we shall see each other again very soon."

With that, the royal visit is over. King Frederik and his daughter take their seats in the carriage, which has arrived to return them to the palace. Everyone at the zoo is waving them farewell. The king waves back and so too does Princess Elina.

Walter feels as if he is walking on air. Is it wistful thinking or was there an extra sweet smile just for him, when the royals said their goodbyes?

"Did you see it too, Rita?" he asks the little bird, who by now has flown back onto his shoulder, "Was this smile not extra special, just for me? Don't you think it was?"

"All the princess's smiles are extra special," Rita twitters, "And yes, maybe you are right, Walter. After all, I do not know much about these things, now do I?"

"No," Walter has to agree with Rita. He cannot expect her, nor anyone else, to understand how he feels. How he even sees every smile from the princess as something very precious and special.

It is amazing how quickly the days speed by after this one. Walter and his friends enjoy every moment of them. 'Why did the days at the farm always seemed so long?' he sometimes asks himself. 'Of course, I worked long hours there and in the circus we gave shows until late. Although I liked the circus, it also, were long drawn-out days. But here at the zoo, time just flies and yet, we work long and hard here as well.'

Deep down, though, he knows why this is. Here, he is happy, while in the earlier days he was not. And the times in between? Yes, they were good, but not like now. Here he is needed. He never gets tired looking after the animals and birds and of nursing them when necessary.

The king, in spite of his busy working-schedule, now and then comes to oversee things and always leaves with a satisfied smile. All is well at his zoo. Yes, thanks to Walter, everything goes better than ever before. Plans for the improvements of the enclosures are also put on paper. Walter does this in his spare time and the king is very impressed with them. Together, they discuss all the possibilities. Sometimes, Walter gets called over to the palace and there, in the library, they talk about the plans some more. Often, Princess Elina also gets called in by the king to give her opinion on matters. They then sit together for long periods and talk. It forms a strong bond between them. How Walter enjoys these meetings.

To be with the king and the princess is such a privilege. Life indeed is very good.

Mostly Rita is also with him, either on his shoulder or on that of the princess. Other times she just sits quietly on a bookshelf, listening to all that is being discussed. And so is Bones, as always, on Walter's side. The king, having two dogs of his own, has no objections to him being there. His dogs have none either. The three of them have a good understanding and are happy in each other's company.

Rita and Mona, now growing up fast, choose more and more to be with their monkey friends in the zoo, playing with them, to their hearts' content. Keenan and Simon always see to it that they can get in and out as many times as they wish. Lorenzo is then here, then there. With his love of the outdoors, he often just parks himself in the big oak tree near the library. Within reach, but still by himself, as is his nature.

Walter does not have to worry about any of his friends. He knows they are never far away. He knows too, Bruno prefers to spend most of his time in his own cabin these days. Sleeping a lot or otherwise visiting his bear friends in the zoo, talking about all the things they have done and experienced.

Meanwhile, the king more and more comes to appreciate Walter. This hard working young man, with his eager face and noble bearing, becomes very dear to him. And Princess Elina? She finds herself becoming very attracted to Walter. Besides his winning ways, he is so handsome and truly nice and honest.

Back in the cottage, Walter often discusses the plans made that day with his friends. Rita and Bones, of course, know about them already. Bruno is not all that interested, because it does not affect him much. After all, he is more than happy already. His life now is pure bliss. As for Lorenzo, he tells Walter to just go on and do what needs to be done.

"For me, it makes not much difference either," he says. "So everything you have in mind is fine with me. I think though, it is great what you are doing for this zoo."

Eventually and at long last, the final plans are ready. All the enclosures will be enormously enlarged to give the animals much more freedom. Trees will be planted and rocks brought in, to provide a natural environment to move around in. Furthermore, the cages will have much bigger and better sleeping quarters at the back. Because the zoo is built in a loose U shape, this is a very practical solution.

The king orders the builders in at once and the work begins. Walter has told the animals about all the changes that are going to be made, and everyone is very excited about this. No matter, it will take quite some time before everything is finished. They can wait. For the birds, it is different. After all, they don't need anything changed, really. Their shelters have no roofs, anyway. They can come and go as they wish.

That the work will take a long time is good news for Walter. For, nearly every day, the king comes by, more often than not, bringing Princess Elina with him. Together, they are brainstorming over the problems that need to be solved. Which method is best and which materials? All the time heeding the good advice of the builders as well, of course. For weeks and months, the work goes on, until at last, everything is finished. And then, it surpasses everyone's expectations. How magnificent it has turned out. The king and princess are very pleased, as is Walter. It is just as he hoped it would be. Lots and lots more space is achieved and the wonderful landscaping has made the whole zoo look much more attractive.

"We shall have a party," the king declares. "A real celebration. We will let all the animals and birds take part in the festivities. It will be great fun."

Princess Elina and Walter wholeheartedly agree and so does every animal and bird. The talk is about nothing else.

"Can we give a concert?" Rita wants to know.

"Yes, indeed," Walter replies; "That is a splendid idea,"

"I want to dance," Bruno joins in.

"And what about us?" Rona and Mona want to know.

"I am going to walk you around in the pram again," Bones promises.

"So, are we doing our old circus show, then?" Lorenzo asks.

"Yes, that should be fun," Walter grins.

"Fine, fine," Lorenzo mutters, "I will be there!"

"Good," Walter tells him, "that is precisely what we want." But he wants more. All the animals and birds must have a chance to perform at this festival. He knows they will love to do so and the whole event shall be the more enjoyable for it. It will mean a lot of training and hard work, but he finds everyone so eager to take part that it really becomes is very pleasant.

Keenan and Simon are a big help as well. And so, after a few weeks, the big day arrives. It is a day full of merriment and wonder. Most of the people present are personnel from the royal household and their families. The builders, having worked so hard on the zoo make-over, are also the king's guests. There is lovely food and lots of refreshments, placed on long tables within the now more of a half circle design of the zoo. The king's own orchestra plays cheerful music. So joyous it all is, with banners flying and smiling faces everywhere.

A sturdy stage has been build a bit away from the tables, but so, that people can see everything that is going on. First to perform are Princess Elina and her ladies-in-waiting. That is a big surprise, even for Walter, because Princess Elina never told him that she and her maidens would take part with a dance. Only at the last moment, just before starting time, Master Roland came to inform him about it. Nevertheless, it turns out to be a wonderful opening of the event.

Princes Elina and her ladies are a vision in misty green garments. The silvery beads on them sparkle in the morning sun. Their delicate costumes make the graceful dancing even more beautiful. Truly a sight to behold for ever. It leaves Walter and everyone else totally enraptured. And Princess Elina easily is the most outstanding of them all. The applause afterwards is sincere and enthusiastic.

Then it is the elephants' turn to make their entrée. As they come running into the arena, the sound of their trumpeting, imposing and forceful, fills the spectators with awe. Following that, it is amazing to see how daintily they climb up onto the stage, while holding each other's trunks. Forming a circle, they dance a little dance as well. Maybe not as graceful as the ones Princess Elina and her ladies performed, but without a doubt, utterly entertaining. They have not forgotten their circus training and know just how to keep everyone calling out for more as they go on with the show. Walter is there with them, speaking softly, letting them feel he is very proud of what they do. Helpers put little stools in a circle on the stage and again, as the elephants sit down, their trunks reach out to each other, forming a second circle. It is all so endearing. Of course they receive a warm applause. After they have left the stage, Keenan and Simon bring them back to their enclosures.

Then it is Gordon and Wosa's turn and who is there with them? None other than Bruno. He and the gorillas have become such good friends. The three of them wanted to do a show together.

Walter, who has been their coach, is rightly proud of the trio. While the orchestra plays soft music, Gordon and Wosa take hands and then bend low down to the ground. Low enough for Bruno to step into those huge hands. This he does and the gorillas carry him round and round the stage. Bruno keeps his balance, and it is a sight to see how careful they are with him. It is indeed most unusual to see three of such huge animals work together in such harmony and their public appreciates that.

They cheer in praise, King Frederik, seated in front, with Princess Elina next to him again, cheers as well, and so does his daughter. They love this show and everyone else does too. After a while, Gordon and Wosa bend down and allow Bruno to step back onto the stage. Then the three of them gratefully bow for the loud applause following their act.

After this, all the other animals get a chance to show what they can do. Even if it is only to prance around a bit, when to old and stiff for anything else. The crowd still loves them and claps and shouts their approval.

The lions provide another sort of attraction. Roaring like thunder, they send shivers down spines, but in a nice sort of way. Of course, no one is really scared because a water-filled channel keeps the lions at a safe distance. The water separation has been Walter's idea.

"And a very clever one too," the king has praised him. It indeed works very well, but the following act has no need for it. From the air, a fluttering of many wings can be heard, followed by the sweet sound of singing birds. Lots of them surging over the crowd, making everyone look up into the sky. These birds, how gorgeous they are. How graceful they fly, circling in grand movements overhead. Swaying up and down, up and down, impressing all and sunder with the beauty of their display.

"How did this perfection come to pass?" they ask one another. "Surely, this could not have been arranged beforehand?"

No, it has not, and it comes as much as a surprise to Walter as it does to the king. The king's invitation for this party was for all animals and birds, yes, but who would have thought so many would show up? The answer to this riddle is not so difficult, though. Some of the sick birds, who did not feel well enough to perform yet, send word to those already cured at the zoo. And the others, the healthy ones, who might one day also make use of the king's help if need be, they have come as well.

And here they are now, in their masses, bringing a message to their king. A message that is understood by all. "Thank you, dear King, thank you," they say. "For all your love and care,"

The king is very moved. Princess Elina, seeing this, takes his hand and so, together with their people, they watch the birds, making patterns in the sky. Then, after a last loop, especially close to the king and his daughter, they fly away, up, up, into the air, until out of sight.

It has left the spectators breathless and is a difficult act to follow. Nevertheless, all the animals do their best. Each one trying to be even more entertaining or amusing than the other. It is Walter and his friends who close the show. As usual, their act is a great success. None of them have lost their skills and they get lots of laughs from their audience. Who can resist the charms of Rona and Mona bobbing up and down in their new frilly dresses, their floppy hats bobbing along as well? They are heart-warming and funny to behold, in their freshly painted pram. Bones proudly wears his new jacket with long tails. It is dark green and has gold trimmings. So very smart, he looks. And so does Bruno, in an identical one, all thanks to Princess Elina. She has seen to it that the seamstress of the royal household made it up for them. While Bones pushes the pram, Bruno dances his old dance routine and their onlookers love the whole display. Walter's outfit is made in the same style as those of Bruno and Bones. Long tails, same dark green colour and gold braiding.

And so, the three of them form a sort of unit. Dashing and dandy, they look. And dignified and funny and endearing too. In one word, splendid, Walter plays the flute while Rita happily sings along. As for Lorenzo, he always is a success. Everybody enjoys his act, with him pretending to be a bit of a bad boy. He gets away with it every time and thrives on it. To top it all, he always draws a lot of applause for behaving cheekily. This time, it is no different. People, as always, just love his antics. They laugh out loud as he screams; "Caramba," over and over, flying than here, then there. Settling on Walter's shoulder, tearing Walter's hair and behaving irritated with him. It makes for a good ending in the performance, leaving everyone in the audience with a smile on their face.

Then the orchestra takes over, by playing some cheery music. The king, in the meantime, has come on to the stage where Walter and his friends still make their bows for the ovation they receive. King Frederik thanks Walter and his helpers for all they have done to make this show possible.

"Of course," he says; "none of this could have happened without the full support of all the fantastic animals from our zoo. Not forgetting the great entry of our feathered friends who brought us so much joy with their wonderful flying display. We have to compliment them all for the success of this morning's performance."

There is loud hand clapping to that, from the listeners. The king does not forget to mention his daughter, the Princess Elina and her ladies-in-waiting either, praising them for their beautiful dancing. "And as for our audience, your encouragement spurred everyone on. All the artists did their utmost best, because of this. So we are thanking you as well. But now, without further ado, please come and enjoy the food and refreshments that are waiting on the tables for us." His words are met with cheers of approval.

Soon, everybody is seated at the attractively decorated tables and munching away amidst lots of laughter and talking. Of course, all the talk is about the wonderful performances of this morning. King Frederik and his daughter, together with the ladies-in-waiting, heartily take part in this happy banter.

Rita, sitting on Princess Elina's shoulder, chirps softly and Walter hugely enjoys the whole scene. Bones is sitting just behind his chair. The other animals and birds are cared for with food and fruit, in their own enclosures. Leesam, together with Walter, Keenan and Simon, have seen to it that each of them receives extra portions of their favourite food on this special day.

Bruno has taken Rona and Mona to the monkey enclosures so that they also get their share of this.

"You do not have to worry about them," he told Walter. "I will also get some of the fruit that is laid out for us there. And then I am going to have an afternoon nap in my own cabin." His words and the care he shows touched Walter's heart, as always.

"You are the best," he told Bruno, "And the show that you performed with Gordon and Wosa, was really excellent."

"Well, yes, everyone seemed to like it," Bruno replied.

"It was good," Walter told him, "and so was our own show. Thank you all. You were really terrific, my friends."

Rona and Mona liked his praise, and at once left their pram for a cuddle. Although, when Bruno picked them up, they gladly went along. Happy to be taken to their friends and the lovely food awaiting them. Aided by all the other good feelings of this day, this is one of the reasons that the look of pure contentment does not leave Walter's face.

When the king, who is sitting not far away from him, asks; "And Walter, tell us, do you not miss the circus and all the people there?" his reply comes swiftly.

"No your Majesty, I am far too happy here at the zoo."

"Good, good," the king smiles.

"Besides," Walter adds, "I still have my music. In the evenings, Rita and me, we often make music, so there is not much time to miss the circus and its people, anyway."

"Aah, yes," the king sighs. "With all the travelling we have done, there was not much time for music at the palace. Add to that the alterations we did at the zoo. No, we have to admit, music was neglected. But we must alter that." King Frederik goes on. "Princess Elina plays the harpsichord rather well. Maybe we must make plans for an evening of music together."

"Can I come too?" All of a sudden, Lorenzo seems to have fallen out of the sky again. Nestling on Walter's shoulder, he asks anew. "Can I?"

Walter, seeing the king look a bit bewildered, wonders what will happen next.

"Aah, well," the king chuckles after a few moments of hesitation, "Yes. We heard what you said Lorenzo, and as long as you do not scream Caramba, then you can come too. Does that make you happy?"

"Yes," Lorenzo nods. "That makes me very happy."

"Good," the king smiles. "We want all of you to be happy on this great day we had together." Raising his voice a bit, he continues; "Please dear people, enjoy the rest of the nice food and refreshments. Talk and laugh some more with each other, on this, your day off. We are content seeing you here so cheerful. Alas, matters of state demand our attention once again. So for now, we have to leave you, with regret, we may add, but it cannot be helped. As for you, Walter," the king with a smile on his face, goes on, "We suppose we are not alone in having some more work waiting?"

"Indeed, your Majesty," Walter now also smiling, answers the king. "Things must get cleaned up and tidied here later on, but it is no problem. Keenan and Simon, along with some other workers, will help me."

"And so will I," Leesam announces. "It should not take us all that long."

"Very well," King Frederik declares. "We will say goodbye for now, then." With a nod of his head to everyone, the king walks away, followed by loud hand clapping from his people. They surely appreciate this day. The wonderful shows, the good food and each other's company.

That the king and his daughter joined them in this, fills their hearts with even more good will for this king they all love so much.

Walter catches Princess Elina's eyes as she turns her face towards him, smiling her most charming smile.

Then, greeting everybody else with a wave of her hand, she calls out, "Not to worry, we shall not be leaving again so soon. The discussions, this afternoon, are at the palace, so we'll be seeing you then. Keep well."

The people cheer her as she follows her father.

"Another perfect day, nearly gone," Walter sighs. Lorenzo also has left him again, flying high up into the sky. But Rita, who has now taken his place on Walter's shoulder, has overheard his sigh.

"There will be many more happy days in this happy place," she chirps.

"Yes, I think so," Walter agrees. "We are very lucky." He reminds himself of this often as days and weeks go by, flowing over into months. Walter's work never bores him. He is happy and content, as are his friends. The king, together with his daughter Princess Elina, regularly comes over to the zoo. They value

Walter's work and the bond between them grows stronger all the time.

It also happens that the king comes back to the words he spoke earlier. Walter gets invited to come and play the flute at the palace, and so this bond becomes even stronger. Of course, Rita is also present at these evenings, delighting the king and Princess Elina with the crystal clear sounds of her beautiful voice. The Princess herself is also very gifted. Her playing of the harpsichord melts Walter's heart. They take turns performing and each one fully enjoys the sheer beauty of the other's music.

And the king? For him, to just sit and listen is pure bliss in itself, enabling him to forget about those worrisome matters of state, even if it is only for a short period.

While Bruno takes care of Rona and Mona on these evenings, Bones always stays close to Walter. Lying just behind his chair, happy to be near him. Even Lorenzo, unusually quiet, is there most of the time as well, calmly sitting on one of the many bookshelves in the library. It is only when all this music making becomes a bit too much for him that he, again, very unlike himself, softly, flies away through an open window. The king's words clearly made a deep impression on him. Not once does he cry out Caramba! No, he really behaves very well.

When they are back at the cottage, Walter always praises Lorenzo for this.

"I know what good manners are," Lorenzo then replies, "And when we are at the palace, I like to be a very well-mannered parrot It is because I have so much respect for the king. I would not like to behave otherwise."

"Splendid," Walter tells his friend. "I am really proud of you."

Well, Lorenzo is also very proud of himself and makes no secret of this. Sure enough, he has to let everyone else know what an excellent sort of big bird he is. So much so that everyone in the end tells him to just fly somewhere in a tree or something.

"Truly, such a goody good parrot can really be a bit too much, don't you think so, Walter?" Bones mutters to Walter.

But Walter just smiles. He smiles so much these days, his friends can't help wondering what this is all about. Even the king takes notice.

'Might it have something to do with his daughter, the Princess Elina?' he asks himself. Having seen the glances these two give each other, it makes him think. But the laughter of his daughter brings happiness into the king's heart. He has never before seen her so joyful.

'Can it be the evenings of music making that give her this glow? No, it can't be that alone.' Pondering about this, the king has to admit that he himself starts liking Walter more and more. "And, who knows," the king sighs at the thought of it, "Well, maybe."

Walter could be just the person he has been looking for, for ages. Honest, reliable, hardworking and much, much more than that. Walter has these special gifts. Not only of understanding animals and birds, but also of making everyone around him feel good. There is a glow from within about him. Furthermore, he can make things happen in a calm sort of way.

"Yes, maybe, he can make things happen for our kingdom too," the king contemplates. "But we have to wait. Walter is a bit young still. He first has to grow up some more."

Chapter XIII

And so time goes by.

Every now and then Mr. Landini and his circus arrive in their nearby little town. For a few days, this adds extra excitement to everyone's lives. Walter and his group sometimes even give a guest performance when asked to do so by Mr. Landini. But with Rona and Mona growing up, they don't seem so eager to perform anymore. To be in the zoo with the other monkeys is all they really want.

And Bruno is getting tired very quickly. His age is starting to tell. Even Bones has lost a bit of his earlier enthusiasm, Walter notices.

As for himself. Yes, it is nice to see again the friends he made in the circus. To talk about old times and have a good laugh with them. To be part of the circus for a short while and receive the public's applause. But, things have changed. Everyone is going on with their own lives. Leila and Lena are engaged to other circus people. They seem to keep their distance a bit, and even Ingrid behaves differently. She has found another very good friend again. He is also an acrobat, working together with her and her brothers now. Pico is very busy as always and so is Pedro.

"Indeed, it might be that we have outgrown the circus," Walter tells his friends, and they all agree that it could very well be so.

Rita does not mind one way or the other. As long as she is free to come and go wherever she wants, singing she does anyway, be it in the circus or when she is with Princess Elina or Walter. It is part of her being.

Lorenzo, though, is quite outspoken. "The circus is part of the past," he declares. "We live in other times now and they are the best I have ever known."

'And yes, how true this is,' Walter thinks by himself.

King Frederik and Princess Elina always come to watch the evening performance when the circus is in town. They love the special circus atmosphere.

They also, always visit the circus animals. Mrs. Landini accompanies them on these tours. The three then might decide if one of these animals or birds could be sick or getting too old to perform. Mr. Landini has the last word on this, but he usually does not object to having a placement in the zoo arranged. And yes, that's what is at long last decided for Jumbo.

Walter is very pleased to see his old friend arrive at the zoo, and so is Jumbo himself.

"It all came true," he says to Walter, "All that I hoped for, to spend the rest of my days in this place. Well looked after by you and your helpers. Meeting some of my own good old friends again and sooner or later, I hope to see the ones I left behind in the circus, here as well."

"Yes, that is very possible," Walter agrees. "In the meantime, enjoy your rest. You have earned it, having worked so hard, for so many years, Jumbo,"

But while all this is taking place, there is something else as well.

Over and above what is happening at the zoo, the circus or at the palace, another situation is building up. Walter knows it. He has grown so close to Princess Elina and the king. Has the time arrived for him to tell of the love he has for Princess Elina? Surely he has to, soon. For he understands she loves him in return,

The king also becomes more and more aware the time to act has arrived. So, one early morning, a messenger is sent, telling Walter, to come to the palace. His words cause quite a stir in the cottage. As soon as the man has left, they all are starting to ask questions.

"What can it be?" Rita wants to know.

"Does it have something to do with the princess?" Lorenzo asks, being curious enough to go inside. Expecting an answer, he places himself on Walter's shoulder.

"I really don't know," Walter replies. Having just cleared the breakfast table, he hastens to put on some suitable clothes for this special occasion.

"Can we come too?" Rona and Mona cry.

"No, you cannot!" it is Bruno, answering them. "You are going with me to the zoo, my dear friends. How long will you be?" he probes, turning to Walter.

"I have no idea," Walter tells him.

"I come with you", Bones declares.

"And so will I," Rita utters.

"Lorenzo, can I ask you to let Keenan and Simon know I will be a bit later than usual for work?" Walter appeals to the big parrot.

"Yes, yes," Lorenzo shrieks. "I shall do that, but mind you, after that, I fly to the palace as well. You will see me sitting in that big oak tree nearby. I want to know what is going on there."

"I will tell you as soon as I know myself," Walter promises.

"And what about me?" Bruno mutters.

"And us?" Rona and Mona cry.

"I let all of you know at once," Walter assures them.

With Rita on his shoulder and Bones trailing close behind, he hastens to the palace.

Master Roland, somewhat agitated, ushers them into the library, where Rita quickly seats herself on one of the top bookshelves. Master Roland, although not officially informed, knows what is about to happen. Being the close confidant of the king, he is indeed familiar with everything taking place in and around the palace.

Walter senses he is here for a very special reason. "Can it really have something to do with what he wishes for most?" he wonders. Waiting for the king to appear, he paces up and down in the room. At last, coming to a halt in front of the rows and rows of books placed on the shelves all around the library. His eyes wander over these volumes with their hidden treasures of wisdom and knowledge. "Aah," he sighs; "How I would love to read them."

"That is not impossible, Walter," he hears suddenly,

As he turns around, the king, who has just entered, walks towards him. To Walter's great surprise, a royal arm is placed over his shoulders. "All the things you dream of can come true, Walter," the king says. "But first, the two of us must have a long talk." He then leads Walter to a desk on which a large map lies spread out.

"Look," the king says, "This is our country. Can you see? Now, take note. The Yanta river divides the country into two. The northern part where we live is smaller than the land south of the river."

Walter nods his head, "Yes, your Majesty," he utters; "I see!"

"Well," the king continues, "All this land, north as well as south, belongs to us. It is one country. However, the terrible truth is, it has indeed been torn in two!"

"Ooh?" Walter's face displays his dismay. But then, his thoughts take him back to the days at Judge Martin's place. There he had read something about this in a book. Only neither Judge

Martins nor father Tobias could give him much further information. 'Or maybe they did not want to,' he wonders now.

Looking up at the king, he asks; "But why was the country split in two, your Majesty? How did that happen and when?"

"That is what we must talk about." The king replies. Loosening his grip on Walter's shoulders, he walks over to a big armchair near the window, where he sits down. "Come, you take this chair," he beckons Walter, pointing to the one opposite him.

The king smiles as Walter respectfully obeys. They both look out over the beautiful garden outside. For a while, none of them speak. Then the king rings the bell, which is on the small table next to him. At once, and as if he has been waiting behind the door, master Roland enters the room. Pushing a trolley, loaded with refreshments, he first serves the king, then Walter. Master Roland treats Walter with utmost regard, for Walter has become a very important person at the king's court. Moreover, he might even become the husband of Princess Elina. One only has to observe the shy smile. The way the princess smiles at Walter. The way these two look at each other, it is all very telling.

"And yes, it would be a good thing this marriage," that is what master Roland thinks, and he is not alone in this. There are many people feeling the same and they talk about it with each other. No matter that, Walter is not nobility. As a person, he is noble enough. Everyone has come to like him and besides all this, the thought of having a splendid, right royal wedding feast is something all people delight in.

Aah, but there are other matters to be dealt with first. After master Roland has left, the king, with a sigh, turns to Walter, saying. "Well, let's eat and drink a bit of what master Roland brought us, while we relate a story to you. A story that needs to be told. It is not known to very many people, because we thought it better to try to keep it a secret so as not to upset our people too much. Anyway," the king continues after taking a bite from one of the tasty snacks in front of him. He watches as Walter also tucks in and only then, goes on.

"For us, living as we do, in the northern part of our land, everything goes very well. Sadly, in the southern part, things are altogether different. This all goes back many years when I was still small. My mother, the queen, had died a few years earlier and my father, the king, was a lonely man."

Walter suddenly realises the king has changed his way of speaking, talking about me and I now. Can this mean he is accepted as family? But, being deeply interested to hear the rest of the king's tale, he bans this thought from his mind for now. Instead, he listens intently as the king's story goes on.

"We lived in our large castle on the south side of the river then," the king tells Walter. "It was a wonderful place to live in and the land was fertile. My father was a kind and good king. The people were prosperous and they all loved him very much. My father was also a forward-looking man. He made plans to construct a bridge over the river Yantai. This would be of great advantage for the whole country and all its people. Indeed, lots of wooden beams and other material, had already been ordered and delivered for it. Work on that bridge was soon to begin. The material could still be there," King Frederik sighs anew.

"But this bridge was never built," the king continues. "For one night, as my father and I were sitting in front of the fireplace, a storm came up. A storm as we had never experienced before. The wind was howling and raging around the castle. Then, all of a sudden, it became extremely cold. The fire gave us no warmth anymore. I became scared and could see my father, the king, became uneasy too. Thunder struck over and over, with light flashes piercing through the room. After that, it started to rain. A pouring rain, beating against the windows. And unexpectedly, in the middle of all this, we heard a knocking at the door," the king pauses for a moment.

Walter is hanging on to his every word. "Yes, Your Majesty?" he asks, the tone of his voice begging the king to go on with his story.

"Well," the king continues. "We heard the knocking very clearly. It was loud and urgent. Before any of the servants could answer, my father stood up and, grabbing one of the torches from the wall, went to open the door. Frightened of being alone, I followed him. After my father turned the lock, the door flew open. The wind gushed into the passage, whirling round and round. In the light of the torch, dripping wet, stood a woman. Draped in a large dark shawl, she just stared at us without uttering a word. My father invited her to come in and led her into the study. Still, our servants were nowhere to be seen. The woman walked straight to the open fire. Standing in front of it, she unwrapped her shawl, letting it drop to the floor. Before us stood a woman like I have never seen before," the king almost whispers.

"Even though I was small, I could see she was beautiful beyond words. Her long hair was flaming red and curly. It was hanging loosely around her shoulders and shone with an auburn glow. Strangely enough, it was not wet at all, but danced in playful ringlets over her face. So delicate a face, with sparkling green eyes and a smile to take your heart away. It was not mine though, I can assure you," the king says in a sombre tone of voice. "It was my father's heart she took, that same instant. Eerily, after that smile, the storm subsided and then was gone. From that day onwards, everything changed," the king sighs again. "My father no longer took much notice of me, whereas previously, we always were together. And with regard to that bridge, well, as I said, it was never built. The woman, who called herself Miranda, took over the royal household. Things had to be done her way. The building of a bridge would interfere with the plans I am sure she already had then. It also meant the end of the early morning rides, far out into the fields, that my father and I always so enjoyed. Me on my pony and him, on his proud white horse. Instead, there were grandiose festivities attended by many strange people. There was one ball after the other, with guests dancing the night away. Expensive and outrageous alterations to the castle took place, costing fortunes. The most lavish ball gowns, as well as other clothes, were ordered, along with priceless jewels. The castle was always filled with people who stayed for long periods of time. There were hunting parties, with sumptuous dinners afterwards," the king pauses for a few moments, then he slowly nods his head.

"Yes," he goes on; "that is how it was, Master Roland, in his own good time, later told me many tales about these happenings as well. But strangely enough, the most outstanding thing I remember is that this woman, Miranda, did an awful lot of painting. And when I say awful, that is exactly what I mean. She always painted the same scene. Something with an island and a small boat. The colours were horrid too. Very harsh reds and greens and purple."

"How odd," Walter brings out.

"Very odd indeed," the king agrees. "As for me," he continues, "I was always kept in the background and only cared for by servants. Luckily, master Roland, being only a young man himself then, was never far from my side. He helped me through this whole period of misery and pain. It was he who choose my tutors, seeing to it that I received a very good education. And all the while, my father seemed bewitched by this woman Miranda, as indeed he was. He made her his queen, and I saw less and less of him. For 'Queen Miranda', I just did not exist. She was always avoiding me where she could. In the meantime, the state coffers became empty and the country poorer. So did the people. They had to pay more and more in taxes and interest. The once wealthy land, with its happy population, became desolate and barren. The residents increasingly began to dislike this queen. Time passed. Unable to stop the crumbling down of everything around him, my father aged fast. At the end of his life, he sent for me. He blessed and kissed me and asked to be forgiven for his neglect. Leaving me in the care of servants only. To master Roland, who he knew, looked after me so well, he gave the task of taking me away from the castle. 'Cross the river,' my father told him. 'Go and live there in the other palace with my son. Teach him all he needs to know about life and how to rule our country. Make him wise and brave, so that in time, he will become a good and competent king. And who knows, maybe, one day, things will turn out for the better.'

"Well," the king ends his tale, "let's hope that day is not far away now anymore!"

"Your Majesty?" Walter asks. It still is not very clear to him where all this is leading up to.

"Yes," the king replies, "you are my hope now, Walter."

"But your Majesty," Walter stammers. "How? What?"

"No, no," King Frederik answers. "Let me first ask you a question. Do you love my daughter, Princess Elina?"

Walter is lost for words. "Yes, your Majesty," he utters at last, "I love her more than I can say. But …."

The king looks at him sharply before he says. "Do you love her enough to go across the river Yanta and take back the land that belongs to me?"

Again, Walter is speechless.

The king, seeing this, goes on. "I know that my daughter, the princess, loves you. To tell the truth, I myself have almost come to think of you as my son. So, I promise you my daughter's hand in marriage, if you succeed in returning this region to me. It was one country always and should be so, forever! It has been written into the laws of this land. My father's will, which is in my possession, makes this very clear!"

Walter has listened closely to the king's every word, but from all the words spoken, those, 'I promise you my daughter's hand in marriage,' are the most magic indeed. His heart is bursting with joy. For this marriage to take place, he is willing to do anything. Anything at all!

With youthful confidence, he is certain the king's wish can be fulfilled by him. "I will succeed, your Majesty," he declares in a steady voice. "Just tell me when I can go." For the sooner this mission is completed, the sooner the wedding can take place. So there should not be any delay!

The king has to smile over Walter's eagerness to deal with this new situation forthwith. Although, if truth be told, this is precisely what he hoped for and expected. "You can go tomorrow if you wish," is the royal answer. "Keenan and Simon should be able to look after the zoo while you are away. Thanks to you, they have become very skilled at their work."

"Thank you, your Majesty," Walter responds gratefully. He adds; "Yes, I believe our wardens have become very competent. I am sure the day to day running of the zoo will not be a problem for them by now. Also, there is Leesam as well to help out, if necessary."

"Excellent," the king beams. He continues; "Well, there is not much time left to prepare for this journey if you want to leave tomorrow. So you better get ready!" With this, the king stands up from his chair. Walter does too, knowing he has to go now.

"I must warn you though," the king says, while walking him to the door. "Take care. Take great care. This woman, Miranda, is indeed a witch, as you will have gathered. For instance, and to give you an example of her cunning, she has put a spell over and all round the river, so no one can cross it. And it is not the river alone, I tell you. She did this even along the whole coastline. Nothing can enter there. No ships, no people, nothing can, Also, she has spies everywhere."

"In that case," Walter answers, "she will know who I am. If she finds me wanting to cross the river, surely, she will let me, if only to find out why."

"My thoughts exactly," the king agrees. "For that reason, I have a boat at the ready for you. You will have no problem finding it. Just ask for Adrian, my old boats man. Then, for now, a carriage is available for you here as well. Is there anything else I can assist you with?"

"Thank you your Majesty," Walter replies; "But no, I think it is better for me and my friends to go on foot. That way, we can travel at our own pace. I love getting to know the people of this land better."

"Good thinking," the king praises him. "Be careful, Walter," he warns again. "You have a dangerous task ahead of you!"

"I will, your Majesty," Walter promises the king. As the front door swings open, Rita is already sitting on his shoulder, chirping her goodbyes, which are returned by a royal smile. Walter bows for the king, which the king answers with a smile. Bones gets stroked behind his ears by King Frederik and then there are the farewells, as Walter and his friends leave.

"And what now?" Bones asks.

"Now we are going wandering, like in the old days, my dear Bones," Walter replies with a big smile on his face.

The three of them suddenly fall silent as this reality sinks in. They now start pondering about the new turn their lives are going to take again.

"What is this wandering thing?" they hear suddenly. It is Lorenzo. He has left his hiding place in the big tree near the palace. Briskly diving now onto Walter's other available shoulder, he asks anew. "What is this wandering about, then?"

"It is going away. Going on a journey to somewhere else," Rita tells him.

"Is that so?" Lorenzo utters. "That sounds interesting, I must say," he muses. Nodding his head, he repeats; "Very interesting indeed."

Walter, while stroking the big parrot, says, "Yes Lorenzo. It means I have to leave from here. Are you also coming?"

"Aah, well, yes, ai, Caramba, I should think so!" Lorenzo responds.

"Ooohhh and I so hoped you would not use this awful Caramba word anymore," Rita sighs.

"If it annoys you so much, I won't," Lorenzo promises graciously. In his excitement over the news of going on a journey, he wants to avoid any arguments.

"Well, thank you," Rita replies pertly.
Bones, looking up to Walter, keeps wagging his tail.

"Yes, Bones," Walter laughs. "Are you ready for another journey?"

"With you, always," Bones responds, with eager eyes. "And we are going tomorrow?" he asks, just to make sure.

"Yes, my friend, tomorrow it is," Walter answers. "Come, let's now tell the others."

The others are waiting at the cottage. "Why did the king want to see you, Walter?" Bruno wants to know. He is sitting with Rona and Mona in his arms. They have come back early. Being with their friends in the zoo is all very fine, but things here are now demanding their attention. They want to know what is going on.

"Is something the matter?" each asks in turn.

"Yes, yes, indeed," Walter tells them. "There is."

"What? What is it?" are the following questions.

Walter sets himself on a chair next to Bruno. "Right," he says. "Here it is. Are you prepared for it? Well then, the king has told me I can marry the Princess Elina. Isn't that wonderful news?" With an ever-growing smile, he listens to the effect his words have Utterances of amazement and surprise, mixed with congratulations, coming from his friends.

"But you did not even tell me about this, just now," Lorenzo grumbles.

"No, you just asked if I wanted to go on a journey with you," Bones joins in.

"Journey? What journey?" Bruno wants to know.

"All right," Walter says. "Let me explain. Before I can marry Princess Elina, the king wants to send me on a very important mission. Of course I agreed. We are leaving tomorrow morning."

"To where? What sort of mission?" they all want to know.

"Well," Walter answers, "I must first travel across the Yanta river and from there up to a castle where Queen Miranda lives. She took the land south of the river. And by doing so, divided it into two, which was wrong. Although married to King Frederik's father, she had no right to do that. This whole country belongs to King Frederik only. The king told me Queen Miranda is a witch. She makes the people who live in that region suffer very much. My task is to remove her."

"And then you can marry the Princess Elina," Lorenzo shrieks. "Is that not what you want most?"

"Yes," Walter answers him. "It really is."

"Are we going to have a party?" Rona and Mona shout.

"But this Yanta river, or whatever its name is, is it far?" Bruno worries.

"We want to come too," Rona and Mona both yell.

"There's another thing," Walter says, "But firstly Bruno, yes, it is far. We have to walk long distances. It will be exhausting and, to be honest, I think it will be better if you take care of things here. I would like you to stay at the cottage. You can help me by helping Simon and Keenan to look after the zoo. Visit the animals and the birds every day, as I always do. See if they are happy, as I am sure they will be. Especially when you talk to them, for they all like you very much. Will you do that for me?"

"Yes, yes, of course," Bruno replies. "But …."

"No Bruno, no buts," Walter urges. "It is better so, believe me."

Bruno does not resist any more. He knows Walter is correct in wanting him to stay behind, for he is old and will only slow them down. Apart from that, Walter has given him work to do while he himself is away, and Bruno feels good about this.

And there is more to come, because Walter is not finished with him yet. He adds, "Also, I would be very thankful if you could look after Rona and Mona. I know they are happy here at the zoo, being together with the other monkeys. Still, it would make me happy to know you are keeping an eye on them. Be with them in the evenings, see that they eat their food, all those things. Will you do that too?"

"Of course I will," Bruno promises. He goes on, "Seeing I cannot come with you, I will do my best also, with the other things you ask of me, my friend!"

"I know I can depend on you, Bruno," Walter says gratefully. "You are the best. Really and truly the best!"

"Ooh, and what about me?" Lorenzo shouts.

"Yes, and us,?" Rona and Mona cry.

"Well, all of you are the best," Walter assures them. "Really, all of you are the best friends one can wish for."

"But then, why can we not come with you? Why do you leave us here?" Mona and Rona ask.

"Because it is better so, my dears," Walter tells them. "Please trust me on this. Bruno loves you and will take good care of you. And more than that," he goes on, "Bruno might otherwise become a bit lonely. So, you keep each other company. You can help Bruno at the zoo as well. And you know, there is no greater place to be than here. Moreover, you staying here will give me much more freedom to do what has to be done!"

The monkeys, upon hearing Walter's tone of voice, know it won't help to cry, so, instead, they cling even closer to Bruno.

"Honestly, I come back as soon as possible," Walter goes on. "And then, think of it, what a nice party we all are going to have. A wedding party! Now, won't that be fantastic?"

"Ooh yes, that will be fun," Rona and Mona shout, for a moment forgetting all other things. They do not know exactly what a wedding is, but it sounds like there could be a lot of excitement and that is what they thrive on.

"A wedding will be great," Lorenzo joins in.

"Can we all come?" Bruno asks.

"But sure," Walter laughs. "What will a wedding be without all of you?"

"Aren't you a bit hasty talking about a wedding already?" Rita chirps.

"Ooh, don't be a spoilsport, Rita," Lorenzo calls out to her.

"She is right though," Walter responds. "First of all, we must outsmart this wicked woman, Queen Miranda!"

"So, it will be just the four of us going," Bones remarks.

"Yes, just the four of us," Walter replies.

"It should be a great adventure!" Lorenzo shrieks.

"It could be dangerous," Rita says

"Yes, it should and could be all that," Walter agrees. "But before we start thinking too much about these things, let's go over to the zoo. We must say goodbye to our friends there." On this, they all agree.

The zoo animals and birds are a bit sad when Walter tells them he has to leave for a while. Keenan and Simon, although a bit upset at hearing Walter's news, promise to look real well after all the zoo's inhabitants.

"And so will I," Bruno adds.

"And me, and me," Rona and Mona shout. All three of them feel useful and important now that Walter has given them a duty to perform.

"Good," Walter declares. "Then I can go without worrying too much over you all!" Gordon and Wosa don't want to let him go once Walter is in their embrace, but eventually, he manages to struggle free. After having said goodbye to everyone, including Jumbo as well as the other elephants, they finally return to the cottage. Jumbo's words of farewell, though, still linger in Walter's mind.

"Remember, we all will miss you very much. Please come back soon! We have heard about what you are going to undertake. Yes, news travels fast, especially here in the zoo. Well, all of us wish you a successful journey. And all of us are with you every step of the way!"

Walter feels humble and very thankful to have so many good friends. But, before they can get underway, there is still much to do. After their evening meal, the packing and sorting out of things that need to be sorted out last for quite a while.

Rona and Mona have gone to sleep and Bruno, lying on his own cosy bench, has also dozed off. Bones is resting in a corner, but Lorenzo watches Walter's every move.

"What is all this packing for?" he asks. "Why do you take so many things? Look at me, I never carry anything."

"I know," Walter answers him with a smile, adding; "neither do Bones nor Rita, but people always seem to have so much that they cannot do without. For instance, I need to pack some nice shirts and trousers, shoes, socks. One can't go and visit a queen without having to dress up a bit. This may seem strange to you, but that is how it is."

"Yes, that's how it is," Rita mutters, from under her feathers. She is, as usual, sitting on a nearby shelf, half sleeping, half listening to Walter and Lorenzo's conversation.

"My, my, Rita," Walter exclaims. "I thought you were very deep in dreamland, but no, come what may you always must get your say."

"It's true, my friend, it's true," Rita answers, now fully awake.

"Yes, well, my dears," Walter remarks, "I think we all need some rest now before tomorrow's journey." He puts out the lights and soon everyone in the little cottage is fast asleep.

Early the next morning, there is a knock on the door. It is a messenger from the palace who, with a respectful bow, hands Walter a small package.

"The king wants you to have this for travel expenses," he says. After a second bow, he quietly and quickly, is on his way back to the palace again. Inside the parcel, Walter finds a pouch filled with silver and gold coins. A real royal gift. Walter, being used to earning his own living, is a bit overcome by this. Nevertheless, he realizes, it could come in handy.

By this time, everyone from the Walter's household is up and about. They are not all that impressed by the king's gift. None of them value money very highly. Only Bruno seems to understand. "This is very good," he says. "You will be able to travel faster now that you don't have to depend on earning money for a living."

"Absolutely," Walter smiles, adding, "and the king wants us to move fast. That is why we should not dally any longer, my friends."

Upon hearing this, Bones is already at the door, eager to go.

"Well," Walter laughs; "I can see you are in a hurry, my friend, but no, we are not ready yet. First, we must have something to eat before we start out."

And so, after a bit of a hasty breakfast, in which Bones as usual does not take part, they leave.

With a flutter of wings, Rita and Lorenzo each take up their position on one of Walter's shoulders. Other than that, Walter also carries his rucksack. His money belt, used in earlier travels, is safely tied to his body. It contains the coins given to him by the king. In spite of this fortune, which should make him feel rich, Walter instead, suddenly feels sad. Sad to leave Bruno. Sad to leave the two monkeys, Bruno holds in his arms. Those two unhappy little monkey faces don't help much either. Bruno's shoulders are drooping. Altogether, the three of them look very downhearted.

After the goodbyes have been said, they wave their farewells as Walter starts the journey. The waving only stops when they turn the bend of the path leading to the palace.

With Bones next to him and Rita and Lorenzo on his shoulders, Walter knows a small part of him stays behind with Bruno and Mona and Rona. But go on, he must. It is only when nearing the palace that his thoughts take another direction. It is for Princess Elina that he undertakes this journey. For her, he will do almost everything. Hoping to chase away the last of his sad feelings, he reaches for his flute. Who knows, maybe Princess Elina will hear his music and come to wave him goodbye as well. And indeed, the princess is already standing on the balcony, smiling and waving to him. Even the king is there, along with master Roland and some servants too. They all wave and smile and Walter does the same.

Rita and Lorenzo have left his shoulders and start circling around the balcony. Rita perches herself on Princess Elina's shoulder and, like so many times before, is welcomed and caressed by her. Lorenzo would love to get the same attention from the princess, but no, he does not think it will be a good idea to fly onto her other shoulder. Instead, he settles himself on the balcony's railing, a bit further away. Does the princess sense his longing for her attention? Indeed, for she walks up to him and softly strokes his beautiful coloured feathers. "You are very handsome," she tells him. "And more than that, you are one of Walter's best friends. That is why you are one of my best friends as well."

In spite of his sometimes brazen manner, Lorenzo, at this moment, does not know what to do or say. Instead, he quietly looks up at the princess. Her words almost melt his little heart.

The king has come closer as well. He puts one arm around his daughter and says. "Yes Lorenzo, the words of my daughter, the princess, are very true. You and Rita here, together with Bones, are true friends. As is Bruno. We understand that he is getting a bit too old to come along on this adventure. We heard he is going to help Keenan and Simon with their work at the zoo, while keeping an eye on the monkeys, Rona and Mona, too. Everything has been taken well care of by Walter. So now, we bid you farewell and hope that this journey will be successful."

Lorenzo just nods his head before taking off into the air again, followed by Rita, who cheerily chirps her goodbyes.

Walter has stopped playing, and now only has eyes for his beloved princess. Does he see a bit of a sad expression on her face behind the smile? Could it be she is troubled over the outcome of this expedition? Over the dangers that lie ahead? Walter has not allowed himself to think about them much, but now, all sorts of thoughts flash through his mind as he passes the balcony.

Admitting to himself 'I must have sounded eager to leave. Why was the king so more than willing for me to go today already? Was it because this would prevent his daughter from speaking to him before his departure? Surely, the princess knows about Queen Miranda. Was the king scared his daughter would have objections? Well, whatever the reasons, I am on my way now,' he says to himself. 'I am going to do what needs to be done and hope for a happy outcome and a speedy return.'

To the princess he calls out, "I will soon be back!"

The princess throws him a kiss, and he clearly hears her answer.

"Yes, yes, please come back soon! I'll wait for you. I'll wait for you!"

With these words ringing in his ears, Walter's new adventure begins.

Once past the palace, he becomes aware of how good it feels to be on the road again.

"Do you feel it too, Bones?" he asks. "Don't you think it is great that we are on our way now?"

"Yes, yes," Bones replies. "It is wonderful to go wandering and see a bit more of how things are, away from the palace grounds."

"Exactly my thoughts," Walter grins.

Rita and Lorenzo, meanwhile, have come back and settle on Walter's shoulder again.

"The king hopes we will be successful," Rita twitters.

"Yes, I hope so too," Walter replies. "And the princess?" he asks. "What did the princess say?"

"The princess said that I am very handsome," Lorenzo shouts.

"Oh, yes, so you are," Walter replies. "What with all your beautiful coloured feathers and your proud bearing. I also think you are very handsome."

"Good, good," Lorenzo remarks. "I am very pleased now."

"That's great," Bones says, "It really is Lorenzo, but…."

"No, no, I don't want to hear any buts," Walter smiles. "It is true. Lorenzo is beautiful and the only but I allow is to state that you all are truly beautiful. Inside and out. That is the wonder about you, my dear friends. Inside and out!”

“Hmm, well, I can live with that,” Bones declares.

“And so can I,” Lorenzo responds while taking off into the air again,

“Me too,” Rita sings.

“Me too!” Walter laughs. “Sometimes these things have to be said,” he declares, stroking the little bird who snuggles against him. “Tell me, did the princess say anything else?”

“Yes,” Rita answers him. “The princess also said that we are her best friends because we are your friends.”

“Hmmm, yeah, well, that is nice,” Walter smiles, “But then, the princess is nice. Very nice,” he adds. Thinking of her, the smile stays on his face as they move on. They see lots of people on their way, most of them looking happy and content. Walter makes it his aim to talk with as many as he can. He finds them friendly and finds out they are hardworking persons, who love their country and their king.

He also sometimes hears them speak about the king’s lovely daughter, the Princess Elina. They seem to know she has lost her heart to a young man who works at the king’s zoo. “Yes, all these rumours one hears,” they tell him. “It appears he is a nice young man, though. At least, that is what we have been told by some folks.”

Walter only smiles when listening to these tales. He does not want to reveal that he is the one they are speaking of. He listens and at other times, plays the flute when crowds are gathering at a Village square. Of course, Rita sings along and Bones does the dancing all by himself now. He does it rather well, too. There is no pram to support him. No Bruno who assists him. Taking all this into consideration, Bones does fine.

The people love it. Lorenzo always adds a bit of his own magic to these shows. It is the same old Lorenzo, with his same old, bizarre behaviour. He just knows how to get everyone's attention and make people laugh. As Walter tries to calm him down, he gets more and more agitated. Shouting and flying around in circles. Of course, it is all make believe and as such, is hugely enjoyed. But with all these goings on, Walter never loses sight of his mission. He wants to get information. Wants to find out how things are with the country and its residents. Get people talking.

And they do. They laugh and talk a lot, but not about Queen Miranda.

"Don't they know that Queen Miranda lives on the other side of the Yanta river?" Walter asks his friends.

"They do," Rita tells him, "But it is believed to bring bad luck to even speak her name out loud. She seems to know everything that is going on here. I overheard people whispering about this to each other. Some folks even talk about a mirror that can reflect all the happenings, here, there, everywhere!"

"Ai," Lorenzo utters. "I have not heard that one yet." He feels a bit envious about this saucy bit of information Rita comes up with. Not to be outdone, he declares, "Did you know there are spies around here? I heard talk about that."

"Hmm, revealing mirrors, as well as spies. It is all very interesting," Walter remarks. He goes on, "Now, if the queen has spies, so do I. You make good spies, my friends. You can go where I cannot go. You can hear people speak to each other when they sit underneath trees. Please, just fly up there and hide in the tree branches. Go wherever people gather and listen to what they say. But be careful. Don't take chances. Don't come up to close!"

"Fine, I like doing this," Rita chirps.

"My, my, I am a spy!" Lorenzo shouts. "That is great."

"And what about me?" Bones asks. "Can I also be a spy?"

"No Bones, I want you here with me," Walter tells him. "You are my bodyguard. No one will attempt to harm me, with you on my side!"

"Indeed," Bones utters. "Don't let anyone even try!!!"

And so it happens that Rita and Lorenzo, while flying then here, then there, in their usual way, pick up a lot of information. This they report back to Walter. They tell him that every so often, people from the other side of the river Yanta come over to buy supplies. Food and materials. Silk and satin and brocade. Everything a royal house may need.

"But how do they manage to cross the river?" Walter wonders. "The king told me no one is able to do that."

But his friends have an answer to this question as well. "It is a big secret," Lorenzo says. "It seems those spies carry a chain with a badge around their necks. It has strange symbols on it, I hear. With this medal, they can cross the river anytime they want."

"My, my," Walter sighs. "Things get weirder and weirder."

"It's not only that," Rita comes with some other news. "Apparently, stories go round about you being an agent of the king! I just heard this today. If I heard it, those spies must have too!"

"Well, that does not sound too good," Walter sighs. "I had hoped we could go unnoticed as such, but now I know we did not. What else do the people say, my friends?" he asks.

"They think you are the one who captured the heart of Princess Elina," Lorenzo answers. He goes on, "They guess you are sent to try and get the land back that belongs to King Frederik. No one thinks that you can do it, though."

"Ooh, is that so?" Walter responds. "Hmm, well," he goes on, looking at each of them in turn. "And what do you think?"

"I am sure you can," Bones replies at once.

"I don't know," Lorenzo hesitates.

"We must try," Rita says simply.

"And so we shall," Walter declares. "Together, we will be able to do it. I am certain of it, whatever people may whisper or wonder." He leans back against the tree, under which they have made camp for the night. Thousands of stars shine down on them.

"Aah, so beautiful it is," Walter sighs, taking it all in. The stillness of the landscape surrounding them. The trees, a lake. A pale moon helps to create a dreamlike scenery.

"Yes," his friends agree with him. "It is truly awesome,"

The next morning they travel on again and so it goes for many days. The evenings are warm and most nights they sleep in the open air. On the edge of a forest or sometimes in a farmer's barn somewhere. News about Walter and his secret mission seems to have spread like wildfire now. Everywhere they go, people try to speak to him about it. But Walter keeps quiet. Friendly, yes, but he never says anything about them being right or wrong when confronted. He just laughs away their questions and inquires, while making a point of it, to instead ask how they are and what their trade is.

Then one night, they find themselves at a large farm. A huge barn is standing aside the farmhouse. Just as Walter decides to ask permission if they can spend the night in the barn, the farmer and his wife come towards them. They are followed by some workers who have spotted them already from afar. So friendly is their welcome. So well-meant their invitation to come and spend the night at the farmhouse itself.

"I thank you for your offer," Walter tells them. "I do apologise, but really, we prefer to spend the night by ourselves in the barn." Having become so used to each other's company, they truly do. Also, apart from that, Walter does not want to answer all the questions these people surely are also going to ask him. So, after a bit of a discussion, at long last, the barn becomes their resting place for the night.

They are spoilt though, with food, meat and fruit, bread and butter. The farmer and his wife can't do enough. They like this young man with his birds and the large dog. They know almost for sure who he is, even though he does not utter a word about this. Nor what he plans to do. His smile is so endearing and charming. One can only hope, he really is the king's envoy. Not only that, but maybe even the future husband of the Princess Elina.

"To think, we may have a member of the royal household here with us," they say to each other. "Imagine that!" Walter and his friends, in the meantime, have gone to sleep. After enjoying the tasty food, they feel tired. So do the animals, sharing the barn with them. They usually have early nights and do not talk much, anyway.

It is a few hours later when Bones starts to growl. First, softly, then louder. Lorenzo and Rita are awake at once. They fly around Walter, waking him up too. Bones has left them already. He is going straight in the direction of the very faint sound he heard. Creeping up to it, silent now. It is not long before he detects what interrupted his rest. A sly figure is moving towards the barn. Bones sees the glimmering of an object in the dim moonlight. With one big leap, he moves forward to overpower this intruder. The knife, because that is the object Bones noticed, slices towards him. No matter, Bones is upon the man already. He does not even take notice of the sudden pain in one of his hind legs. The knife has wounded him there, but more important to him is the fact of having control over his suspect. And that he has!

The man is totally taken by surprise. Being unarmed now as well, he does not stand a chance against Bones, who holds him in a breakneck grip. By this time, Walter has arrived at the scene. With one glance, he takes it all in.

"You did well, Bones," he tells his friend. "Very well. For sure, you saved my life tonight. I can never thank you enough for that!"

Bones wags his tail and immediately obeys when Walter tells him, "You can release the man now, Bones."

He keeps within the shortest distance, though, just in case. Meanwhile, pandemonium overtakes the night's serenity.

The farm dogs have started barking. Sheep are bleating, cows mooing. People are shouting and running towards the barn.

"What is going on?" they want to know.

"What is happening?" The farmer, oil lamp in the one hand, a wooden club in the other, grasps immediately what is going on.

"He wanted to kill you," he says to Walter. "He must be a spy from the other side of the river!"

"Very likely," Walter responds. Looking closer, by the light of the lantern, he sees the glimmering of a chain on the man's neck. Coming nearer to the intruder, with Bones watching and growling, he grabs it. The man howls and starts protesting loudly while Walter examines the symbols on the chain's badge.

"No matter what you say," Walter tells him, "This badge here, proves who you are. You are indeed a spy for Queen Miranda!"

People gasp for breath all around them.

Lorenzo screeches and wildly flaps his wings while circling into the sky.

Rita, agitated, twitters on Walter's shoulder.

"What shall we do with him?" the farmer asks. All sorts of answers come after his question, from, "Beat him, bash him," to; "let's put him in prison."

Walter shrugs his shoulders. "We should not beat him nor bash him," he says. "The best thing we can do is to put him in prison for a while. Maybe he will come to his senses there. After all, we are one country, with one people. Why should we fight and try to harm each other?"

"Well said," the farmer agrees. "Indeed, we are one country. All of us are citizens of this land. Our hope is that we can become one again!"

The farm workers like what they are hearing. Apparently, so does the queen's spy. Addressing Walter, he cries out, "Forgive me, please. I never thought about it that way. I wanted to kill you, yes, but only because Queen Miranda instructed me to. I do not hate you. I am a peace-loving man. Please believe me!"

"You have been trained the wrong way," Walter responds. "I forgive you, because there is no place for hate in my life. But still, I think it might be better to have you locked up for a while. To keep you at a safe place might be better for me and also for you!"

The intruder has no answer to Walter's words. He is very aware of Bones watching him and of the farm workers, who are coming closer and closer. That's why he decides that this might be his best option.

"Well," the farmer addresses Walter. "Now, we know the truth. You are indeed the king's envoy. You are the one who is going into battle with Queen Miranda."

"But how are you planning to do that?" the farmer's wife asks. "You have no army. We see no soldiers on your side. You only have these birds and this dog with you!"

"That is more than enough," Walter answers her. "These birds and my dog are my friends. They talk to me, they help me. Like my friend Bones here has done now tonight. Without him, I might have been taken by surprise. I could indeed have been killed. And by the way, I am not going into any battles. That is not my plan at all."

"Well, we wish you and your friends the best of luck," the farmer responds. "If I may say so," he adds, "You really and truly need it."

"That is for certain," everybody around him agrees.

"Can we help you with anything?" the farmer wants to know. "Please say so. We're only too willing."

"Thank you, but no," Walter replies. "The only thing I ask of you is to take this spy away from here. Watch him. Put him in safe custody so that he will not be able to contact anyone."

"Consider it done," the farmer assures him. He signals a few of his workers to take care of this task. Bones keeps growling as they bind the spy.

"I will take it from here," the farmer tells Walter. "You just go and rest some more. It is still early night and you need your strength. I will have my foreman and two of the other workers stand guard over you, so that this sort of thing won't happen again. Ooh and by the way, you are not far away from the river Yanta anymore. Depending on how fast you travel, of course, I would say it is not even a day by foot."

"Great," Walter answers.

"Can I just ask you one more question?" the farmer's wife says.

"And that question is?" Walter smiles.

"Eeh, I wonder, you must be also the young man everybody talks about. The one that maybe one day is going to marry our Princess Elina?"

"Aah," Walter chuckles. "Even this secret seems to have leaked out. But talking about maybe. Maybe if my mission is successful. Then maybe, who knows? Anyway, I'll bid you all good night once again. Come Bones, Rita, Lorenzo, we are going to try and sleep some more."

As he moves away, the people he leaves behind start calling after him. "We wish you success!" they shout. "We wish you all the best. Please come back safely."

Walter is very moved by this.

Lorenzo, who is circling overhead, suddenly sees a glimmering object near a bush. Diving closer to have a better look, he shouts, "A knife, Walter, I see a knife lying there near you!"

Aided by the moonlight, Walter also sees it. As he picks up the dagger, he notices Bones limping closer as well. "What happened to you, Bones?" he asks. "Don't tell me this knife was thrown at you?"

"It was!" Bones admits. "It just hit me on the side of my leg. Nothing serious though, I would think."

"Not serious?" Walter gasps. "My, my, I think it is. Let me have a look at it."

"It is nothing, really," Bones replies.

"But you are limping," Walter argues.

"Let him be Walter," Rita chirps from his shoulder. "There is nothing you can do now. Let's wait until tomorrow morning, then you can see if it is bad or not."

"Yes please," Bones joins in. "Tomorrow morning is good enough,"

In spite of Walter's protests, he manages to escape further inspections by limping back to the barn. There he hides, burrowing himself deeply into the hay. His friends who followed him, decide to leave him be. Walter, though, is far from happy with this situation and keeps grumbling about it for a while.

"You are a very self-willed dog," he says. "Self-willed and stubborn, too."

"That's what I am," Bones mutters back. "I told you so, a long time ago. Remember?"

"Yes, yes, indeed, I do now!" Walter answers. "Hmm, yes, well, I suppose you were born that way! Sadly, there is nothing one can do about that!"

"No. Nothing!" Bones agrees.

Then, wisely, Walter decides to end the argument. Turning to one side, he closes his eyes and so, at long last all of them fall asleep again.

The next morning, they are up very early. Walter knows life at the farm starts even before daylight. Wanting to be gone by then, he packs his belongings, while telling his friends they must make haste. There is no need for that though, because Rita and Lorenzo have already left the barn without Walter noticing. Bones also stands at the ready.

"How is your leg?" Walter asks his friend.

"Better, a lot better," Bones answers.

"Good," Walter replies. "I will have a look at it a bit later, then. Let's get away from this place first. The people here are really nice, but I do not want to answer any more questions."

"That's fine with me," Bones responds.

They quickly leave the barn, and once outside, Walter greets the farm foreman and his helpers. "Good morning," he calls out to them.

"Good morning," their responses come back.

"Thank you for keeping watch over us," Walter adds. "We have to leave now, but please give my regards to your nice boss and his wife. We are very grateful for all their help. Please tell them that as well!"

"I will," the foreman promises. He goes on; "The spy who came here last night is in prison now, sir. I am sure we can keep him there for a while." When he sees Walter nodding his head, he says, "We wish you all the best, sir."

Amid smiles and more good wishes, goodbyes are waved and soon afterwards, they are on their way again. It is a quiet rural area the four of them go through now. Here and there they see a farm with workers busy in the fields. They greet Walter by waving their arms and shouting a greeting, which always is answered by him in the same way.

Not many people cross their path, though. "Which is just as well," Walter remarks. "We can do with a bit of privacy after all the commotion of yesterday."

"Yes, indeed," his friends agree. They once again are resting in the shelter of a big tree. Here, out of the sun's glare, Bones, at long last, let Walter have a look at his leg.

"See," he says. "The knife just scraped it. I do not even limp anymore,"

"Yes, I noticed that," Walter replies. He goes on, "Well, you were very lucky, my friend. Thank goodness for that. It could have been much worse."

"True," Bones admits. "That is very true."

Propped up against the tree, they eat their lunch, while gazing into the sky where Rita and Lorenzo are circling a bit further away.

These two usually still find their own food of seeds and fruit, while Walter always buys for himself and Bones. At farms, at farm stalls, wherever it is available.

"Now, today, we have more food than we can eat," Walter remarks. "This will last us for quite a few days. The farmer's wife gave us so much last night, we still have lots and lots."

"You packed what was over in your rucksack, did you?" Bones asks.

"But of course," Walter answers. "All that wonderful food. It would have been a pity to leave it behind!"

"No, for sure," Bones mumbles. "That would have been a pity indeed!"

It is at this time that Rita and Lorenzo fly back to them. Rita on Walter's shoulder, Lorenzo settled just above their heads on a tree branch.

"We have seen the river," Rita twitters.

"It is not far anymore," Lorenzo shrieks.

"My, my," Walter cries out. "That is good news. So the farmer was right by saying we are not all that far from it anymore. Tell me, did you see a boat? The king said, a boat is waiting there for us."

"Yes, there is a boat," Rita says.

"I saw it too," Lorenzo declares.

"There was also a man nearby the boat," Rita remarks.

"Well, yes, that must be the man King Frederik told me about. His name is Adrian," Walter replies. "Come on, let's quickly go and see."

It does not take long before they are on their way. Rita and Lorenzo have already flown in the direction of the river again while Bones runs in front of Walter. Within a time span of under an hour, Walter sees the river sparkling a short distance from them. It curves wide through the landscape, with huge trees on its side. Then he notices the boat and the man sitting next to it, clearly waiting for them.

"Welcome," he greets, "My name is Adrian. The king sent word you are coming. I have to row you across the river. Correct?"

"Yes, that is correct," Walter replies. "But first, let me introduce you to my friends. My dog's name is Bones, while my feathered friends are Rita the red robin and Lorenzo the parrot. I am Walter. Is it possible for you to take us over right away?"

"Hmm, right away, you say," Adrian repeats Walter's words. He smiles, but his smile is a bit sad. "I would love to," he confesses. "You seem to be a very nice young man and your friends are very likeable too, but I am afraid," his voice falters a bit.

"Yes?" Walter urges him on.

"It is the spell," the boat's man sighs. "I was wondering all along. How can I get you to the other side of the river? Don't you know Queen Miranda is a witch who put a spell over it?"

His last words, Walter can scarcely hear, as Adrian whispers them, after fearfully having looked around. "Don't worry," Walter assures him. "You will see. There is no spell now!"

"But how can that be?" the boats man argues. "Only the queen's spies can cross over. The weird thing is, I can not resist their call. No matter what I do or where I am, I hear them cry out to me. I then just have to come and row them over. Maybe it has something to do with this strange chain they carry around their neck," Adrian sighs. He goes on, his voice still in a whisper, "I am sure it has a secret sign on the badge in the middle of it. I saw it, because they always keep swaying it around."

"Does it look like this?" Walter asks, showing the chain he took from the spy the evening before. He has kept it in his pocket and when the boat's man sees it dangling in Walter's hand, he gasps for breath.

"Yes, that is one," he cries out. "Where did you get it?"

"It does not matter," Walter tells him. "What matters is that we go to the other side of the river now. Come on Bones, get in the boat. Lorenzo, Rita, are you flying over, or do you want to come with us?"

"I come with you," Lorenzo declares.

"Me too," Rita twitters.

Walter jumps into the boat and, seeing there is nothing else he can do, Adrian also sets foot on board. Installing himself at the oars, he declares. "Now just watch. I row and row, but nothing will happen. We won't move. See?"

"But we do move," Walter informs him. "See?"

Adrian's mouth suddenly starts to hang open in utter disbelief. He rows on. They glide over the water with ease. Only the splashing of the oars into the water can be heard. Walter and Bones sit at the back while Rita and Lorenzo have found themselves a space near the boat's bow.

"Eeh, eh," comes Adrian's voice after a short while. "Eeh, is it the chain, then? Did you wave the chain?"

"No, I did not," Walter replies. "I do not need that chain, my friend."

"Well, this is weird," Adrian remarks. "Very weird." He keeps on rowing, filled now, with a new sort of respect. "This young man must be a really important person," he ponders. What with the king's messenger coming here and ordering him to place himself and his boat under his command? And now this amazing river crossing. Even the way he speaks to Walter changes.

"Sir, believe me sir," he says. "For years, it was not possible to row across the river. For years and years. That is why the king gave me a piece of land, so that I could make a living from farming."

"I believe you Adrian," Walter answers. "It is as you say. But for today, the spell has been lifted. Do you want to know why? Queen Miranda knows I am coming to see her. That is why!" His words startle the boats man Adrian still more. But he rows on. The sooner this whole affair is over, the better he will feel. 'What sort of undertaking is this, anyway?' he asks himself. 'Who, in his right mind, would like to go and see the Witch, Queen Miranda? This young man with his dog and birds surely is not thinking of trying to defeat her? If so, he will surely come to great harm.' These are the thoughts going through his mind while rowing as fast as he can. The river is deep and very wide, with a strong undercurrent. It takes a long time to get to the other side. However, nothing seems to disturb Walter. He is at ease and talks to Bones who does not really enjoy the river crossing. Lorenzo and Rita meanwhile, have taken off into the air, circling above them. "How free you are," Walter calls out to them. "It must be wonderful to be able to fly."

"We don't complain," Rita sings.

"No, not at all," Lorenzo shouts.

Adrian has his own thoughts about Walter talking to his companions. ”Still, it might be better to keep quiet,“ he muses. ”It won't do to upset this stranger who talks to his dog and those birds he has with him. Who moreover, also seems to be totally unconcerned over what might be waiting on the other side of the river Yanta. They at least arrive safely at their destination though. Walter thanks Adrian, while handing him some money.

The boatsman is overwhelmed by this. ”So much money,” he stammers. ”It is too much.”

“No, it is not,” Walter laughs. ”It must have been ages since you last earned some money by rowing people over.”

“Yes, that is true,” Adrian replies with a chuckle. He watches as Walter, followed by Bones, steps ashore.

“Farewell my friend, I am not sure when we will return, but return we will,” Walter calls out.

”I really do hope so,” Adrian answers, although he does not believe any of them shall ever be back. After waving politely, he hastily returns to his own side of the river, grateful nothing unforeseen happens to him on the way.

“Well,” Walter sighs, “here we are then. In the other half of this country. It looks different, don't you think?” he asks his friends. ”It feels desolate and the landscape is so bleak and dreary.”

“It is,” Rita says.

”It looks unfriendly,” Lorenzo exclaims. Both birds have settled on Walter's shoulders again. They find comfort in being near him, for this is a strange place with an eerie atmosphere. Bones is sniffing the air and wriggling his ears. “It feels as if someone is watching us,” he declares.

"I am sure, someone does," Walter agrees. "And we all know, who! But then," he goes on. "That is something I expected."

They start walking, the long road that curves land inwards. From the map, shown to him by the king, Walter knows exactly, how to reach the castle where Queen Miranda lives. It is quite a long way off. In silence they travel on. No people to be seen, no animals nor birds. Now and then, they pass an old farmhouse, but, if anyone is living there, is hard to tell. Rita and Lorenzo sit very still on Walter's shoulders. Only their eyes move and keep looking all around. Bones, tail drooping, stays at Walter's heels.

"This is no good, my friends," Walter declares at last. "We have to get out of this depressing mood. I think, music is what is called for!" Out comes his flute and the first notes, soon fill the air. Walter makes them sound jolly and happy. All at once the feeling around them seems warmer and more friendly. Even more so, when Rita with her sweet voice, softly joins Walter. Bones lifts up his head and his tail starts wagging.

"Good, good," Lorenzo shouts, ruffling his feathers. "This is better. Much better!"

Walter smiles sideways at him. "Yes," his eyes say. "Of course it is." Now their journey is not so gloomy anymore. Walter's step becomes lighter. He becomes aware, that even on this side of the river, the sun still shines. Here and there, a tiny flower has struggled free. It's little speck of colour, cheering up the area around it. "If tiny flowers can survive here, then surely, so can we," Walter says aloud and his friends agree.

That evening, they sleep under the stars again. Near a little stream, as always, and where a circle of trees give shelter from a whirling wind.

CHAPTER XIV

Early the next morning, after a wash and something to eat, they move on.

Before midday, a small village is their next stop. Everything looks terribly run down, the houses, the streets, the people that shuffle by. But, they do find a market. Not like the ones they're used too, but at least, some vegetables and fruit are for sale here.

"Very good," Walter declares. "Let me go and get something."

He buys a few apples and pears and, after having paid for them, asks the stall holder, "Please tell me, how are things these days?"

The man mumbles something that sounds like 'bad, bad.'

"I am sorry to hear that," Walter responds. He goes on, "I wonder where all the people are? There are not many here and on our journey, we did not see many either. We passed some farms on our way, but they all seemed desolate."

"This is so," the man agrees. "Many farmers have gone elsewhere, looking for work. They," here he halts.

"Yes?" Walter urges him on, hoping to find out more.

"No, nothing," the vendor replies, looking at Walter with distrust in his eyes. "Why do you want to know all these things anyway?" he asks. "Are you from the castle?"

"No, no," Walter laughs. "Not from the one you are thinking of, I assure you!"

"Well, you do look different. Moreover, as it is impossible to cross the river, certainly one cannot come from there," the man frowns. "Please go away," he pleads. "I do not want trouble."

Walter gets the same reaction everywhere. People are clearly afraid to talk. As soon as he starts asking them something, they refuse to answer.

"I suppose, they think, I am a spy," Walter sighs. "Have you noticed how poor and unhappy everyone looks?" he asks his friends. "All this has to change," he adds. "When King Frederik is king over this part of the country, I am sure the people here shall become prosperous again. And this, before long."

"But of course they will," Rita chirps.

"Yes, of course," Lorenzo yells in agreement. "As soon as…."

"Shuush, shush Lorenzo," Walter stops him. "Come to think of it, the less said now, the better. Even the walls and stalls seem to have ears in this place."

"That must be the reason no one wants to talk to you," Bones barks. "They are scared of…."

"Yes Bones, yes we know," Walter stops him too.

They wander on, through lonely streets, until the village lies behind them. There are more to come, all small and sombre. But wherever they go, people refuse to answer any questions.

"What a strange and troubled land this is," Walter remarks to his friends one evening. They have just eaten and sit gathered near a small fire that Walter made. It is more for comfort than for the cold. It cheers them up, taking away some of the gloom surrounding them. The soft murmur of the small brook nearby also helps a bit. They talk and make some music and then drift off to sleep.

Then, after some more days, they at long last are within reach of the castle where Queen Miranda lives. One can see it from far away already. It is situated on top of a hill, imposing and splendid, with high towers, greyish-white of colour. The terraces around the castle are intensely green, in sharp contrast with the barren land elsewhere.

Walter is overwhelmed by the strangeness of it all. Here he is, after a journey without any problems. 'And now what?' he asks himself. 'Will I be able to do what has to be done? But, let me not think too much about this,' he decides, 'Handling each situation as it comes along might be the best way of dealing with it, anyway.'

"I want to go and look around there," Lorenzo interrupts his thoughts.

"Yes, me too," Rita declares. "Can we?"

"Yes, of course you can," Walter answers; "Be careful, though."

"Yes, we will," they both assure him and off they are, flying high up into the air, alongside each other.

"Well, as we are unable to fly, you and I, we just have to walk Bones," Walter remarks. And that is what they do. After a while, a garden path stretches out before them. It leads up to the castle. Then, when nearly there, something very unforeseen happens. As they look at the finely carved wooden entrance doors, those doors suddenly swing open and out, steps the queen. A woman so stunningly beautiful, she has Walter gasping for breath.

With outstretched hands, she walks over to them. Ringlets of auburn red hair dance around her exquisite face. She is a vision, dressed in a long sea-green gown. Sparkling green eyes and a welcoming smile complete the picture.

'Is this true?' Walter asks himself. 'Am I awake? Or is this a dream, I wonder?'

But here is this elegant hand, taking his. "I have been waiting for you," her soft, but clear voice addresses him. "I am Queen Miranda and your name is Walter?"

"Yes, that is correct, madame," Walter replies, while taking her hand and bowing at the same time. He adds, "Dare I ask how it is, Your Highness knows my name?"

A tinkling laugh fills the air. "Ooh, I know all sorts of things," comes the queen's answer. "I have spies everywhere."

"I am sure," Walter responds, looking straight into the queen's eyes. She just smiles, then, bending down to stroke Bones, she remarks, "you are such a watchful dog, I believe."

Walter notices at once how Bones, although trying to be polite, can hardly endure the queen's touch. He shivers and his hair is standing upright.

The queen detects this as well. "Animals usually, do not like me very much," she tells Walter with a most charming smile. "But I hope, you do." Without waiting for an answer, she takes his arm and together they walk to the castle's entrance, followed by Bones. Walter looks up into the sky, but Rita and Lorenzo are nowhere to be seen.

"Your birds are flying around in my tropical garden," the queen informs him. "You will see them just now, but first, let us go inside."

They enter a gigantic hall that has a winding stairway in an outmost corner. Plants with lush greenery are everywhere. They are reflected in large mirrors, which give the impression there are even more of them. The queen leads Walter through an open door, into a delightful, sunny room. Here also, there are plants in abundance. The walls are decorated with colourful images of birds. Only three walls of the room can be seen. Masses of palms and other tropical plants fill the space where the fourth one should be, creating an effect of a dense forest. It is into this area that the queen leads Walter.

"This is my favourite place," she declares. "It makes me feel free and happy. Rain, wind and sunshine are able to come in, to keep it natural. Just look up and see the sky above us. That is how

Rita and Lorenzo found their way in here," the queen ends a bit out of breath.

Walter wonders anew, 'how does the queen know their names as well?'

As if reading his thoughts, she laughs and says, "It is my spies. They whispered them in my ears."

"Indeed," Walter replies. The smile on his face is only half-hearted as he asks. "I suppose your Majesty knows everything that is going on around here?"

"And beyond," the queen answers, looking at him with a disarming twinkle in her eyes. They are now standing in the middle of the courtyard and there, among the luxurious foliage, Walter spots Rita and Lorenzo. They promptly fly onto his shoulders. The queen has loosened her grip on Walter's arm and moves a bit away from him, looking at each bird in turn, as if studying them.

"Good day to you, ma'am," Lorenzo shouts suddenly, with for him, unexpected good manners.

Walter cannot help but laugh.

The queen laughs too. "Good day Lorenzo and good day Rita," she responds.

"And the same to you, Ma'am," Rita chirps.

"Right," the queen says. "Now that we have the formalities behind us, let's go back to the sunroom? I am sure we could all do with some refreshments."

At their return there, the queen asks Walter to take a seat on one of the green wicker chairs with white and pale yellow cushions. Placing herself on the one next to him, she claps her hands and at once, two servants appear. They look very smart in their green uniforms, which are braided with gold. Both servants carry a tray, one with two tall glasses, filled with what seems to be orange juice. On the other, is some fruit. After putting them down onto a small table, standing in the middle of the room, they quickly disappear again.

"You must be thirsty after your journey," the queen states. "I hope you enjoy the drink and the fruit?"

"Absolutely, this is perfect," Walter enthuses, while drinking from the glass in front of him. A third servant even brings a bowl of water for Bones, who promptly and gratefully laps it up.

Rita and Lorenzo already ate from the tempting fruit at the courtyard. This has stilled their thirst and hunger. Each of them has now flown into one of the tropical plants at the end of the sunroom. From there, they keep watch. The queen daintily takes small sips from her glass.

"Have some of the fruit," she urges Walter.

"Yes, thank you, your Majesty," Walter responds, choosing a big red apple. The queen looks on with a smile as he, with great delight, savours it.

"It is good to have you here," she tells him. "It sometimes gets a bit lonely in this place. Can you believe that?"

"Oh yes, I do," Walter answers in between bites.

"Well," the queen sighs. "It has been like this for a long, long time. But I do not want to bore you, so let me rather show you your rooms. As you are my very special guests, I will personally do so. I suppose you like to freshen up a bit?"

"That would be great, thank you your Majesty," Walter replies. He has finished his apple and now bows gallantly for the queen.

She gives away a dazzling smile and says, "Shall we go, then?" Standing up, she moves over to the hallway, followed by Walter and Bones. Rita and Lorenzo also join them, taking their place on Walter's shoulder again.

The queen ushers them to the stairway in the hall's outer corner. Mounting the steps up to the first floor and then taking a turn to the left. "This is the blue wing," she explains. "My rooms are in the white wing, on the other side."

She stops at the last door of the passage and opens it. A room in the softest blue and white colours unfolds itself before Walter's eyes. It is large and even has a study nook, complete with desk. Elegant furniture fills the rest of the area. The floor of white marble has a powder blue carpet. An inter-leading door reveals a bedroom. On the bed is a blue bedspread with white cushions loosely piled on top.

"This is more than marvellous," Walter says, trying to take it all in.

"I am glad you like it," the queen responds. "You will find a closet and wash basin next to the bedroom. I had the servants fill the basin with fresh, rose- perfumed water."

"I do not know what to say," Walter reacts. "To go to all that trouble for me, it is simply overwhelming!" And indeed, he is totally taken aback.

"Ooh, it is nothing," the queen answers. She continues; "As I told you already, it sometimes gets lonely out here. So, it gladdened my heart to learn you were going to visit me. Hopefully, you will stay some time?" Her face, that lovely face, is open and eager, her voice pleading.

Walter is getting more and more confused. 'What is going on?' he asks himself. Surely, this lovely queen cannot really be the bad witch he has heard of so much lately? The one everybody is scared of? Having such an honest character himself, he finds this hard to believe.

As Queen Miranda turns to leave, she pulls a bell cord dangling near the door. Immediately, the figure of a tall, sombre looking man appears in the entrance. He wears outlandish clothes in bizarre colours, is bald and has a strange white face with slanting green eyes.

"This is your personal servant from now on," the queen says. "He comes from my own faraway island. His name is Erwin, and he does not speak. Don't worry though," she goes on, "he can understand everything you say and fulfil your every command."

"That is not … e … I do not need a personal servant," Walter mutters, while Bones, meanwhile, silently bares his teeth.

"I insist," is the queen's reply. Then she says, "Well, I hope to see you in the sunroom just now? I will be there, keeping myself busy, with one of the many seascapes I paint. Didn't you notice my painter's easel standing in one corner?"

"No," Walter replies, shaking his head. "I did not, your Majesty. It must have escaped my attention."

"Ooh, maybe I put it a bit out of sight," the queen laughs. Then she adds, "To tell you the truth, my paintings are not all that good. It is just something I do to while away the time."

Now Walter remembers, the king talked about paintings of the sea, which the queen painted over and over.

"No matter," the queen sighs, "you will see it just now then. I would like to hear your opinion regarding my work." With these words, she is gone.

"You can go to your own quarters for now," Walter addresses Erwin. This figure, who with folded arms, is still standing near the doorway, is not who he wants or needs. With a slight bow, the man departs, leaving Walter alone with his friends at last. Rita and Lorenzo have flown over to a bookcase, settling themselves there. Bones lies down on the blue carpet.

"Yes, well," Walter utters. "Please tell me, my partners, what do you make of all this?"

"I don't know," Bones begins. "But there is something about this queen that makes my hair stand on end."

"I saw that," Walter remarks. "Well, I think we all feel a bit uneasy in her presence," he continues. "But let's watch the goings on a bit longer, I would say. Let's see what happens next?"

"Yes," Rita chirps. "That might be best."

"Well, I can tell you already. This queen is not as nice as she pretends to be," Lorenzo declares. "There is something very odd about her."

"Indeed," Walter sighs. "That is true. How, for instance, can she be so young and beautiful? When King Frederik's father died, she could not have been that very young anymore. But here she is, looking so ravishing and stunning. Time must have stood still for her." He shakes his head, while pondering about this. Feeling a bit disturbed over everything that had happened so far, he walks over to the small side room. There he finds the sweet-scented water the queen spoke of. After splashing his face and hands with it, he feels better.

"Yes," he calls out to his friends. "It might indeed be a good idea to go along with the situation here for a while. Things will sort themselves out soon enough, I believe. So let us join the queen in the sunroom and see how we go from there."

The servant Erwin is waiting for them on the other side of the door.

'What did he hear?' Walter wonders. 'And can he really not speak?'

As they start moving away, Erwin goes inside, leaving the door open. Walter, looking back, sees him picking up the rucksack, which is still lying on the marble floor. 'Ooh well,' he thinks to himself, 'that at least will give our strange servant something to do.'

While walking to the staircase, Rita whispers from his shoulder, "You must be very careful, Walter. Things are not what they seem here."

"Yeah, it is a make-believe world all around us," Lorenzo mumbles, trying to keep his voice down.

"And that Erwin is not for real either," Bones grumbles. "I don't know why, but I really and truly dislike him."

"Oh, well," Walter replies absent-mindedly. He is still struggling to figure things out. "The welcome we received," he ponders. "I expected anything but this. Only the red carpet was missing. It is absolutely perplexing."

"I think that is the whole idea," Bones mutters. They have reached the staircase by now and descend towards the hallway and once there, cross over to the sunroom.

"I am here," the queen calls out to them. Her voice comes from behind some plants. Going into that direction, Walter finds the queen sitting in front of a large easel. He looks in disbelief at the painting she is working on.

'This is it,' he thinks. 'The painting the king talked about.' It is just as he described it. Sinister and brooding and yes, those shocking colours. Red and lilac, with green and blue. Some yellow for the beach. A bit of white for a small boat on the shore. The sea and sky flowing over into each other and in the middle of it all, a tiny island.

"How do you like it?" the queen asks, looking up at him.

"Err … e … yes, I suppose, e, I don't really know," Walter stammers.

"You do not like it?" the queen says. "Well, let me tell you, neither do I," she adds. Her eyes are playful and shining with mischief. "It really exists, you know," she adds. "The island, I mean. That is where I come from. Sometimes it floats over the ocean, while at other times, it is down on the seabed."

"Please tell me more about it?" Walter responds.

"I wonder, no, I do not think you will understand," the queen muses.

"Your Majesty means I won't understand why this scene is painted over and over?" Walter challenges her.

"You know then?" the queen urges him on.

"The king told me," Walter says simply. It is the first time the king is mentioned, and it seems to have a really strange effect.

The queen stands up, a brush with red paint still in her hand. "Well, well," she sighs.

Walter can see there is more to come after these few words, but, just at this moment, Rita and Lorenzo decide to fly away and take off to the courtyard. The queen and Walter watch in silence as they lose themselves in the greenery. And Bones watches the queen. He seems to sense something else is coming as indeed it does. As both he and Walter look on in amazement, queen Miranda lifts the brush and starts splashing red paint all over her art work.

"Ooh, this feels good," she says. "I should have done this a long time ago already because whatever I try, it is all in vain, anyway."

Observing the look on Walter's face, she goes on, "Come, we have to talk, you and I. But first, let's sit down." Once the two of them are seated, two servants appear.

'Could they have been waiting behind some of the enormous plants here?' Walter wonders. Ignoring Bones, who lies in the middle of the room, the servants serve fruit juices again and also some tempting snacks.

"You must be hungry," the queen declares. "Please try some of these."

"Yes, thank you your Majesty," Walter replies, only now becoming aware how hungry he is.

The queen, waving her servants away, hands Walter a plate and a napkin which has been put on the table in front of them. Giving the example, she places some of the savouries on her plate and daintily starts eating. Walter also chooses a few delicacies and enjoys every bite.

"Now then," the queen says after a short while. "I might as well tell you the rest of my painting dramas. For that is, what it is, one big drama. As you may guess, I painted quite a few paintings by now."

"Yes," Walter nods, "One would think so." He cannot prevent the slight smile on his face, nor the twinkle in his eyes.

The queen opts to disregard this, while continuing, "Well, the thing is, I want the island, this island where I come from, to disappear. But, for that to happen, all the colours of this painting must be absolutely correct. Not a single stroke should be wrong. Every line has to be in its precise place. Otherwise it cannot happen. So, every time I finish this painting, I wait. I have to wait for twenty-four hours and if nothing has happened by then, I start anew."

"It all sounds very weird to me," Walter responds. "I don't understand."

"I am sure you don't," the queen replies. "But," and here she lowers her voice to a whisper. "I am going to tell you a great secret. A secret I have never told anyone else before." She pauses while looking straight into Walter's eyes. "This is because you are very special to me," she says.

"Ooh, and why is that?" Walter wants to know.

"Because you are my stepson's messenger and I want to put things right," the queen answers. "King Frederik as well as everyone else and maybe even you, think I am a bad witch. But I am not!"

"Your Majesty is not?" Walter half whispers.

"No," the queen replies. "Well, e, actually, to tell the truth, I am what one would call a good witch. Have you ever heard of those?"

"Yes, I have," Walter admits.

Queen Miranda continues, "Now let me tell you about this island, which was my home a long, long time ago. A coven of luckless witches live there, and I was one of them. Yes, I was," the queen sighs. "But I did not want to be one. I wanted to get away from there and live my life as a good witch. How happy I was when I was sent here. Even though they brought me to this land with harmful intent, I planned to outwit these miserable old vixens. Having found some long forgotten old scrolls in a nook somewhere, I read those and learned about a spell. A spell that said; 'If any person is able to paint, in every minute detail, the island and its surroundings, it will disappear,' And so will all who live on it. That is why I tried so hard, and for so many years, to do just that. Had I been successful, that shelter of wickedness would simply have vanished. I would have been free to become the good witch I really am."

"But how would your Majesty have known the island was gone?" Walter asks.

The queen smiles a weird smile. Her eyes glitter emerald green as she answers. "Ooh, I would have known." Not explaining this further, she goes on; "Well, you're coming here, has changed everything. I no longer have to keep painting this awful painting. You are my hope for the future, I will tell you. You and my stepson, the king! Together, we can put things right and turn everything back to normal in this beautiful land."

Bones, lying at Walter's feet now, yawns while looking up at Walter. His eyes ask, 'What sort of tale is this?'

Queen Miranda apparently does not notice Bones' reaction, or maybe just pretends not to. She calmly continues. "If only we could convince the king that his presence is needed here. That is why I say you are my hope, for you are the one person who can persuade him to come."

"I am not so sure," Walter responds half-heartedly.

"Well, I am," the queen declares. "Please think it over? In the meantime, can we be friends? I am looking forward to having dinner with you tonight. Then maybe afterwards we can make some music?"

"Yes, that will be nice," Walter agrees.

"Very good," Queen Miranda smiles. "Dinner is served at seven. The gong will chime some time before. Erwin shall escort you to the dining room. If you like, he can also show you around the castle a bit." She claps her hands and within seconds, the brooding figure of Walter's new man–servant, stands next to his chair.

Bones' hair on end, his teeth bared. He just knows something is wrong somewhere.

Walter pats him on the back and, rising from his chair, politely bows before the queen as he takes his leave.

Smiling her dazzling smile again, Queen Miranda watches as they move away. Erwin bows them out of the room, then taking the lead, guides Walter and Bones towards the hallway.

Here, Rita and Lorenzo promptly join their party, flying straight onto Walter's shoulders. They both are very nervous, just like Bones. What is it that makes them feel so uneasy? Is it the overwhelming influence of Queen Miranda, or maybe the looks Erwin gives them? The glare of those fierce green eyes in that blank face? They are not sure, but it is good to be near Walter now. His calmness has a soothing effect on them.

Walter decides to make use of the queen's offer. He wants to become familiar with the castle's outlay and its surroundings.

"Yes Erwin, you can show us around," he addresses the mute servant in front of him. There is no response from this odd figure who just keeps plodding ahead. Up the staircase and then through the passage, from room to room, he leads them. Although beautifully furnished, each one seems gloomy and is of no interest to Walter. He has noticed other staircases leading up to the castle's towers and wants to look around there.

"Can we go further up?" he asks Erwin. But Erwin just shakes his head and refuses to go on. Instead, he turns around, leading them towards their own rooms again. It makes Walter wonder what secrets will the floors above them hold, but, not wanting to cause any problems at this stage, he just follows the man.

Rita and Lorenzo are still on his shoulders, while Bones strides in between him and the mute servant. Upon arriving at their own quarters, Erwin opens the door and waits until they are inside. With a heavy thumb, the door is closing behind them.

'Just as well,' Walter can't help thinking, while staggering to the bed in the adjacent room. Worn out and maybe, because of that, suffering from a bit of depression and despondency. 'What am I to do? What is really happening here?' he asks himself again.

As he lies down, Rita and Lorenzo scuttle onto some cushions next to him. From there, they examine his pale face. So does Bones, who with his forepaws on the bed, leans over to Walter.

"Are you all right?" he wants to know.

"Yes, yes, I am fine now," Walter answers. "Maybe just a bit tired. We have travelled long distances, and it has been a hectic day so far, with more to come, I am sure."

"Don't worry too much," Rita tries to encourage Walter. "After you have rested for a bit, things might not feel so gloomy anymore."

"I suppose so," Walter responds. "I think it is best if we all sleep a little."

"Good idea," Lorenzo retorts. He immediately tucks his head underneath his feathers, already on his way to dreamland. Rita follows his example and Bones does not need any urging either. Making himself comfortable on a soft rug next to the bed, he is asleep within seconds and so is Walter.

The gong for dinner awakens them. By then, it is already getting dark, as Walter discovers. No matter, thanks to Erwin, who has laid out his clothes beforehand, it does not take him long to get dressed. In the shortest possible time, they walk out into the passage, where their silent servant is waiting. With him leading the way again, they go downstairs and walk over to the dining room.

Bones, as usual, is at Walter's heels and Rita and Lorenzo are each perched on one of Walter's shoulders. A festive sight greets them. Candles are flickering everywhere, their lights sparkling and dancing merrily in the profusion of crystal chandeliers and vases. The vases are filled with flowers in an abundance of colours. Servants, smartly dressed in white uniforms, are lining the walls. Queen Miranda adds even more magic to this whole fairy tale atmosphere. Coming towards them in a glittering, silver evening gown, she looks like a dream.

"Aah, there you are," is her welcome. "Did you have a nice rest?"

"Yes, very much so, thank you, your Majesty," Walter answers while bowing slightly. On the queen's outstretched hand to him, he places a gallant kiss. His reward is the dazzling smile that so enhances the queen's beauty.

"I hope you have built up an appetite," are her next words. Without waiting for Walter to answer, she takes his arm and continues. "Shall we then take our place at the dinner table?"

"Only with pleasure, your Majesty," Walter responds. Soon, they are seated. Walter is next to the queen, while Bones lies down close by, but out of the way. This is just as well, because at once, all the servants spring into action. Having first assisted with placing the queen and her honoured guest at the long table, they now start bringing on one silver platter after another with fine food. All pleasing to the eye and spreading the delicious aromas of exciting spices around.

Rita and Lorenzo, meanwhile, have left Walter's shoulders and flown to the courtyard. The extensive amount of fruit and seeds there are actually more to their liking than the food on the queen's table.

"They will come back after dinner for our evening of music making, I hope?" the queen asks.

"But of course they will come back in time, your Majesty," Walter assures the queen. "Rita would not want to miss out on this and Lorenzo surely will also be at the party. Only, please do not expect him to make any contribution to it at all! He can sometimes act very strange when asked to perform."

"I won't," the queen laughs, and Walter anew wonders, "How much does Queen Miranda know about them all? Does she really have a magic mirror and can it show her what happens even in places as far away as the palace of King Frederik?" He does not get much time to ponder about this, because the queen demands all his attention. Asking him how things are on the other side of the river and telling him how she enjoyed the time when King Frederik's father was still alive.

"You may have heard. We had enormous festivities then, with lots of people coming over who stayed for a long, long time. Aah, yes, they were good times," the queen sighs. She then asks Walter about his past and how he eventually came to the palace.

"How interesting," the queen cries out, when Walter relates to her his time with the circus of Mr. Landini. She just can't hear enough of it, asking for more and more tales about what took place there. "Tell me which circus acts were performed, please, and what did you do?" Her laughter is genuine when hearing what Lorenzo always did. Playing up by throwing tantrums and how people loved it. All these stories amuse her enormously and so, dinner time passes quickly, while the queen and Walter enjoy each other's company.

"Great," the queen remarks at last. "I had a great evening and even greater, it is not over yet. Shall we go to the music room?"

"Only with pleasure, your Majesty," Walter answers, returning her smile and bowing. Then, taking the queen's arm which she holds out to him, the two of them leave the dining room.

Through the passage they go and Bones quietly follows. By the flickering light of torches adorning every nook and cranny, they soon enter another beautifully furnished room. Most eye-catching though, is the variety of musical instruments on display here. In all sorts and sizes, they come. Hanging from the walls, standing in corners. Walter is very keen to study them one by one. But the queen has other plans.

Walking over to a spinet with a small seat in front of it, she settles down and starts playing.

Walter is amazed by the exquisite performance that follows. A simple folk tune, he knows well, cleverly adapted and enhanced by the queen into a light-hearted tune.

The Queen, as she gazes up to Walter, smiles at the surprised expression on his face. "Years and years of practice and lonely evenings," she calls out to him.

Walter can only nod. Yes, he understands.

At this moment, through the open door, Rita and Lorenzo make their entrée. Rita, at `once, flies over to Queen Miranda and perches herself on the back of a nearby chair. Enchanted, she listens. Lorenzo has found a place for himself on one of the window sills and wisely decides to keep quiet, very quiet.

When the queen ends her performance, she turns to Walter and gracefully, with a bow of her head, accepts his applause and compliments over her magnificent playing.

"And now I want to hear from you, my dear friends," she then addresses both Walter and Rita.

"Yes, I will get my flute, your Majesty," is Walter's answer, but the queen waves her hand while uttering, "No need, it is here already."

Erwin, carrying Walter's flute, enters the room and hands it over to him. Bones softly growls from deep within his throat, because he does not like this man so close to Walter, upon which this weird figure hastily makes his retreat.

Rita is on Walter's shoulder as he puts the flute to his lips. As so many times before, their sound melts in perfect harmony. One lovely melody after the other, dazzling and joyful. The queen does not want them to stop. Over and over, she waves them on. Her face glowing with happiness. When at long last, Walter takes the flute from his mouth, Rita also stops singing. The queen's applause for both of them, is long and well meant.

"This was absolutely splendid," are her words. "Fabulous and splendid."

"Thank you, your Majesty," is Walter's answer to this praise, while Rita also thanks the queen by bowing her little head.

"And now we can make music together," the queen announces. "I have been looking forward to this for a long time! But first, let's have something to drink. I am thirsty and so, I suppose, are both of you." Pulling a nearby bell cord, immediately has the result of a servant entering the room. He carries a tray full of refreshments.

Serving first the queen and then Walter, he also puts a little bowl of water on the table. "This is for you Rita," Queen Miranda laughs. "Surely, we must not forget our other guests now, must we?"

"Thank you, your Majesty," Rita chirps while flying over to the water bowl.

The queen and Walter both watch as she, little by little, drinks. Another servant, in the meantime, has rolled out a little carpet in a room corner. On this, he puts a large bowl with food for Bones. "You must be hungry by now, Bones," the queen remarks.

"Yes, I sure am," Bones responds, and the queen seems to understand.

While Bones enjoys his meal, the queen turns her attention to Lorenzo. "What can we arrange for you, my dear?" she asks.

But Lorenzo, who is still sitting on the windowsill, just shakes his feathers. "Nothing for me, your Majesty," he answers. "Thank you very much, but I really have no need for anything."

"Ooh well, then we can go back to what we came here for, making music together," the queen declares. Having finished her drink, and noticing Walter has as well, she goes on, "Shall we?" Placing herself in front of the spinet again. she lightly plays a few notes.

Walter recognises them. This is how the national anthem begins. While walking up to the spinet, flute at his mouth, he has no problem following the tune. Neither has Rita, who has taken her place on his shoulder again.

As Walter stands next to the queen, the three of them play in perfect harmony, this old, old melody. This song, that has been sung for so many years by all the people of the land. And afterwards, the queen goes on, playing to her heart's desire, the music she likes most. One ballad after the other, while Walter and Rita accompany her effortlessly. For a very long time they go on, until, at last, the queen lets her fingers rest on the spinet.

"This will do for tonight," she says, "Or, what do you two think?"

Rita bows her little head in agreement while Walter sighs. "I think so too, your Majesty." He is more than impressed by the queen's playing. And also again, by her great beauty, as she shakes her flaming red curls while looking at him with those enormous brilliant green eyes.

"It must be quite late," the queen adds. "Bedtime, I suppose. You must be tired after your long journey and then this busy day here at the castle, on top of it, as well."

"It has been a bit overwhelming indeed," Walter responds.

"Well then, you are excused," Queen Miranda smiles. "It was a remarkable day for me, too. So, let's say goodnight for now. We can all go upstairs together. Tomorrow will be another day for us to get to know each other even better. Shall we go then?"

After first bowing gallantly, Walter follows the queen as she leaves the music room. Bones trails behind them, while Rita is still on Walter's shoulder. Then Lorenzo takes his place on the other available one. Walking through the wide passage, they soon reach the stairs. Up, they go again, with the queen talking about the weather and how nice it is that the long summer days keep going on and on. At Walter's rooms, where Erwin already is waiting, she halts.

"Sleep well, my dear friends," she says. "I hope you have a good night's rest."

"Of that, I am sure, your Majesty," Walter answers. "Thank you for a delightful day and evening."

"The pleasure was mine," the queen assures him. Walking away to her own apartments, she looks back with a smile and a wave of her hand. Walter again, bows. Erwin opens the door and again, Bones can't help growling at him. One can see this servant is not mad about Bones, either. He almost looks ready to run away. Instead, he quickly closes the door once they are all inside.

"I can smell him, even from here," Bones mutters. "Or what am I saying," he goes on. "Even when he is much further away, I can still smell him. I do not like it. I do not like it at all. It reminds me of something, although I can't recall exactly of what! But here he is, by day and by night, spying on us all the time, I think."

"Yes, you may be right, Bones," Walter admits. "Well, we have to talk things over, the four of us. Let's just do it softly so no one can hear us. We must try and sort out our position." With these words, he walks down to the next room and sits down on the bed there. His face bears a bewildered expression.

Lorenzo is the first to speak, talking as softly as he can manage. "Right," he says. "Rita and I found out lots of things."

"Good," Walter replies. "Let's hear all of it."

"Now," Lorenzo begins. "Tonight, as you know, we flew off into the courtyard. For some time, we took shelter in the greenery, just in case someone was watching us. However, after a while, it became clear, no one did, not even Erwin."

"I suppose all the servants were busy in the dining room or kitchen," Walter says. "I don't know about Erwin, though. Anyway," he goes on. "What happened next?"

"We flew away again," Rita utters. "We wanted to try to find out of what is really going on around here."

"And we did!" Lorenzo chips in.

"Yes?" Walter urges him on.

"Now wait for it," Lorenzo responds. "It is indeed, as the king told you. This Queen Miranda is all he said she is."

"You mean she truly is a bad witch?" Walter whispers.

"Yes, that is the truth," Lorenzo states simply.

"My, my, in what sort of make believe story are we finding ourselves in then I wonder?" Walter cries out. Adding, "It is all so confusing. I don't know what to think of it anymore. The way we were received, the warm welcome and the queen's kind words. Can anyone be so deceiving? But go on Lorenzo. To whom did you speak and what was said?"

"I spoke to Oscar, the wise old owl who lives in one of the towers," Lorenzo answers. "When Rita and I flew up there, he was waiting for us. Oscar knows everything. He knows how friendly the queen behaved towards us. But Oscar says it is all play-acting, a fantasy, that's what it is,"

"Can it really be so?" Walter sighs. "She seems so truly nice. I almost started liking her."

"The king did warn you," Rita chirps.

"Yes, yes, I know and that is just it," Walter sighs. "How could I, even for a short time, have failed to heed his words? But she seems so sincere."

"The queen must have put a spell on you," Bones moans.

"No, I don't think so," Walter replies. "But let's go on, my friends. What more did the owl have to say?"

"Ooh," Lorenzo continues; "Oscar advises us to leave as soon as possible. He says you should forget about trying to defeat her. The queen is wicked and cunning. She scares everybody around here. Farmers and townspeople alike. She takes all the money she can get from them. That is why the population is very poor and the land barren. The servants at the castle are paid a pittance, and they all dislike her."

"Yes," Rita takes over from Lorenzo. "At first, the queen gave all those lovely parties the king told you about. But that changed after the old king died. From then on, she started stashing money away. Oscar tells us she hides it in the towers."

"My, my," Walter sighs. "Isn't this awesome? I most certainly like to meet this Oscar."

"Yes, we must arrange that," Rita agrees.

"Oscar wants to speak to you too," Lorenzo joins in. He goes on, "Oscar also told us the queen spends hours and hours looking into a magic mirror. Not only does it show her what is going on in the land, she also talks to this mirror."

"Yes, and the mirror talks back to her," Rita adds. "What?"

Walter reacts, not believing his ears.

"Yeah, Oscar heard the queen speaking to another witch. He saw an old woman's face appearing in the mirror. That woman tells her what to do."

"My my," Walter utters again in total amazement. "Could Oscar hear what they were talking about?" he inquires.

"No, not all of it," Lorenzo answers.

"He did hear some things," Rita says. Oscar says the witch in the mirror talked about giving the queen another hundred years. But only if she can deliver something or someone.

"Another hundred years?" Walter responds. 'For delivering something or someone? Hm, it makes me wonder. Could this someone be King Frederik? Well, this throws a whole new light on the situation here.'

"Anyway," he goes on, "Thank you Rita and Lorenzo, you did very well."

"Ooh, but this is not all," Lorenzo declares.

"So, there is still more to come, then?" Walter gasps.

"Yes, there is," Lorenzo answers. "The first thing we should do tomorrow morning is to take a walk, Oscar says."

"Why?" Walter wants to know.

"Because," Lorenzo replies dramatically. "At the back of the castle, behind the first rows of trees, lies an army in waiting."

"Ooh nooo," Walter wails.

"Oooh, yes," Rita chirps.

And Lorenzo concludes, "That's how it is!"

"What do we do now?" Bones, who has just been listening so far, asks.

"We have to confront Queen Miranda," Walter declares. "It is the only way."

"When?" Rita wants to know.

"Why not now?" Lorenzo asks.

"We can't," Bones grumbles. "Erwin is still on guard at the other side of the door. I can, of course, try to overpower him," he adds hopefully.

"No," Walter says. "It is late. It might be better to leave things for now. Tomorrow we should feel calmer and better able to make the right decisions."

"Yes," Rita speaks up, "I agree with Walter."

"I have no problem with that," Lorenzo replies.

"And neither have I," Bones admits. Putting his head on his front paws, and with one ear pointed upwards, to hear even the faintest sound, he dozes off.

"I think we should follow Bones' example," Walter suggests. "We need our strength, because there lies a busy day ahead of us, if you ask me."

It takes him a while to fall asleep, though. There are so many things to be concerned about. What will happen tomorrow? Will they be capable to get the upper hand over Queen Miranda? Over her, who acts so endearing, but has brought so much suffering to this land. And now she might even be planning to make King Frederik her prisoner.

Chapter XV

Erwin wakes them the next morning with a sumptuous breakfast tray. Fresh baked, crusty bread, butter, creamy cheese and boiled eggs, milk and fresh fruit. It is curious to see how Erwin looks at Rita and Lorenzo. They, in turn, shy as far as possible, away from him.

On the other hand, this weird creature tries at all costs, to keep at a distance from Bones. 'Well, that is no wonder, actually, seeing the way Bones behaves towards Erwin,' Walter ponders.

After breakfast, the four of them decide to go on an inspection tour. With Oscar the owl's words in mind, Walter first wants to find out more about this army, he mentioned. They go downstairs, into the hallway again. Here and there, a few servants are moving around, busy with some chores. They greet Walter respectfully.

Strangely enough, Erwin is nowhere to be seen. Walter, who half expected the mute servant to follow them, now wonders if Erwin is fearing Bones so much that he is unwilling to do so? 'It could very well be,' he muses.

By this time they have reached the front door, which is standing open, and they move on to the terrace. From there, down the steps leading to the gardens.

"Can you imagine it was only yesterday that we arrived here?" Walter asks his friends. No, they can't!

"It seems much longer," Rita chirps from his shoulder. Walking on, they soon round one of the castle's corners. A bit further still, rows of trees come into sight.

"It is just as Oscar described it," Lorenzo calls out.

"I suppose the army will not be far then either," Walter utters. And indeed, after going on a bit more, they see them. Rows and rows of army tents, with soldiers moving to and fro. It all looks very sinister to Walter and clearly, Rita as well as Lorenzo, feel the same. They at once fly up into the air, preferring rather to watch things from a safe distance.

"It might be wiser if we turn back here," Walter tells Bones.

"Good thinking," Bones answers. Just like his master, he is brave, but does not believe in needless risk taking. So the two of them turn back to the castle. Rita and Lorenzo follow their example.

"Interesting," Lorenzo remarks, after having settled himself anew on Walter's shoulder. He goes on. "Why is it that Queen Miranda has so many troops on her doorstep? Where does she need them for if it is not to take King Frederik prisoner?"

"A whole army to capture the king?" Bones asks.

"As far-fetched as this may seem, it could be true!" Walter responds.

"Yes and remember, the queen wants the king to come over here," Rita, giving her opinion, mutters. She has settled herself on Walter's other available shoulder, and starts pecking him lightly with her beak.

"Yes Rita, I remember. Stop pecking my ear, please," Walter laughs. "Anyway," he goes on, "Let's go inside and see how things go from here. I suppose the queen will be up by now."

He is right. Queen Miranda meets them as they enter the sun room. "Aah, there you are," she greets them. "Good morning. Did you have a nice walk?"

"Good morning your Majesty," Walter answers. "Yes, indeed, we did. It is always so interesting to explore one's surroundings. My friends and I are really impressed by the lay-out of your Majesty's gardens."

"Thank you," the queen, with a bit of a puzzled expression on her face, replies. "Did you sleep well?" is her next question. But, without waiting for an answer this time, she goes on, "And your breakfast? Was everything in order?"

"It was a great breakfast, thank you your Majesty and yes, I slept very well," Walter informs the queen.

"Good, good," Queen Miranda responds. She leads them to the same corner of the room where they had their chat the day before. Sitting down, she invites Walter to do likewise.

As Rita and Lorenzo make their way to the courtyard again and Bones finds a place at Walter's feet, the queen asks, "Well, have you thought about our talk of yesterday?"

"Your Majesty?" Walter is stalling. He plans to take things very carefully from here.

"Surely you haven't forgotten?" the queen urges. Although she is just as beautiful as the day before, something about her has changed. Her hands seem to shake, her eyes are evasive.

"No, I have not forgotten, your Majesty," Walter answers. "It is just, I am not quite sure."

"What do you mean?" The queen inquires, her voice suddenly sounding tense.

"Well, I am not sure if it is such a good idea to have the king come over here," Walter answers calmly.

"Please tell me why not?" the queen reacts, her eyes glaring. She is looking at him directly now.

"Because," Walter answers. "I do not like the preparations that are being made for the king's arrival here."

"I do not know what you are talking about," the queen tells Walter. "Please explain!"

"I have seen your army at the back of the castle," Walter responds. "My friends and I went over there on our morning walk."

"You did?" Queen Miranda almost cries out. She brings a hand to her mouth as if to stop herself, but to late. "You were not supposed to," she whimpers. "Whatever happened to my servant, Erwin? He was expected to prevent you from going there."

"Erwin seems to be very frightened of Bones, your Majesty," Walter replies dryly. Bones, having followed the conversation, looks up and growls softly.

The queen, ignoring this, continues, "It does not matter now. However, I assure you, the army you saw has nothing to do with the king's possible visit. My army is busy with a training exercise, which is held here each year!"

"That might be so," Walter responds. "But I believe there is more to it than that. Strange things are going on here. Things that need to be clarified! Why, for instance, is it that your Majesty spends so much time in one of the tower rooms, speaking to a mirror?"

"How do you know about this mirror?" the queen asks in bewilderment.

"Oscar the owl, who lives in one of the castle's towers, told my friends Rita and Lorenzo. I am sure your Majesty is informed of me being able to understand and talk to animals and birds?"

"Yes I am," Queen Miranda admits simply.

"Well, this puts me at an advantage, of course," Walter goes on. "My friends are always on the look-out for me. They tell me Oscar saw many things, and this was one of them. He also told them, someone in the mirror talks back to your Majesty. It seems there was some talk about another hundred years if your Majesty could deliver something or someone. I have a feeling this someone is no other than King Frederik himself, am I right?"

"Ooh no," Queen Miranda wails. "This is too much. You seem to think you know everything now!"

"Not everything," Walter replies. "I must say, this story with regard to all these paintings is not very clear to me yet. What does it all mean? Firstly, this island. Why should it disappear?"

"Because, once the island is no more, I am free," the queen cries out.

"Free from what?" Walter urges.

"Free from ever having to go back there, of course. I told you so," the queen exclaims. There are tears in her eyes as she looks up at him.

"But why would your Majesty have to go back there at all?" Walter wants to know.

"It is our law," the queen sighs. "Every witch receives one chance only. To gather a fortune and a kingdom if possible. We get one hundred years. After that, we must return."

"Aah, now it begins to dawn on me," Walter declares. "Let me guess, maybe those hundred years are coming to an end now. My, my, and in all those many years, the efforts to paint this island the correct way failed. Hmm, and then your Majesty's spies came with information about the journey I was going to undertake. Surely, everything about me and my stay at the court of King Frederik was known already to your Majesty. This wonderful magic mirror was a great help with that, I am sure. The rumour goes that this mirror can see far beyond anyone's imagination. So my coming here must have been great news, for it gave your Majesty another plan to work on. That is why you said; I am the only hope left now. Is it not so?"

The queen slowly nods her head.

"Right," Walter continues; "Now we come to the army that is stationed at the back of the castle. Why are they there? My conclusion is Your Majesty wants the king to come over here, so they can imprison him and his men." Although Walter is very polite, he is very determined as well.

The queen can see it in his eyes. While her attempts to trick Walter have come to nothing, she nevertheless does not give in yet.

"It is all such a pity," she sighs, "Yesterday was so perfect and I was so looking forward to spend some more time with you. Just think of our dinner last night. The music we made. Can't we go on like this together? With the vast fortunes I gathered, I could offer you a great life here, you know."

"No, no," Walter says firmly. "Please, your Majesty, this won't do. I think we must get back to what Oscar told my friends. About this other witch. Is she in charge of your Majesty?"

"Yes, she is," the queen admits.

"Well then, I wonder," Walter continues. "What was it that Oscar overheard? He told Rita and Lorenzo, this witch in the mirror spoke over another hundred years and a sort of agreement." Looking at the queen sharply, he sees her eyes widen and her mouth sag.

All at once aware that here lies the answer to his questions, he cries out, "Aah, that is how it is. I've got it! The first hundred years have more or less run out, but your Majesty has been given another chance for some more of the same. Another hundred years to live in this land would be great, I take it. Now, let me go on with this notion. Certain conditions had to be agreed to, of course. This entails securing the whole kingdom, which demands the arrest of King Frederik. As I said; that is why the army is here. Am I correct?"

The queen does not answer, but going by the expression on her face, Walter knows he is! "My, my," he goes on, "With the king as prisoner, Your Majesty could very well have succeeded in taking over this whole country. No doubt Princess Elina and I would suffer the same fate afterwards. Imprisonment and goodness knows what else. No wonder my coming here must have been such good news. No wonder I received such a warm welcome!.

"'You are my hope now,' your Majesty said. Indeed," Walter pauses for a moment, then he adds; "One thing though, aside from all this, what lies behind the hoarding of these fortunes your Majesty spoke about? Surely, it cannot be spent on this island alone?"

The queen suddenly laughs a very unpleasant laugh. "Ha, we do not really need it, you know. We just throw it into the sea," she says. "All these monies that you people work so hard for and cannot do without, it means little to us. No, our pleasure is in scheming it away from you and see people suffer from the lack of it."

It is another face Walter sees in front of him now. A cruel face with cold eyes and a strangely twisted mouth. Suddenly, Erwin, the bald servant, makes his appearance. He hides something behind his back and Walter senses it is a weapon. Maybe a sword?

The hairs on Bones back, at once, stand up straight. He bares his teeth and growls as Erwin slowly slinks towards them.

Standing up, Walter addresses him, "If you think of attacking me, Erwin," he says calmly. "Don't! It would not be very good for your health, nor for that of your queen. I advise you to turn around. Go back the way you came. Yes, to the hallway again, but not too fast."

Erwin, unexpectedly weak and timid, immediately surrenders to Walter's command. And indeed, as he turns, the sword he carries in his hands is there for all to see.

"Please, Your Majesty, follow your servant?" are Walter's next words.

Bones has had enough. With one leap, he is upon Erwin, yanking the sword away from him and placing it into Walter's outstretched hand. It is done in seconds.

"Thank you Bones, that was good work," Walter praises his friend. "My, my, just what I thought," he goes on. "A sword indeed."

Pointing it at the queen has the desired result.

The queen slowly stands up and, although furious, can do little else, then obey Walter's orders. They walk in eerie silence. The castle seems deserted. No servants to be seen. Most probably, they have taken cover somewhere, wondering what will happen next.

After the hallway is entered, the far corner is reached. Then Walter gives the next order. "Up the stairway, if you don't mind,

Your Majesty," are his words. With a wave of his hand, he spurs Erwin on to do the same.

The queen, while minding this sudden turn of events very much, does not say a word. The iron undertone in Walter's voice startles her, and she meekly follows his directions. There are more stairs to climb. Past the servants' quarters they go, but again no one comes into sight. However, Walter is sure many eyes are observing them.

It is a long way up before, at last, they come to a halt in front of a heavy bolted door.

By this time, Bones has moved on into the narrow passage where they now find themselves with Queen Miranda and her servant in the middle. It is closed off by Walter on the one side and by Bones on the other. There is no way out.

"Will Your Majesty please hand me the key to this door?" Walter asks.

The queen hesitates, "There is no key," she says at last. Her voice is faltering.

"No key?" Walter responds, "How does one open this door, then?"

"It is a … I have lost the key," the queen tries again.

"Aah, how amazing," Walter reacts. "Please, your Majesty, try to remember where it can be?"

"I have forgotten," Queen Miranda replies, avoiding his eyes.

But then they hear Lorenzo's voice, coming from an opening above their heads. "I know where it is," he calls out to them. "Rita and I are here. We both know that the queen hides this key in the magic room. Oscar told us. He says, it fits all the locks, and he showed us where to find it. Wait, I'll get it for you."

While he flies off, Walter addresses the queen. "See," he says. "That is what friends are for. And really, it does not help to resist us."

Soon Lorenzo is back. A yellow cord with a key on it dangles from his beak.

"Thank you Lorenzo, very good work," Walter praises him. Taking the key, he at once inserts it in the lock. After a few turns, the heavy door slowly swings open. It is not a large room that comes into view, but is filled with large bags.

Walter, stepping inside, sword still in hand, slits open one of them. Gold coins tumble out. Seeing some other bags are open, Walter puts a hand inside one of them. "My, my, this one is full of diamonds," he utters, holding some sparkling stones up into the air.

He finds pearls, rubies and sapphires and many other jewels gathered in the small room, all neatly in their own bags.

"There's lots more," Rita reports. "All the tower rooms are filled with treasures."

She, along with Lorenzo, flies in and out of the numerous slits and air vents each tower room has.

"Good," Walter responds; "Let's go and inspect those as well, shall we?"

Bones, constantly on the alert, while watching the queen and Erwin, now follows them further into the passage. Walter locks the door behind him and then follows close behind. It is indeed the same everywhere. All the rooms contain enormous wealth.

"Well, what Oscar said turned out to be very true," Walter remarks after some time.

"But of course," Lorenzo replies.

"Yes," Rita declares, "Oscar knows everything. He has been living in these towers for years and years,"

"And all alone too," Lorenzo adds. "Most other birds have disappeared, for this is not a nice place to be in anymore."

"No, the land and everything in it has gone to waste, as we saw for ourselves," Walter responds.

By now they have reached yet another tower room and Walter again tries out the key. Indeed, it unlocks this door as well. "My, my, it is hard to believe what my eyes see," Walter utters, as here too, bag upon bag, standing in rows, comes into view. All of them also, filled with gold and precious stones, as Walter soon discovers.

By this time, queen Miranda seems to have become very angry. "What If I were to call for my servants now?" she asks. "I have many of them, as you might have noticed."

"Yes, what if?" Walter responds, "I am afraid it would not help at all. Had they wanted to assist Your Majesty, no doubt they would have been here already. Does Your Majesty not think that behind those closed doors of the servants' quarters and everywhere else, we have not been seen or heard? I am sure the servants know what is going on. No Madam, I declare, they are no willing to come to your Majesty's rescue. From what I heard and observed, they are only too pleased with what is happening now."

"That's it, that's it," Lorenzo shrieks. "They don't like the queen at all!"

"Yes, yes," Rita chirps in. "If they were to come, it would be to help us!"

"Is that what Oscar says?" Walter laughs.

"Exactly," Lorenzo replies.

"Well, in that case, we won't worry too much about Your Majesty calling the servants," Walter says. He adds, "I think they are scared and are just waiting to see how things work out. As for Your Majesty's army, I do not believe they can be depended upon, either. Didn't Oscar have something to say about them too?" he asks his friends.

"Ooh yes," Rita offers some more information about this. "Oscar told us that the army is just waiting to take matters into their own hands. They have not been paid for months and are hungry and desperate,"

"My, my," Walter responds again. "As I expected, no help from the army either, Your Majesty. It seems to me, everything is lost. Not even the servant Erwin can assist anymore. See how he stands trembling there, next to Bones. I believe he is scared to death. But, let's not while away our time with all this," he adds. "There is so much to do still. May I ask Your Majesty to show us the tower from where this country is being watched? I suppose that is from where all the magic is performed? The spells, the abracadabra? The magic room with even a magic mirror?" Walter sees the queen's eyes light up.

"No, no," he says, "Please madam, don't get any ideas. Your Majesty will not be allowed in. Not with all this sorcery stored away in that place. There will be no change of putting a spell on me or my friends. No. We can't have any of that. Please, will Your Majesty lead the way, then?"

Much to her chagrin, the queen has to do as Walter asks. From the inner balustrade, they climb one stairway higher,

"This is it," the queen declares, surly at last, as she stops in front of yet another door.

"Right," Walter replies cheerfully. "And what is behind that small door here on the side?" he inquires.

"That is just a storeroom," the queen answers.

"Great," Walter responds. Then he says, "It grieves me to do this, but will Your Majesty be so good as to step inside after I have opened it?"

Unlocking this door takes only a moment. Walter makes a courteous bow and, with a gesture of his hand, invites the queen to enter. Without a word, Queen Miranda obeys.

"I see there are window slits here as well," Walter remarks. "They will provide enough fresh air and light, I am sure. And look," he adds, "As luck will have it, there is even a bed with cushions and blankets as well as a table and a chair to sit on. So, it has all the comforts one could wish for."

The queen still refuses to speak, but the disapproving expression on her face says more than enough. Walking over to the window slits, she starts staring through them. Walter softly closes and locks the door again.

A bit further away in the passage, they find even more storage rooms. "Very useful this," Walter remarks while looking at Erwin. "I am afraid it is your turn now," he says.

The strange figure, still shaking with fright, offers no resistance. He willingly steps into the small room that also has a settee and a little table.

"Not too bad. It really is not bad this," Walter utters as he also closes and locks that door behind him. "I almost feel sorry for them," he goes on. "How things have changed for Queen Miranda and her servant. And all in such a short time."

"It can't be helped," Rita chirps.

"One has to do what one has to do," Lorenzo utters.

"And this Erwin is not what he makes out to be," Bones growls. "I can just feel it."

A few moments later, they enter the magic room. Bones lies down, positioning himself so that he can oversee the whole passage. This way, nothing will escape his attention.

Rita and Lorenzo follow Walter and settle each on a windowsill.

Walter tries to take in all this room reveals. There are lots of books, some old and tattered, lying on tables. Shelves, with pots in all shapes and sizes, many of them, it seems, filled with herbs. Others have substances in garish colours. There is a fire grate which has embers still smouldering in it. An eerie green haze emerges from the large pot hanging over this fire place. It gives off a sickly sweet smell. Then Walter sees the mirror.

Slowly, he steps closer. Almost as in trance, he stares into the large looking-glass, forgetting everything else. It is not his own face he sees. No, far from it. It is a landscape that stretches out before him. Miles and miles of it. He sees hills and farms. Tiny villages and people in market places. Even the Yanta river, he observes further away. It is awesome and magnificent, stunning and alarming, all at once.

"How can this be?" Walter whispers. "How is it possible to see so much in a mirror?"

"Remember, this is not an ordinary mirror," Lorenzo howls.

"Hmm, yes, this is a magic mirror. It truly is," Walter sighs. He finds it difficult to turn away from these astounding visions.

Rita's sweet voice brings him back to his senses. "Come and see the landscape at this side, Walter," she urges. "From here, one can also look very far."

As Walter joins her. He finds out this is correct. Actually, the scenery unfolding before his eyes through the window slits is very appealing as well. The castle's lovely gardens with so many flowers and green lawns, the hazy hills further away. It is soothing and serene. By contrast, the magic mirror's images seem spooky. Still, Walter can't help himself. He just has to have another look. Standing in front of the mirror again, he stretches out his hand and touches the heavy wooden frame around it. To his amazement, the glass seems to cloud over and then starts revealing a different view.

"It is the king's palace," Walter gasps. "And there is the king, walking in the garden."

Rita and Lorenzo at once fly onto his shoulders and they see it too.

"Isn't this fantastic?" Lorenzo shouts. "Ai, Caramba, Caramba!" He has not used these words for a long time. Uttering them now shows how impressed he is.

"Yes Lorenzo, it really is miraculous," Walter declares. "No wonder Queen Miranda knows so many things."

"Indeed," Rita sings. "No wonder at all!"

For quite some time, the three of them get lost in the scene before them. It is so good to see the trusted figure of King Frederik calmly walking through the palace grounds.

"But come, let's go," Walter says at long last. "This is a weird place to be and we have other things to do."

Bones is glad to see them re-appear again. "Can we leave now?" he asks.

"Yes," Walter answers, "I think that will be best."

Going down the landing, they are in for another surprise. All the servants are standing lined up against the walls. They start clapping their hands and burst into cheers as Walter and his friends pass by. There are smiles on every face. No one has to tell them anything. They know what has taken place.

"Well done," they cry out. "Well done."

It truly pleases Walter and his group. "Thank you, thank you, I am sure it must be great to be free from Queen Miranda." Walter beams. "You will never have to serve under her again, that I can promise you. Soon, very soon, King Frederik shall rule this land anew."

"Hurrah, long live the king. Long live King Frederik," the servants joyfully shout back.

Walter raises his hand to calm them down. "This calls for a celebration," he announces. "You are free for the rest of the day. Have some fun, enjoy yourselves."

Loud cheers go up again after these words. "Hurrah, hurrah," the servants call out again, "Thank you." Laughing and talking excitedly, they run down the stairs. Walter and his friends are caught in the rush as well. A great feeling of happiness is spreading through the castle. It is stimulating and thrilling. When they land on the first floor, Walter stops in his tracks. Rita and Lorenzo are still on his shoulders, Bones on his side.

"I saw a balcony when we were at the back of the castle this morning," Walter utters. "Let's see if we can find it." He goes on, "I think it might be a good idea to address everyone from there."

As the servants rush on towards the ground floor, he starts opening a few doors. Soon, the room with the balcony is found. In no time at all, Walter finds himself looking down over the lawn, where the servants are gathering now. Soldiers are running towards them, curious to know what is going on.

"We are free," the servants call out to them. "The queen has been taken prisoner. Yes, yes, we are free!"

Their calls have the result of many more soldiers coming forward. They throw their soldier caps high into the air on hearing this news. And more and more are arriving. Every one of them wants to hear this good news. They can hardly believe it.

Bones is getting excited too and suddenly starts barking. This makes everybody look up to the balcony. By seeing Walter and his small group, a silence falls over the crowd beneath. Then, a spontaneous applause rises up. Hands start waving up into the air, followed by shouts of joy. Soldiers and servants stream closer to the balcony where Walter is waving back.

"Yes, it is true," he announces in a loud voice. "Queen Miranda's rule has ended! Long live King Frederik!"

A mighty roar of approval rises towards the balcony. "Long live the King," Walter hears. "Long live King Frederik!"

"How absolutely wonderful this all is," Walter says to his friends.

"It truly is," Rita sings.

"For sure," Lorenzo yells. "Oscar was right. It makes everybody happy that the queen is gone."

Bones has stopped barking but keeps on wagging his tail. He is so glad to be standing here next to Walter, away from the queen and, better still, away from Erwin. Walter raises his arms above his head to get the attention again of the people gathering on the lawn below. After a last; "hurray," they quieten down, eager to hear what Walter's message will be.

"Today is an outstanding day for our country," Walter begins. "At long last, you and we, from the other side of the river Yanta, have become one nation again. Being sent here by our king, to try to make this happen, I am very pleased to tell you, that is exactly what we did! I must add," he continues, while loud cheers are rising up anew. "I must add, my friends played a large part in this." Walter points to the birds on his shoulders.

"This," he says, taking Rita into his hands and showing her off to the crowd, "This is Rita the red robin."

Soldiers and servants shout their approval as Rita dives out of Walter's hands, flies over their heads and then after finishing a graceful circle, lands back on his shoulder.

Next, Walter presents Lorenzo. "This is Lorenzo," he announces. Lorenzo follows Rita's example, only, he circles a few times over the spectators while shouting; "Well done, well done," This brings about loud laughter from everyone. As Lorenzo also flies back onto his shoulder, Walter goes on, "My flying friends made exceptional spies, I can tell you. And here we have Bones. He is a dog like no other I know of. A true friend and buddy who protected me all this time and also, with great danger to himself, saved my life."

After these words, the cheers seem unending, and Walter and his friends are a bit overcome by all this enthusiasm. More of the same results, when Walter goes on to say, "You are all off duty for the rest of the day. Let's have a celebration!"

As Walter and his group withdraw from the balcony, joyful singing follows them. "Good, that's that," Walter sighs with relief. "Now, let's see what next needs to be done."

They go down the last staircase and find the kitchen staff gathering around them. Eager to help with the celebration, they have come back in. Everyone is in a festive mood and the head chef wants to know what he can do first.

"First, you do what you like doing most," Walter answers with broad smile. "You people can brew and cook up everything you can think of, for lunch, midday snacks, dinner. As long as it is extra special, not alone for us, but for everyone around here. Do you have enough supplies for that?"

"O yes sir," is the head chefs reply. "More than enough. The kitchens store rooms are overflowing with food. Come on, all of you," he calls out to his helpers; "Let's start at once!" With that, he and his staff march on to the kitchen, singing and smiling while they go.

"Right," Walter chuckles; "And that takes care of that! Now from you Lorenzo, I would like to hear, can you take a message to the king?"

"Only with pleasure," Lorenzo answers. "It will be an honour to do so. What is it you want me to say?"

"Whatever you want, as long as you ask the king to come over here to take possession of this land. It is all his again. And another thing," he adds, "You better return together with the king and his entourage. Otherwise, it will be too tiring for you. Tell the king, I will have three coaches waiting for his Majesty, at this side of the river. I am sure this can be arranged. There must be some coaches available around here. I will see to that, of course."

"Of course," Lorenzo replies. Then he asks; "When can I go?"

"It is very urgent," Walter responds.

"I am on my way!" Lorenzo declares at once.

Walter walks with him to the courtyard, and from there, Lorenzo takes off.

"Goodbye, we wish you luck," Walter calls after him, as do Rita and Bones.

"Goodbye," Lorenzo calls back. He is happy and proud. Walter has chosen him to bring the king the good news.

"Well, what else?" Walter asks out loud, even before Lorenzo has faded from sight.

"What about Queen Miranda?" Rita wants to know. "What is going to happen to her? Does she have to stay in that tower room?"

"Yes, sadly, I cannot think of another solution," Walter answers. "I will make sure though, a fine supper is prepared for the queen and shall deliver it myself."

"That sounds good," Rita chirps.

"And let's not forget Erwin," Walter says.

"That is very hard to do," Bones grumbles.

"I still can't get over it. How smooth everything went," Rita remarks. "Why did the queen just give in?"

"I think it all came too sudden," Walter replies. "Moreover, the queen was so sure of having deceived us. She never foresaw that a very wise owl would give her game away. When I confronted Queen Miranda this morning already, she was unprepared for it. From that moment on, she had no chance of doing anything else than following orders. And," he goes on, "As luck would have it, our coming over here happened just at the right time."

"Ooh?" Bones utters. "What do you mean?"

"Well, I don't think to be mistaken by guessing, the queen's first hundred years here are more or less over!" Walter replies.

"Aah, if that is so, then the queen spoke the truth," Rita reacts. "Her Majesty did indeed pin her hopes on you and the king."

"Precisely," Walter agrees. "Only, she did not tell us the whole truth, though."

"No, the queen tried to keep that a secret but it came out soon enough," Bones utters.

Suddenly, there is a rustling of leaves in the tree branch above them. Looking up, they see a lonely owl.

"Hello, you must be Oscar," Bones greets him.

"Yes, that's me!" the owl answers.

"Hello," Rita sings "Good to see you, Oscar. It is so nice you have come to meet Walter and Bones."

"The pleasure is mine," Oscar replies.

Walter smiles at him. "I am glad and grateful you have come," he says. "Your warnings about Queen Miranda, to my friends Rita and Lorenzo, brought me to my senses. It made me face the truth again. Thank you for that."

"I am happy it worked," Oscar answers. "Maybe this was the reason I stayed on here, all those long years. Anyway," he goes on, "Congratulations, that you acted so quickly and took the queen prisoner. Now I am free to go. I can tell you, it became very lonely in the end. I would love to see some other owls for a change. Do you think I may find any somewhere? They all seem to be gone, as are the other birds."

"Where we come from, there are lots of birds, including owls," Walter replies. "I am sure they will soon come flying over here, now that this land belongs to King Frederik again."

"Good," Oscar sighs, "I think I will go and look for them then. In the meantime, keep well and goodbye to you all!" Slowly flapping his wings, he takes off into the air.

"Farewell," Walter calls after him, and so do Rita and Bones.

Once he is gone, Walter wants to move on as well. Lots of matters still need his attention. Turning around to leave the courtyard, he sees someone marching towards him. It is a man in uniform. Bones growls from deep under his throat. "It is all right, Bones," Walter quietens him. "Let's hear what the man has to say."

Coming nearer, and after a respectful salute, the person in front of him says; "Sir, may I present myself? My name is Captain Olivier Smith. I have come to put my troops under the king's command."

"Good, that is great," Walter responds. "I am glad you came, Captain. As it happens, I was at the point of going over to your army camp."

"Yes sir," the Captain replies, standing at attention while saluting Walter again. "What are your orders, sir?"

"Well," Walter answers, "There are several things that need to be done. Firstly, I need three coaches with horses, in a hurry. King Frederik needs those once he is on this side of the river. For the heralds, there should be at least four extra horses as well. Please see to it. The coachmen may have to wait a while for the king to arrive. Enough food and tents for shelter must be provided. The royal kitchen, I am told, is very well stocked, so food should be no problem. Tell the head chef I send you, he will be pleased to help."

"It will be taken care of, sir," the Captain assures Walter.

"Fine," Walter replies. "Then, I want you to select a group of your men to go from farm to farm and village to village. They have to spread the good news. The good news is that King Frederik is coming here. That he is king of this whole country now, because Queen Miranda has been defeated!"

"Yes sir, straight away sir," the Captain answers. Looking into Walter's eyes, his face suddenly broadens with a warm smile. "Asking your pardon sir," he says, "but my staff and all my soldiers asked me to let you know how pleased we are about this change. My men and I have great respect for what you did, sir, and we want you to know that!" Saluting smartly again, he deftly turns around and marches away.

"Nice," Bones says. "Very nice!"

"Yes, isn't it just?" Walter laughs, while Rita, who is still on his shoulder, happily chirps along.

Noticing Bones sniffing the air, she teases, "You are smelling food, is it not?"

"Hmm, hmmm, yes," Bones admits and indeed, Walter smells it too now. A tempting aroma wafts over and up into the courtyard.

"Shall we go and see what is cooking?" Walter asks Bones.

"Only with pleasure," Bones replies eagerly.

"I rather stay here," Rita announces. "This is a much better place to be, for a little bird like me."

"Fine," Walter agrees as she flies away from him. "Bones and I will see you later, then."

Following their nose, they soon find the kitchen, where lots and lots of pots are simmering and bubbling on large stoves. The head-chef and his helpers are busy with stirring and chopping, kneading, and many other tasks. As soon as Walter and Bones arrive, the whole staff seems to bubble over from pleasure as well. They start clapping their hands, while the head-chef welcomes them with a big smile. "Sir, it is a real honour to have you here with us."

"Thank you," Walter smiles back. He adds, "I must admit, hunger also played a part in this. With all that happened, we completely forgot about lunch."

"Ooh, but please allow me to prepare some food for you, sir. Some delicacies on a plate, perhaps? Just enough to still most of the hunger pangs without spoiling the appetite for tonight's dinner?"

"Yes, that sounds splendid," Walter replies. "And could you give my friend Bones something to eat as well?"

"But of course, sir," the head-chef enthuses. "We'll do that at once!"

He gives some orders to one of his helpers and in the shortest possible time, a bowl of delicious food is placed in front of Bones.

"Oh good, good," Bones raves, eating with gusto.

"Please forgive me, sir," the head-chef addresses Walter again. "Your platter just takes a little bit longer to prepare, because of the different savouries I like to put on it."

"Don't worry, I can wait," Walter smiles. Leaning against the table where the chef prepares his food, he asks, "By the way, what is your name? Did I hear someone call you Master Bernard?"

"Yes, that is correct, sir," comes the answer back to him. Without even looking up, Bernard goes on with his work. He wants everything to be perfect for Walter, who already has won everybody over, with his charm and ready smile.

"Can we lay the table in the dining room?" one of the helpers wants to know.

"For one plate of food?" Walter replies. "No, there is no need for that. I will take my plate to the sunroom and eat there. You all just go on with the preparations for tonight's dinner. Oh, and before I forget, you can expect Captain Olivier Smith here as well this afternoon. He will require extra food supplies for the coaches that are going to fetch King Frederik from this side of the Yanta river. I told him there is enough?"

"For sure, sir," Bernard answers. "The king is coming then?" he asks anxiously and Walter notices the whole kitchen staff listens with full attention.

"Yes," he smiles. "Indeed, King Frederik will be here shortly."

There is even more excitement now in the kitchen. Master Bernard sums it all up when he says. "We can hardly wait, sir. It will be such a great occasion."

"Absolutely," Walter agrees. "I am just as thrilled about this as you all are." He goes on, "Oh, there is something else I would like to ask you."

"No problem, sir," Bernard replies. He adds, "Things go so smoothly here. Dinner will be served on time, and I still have enough free moments left for any other requests."

"Well, in that case, you can prepare two more trays with food for me," Walter says. "I want to take them up to our prisoners, Queen Miranda and her servant Erwin. And, thank you Bernard, this plate of food which you are preparing for me, it is more than enough now. Thank you."

"Right, sir," Bernard replies, while handing the tray to Walter. "Do you want those extra trays brought to the sun room sir?" he asks.

"Yes, that will be great," Walter declares.

Bones, who has already emptied his bowl of food, is waiting for him at the door.

"See you all later again," Walter calls out, as they leave. The return greetings follow them well into the passage. Once in the sunroom, Walter places his tray on one of the small tables next to a settee. "This is nice," he sighs, sitting down. "Would you like some of my food, Bones?" he asks. "There is so much, I won't be able to eat it all by myself."

But Bones has had enough to eat. "No thank you, I am full," he replies, stretching his whole length on the floor.

"O well, that's good then," Walter laughs. "Ah, this tastes delicious," he declares after taking a few bites. "Master Bernard sure knows what he is doing."

"Ahem, you are talking about me, sir?" a voice behind him wants to know. Master. Bernard, followed by an assistant, has walked in. They each carry a platter of food on a tray.

"Indeed," Walter admits, turning towards them. "My, my, these platters look superb," he remarks. Pointing to a large table in a corner, he says; "Yes, you can put it there. The other one as well, please," he tells the assistant, who wavers a bit in the background.

"Right sir, right away sir," the young man answers nervously, while doing as Walter asks. He is overcome by Walter's presence and by what he has achieved. That he defeated Queen Miranda, this person, who maybe even younger than he is. It is remarkable, truly remarkable. As far as that is concerned, he, like all the other people in and around the castle, share the same thoughts.

"Is everything in order, sir?" Master Bernard asks,

"Absolutely," Walter declares, adding, "I wonder if we could have some milk as well? Some for myself and also some to go with the other two platters?"

"Of course, sir, it will be brought directly," Bernard answers.

"Good and thank you," Walter says. "You did well."

After bowing respectfully, the head chef and his helper return to the kitchen. Within minutes, they are back. This time, bringing three jugs, filled with milk and also three glasses.

"Aah, excellent," Walter exclaims. "I am very thirsty now." He watches as the head chef pours some milk for him and then drinks eagerly. Wiping the last drops from his lips, he adds; "I need some help to carry these trays with food and the milk upstairs. Can I borrow your assistant for a while, Master Bernard?"

"Yes sir, of course you can," comes the answer at once. "His name is Edward and he will be very happy to help out, aren't you Edward?"

"Yes Sir, I am," the young man hastens to answer.

"Good," Walter declares. "Thank you Bernard. Edward will shortly join you in the kitchen again, then."

"Thank you sir," the head chef replies, before he, with a bow, disappears. Just after he is gone, a somewhat older servant enters the room. "My name is Ruben, sir," he presents himself. "Master Bernard told me you may need some more help with those trays."

"Good man," Walter smiles. "If we each take one, then Edward can carry the milk."

So it is done and soon the small group, followed by Bones, starts mounting the many stairs to where the prisoners are kept. A bit out of breath, they at last reach the room that holds Erwin.

"Right," Walter says. "Let me first get the key now." He puts down the tray and reaches for the yellow cord dangling around his neck. For such a valuable item, he finds this the safest place. So, after opening the door, the key on its cord returns there again. Edward follows him into the room while Ruben and Bones wait outside. Walter puts the tray with food on a small corner table. He then takes one glass and one jug with milk from Edward. "Please place the other jug and glass on the floor next to Bones," he tells him. As Edward does so, he adds, "You may go now, because I think you are urgently needed in the kitchen. That goes for you as well, Ruben," he addresses the other helper. "Thank you both for your assistance, but it is better that you leave now."

"Yes sir, goodbye sir," they answer almost as with one voice. Both of them seem a bit scared and, rather hurriedly, they scurry downstairs again.

"Well," Walter says, "Let's see then how our servant Erwin is. Erwin?" he calls out. Coming from the lighter outside into the small, darker room, he only now detects a cowering figure huddled on the floor, making no attempt to respond. Coming nearer, Walter observes shivers raging through the body in front of him.

'Something very weird is taking place here,' he feels. Something beyond his understanding. Bones is in the doorway now, growling with bared teeth. Still, there is no reaction from Erwin. He does not even seem to notice them. 'The best thing to do,' Walter decides after a short while, 'is to leave him be.'

Bones' growling has become a soft whining from deep within his throat.

"My, my, let's quickly go Bones," Walter utters. Acting upon that, they both turn around and Walter carefully closes and locks the door behind them.

"Phew, that was dreadful," he says with a shudder. After this, they come to the room where Queen Miranda is. Very cautiously now, Walter unlocks the door. Queen Miranda's back is turned towards him. She is seated near the window slits, looking out over the land she once possessed. While Bones takes his post at the door, Walter places the food and milk onto a nearby table.

"Good afternoon your Majesty," he greets. As before, with Erwin, he gets no answer. "I brought a tray with food and milk," he tries again. The queen does not react. An eerie silence fills the room. Although Walter can only see Queen Miranda's back, he still notices some changes. Her whole figure has slumped and her golden red hair has lost much of its lustre.

'What is going on here?' he wonders.

"You must promise to bring me back," he hears the queen addressing him at last. But even here, he observes a difference. The queen's voice no longer is pleasant and sweet. Instead, it sounds cracked and very tired.

"Back to where, Your Majesty?" Walter asks.

"I must return to the witches' island," the queen says. "I told you, don't you remember?" Her last words almost end in a cry.

"Yes, Your Majesty," Walter replies, "I remember now!"

"Tomorrow morning, very early," the queen insists.

"Tomorrow morning," Walter repeats after her. He cannot do otherwise. The queen seems to be so desperate.

"I will have a carriage ready," he says

"You will bring me?" Queen Miranda urges.

"I will," Walter promises. "Can I get the servants to pack some things for your Majesty?"

"Ha, ha, no, no," the queen almost cackles. "Where I have to go, no baggage is needed. Only Erwin must come with me."

"It shall be done as Your Majesty requests," Walter agrees. He walks back to the door where Bones stands waiting. "I have to leave now, your Majesty," he says, "But," he adds, "luckily, I see there is even a bed in this room together with blankets and cushions. I hope your Majesty may have a good night's rest." With these words, he closes and locks the door behind him.

Going down the stairs again, he ponders, 'Can the promises he made be kept?'

"Is it the right thing to do?" he asks Bones, who has overheard every word spoken to the queen. "Should I not have handed her Majesty over to King Frederik rather?" he muses.

"I don't think so," Bones replies. "As far as I can make out, that island must be a horrible prison, anyway."

"Indeed," Walter agrees. "I believe it is better so. And another thing," he goes on, "It solves the problem of us having to imprison the queen and also, that dreadful Erwin. By the way, what do you make of him, shivering and shaking so much? Why was he crouched into a corner on the floor and did not even want to look up?"

"Yes, it was very strange," Bones answers.

"And the queen," Walter goes on, "She kept staring outside."

"Yes, she did." Bones mutters.

"Perhaps they can't stand the sight of us anymore," Walter remarks.

"Perhaps? I would say for sure," Bones declares.

"Yes, yes, of course, that is true," Walter admits. "But it does not explain everything. I feel there is more going on here than we can imagine."

So, it is a very quiet and puzzled twosome who arrive back in the hall where Rita is already waiting for them. Sitting on one of the stairs banisters, she is full of cheer.

"You must come and see," she enthuses. "Everybody is so happy, and Master Bernard is making so much food. And the army cooks are also busy with cooking enormous meals. They are all waiting for you now, Walter. They want to know what to do next."

"What? Ooh," Walter responds, a bit absentmindedly. "Yes, yes, of course, the food. Ah, that reminds me, I still want to drink some of that milk Master Bernard brought me. One gets thirsty after walking up and down all those stairs."

Entering the sun room again, he finds the half empty food tray and the glass with milk, just as he left it. Emptying the glass in one go, and feeling better after that, he utters; "And now, I want to forget about Queen Miranda and Erwin for a while. Let's see, where are all those people you say are waiting for me, Rita."

"On the lawn, are you coming?" Rita chirps, while flying in circles above his head, "Yes, yes," Walter laughs. "I am coming."

Along with Bones, he follows Rita to the lawn at the back of the castle. Soldiers and servants, each in their own colourful uniforms, are milling around. Army cooks tend to large pots, steaming over camp fires. The smell of food drifts through the air.

As soon as Walter is spotted, everyone is trying to get near him. They all want to shake his hands. Walter does not mind, for he is just as happy as they are.

"When will the king come?" is the most asked question to him. And, "I expect him in a few days," is Walter's answer every time. And, "Hurray to that," is the response he hears most often.

Then it is Master Bernard, the head-chef, who arrives at Walter's side. He looks a bit worried. "Excuse me, sir," he utters. "Dinner is ready. Will you come?"

"Aah," Walter reacts. "Dinner yes, of course." After thinking for a moment, he adds; "Wait, I have an idea. From what I heard and saw, there is an enormous amount of food prepared. Far too much, I would think, for just me and the workers here at the castle. Why don't we share with the soldiers? They have food shortages, I believe."

"Yes," master Bernard agrees. "That is a very good idea, sir. Having had a look at what is cooking over there in those pots hanging over the fires, it is really not all that good and very far from festive.”

“Well, you see?” Walter replies. “Let’s bring on the castle’s food, then. Bring it all here, ooh and don’t forget, we need something to drink also! Find tables and benches for us all, so that we can eat together and have a real good feast!” His words are followed by a spontaneous applause. Clearly, everyone within hearing approves. “Yes sir, it will be done as you say sir,” Bernard bows. He goes on, “I may need some extra help, sir.”

“No problem, I am sure,” Walter laughs. “Attention, attention,” he call’s out. “We need some volunteers. Anybody willing to help with the fetching and carrying of food, tables and benches, please come forward.” As Walter expected, there is no shortage of eager hands. Soon, headed by master Bernard, soldiers and servants, march off to the kitchen. “Good,” Walter smiles. “Now, let’s move about a bit, Rita, Bones, shall we?”

“I think I rather watch from that tree over there,” Rita responds, flying away from him, into the branches of a nearby old oak tree. Bones, as always, stays on Walter’s side. A lot of action is taking place all of a sudden. Tables and benches appear and are carried to open places. Army officers shout commands, but it all happens in a sort of agreeable way. There is a jolly mood all round.

Walter, strolling then here, then there, is warmly greeted by everyone. Greetings, which he returns in the same good humour as they are uttered. One of the army officers walks over to him. Saluting respectfully, he asks permission to speak. “Excuse me, sir,” he says, after a nod from Walter that he can go ahead. “My name is lieutenant Fernando Lopez, at your service, sir. My men and I, we thank you from the bottom of our hearts for freeing us from the reign of Queen Miranda.”

"You are very welcome," Walter smiles. He continues; "I am pleased to meet you and as a matter of fact, I think your services could come in very useful."

"Sir?" lieutenant Lopez asks.

"Yes," Walter replies. "I need a carriage and horses. Tomorrow morning at sunrise. Can you take care of that?"

"Yes sir, leave it to me sir," the lieutenant answers. Standing at attention, he again salutes and then marches off. No doubt, on his way to the stables, to command a carriage and horses for the next day.

"Good," Walter remarks to Bones, "I am sure that is going to be arranged." Bones wags his tail in agreement. Other officers come up to Walter as well, making themselves known and offering their services. They also invite him to join them at their table. All of them want to declare their loyalty to King Frederik and to Walter, his ambassador. Walter accepts and soon is seated at the head of the officers' table, taking part in a lively debate. Captain Olivier Smith is also present and informs Walter his orders have been fulfilled.

"Ai sir," he says; while standing up and saluting smartly. "A large group of our soldiers are on their way to spread the good news of King Frederik's return. Also, the coachmen, with their coaches and finest horses, have gone to meet the king at the river Yanta. Master Bernard has supplied all of these men with enough food to last for days on end."

"Marvellous," Walter compliments the Captain. "Thank you, this sounds like you have done excellent work," With a chuckle he goes on; "Please sit down again, Captain, so that we can all have a discussion together. I want to find out more about the circumstances here."

"Yes sir, as you say sir," the Captain replies and, after saluting Walter, takes his seat at the table again.

Now a question-and-answer session starts. The officers want information about the situation on the other side of the river. Walter wants to know why everything on this side is in such a shocking state. Why was there no uprising? No protests? The answers he gets all come down to the same thing. Queen Miranda kept everyone under her spell. Only now that the spell had been broken by Walter, can things turn back to normal. This brings the discussion to the point where the matter of assistance comes up. Does Walter need any help? "You know, the army is at your command, sir."

But Walter declines. Apart from the messengers and coach he requested Captain Olivier Smith to take care of, he needs no further help at this stage. Of course, there is also the carriage and horses he requires for the next morning, but that has been attended to, as well.

"It is best to leave me and my friends on our own until this whole affair has been dealt with," he declares. "As you will understand, some things still need to be done. But, as before, we have to do them by ourselves."

At this precise moment, Master Bernard and his staff arrive with fare that really is enough for a whole army. They carry meat and fish and salads, pastries, refreshments and still more food. The army cooks bring what they have prepared as well. This exists mainly of potatoes and leeks, but is welcomed anyway.

So, with all this sustenance, it becomes a huge feast. Everybody is happy and in a merry mood. There is much singing and now and then, a fresh; 'hurray, for king and country' can be heard. Many praises are also heaped on Walter and his friends, for they made it all happen.

The three of them become a bit overwhelmed by all this. Bones hides his head between his forepaws, while Rita, who is on Walter's shoulder again, tucks her head between her feathers.

Walter just smiles and waves his hands in front of him to indicate 'enough, enough.'

The festivities go on and on, but Walter later excuses himself and, together with Rita and Bones, slips away. Exhausted, he, at long last, arrives in his room at the castle. There, he gratefully tumbles into bed. Bones immediately falls asleep on the shaggy carpet in front of it and Rita, on the bed's headboard, is soon in dreamland as well. It is still half dark the next morning, when a knock at the door wakens them. Bones growls, but becomes silent when he recognises the voice of lieutenant Lopez.

"Good morning sir," they hear. "Your carriage and horses are waiting."

"Yes," Walter answers, at once wide awake. "Thank you, I am coming."

"At your service, sir," the lieutenant's voice comes from the other side of the door. "Will there be anything else, sir?"

"No, nothing else, lieutenant," Walter responds. "Thank you for your trouble. I do appreciate it."

"Not at all, sir," the answer comes back. "I am glad I could be of help, and a good day to you, sir." Then they hear his footsteps moving away.

"A good day?" Walter repeats out aloud. "I wonder how good a day it will be."

He is up by now and moving to the adjacent bathroom. "Are you coming with us?" he asks Rita. "Thank you, but eh, if you don't mind, I really can think of more pleasant things to do today," Rita replies.

"Yes, so can I," Walter declares. "O well," he goes on; "Then it is just Bones and me, this time."

Bones is ready to go. They leave the door open, so Rita will be able to fly over to the courtyard if she wants. There is no thought or time for breakfast. Shortly, they climb the stairs to the tower rooms again. All is strangely still in this very early morning hour.

Walter's heart is heavy with foreboding. How will the queen be? She behaved so weirdly the previous day. And Erwin? Will they find him sick? What with all the shivering and shaking? The answers to these questions lie beyond the massive doors they finally arrive at.

First, Walter opens the door of the room where Queen Miranda is. Like the evening before, she sits near the window slits, looking outside. The tray with food and milk, are untouched.

"Your Majesty?" Walter utters. There is no answer. "Your Majesty, the carriage is waiting," Walter tries again. The first rays of sunshine are now creeping into the room. As Queen Miranda slowly turns around, they touch her face and hair. Walter hears himself gasping and then, holding his breath, for, never in his life, has he been so shocked as at this moment. The queen's hair has gone silver grey. Her beautiful young face is no more. Instead, it is sagged and wrinkled. She seems to have shrunk too. This he sees, as she stands up and starts walking towards him. Long bony arms outstretched, as if to keep her balance. Those arms are horribly thin.

'This is like something out of a nightmare,' Walter thinks. He just stands looking, unable to speak. The queen, he knows, has vanished. This is the witch Miranda!! The queen does not speak either. She keeps on walking, avoiding his eyes. Past Walter and Bones she goes.

Bones seems to be just as astounded as Walter is. His bearing is stiff and tense, while his eyes follow the queen into the passage. In front of the door where Erwin is, she halts.

"O yes, Erwin," Walter trailing behind her, remarks. "Let's see how he is."

As he opens the door, Queen Miranda slips in before him, straight into the corner, where she picks up the little dark bundle lying there. Again, Walter putting his hands in front of his mouth, to not to make a sound, can hardly believe what he sees.

Bones, who is standing next to him now, cannot help growling The wretched old woman, turning towards them, is holding a miserable black cat in her arms.

"Erwin?" Walter asks. Only the slanting green eyes have not changed. They look at him and Bones with the same resentment and dislike as before. In dead silence, this small group, proceed to move on. Down the stairs, taking the first steps, to an awkward journey. The queen with her cat in front, Bones behind them,

376

followed by Walter. Because nobody is around so early yet, they reach the carriage without being seen.

Walter helps the queen inside and then Bones jumps on the bench opposite her. The black cat on the queen's lap cowers in fright, barely able to suffer Bones' presence so nearby. Walter takes the reins and spurs on the horses. Even they seem frightened.

With haste, they go galloping away. Walter knows it is his ghostly passengers that make them behave as they do. Only his soothing words keep them from bolting in fear. For hours they drive. Over fields and hills, on and on.

At long last, the horses get tired and slow down a bit. Still, there is no end to their journey in sight yet. No sea to be seen. The sun is already high in the sky before Walter notices the first sand dunes. He breathes a sigh of relief. The sea must be near now. Soon afterwards, they halt on top of a sloping dune. Walter is thrilled to be looking at a sparkling green sea, just below. Climbing down, he opens the carriage door and helps the queen to step out. Erwin, the black cat, lies still motionless in her arms.

"Well, your Majesty," Walter declares; "I suppose this is it. Here is the sea. But I wonder, where is Your Majesty's Island?"

While he speaks, something is happening. The sea begins to rumble, spewing up large masses of white foam. Round and round, the water starts to whirl. Then, waves are breaking with the sound of thunder. The sky begins to glow with eerie colours. Green and red and purple. Layer after layer, on top of each other.

'Somehow, these colours look familiar,' Walter can't help thinking. Then, suddenly, a small island arises from underneath the storming, shifty sea. But there is another image as well. A brooding dark cloud is slowly taking form into the sky.

"Oooh, nooo," Walter hears Queen Miranda cry out. "That is what I always forgot to paint in my paintings. It is the cloud! The dark cloud of doom that hangs over us, witches. Ooh noo."

Walter has no words, for words fall short by so much despair.

There is a long silence as even the sea becomes still again. When at long last the queen speaks, her voice, besides being crackled, now also sounds hollow. "We have to bid you farewell," she utters, and despite the things she has done, Walter again almost feels sorry for her.

"Goodbye Your Majesty," he says. "And yes, goodbye to you too, Erwin," he adds. There is no response.

The queen stumbles off the dune, towards the tiny white boat. Walter only now notices it. Of course, it has to be there, waiting for the queen to go on board, along with her cat, Erwin.

Both Walter and Bones watch as they take their place in the small vessel. Soon, it drifts out over the sea. Closer and closer to the island. The figure of Queen Miranda, so desolate and forlorn, is a sight Walter will never forget. The island is like a magnet, seeming to draw the boat nearer and nearer to it. Then, suddenly and unexpectedly, the dark cloud of doom falls down on them. Grabs them, absorbs them. Makes them disappear from sight when approaching the island.

Slowly, very slowly, the Island is disappearing as well. Sinking back into the ocean. The water whizzing and whirling, while the creepy colouring of the sky, returns to normal. Gone are the shrill, bizarre tinges of just a while ago. Gone too, is the dark cloud. It is as if nothing strange has happened here at all. The ocean is calm again, the sky blue and the beach sand yellow. But Walter, not able to tear himself away yet, keeps staring over the now still sea. "How is it possible?" he asks Bones. "I find it hard to believe what took place here just now."

"Yes, I can't believe it either. It was very, very weird," is the only answer Bones can find at this moment. After a last look, they at long last, drive off again in the coach. Bones sitting next to Walter in the front.

Walter's thoughts, meanwhile, keep going back to Queen Miranda. How fast everything changed. One happening following another. "To think that just until a few days ago, Queen Miranda was still the queen of this land," he says to Bones. "And now her reign is over!"

"Yes, she is gone and so is Erwin," Bones utters with satisfaction. He goes on, "I knew all along there was something very weird about this Erwin. I constantly wanted to go for him."

"Well, keeping in mind, he turned out to be a cat, I am not too surprised about that," Walter smiles.

"Mmm," Bones grumbles. Pondering over this for a while, he utters, "Rita felt it too. She was very scared of him."

"I know," Walter agrees. Again they drive on in silence, but all sorts of thoughts keep tumbling through Walter, head.

"I am still trying to get a better understanding of what happened," he utters. "King Frederik told me about lavish parties being held at the castle. Fortunes were spent. Later on though, after the old king died, this seemed to have stopped."

"Maybe it became boring?" Bones offers. He has no idea what Walter is going on about.

"Yes, maybe," Walter muses. He continues; "It could also be that after King Frederik's father died, people lost interest in Queen Miranda and her parties. Or," he gasps at the thought. "It might even have been, because the queen loved her husband so much, that she did not feel up to these festivities anymore. Not on her own, I mean. What do you think?"

"I suppose we will never know," Bones replies.

"I agree," Walter sighs. He goes on, "Her not being able to get the painting right, in order to get her freedom, must also have been very frustrating. All the riches she gathered did not help either. They were not meant to be hers, anyway."

"Would it have helped Queen Miranda if all those fortunes had gone to that island?" Bones asks.

"Of course, yes, it would have given her a higher standing and respect among the other witches, I am sure," Walter responds. "Now, she has to start all over again, I would think."

"You don't mean she might come back one day?" Bones shudders.

"Oh no, we do not have to get upset by thoughts like that," Walter answers. "No witch would even think about coming here again. People have suffered too much and for to long. They simply would not allow anyone to behave in such a way anymore," Walter ends his comments.

"True, true," Bones mutters. For a while, they drive on without speaking. The horses are glad their spooky passengers have gone and move at a steady pace. Bones stretches out on his seat next to Walter while mumbling a bit to himself.

"Anything wrong?" Walter wants to know.

"I am thirsty," Bones confesses.

"Now that you mention it, I am too, actually," Walter responds. Keeping on the lookout, they soon enough find a little stream. Stopping at the water's edge, they drink eagerly. Of course, the horses get their turn as well.

"You really have earned it," Walter tells them. "Thank you for being so good and for not bolting away with our uncanny passengers." The horses are grateful for Walter's praise.

"Yes," they admit; "It was hard not to run off, but now we feel much better."

"Good," Walter declares. He goes on; "Water is all we have at the moment. Sadly, for food, we have to wait until we are back at the castle."

"No matter," the horses whinny, "We'll make it, now that we are no longer thirsty."

"I am glad to hear it," Walter replies, adding; "well, let's be on our way then,"

That's what they do. On and on again, the horses go. It is already late in the afternoon when they get back to the castle. Somehow, news has spread. People have gone up to the castle's towers to see the carriage arrive.

That Queen Miranda is not in it, they hear soon enough, from Lieutenant Fernando Lopez. Out of curiosity, he watched the goings on this morning. Hiding behind a tree at the back of the castle, he saw Walter helping Queen Miranda and her cat into the carriage and then driving off. Before long, everyone at the castle was informed about this. Lieutenant Lopez described everything in the finest details, saying that he did not even recognise the queen, nor her cat.

"But is must have been them, of that I am sure," were his words. "Bones, the dog, was also there. He took a place inside the carriage as well. I suppose he had to keep guard over these two."

For the rest of the day, lieutenant Lopez has been waiting for Walter's return. He wants to be the first to tell everyone what has happened. With Walter's carriage coming nearer and nearer, the lieutenant starts running towards and then next to it. Scanning the carriage interior, he sees no one inside. After saluting both Walter and Bones, he beckons to the people at the towers. "She is not here," he shouts. "The queen is gone!" Now everyone knows, Walter has delivered them from Queen Miranda. They are free!

"She is gone. She is gone," the word goes on and on. "We are free from the evil queen from now on. What a relief. Now King Frederik is our king again!" All of a sudden and without anyone touching them, the bells in the bell tower start ringing and ringing. "Ding dong, ding dong, Queen Miranda is gone, is gone!"

The whole household, along with the army troupes, is waiting for them. Such a welcome, with waving and shouts of joy, as soon as he and Bones alight from the carriage. Everyone is trying to shake Walter's hands. Grooms take the horses and carriage over from him. However, before they lead them away, Walter tells them, "I will come soon to take a look at the stables."

"Please do, sir," one of the young men, who seems to be in charge, answers back.

"And your name?" Walter wants to know.

"My name is Conrad, sir," is the reply.

"Right, thank you Conrad, I will see you then," Walter says.

"Yes sir, thank you sir," the young man responds.

As Walter turns around, he sees Bernard, the head-chef, trying to get his attention.

"Good afternoon, sir," he greets. "Begging your pardon, sir, but you must be hungry. Can I prepare something for you to eat?"

"Yes, yes, a good day and a good idea Bernard," Walter laughs. "I am indeed very hungry and am sure, so is my friend Bones. Will you bring our food to the sun room again? Make it the same as yesterday's, because that was very nice!"

"Yes sir, I attend to it at once," Bernard answers. "And for tonight, sir?" he asks. "Where would you like dinner to be served?"

"No, no dinner tonight," Walter replies. "It is quite late already. After the food you are going to bring us just now, I only want a good rest. I think an early night is our best option. First though, I have this one question. Where does all this food that seems to be here in abundance come from? The farms we saw thus far looked desolate, with nothing growing in the fields."

"That is correct, sir," Master Bernard responds. "Everything has gone to waste, except the queen's own estate."

"Ooh and where is that estate?" Walter wants to know.

"It lies just east from here, sir, beyond those hills over there," Bernard points out. "It is a very large farm which supplies us with everything we need."

"Thank you," Walter says. He is already planning to go there as soon as possible.

"My pleasure sir," Bernard replies and after making a respectful bow, he returns to the kitchen.

Walter slowly makes his way towards the castle, here and there, stopping to shake hands or talk to someone for a while. He is glad though, when at last they reach the sun room and he is able to let himself sink into the first chair in sight. Bones lies down close by. Both are worn out from the many emotions of this day.

It is then that Rita flies in from the patio. After they have greeted, she sets herself on the armrest of Walter's chair. She then explains; "I wanted to come over to you earlier, but there were so many people about. It made me decide I rather wait for you here."

"Good thinking," Walter praises her.

"How did it go?" Rita asks. "Did you bring the queen safely back to her island?"

"Yes, we did," Walter answers.

"I've got some news for you," Bones tells Rita. "Remember how scared you were of Erwin?" he asks.

"Yes, I do," Rita responds. "His presence made me feel very uneasy indeed. You did not like to be near him either, Bones," she remarks.

"That is true," Bones admits. He goes on; "do you know why this was so?"

"No, why then?" Rita exclaims.

"It was, because, because Erwin was a cat!" Bones gloats.

"No," is Rita's shocked reaction. "He couldn't be!"

"He was," Walter confirms Bones' words.

"Ooh, ooh, now you two must tell me everything about this, please," Rita cries.

"Right," Walter agrees, but just then Master Bernard arrives with the food tray, trailed by Edward, his helper. Edward carries a glass jug with milk in one hand and in the other a bowl with food for Bones.

"Thank you, that is great," Walter says as Bernard places his tray on the table in front of him. As soon as Master Bernard and Edward have left, Bones devours his food, even though he understands that Rita longs to hear how the rest of their day went.

Walter eats unhurriedly. Drinking some milk in between makes him soon start feeling better.

"It has been a day full of surprises," he at last reports to Rita.

"There were more?" Rita wants to know.

"Absolutely," Walter answers. "The first one was, when we saw this morning how the beautiful Queen Miranda, overnight, had changed into an old woman!"

"What?" Rita brings out. "Erwin the servant, became a cat and Queen Miranda an old woman? Ooh, how weird and how eerie it must have been to travel with them!"

"Yes," Bones grumbles. "Most of all, for me. I'd say I had to sit near both the queen and the cat to watch them the whole time. I tell you, it was very difficult."

"It must have been," Rita agrees. "Just as well I did not come along," she adds.

"Absolutely," Walter responds. "That was very wise."

"Now, what happened after you arrived at the sea?" Rita inquires.

"Well, first, we saw those strange colours appearing in the sky," Walter says. "Layer upon layer, exactly the same as in the queen's paintings."

"Yeah, but she forgot the cloud," Bones utters.

"Cloud? What cloud?" Rita twitters.

Walter explains; "The queen called it the cloud of doom which hangs over witches. Because it was missing from her paintings, she could not win her freedom. It had to be just right, remember?"

"Yes, I remember," Rita answers. After a moment's thinking, she goes on; "Still, I wonder, would it have made any difference at all? Would Queen Miranda have behaved in a better way after gaining her freedom? Was she really a good witch at heart?"

"I suppose we will never know the answer to all these questions," Walter replies. "What I do know, though, is that no one has the right to make so many people suffer as she did, bad witch or not. But, my friends," he goes on, "It is getting late. I think what we need is a good rest after all we went through today and the days before that." Rita and Bones agree. They leave the sun room and head for their chambers upstairs. Once there, it does not take long before the three of them are fast asleep.

Early the following morning, Walter finds himself wondering if he is awake or dreaming? He sees Princess Elina standing in the doorway, smiling at him. He smiles back, but then, she is gone! "Ooh no," Walter groans, "It wasn't for real!"

Being fully awake now, he starts thinking about how things will go from here. Will the king be true to his word? Will he truly allow him, Walter, to marry his daughter, the Princess Elina? Since leaving the palace, he has tried not to dwell on any of these thoughts. Other important affairs had to be dealt with first. But it is different now. He has done what he came to do, so, rightfully, Princess Elina should become his bride.

With these thoughts, he steps out of bed to prepare for whatever may lie ahead. 'When will the king arrive? And will Princess Elina accompany him?' He asks himself, hoping and expecting that this will indeed be so. After all, the princess always joins her father on his travels. "And now, more than ever, she will for sure," he tells himself while hoping and praying, that it shall be soon. King Frederik's party, travelling by coach, will move much faster, of course, than he and his friends could.

After breakfast, which this time is served in a small dining room, by Master Bernard and a few helpers, Walter and his friends set off to inspect the stables. They find everything there, spic and span. Conrad, the young groom they met the day before, proudly shows them around.

"This is great," Walter compliments him. He continues, "I see you have three coaches left here. Then, of course, there are the ones that have gone to the river Yanta to fetch King Frederik and his entourage?"

"Oh yes sir," Conrad replies. "My supervisor, Mr. Goodman, went with them. He took two of our other grooms with him. They are all very good men, sir. Also, the horses are the very best of the royal stables. As for the coaches, they were cleaned and polished to perfection before leaving."

"Good, I am glad to hear it," Walter smiles. "Now, I'd be grateful if you got one of these other coaches ready for me again."

He adds, "I like to visit the estate that provides the castle with food."

"Yes sir, of course sir," the groom answers. He gives some orders to a few stable boys and within a short time, the horses are harnessed in front of a carriage, ready to go.

As before, Walter takes the reins himself. With Bones next to him and Rita on his shoulder, he leaves. They enjoy the pleasant drive through green fields and shady lanes. "How different from what we saw when coming here," Walter and his friends remark to each other. They appreciate their time out and happily chat away. All three are grateful for the break from pressure for a while.

After about an hour, a farmhouse, surrounded by large trees, comes into sight. At a nearby shed, people are busy unloading bales of hay from a wagon. One of the men walks over to them as Walter brings the horses to a halt.

"Good day to you," Walter greets. The man greets back in the same manner, while the others stop with what they are doing, to wave at them. "I would like to see the farmer, please," Walter says.

"That's me, sir," the man answers. "I am Farmer Triska. Forgive me sir," he goes on, "But, are you the person, eh, the person that those messengers who came around, told us about?"

"That must be me," Walter smiles. "I am the one who, in the name of King Frederik Lamonte, took back this land from Queen Miranda!"

"Hurray, hurray, it's him, it's him," the workers shout while running towards Walter's coach, circling around it, laughing and talking. Everyone is excited.

"Right," Walter says, stepping down from the carriage. "Nice to meet you, too. I have come to find out more about this farm and, of course, about you as well. The fields we saw on our way over here are very well looked after. Also, the food supply to the castle is excellent."

"Thank you sir," Farmer Triska answers, adding, "We are doing our best, sir."

"Indeed," Walter responds with a warm smile. He goes on, "I expect the king shortly and in the meantime, would like to be shown around the farm. That way, I can report back to King Frederik concerning the overall situation here."

"You are very welcome sir and it will be an honour for me to take you myself," Farmer Triska replies.

"Good," Walter declares. "Shall we go then?" Climbing onto his seat on the carriage again, he takes the reins. With Farmer Triska on one side of him and Bones on the other, they drive away. The laughter and waving of the workers follow them for quite a while, Walter of course, is waving back and so does Farmer Triska.

Bones is barking and Rita flies overhead. Everyone is in a jolly good mood. The horses, happy to be in such pleasant company, gallop at a steady pace. Farmer Triska proudly shows Walter the whole farm estate. From the one end to the other they go. Everything is well kept and tidy. "Very good. This is an outstanding place. The other farms we have seen seemed so neglected and deserted," Walter remarks.

"They are," the farmer agrees. "Queen Miranda wanted far too much in taxes and goods out of them," he says.

"So I understand," Walter replies. "Ah well," he goes on; "From now on, things will be different."

"Yes sir, I am sure," the farmer laughs. "We all have hoped for this, sir. It was not easy working for a person such as Queen Miranda. Or rather, not so much a person as such. The rumour goes, she was a witch. Is that true, sir?"

"Yes, it is true," Walter answers. "But," he adds, "let's not go into that any further. Let us rather enjoy our drive through this beautiful landscape."

And this they do. Each field is neatly laid out, with workers tending to them. They all wave as the coach passes by. Bones, tail wagging next to Walter, sometimes hops off and runs beside the carriage. His barking then only reveals happiness.

Rita is equally content and keeps singing above their heads or now and then, on Walter's shoulder. It is the same everywhere. Everyone seems to know who Walter is.

"Yes, news travels fast in this region," Farmer Triska smiles, and his remark makes Walter smile as well.

It is already past midday, when at last, they turn back towards the farmhouse.

"I am hungry," Farmer Triska informs Walter. He goes on; "My wife makes the most tasty soup one can think of. Would you like to come in and try some?"

"I won't say no to a good bowl of soup," Walter chuckles.

"Right," Farmer Triska answers. "Let's go for it then!"

Two of the young men Walter saw working at the barn this morning, are waiting for them.

"My sons Gerhard and Alexander," the farmer introduces them proudly. The farmer's wife, appearing in the doorway, is also presented in the same proud way. "My wife's name is Martha and mine is Orin," Farmer Triska pronounces while smiling from ear to ear.

"Glad to know you all," is Walter's response and after much handshaking, he is ushered into a large kitchen. A warm aroma of good food welcomes him there and soon all of them are seated at the table.

Bones, grasping that Walter is among friends here, decides to stay outside. After drinking some water from a nearby fish pond, he finds himself a cool place under a tree. Lying down, he observes how a few young boys take care of the coach's horses. They give them water to drink and lots of hay to eat.

Rita, meanwhile, is still on Walter's shoulder, listening to the lively talks around her. It is all about the years and years of Queen Miranda's reign. The good and the bad, but mostly the bad things she brought over this land. Farmer Triska and his family have been lucky. They, as always before, were able to keep delivering their produce to the castle. But even for them, it has not been easy.

"Queen Miranda was hard to please and underpaid them severely," Walter hears. But now, hopefully, this is all in the past and everyone is looking forward to a better future.

Walter listens while enjoying the real good bowl of soup in front of him. He also tucks into the delicious bread, warm from the oven, that goes with it. After lunch and after thanking the farmer and his family for their hospitality, Walter excuses himself. "Although I do not like to leave you so soon," he says; "I have to go now. There is still much to do."

Of course, all of them understand this, so soon, Walter and friends take their place at the coach again. Every one of the family and all who are working at the farm, wave them out, as they go.

"This was a very pleasant day," Bones says.

"Indeed it was," Walter agrees. "What do you say, Rita?"

"Yes, I loved it too," Rita chirps.

The three of them enjoy the ride back, and so do the horses. Refreshed after a good rest and having eaten good hay, they love this being out and about. Doing so with Walter makes it even more of a feast.

But, from the moment they return, Walter's time is not his own anymore. He gets called on and asked for, from all sides. Each member of the household, and even those of the army or their spokesmen, is seeking his advice. It all comes down to the king's arrival. What do they have to do? What can be done? Which food must be prepared? And so forth and so on.

Walter manages to calm everyone, solving one problem after another. He holds meetings with the castle's staff and army personnel, winning them all over again, in the process. They like his kind manners and ready smile. The result? Every person feels a part of a team, trying to do the best they can, to make the king's homecoming an outstanding event.

Such a busy time it is, with the days speeding by, but when will the king arrive? The magic mirror in the tower room does not give any answers to these questions, either. Yes, Walter sees the palace when he turns the mirror, but everything seems very quiet over there. Now and then he notices servants going in and out, but the king is nowhere to be seen and neither is Princess Elina.

For him, no old witch's face appears in the mirror like it did when Queen Miranda was still in power. 'This witch, most likely, was telling her what really was happening at the scenes she was looking at,' are Walter's thoughts about this. But for him, no such luck, so he just has to be patient and wait.

CHAPTER XVI

Lorenzo is the first to appear.

He flies straight onto Walter's shoulder, finding him walking up and down the garden path in front of the castle, wondering how much longer it will take for King Frederik's party to reach the castle.

"We're here," Lorenzo shouts. "We're here. How are you Walter?"

"My, my, Lorenzo, ah, it is so good to see you," Walter calls back, laughing with relief. "I am well," he answers then. "And you?"

"Fine, fine," Lorenzo hollers. "So, the king is coming?" Walter asks eagerly.

"Yes, the king is here and Princess Elina too," Lorenzo replies.

Walter, hoping for and expecting this all the time, is overjoyed. "Oh my, my, that is marvellous," he exclaims with a wildly beating heart. "How wonderful it will be to see my beloved princess again! Now everything is totally perfect."

Rita, flying over from a nearby tree, hovers above them. "How nice to see you Lorenzo," she sings. "How are you and how are Bruno and Rona and Mona and all the others?"

"I am fine," Lorenzo answers, "And Bruno and Rona and Mona and the others are fine as well. We are all fine."

"Good," Bones, who is standing next to Walter, utters. "It is good that you are back my friend," he adds, "And I missed you all very much as well," is Lorenzo's warm reply. "And everyone on the other side of the river, are missing all of you, very much! They hope to see you soon," he adds.

"Yes, we do hope so too," Rita chirps. Then she announces; "Well, I am leaving. I want to be the first to welcome the king and Princess Elina," and away she flies, singing while she does so.

Walter, hands above his eyes, looks after her. At the same time he also searches the landscape in front of him. The trees on the road winding down from the castle prevent him from seeing the royal party as yet. But soon, the wind blows the sound of trumpet over to them and then, yes, there are the heralds, riding in front of the carriages. They and their instruments, announcing the arrival of King Frederik.

People start appearing from everywhere. From the castle, from the gardens, from the army camp. Walter, meanwhile, is running as fast as he can towards the royal convoy.

Lorenzo has flown away, circling high above him in the sky. Bones runs beside Walter. After a short while, they see both the king and Princess Elina, leaning out of the window of their carriage. They smile and wave. Of course, Rita is also there, cheerfully singing on Princess Elina's shoulder.

As soon as Walter is near enough, the king draws back from the window and gives the order to stop. The carriage door swings open. With one big step, Walter is inside, shaking hands with King Frederik, who then puts an arm around Walter's shoulder. "Well done, well done my son," he praises.

"Thank you, Your Majesty," Walter answers. He turns to Princess Elina, who looks at him, still smiling, but with tears in her eyes.

"It is so good having you here, dear Princess," Walter brings out. Princess Elina offers him her hand and Walter, bowing deftly, places a kiss on it. "How lovely my Princess is," he whispers, at once shy, for daring to say something like this. Princess Elina, while slowly drawing her hand away, still keeps smiling at him through her tears.

Rita, on her shoulder, tweets cheerfully, foreseeing a real happy ending for these two people she loves so dearly.

King Lamonte pulls Walter onto the seat next to him, then gives the order to continue the journey. As the royal entourage moves on, he declares. "And now we have reached our destination, our dearest wishes have come true. We are back at the place where I was born. This castle where I grew up and lived with my parents. Here in this land that all of us loved so much!" His voice is full of emotion and his eyes are not dry either.

Soon, the carriages swing round the flowering garden beds in front of the castle. Bones, cheerfully running alongside the king's coach, with Lorenzo on his back, brings more smiles to the lips of the passengers inside,

The heralds are still blowing their trumpets. Loud whip-lashes crack over the horses' heads. Yes, the king is back! And see, the whole army regiment is waiting for them. All the army officers, and every last man. Standing at attention and saluting their king. The king's smile broadens, as he, in turn, answers their salute. In front of a rolled out red carpet, they come to a halt.

The castle's servants are lined up on each side of this carpet. Their loud "Hurrah, Hurrah," fills the air. The castle's grooms running towards them, hastily help to open the carriage doors. First, King Frederick alights, followed by Princess Elina and Walter.

The waving and shouts of joy go on until the king raises his hand. At once, there is silence. Then the king starts to speak.

"Dear countrymen and women," he begins. "This is a memorable day. For the first time in many, many years, we are together again. One nation, one people! We can't begin to tell you how happy this makes us."

"And us, and us," his listeners cheer.

"Right, right," the king laughs. "And you," he continues, "We are so glad to hear this. We know how difficult your lives have been and announce hereby that all this will change. From now on, things will improve. Together, we are going to rebuild this land. We will make it a pleasant place to live in, for all of us!"

His words are greeted with loud clapping of hands and shouts of glee and delight. Clearly, everyone loves what the king is saying. Servants, soldiers and officers, they are all overjoyed to see him and his entourage. Of course, this also includes the lovely Princess Elina, whose charming smile, at once, steals their hearts.

The King understands. He is just as happy as they are. Placing his arm around Walter again, he says, "This young man made it all happen. He is the one who undertook to bring this about."

Anew, a loud "hurrah, hurrah," swells up from his audience. The king's other arm slips over Princess Elina's shoulder and while hugging them close to him, the king says; "These two young people are the light of my eyes. It so happens that they love each other. I, King Frederik Lamonte, have promised my daughter's hand in marriage to this young man, who ended Queen Miranda's reign over this land. My dear people, I am going to keep that promise. Soon, there will be a royal wedding!"

Now there is no end to the joy and merriment. Soldiers' caps fly high into the air and even the officers forget their usual reserve and join in with the rejoicing. Like all the others, they have been completely won over by Walter's gallant ways and charm.

The king places Princess Elina's hand into Walter's, saying; "This day is the most memorable day in our whole life."

Princess Elina and Walter just smile at each other, their hearts overflowing with love and happiness.

Under cheers and amidst lots of gaiety, they walk towards the castle's entrance. The king is beside them. The others in the king's entourage follow closely behind. They are the king's advisers. Wise men who will help decide on how to restore this land.

Rita chooses this moment to take her leave from Princess Elina's shoulder. Princess Elina smiles as the little bird chirps a goodbye. Her smile deepens by observing how Lorenzo flies away from Walter's shoulder too and joins Rita. Along with Walter, the King and others in their group, they watch as wing by wing, those two take off into the sky. However, as both Rita and Lorenzo love to keep an eye on all that is going on, they soon choose to settle down in the courtyard again. On a tree branch nearest to the sunroom, they find just the right spot. Bones rightly has decided to disappear from sight as well. Clearly, Walter can do without him for a while now that he is in this royal company. But just to be on the safe side, he chooses the courtyard as his destination too. Near the open door of the sunroom, Lorenzo and Rita see him lie down. "We're all together then," Lorenzo cackles. "Yes, luckily, we are," Bones answers, looking up at his friends.

"Bones does so love good company," Rita twitters.

"Absolutely," Bones replies. "I do indeed." Together they keep watch now and while doing so, Lorenzo speaks about his journey to the palace on the other side of the river Yanta. He has lots to tell and Rita and Bones are good listeners. They hear how exhausted he was upon arriving. Luckily, though, the king saw his landing in front of the library window and quickly took him inside. Lorenzo also relates the king's joy upon hearing of Queen Miranda's defeat.

While Lorenzo tells his tale, they see the king and his gathering enter the sun room. They notice how happy Walter looks as he shakes hands with all the king's men.

Master Roland is one of them. For him, this is a great day too. "So many memories come back now," he says to Walter. "So many fine and happy ones, along with the others who were sad."

"I understand how you must feel," Walter assures him. He continues; "It is good to have you here, Master Roland. Please make yourself at home again. We need an organizer like you in this castle." Master Roland is only too happy.

Within a short time, the tables in the sun room are put together and bedecked with crispy white linen tablecloths. Soon, food is brought in by a beaming Bernard and his helpers. Other servants hover about, eager to lend a hand, for all of them love to serve the king and his guests.

Then suddenly, Bones hears Princess Elina call his name. He is at her side in a second and is thrilled when she says, "I want to thank you, Bones, for being such a good and faithful friend to Walter. He has told me all about what you have done. How well you protected him without concern for your own safety. Because of this, you will also be my very special friend for always!"

Although she is not aware of this, Bones already loves and adores the princess. Now, wagging his tail while looking up at her, his eyes say it all. The princess and Walter both understand and are very moved. Their warm smile follows him as he moves away to lie down in a nearby corner of the room. From there, he can watch everyone going in or out. Walter and his bride to be, each sit on one side of the king as they take their places on the table. The king's advisers assemble around them. While the servants serve snacks and refreshments, a lively conversation is starting to take place. Also, a flood of questions and answers, fly to and fro.

"Yes, all is well with Bruno and Rona and Mona, the monkeys. They send their love and hope to see you very soon," Princess Elina confirms Lorenzo's utterances.

To hear this anew soothes Walter's concerns about the friends he left behind. Then, of course, the king wants to know everything that had happened since Walter left the palace to go on his journey. Walter, for his part, willingly reports all that has transpired since they last saw each other. His tale is interesting and absorbing. Also, it takes quite some time to tell it all. His listeners do not mind. They are fascinated and love every detail of his story.

So time goes by with enjoying the lovely food in front of them, while at the same time taking in all Walter has to tell. When he finishes his tale and the light meal they relished is consumed, everyone strolls outside. There, the army officers are gathering, waiting for permission to speak to King Frederik. Master Roland oversees it all.

First, the army commanders get the chance to personally meet the king. Then it is the castle's staff who are introduced. Everyone wants help with their problems and assurances of their positions. King Frederik quietly calms everyone's worries and fears.

Rita has flown onto Princess Elina's shoulder by now. She stays there as the princess a while later withdraws to the chambers Master Roland has put in order for her. He has seen to it that everything is spotless and tidy. It is the same rooms Queen Miranda occupied before. They link up with the king's chambers, which are even bigger. The king's advisers, weary after the long journey, express the wish to take a rest as well. Master Roland, foreseeing this, has made quarters available to them on the second floor. Flowers have been placed on tables and all beds fitted out with fresh linen. Grateful for the care and attention, the king's advisers soon lie down for a well-earned snooze.

King Frederik and Master Roland seem to have boundless energy. Both are so overjoyed to be back at the castle that weariness apparently has no hold on them. After everyone has left, King Frederik and Walter can at long last have the private discussion they long for. Walter is doing most of the talking, though, as he tells the king more of what he found out about Queen Miranda. He speaks of the magic mirror in the tower room and how the queen was able to observe so many things from there. Even the palace on the other side of the Yanta river. Even the king himself and the people around him.

Upon hearing this, King Frederik shakes his head in total amazement.

Then Walter also relates his finds of the unbelievable treasures hidden in the tower rooms. He speaks of the plan to eventually throw all these riches into the sea.

"That would have been a horrendous loss," King Frederik declares. He continues; "But you being able to prevent this from happening is fantastic news. We can use all this wealth to rebuild this land and try to compensate the people. They have suffered so much under the rule of Queen Miranda. Of course, money can never undo their misery and pain, but at least it can bring relief from poverty."

"It will be wonderful to do this," Walter reacts eagerly. "I was asking myself how one could improve the lives of the people here. But luckily, now your Majesty's words, answer this question."

"Good, that is what will happen then," King Frederik smiles. "And now, shall we go up to those tower rooms and see all that you spoke of?" he enquires.

"Yes, I love to show your Majesty around," Walter answers eagerly. Without further ado, the two of them leave the sunroom and start climbing the stairs leading to the tower rooms. Lorenzo is nowhere to be seen, but Bones follows close behind them. Once they have arrived at their destination, King Frederik is totally overwhelmed by all the riches that Queen Miranda stowed away in room after room.

"It really is unbelievable," he utters over and over again as they inspect the one after the other. "How lucky for us all the queen's plans failed," he sighs. "Imagine if all these riches would have been thrown into the sea. How deplorable, how sad. Rebuilding this land without itbwould have been far more difficult. We, our whole country, can never thank you enough for preventing that, Walter."

Strangely enough, at this moment, Walter can't help thinking that King Frederik has gone back to speaking of we, when talking about himself. Coming to the conclusion that this seems to "come and go," he then just shrugs his shoulders.

"Everything just fell into place," he answers the king. "I suppose I was simply at the right time at the right place."

"Be that as it may," the king replies. "Fact is, you succeeded where no one else succeeded before."

By now, they have reached the room where Queen Miranda spent a lot of her time. "The Witch's room," Walter announces. Bones, as before, lies down in front of the door as the king and Walter enter. He knows it will be quite some time before they will leave from there again.

The king gasps in wonderment at the strange sights in front of him. "Look at this," he exclaims. "This place is really bizarre and weird. And that awful sweet smell! Yes, this is a real witch's room, as you call it, Walter. Ah, and this must be the magic mirror you spoke of?" he says, walking towards it.

"Indeed, your Majesty," Walter replies. But the king does not even hear his answer. For it seems that by looking into the magic mirror, one gets totally absorbed by it. This happened to Walter as well and as he joins the king by staring into it, the same thing recurs again. Together, they view the world outside. The hills and the forests, the lakes and the small villages.

"How marvellous! How absolutely marvellous this all is," King Frederik brings out. Just like Walter, he can hardly bring himself to look away from the mirror. But at long last, they do. Then, King Frederik is overcome by the sight of the many old books in the room.

"My, see all this," he says enraptured. "It will be great to research and investigate these." Thrilled, he promptly starts gathering them, with Walter at once assisting. After a while, most of the books are piled neatly together onto a large table. To Walter, who is still rounding up some more, the king says; "This will do for the moment. Come sit here beside me, then we can browse through them for a bit."

"Oh yes, your Majesty, that is a great idea," Walter eagerly agrees. He dusts off some chairs and draws them up to the table. From then on, both the king and he are lost to the outside world. Such mysteries, such riddles, symbols and uncanny tales are unveiled in some of these books. It makes the both of them shudder.

"Burn them," the king utters after some time. "We must burn them! Especially this one. This one is pure poison," the king declares, pointing to the thickest and most disturbing book on the table.

Walter cannot agree more. "We can burn that one now," he suggests. All the things to make a fire are lying there by the grate.

"Good idea," King Frederik comments. "For I cannot stand the sight of it a moment longer."

In no time at all, Walter has the fire going and with gusto, the king and he tear the book apart, throwing the pages in the fire. They are quickly devoured by the flickering flames. But it happens with much twisting, curling and hissing. The flames turn green, bad smelling smoke fills the room, which makes both the king and Walter gasp for breath.

"It protests," the king utters, coughing.

"Yes," Walter answers. "This book does not want to be burned!"

"I agree," King Frederik replies. "But," he adds, "That is exactly what is happening. The flames from this wood fire are now burning away all its magic."

Although nearly choking from the ghastly fumes spreading through the room, both the king and Walter are suddenly feeling much better. They watch the last pages crumble to ash and almost at once, the awful smell and smoke disappear.

Now they get busy selecting the other books, not meeting the king's standards. Those are put together on the large table. "We will have them destroyed tomorrow morning and good riddance, will be," the king exclaims.

Only the rare editions of academic wisdom, King Frederik keeps. Putting those aside on a shelf, he happens to notice another book that looks interesting. After taking a closer look, the king says, "But this is a diary! Can you believe it? It is Queen Miranda's diary that she kept for many, many years. For, eh, let me see, well, well, it dates back more than a hundred years ago. Now, how is this possible? How on earth?" Sitting down again, the king starts to read.

Going over the pages rapidly, he now and then calls out, "My, is this not amazing?" And, "Can this be true?"

Walter, leaning over the king's shoulder to see better, also catches some dates. After some time, the king and he come to the same conclusion. Indeed, the witch, who became Queen Miranda, did indeed start this diary about a hundred years ago. It begins shortly after she left the witches' island and tells the tale of her being placed in a country further up north.

"You read that?" King Frederik exclaims. "Not this country, but another one, further up north, mind you!"

"Yes," Walter answers the king. "I wonder which country that is?"

"Ooh, it could be one of many," the king replies. "It does not matter, though. It seems her instructions were the same, to bewitch the king and enslave him. Gather the riches of the land and eventually return with them to the witch's island. However, as one can clearly read from these pages, there happened to be a problem. The first king, of the first country where she landed, had a twin brother and although the king soon fell for her charm, the king's brother did not. He made her life as unpleasant as he could. Never letting up, never allowing her to do what she came for. In the end, after fifty years of trying, the witch Miranda finally had to give up. Not only that, but orders from the witches' island transferred her to yet another country. Now listen to this," King Frederik reads out aloud, "The witch Miranda writes here, 'I think, the kingdom I am in at present is just the right place to be. Pity I have only another fifty years left to complete my mission. Then, the hundred years allowed to me, are over. I shall have to go back to the witches' island. But before it comes to that, I am sure to think of another plan'!"

"So, this explains a lot of things, is it not?" the king remarks.

"Absolutely," Walter responds, adding; "Now we know why the queen became so desperate in the end. Apparently, her plans were not working and her time here was running out!"

"Precisely and here you are, speaking of being at the right time in the right place," the king declares. "If ever that happened to someone, it certainly happened to you! It is miraculous, no less, that you came here just at this particular instant."

"Yes," Walter smiles. "I agree. It was miraculous indeed." With affection, they look at each other, the king and his soon-to-be son-in-law.

Closing the diary, the king stands up and puts his arm around Walter's shoulder. "We must go," he says; "But before we do, let's have another look at that magic mirror, shall we?"

Standing alongside in front of the mirror, the two of them peer into it again. "To be able to see all this," the king almost whispers. "It truly is amazing."

Then Walter remembers. "But this is not all," he says. "See what happens if one touches the mirror?" He puts his hand on it and slowly, the mirror starts turning, now revealing another landscape. This time, the palace gardens become visible. It is the same as Walter saw it before, but instead of walking in the gardens there, King Frederik is here, standing at his side.

"Unbelievable, that is what it is," he hears the king say. "To think, everything that happened in our country, even on the other side of the river, could be observed from here! Queen Miranda must have laughed at all of us."

"She didn't in the end," Walter utters.

"That is true," the king admits. He goes on, "Tell me, when you met the queen, was she still so very beautiful?"

"She was," Walter answers. "That is, until I confronted and unmasked her. Very soon afterwards, she started to change. I noticed it when bringing her a tray of food. The queen was already a prisoner then in one of the tower rooms. Her hair seemed to have lost its colour, and she looked smaller somehow. However, as the queen kept her back turned towards me, I could not be sure. Although a bit taken aback, I did not think about it anymore. But the next morning, when I came to fetch her, I was horribly shocked by her changed appearance. Overnight, she became an old woman. It really was awful."

"Of course it was," King Frederik agrees. "It was also another sign that the hundred years granted to her were over and gone. From that moment on, everything just collapsed I take it. Which was very lucky for us," the king declares with satisfaction.

"Very much so," Walter grins in agreement. A feeling of wellbeing engulfs the two of them there in this depressing tower room.

"One last thing," the king remarks; "It is about Queen Miranda speaking to the witch in the mirror. How did this happen and would we be able to do the same?"

"I don't know," Walter answers truthfully.

"Oh, well, don't worry about it, Walter," the king says. "Rather, let us leave from here and go back downstairs."

But before they do, both of them are casting a last glance into the mirror. And then, a curious thing takes place. The image in the mirror slowly starts fading. It is as if a mist creeps over it. Everything becomes grey and more and more blurred. Then, the mirror turns black.

"It is finished," Walter whispers. He touches and turns the mirror, but nothing happens. "See, all the magic is gone now. Does your Majesty think it can have anything to do with the book we burned?"

"It could be," the king replies. "It could very well be so. I suppose that particular book, together with the mirror, were mean to help Queen Miranda overpower this land. With that failing and the book gone, it seems the magic of the mirror has ended. Which is just as well," the king smiles. "We do not need a magic mirror here, nor anywhere else in our land. So, come, let us rather leave this sordid room."

Bones, wagging his tail, is only too glad about this decision. It has been a very long wait for him.

Walter locks the door behind them. He then tries to hand the rope, holding all the keys, to the king.

"No, I want you to be the holder of the keys, Walter," King Frederik smiles.

"Thank you your Majesty, I shall take good care of them," Walter replies.

"Yes, I know, that is why I want this so," the king replies.

Walter smiles back at the king. He is very grateful for this trust. On their return to the sunroom, the king wishes to rest for a while.

Settling on a settee facing the courtyard, Walter notices Lorenzo and Rita nearby on a low tree branch. The first thing he does is to stroll over to them. "So where have you two been?" he asks. "I thought you were with Princess Elina, Rita and you, Lorenzo. I did not see you when the king and I went upstairs."

"I was hungry," Rita tells Walter. "Princess Elina is sleeping, so I came here to get some nice fruit, and I dozed off here in the courtyard."

"I have had long flights and very little sleep lately," Lorenzo bawls.

"Oh my, my, indeed," Walter laughs while ruffling Lorenzo feathers.

The king can't help smiling. It warms his heart to see how devoted Walter is to his friends and they, likewise, to him. "You know Walter," he says, raising his voice so Walter can hear him, "I think it will be best if you take charge of the rebuilding of this land."

"Me?" Walter reacts in a stunned voice. "Why me?" he asks, walking back to the sunroom. With a startled expression on his face, he looks at the king.

"Yes," the King continues. "You and your animal friends, including the feathered ones, always seem to be at the right place at the right time. As you yourself said, with you around, things appear to rectify themselves most naturally. Problems are solved and normality restored."

"Oh, that is great," Walter chuckles. "My, my, this sure is news to me. I never thought about it that way!"

"Maybe you don't," King Frederik remarks, "But other people do! And as for the rebuilding of this land, do you accept my offer?"

"Oh yes, I love to Your Majesty," Walter enthuses.

"Good, that is settled then," the king decides. "You will have some of my best people to help and assist you. The army can support you with manpower and practical advice."

"It all sounds fantastic," Walter beams. He goes on, "there are so many things that need to be done. The farmers must be helped to get back on their feet and go farming again. Roads must be repaired and new ones must be built." He hesitates for a moment, but then continues. "Beside all this, something else needs to be dealt with as well though!"

"Yes, and that is?" the king urges him on.

"It is, Your Majesty," Walter stammers. "I was thinking about …."

"About the wedding?" the king laughs. "You do not really believe we are forgetting about the wedding, do you?"

"I, e, I don't know, Your Majesty," Walter admits a bit lamely.

"No, no, we won't," the king says, looking at him with a twinkle in his eyes. "Let me add, young man," he goes on,

"Princess Elina never for a moment lets me forget about it either. She has made all sorts of plans already. Did she not tell you?"

"We did not have all that much time together as yet, Your Majesty," Walter mutters.

The king can't help smiling at the look on Walter's face. "Yes, it is true what you say," he replies, "But do not worry, very soon all this will change. I wonder," he goes on; "What if we give you two months to organize and see to the most urgent matters here? After that, you come over to the palace on the other side of the river. By then, everything should be ready for one of the most lavish wedding feasts one can imagine."

Walter is thrilled. His eyes start shining and Bones, tail wagging, shares his joy. Rita and Lorenzo, sensing something really big is up, at once fly over to Walter. Settling themselves on his shoulders, they wait.

Walter's joy is very catching. "How marvellous," he declares. "How absolutely wonderful this all is. I really am staggered."

"Staggered by what?" the voice of Princess Elina asks eagerly.

"Aah, there you are, my dear," King Frederik smiles at his daughter, who is just now entering the room. "I was speaking to Walter about the wedding plans that are in the making. He really is staggered by it all."

"Don't you agree?" Princess Elina asks, with her eyes laughing into Walter's.

"I do, I do," Walter assures her hastily.

"Well, let's be happy then," Princess Elina says, taking Walter's hand in hers.

"Yes," Walter smiles. "I am very, very happy."

Suddenly, they swirl around the room together. Excited and full of laughter, Rita and Lorenzo, who are still on Walter's shoulder, swirl along for a bit. Soon, though, they fly up and start circling around the happy couple. Bones quickly joins in the fun. Standing on his hind legs, he begins dancing as well. Rita sings and Lorenzo tries to do the same.

Enchanted, the king watches, a big smile on his face.

CHAPTER XVII

The first thing Walter does the next morning is to get hold of some wooden crates.

Master Roland again is a great help, even with a task like this. He knows exactly where to find them. A few servants were soon instructed to bring the crates upstairs to the tower room.

"The king told me there are books to be burnt," Master Roland comments to Walter. "Shall I get a fire going in the meantime? There is an open space on the left side of the castle. It was always used for bonfires and such like."

"That would be great, Master Roland," Walter answers. "We will be there shortly then, thank you!" It indeed does not take all that long to pack the books into the large crates. Two crates are filled with the ones that need to be burned. The other two, with the books King Frederik wants for the royal library.

Walter's helpers, uneasy to be in this gloomy room, work with great haste. They are more than happy when, after bringing the crates outside, Walter closes the door behind them.

The large fire on the left of the castle already draws many people around it. They all want to see what is going on. The rumour that the witchcraft books of Queen Miranda will be burnt has quickly spread. Firstly, though, Walter and his helpers deliver the books meant for the royal library. The king is there, waiting for them. "Just leave the crates here, my good men," he addresses the servants. "Everything will be sorted out at a later stage."

"Thank you, your Majesty," the helpers respond as they place their load on the floor. Bowing respectfully, they immediately leave to get the other books at the waiting fire.

"Look, as luck will have it, the windows here look out onto the fire that Master Roland has going already," the king tells Walter.

"Yes, I see," Walter replies, after walking over to him and looking down at the blaze underneath them.

"I shall watch from here," King Frederik says. "It will give me great pleasure to see all of those books go up in flames."

"Right, Your Majesty, it shall be done straight away," Walter assures the king. And so it does. Book after book is thrown into the raging flames by eager hands. Everyone wants to take part in destroying the last remnants of Queen Miranda's rule. All in all, it becomes quite a celebration, with people cheering as volume by volume, hissing and whizzing, catches fire. It is only after nothing but ashes are left that the by now, quite big crowd, goes back to their normal day chores. Having discovered the king looking on behind the library windows, they wave at him while leaving. Walter and Master Roland also get their share of this and smilingly, all three of them, wave back.

Walter's friends have kept themselves in the background during all these goings on. Fire is something they do not like. For them, it is something to be very frightened of. They have chosen the stillness of the courtyard to wait out all the commotion. Walter knows where to look for them, though.

After finding them, he sits down for a while on a wooden bench beneath a fruit tree. Lorenzo and Rita are sitting on a branch just above his head while Bones quickly takes his place next to him. Stroking Bones' head, Walter utters, "And now, my friends, let's see what comes next."

The next days are filled with discussions and deliberations, ideas and plans. The army officers and their men need further instructions. Farmer Triska is ordered to the castle to talk about matters regarding the estate. Other people come to seek advice. It is a hectic time.

Still, Princess Elina and Walter manage to have some moments together. The evenings are used for making music. Of course, Rita takes part in these sessions as well. Bones is always there too, but Lorenzo often sits a bit further away, usually in the courtyard. King Frederik, though, is a most captivated listener.
But then, after about a week, the time to part has come again. The king and Princess Elina will go to proceed with the wedding arrangements. Walter and the king's advisers are left to organize

things at this side of the river. Two months is not all that long," Walter tells Princess Elina. "After that, we always be together, my beloved."

"Two months seem like a very long time to me," Princess Elina sighs.

Walter pulls her close to him and tries to wipe away the silent tears trickling over her sweet face. "I can't bear it when you cry," he utters while planting kisses on both of her eyelids.

Rita cannot bear it either. Flying from Walter's onto the princess's shoulder, she chirps, "Please do not cry, dear princess. Shall I sing for you to make you smile again?" Looking at Walter, she asks, "What do you think, Walter? Shall I go back as well? Maybe that would help a little?"

"Yes, it might," Walter answer. When he repeats Rita's words to Princess Elina, a smile already starts breaking through her tears.

"Yes," she nods, "It will help a great deal! Would you mind very much if Rita does come with me?" she asks.

Although Walter always finds it hard to part with his little friend, he knows it is the best solution. Rita will be good company. Besides, the work here will keep him very busy. So, to be with Princess Elina now should be much more pleasant for Rita as well. "I have no objections at all," is his reply. "It will be better for both of you, I am sure."

"Thank you, Walter," Rita chirps from the princess's shoulder

"Thank you, Walter," Princess Elina echoes the small Robin's words. Her face is more cheerful now, which gladdens Walter's heart. Still, the sadness about the coming parting lingers with both of them.

At the arranged time and day, master Goodman and Conrad, the groom, both sitting up front, arrive with the carriage. Halting at the castle's entrance, they have come to drive King Frederik and Princess Elina to the river Yanta. There Adrian will row them over. It has been arranged that another carriage will be waiting there for the return trip to the palace.

It does not take long before their passengers board the coach. Master Roland sees to it that a few servants put the baggage in the storage compartment. "Right, now we are ready to leave," King Frederik declares. There is still time for some more farewells, though, which are a bit emotional. Rita and Lorenzo are trying their best to distract everyone and make the departure a bit more light-hearted. They fly around with Rita singing, while Lorenzo shouts, "It's not so bad, it's not so bad. We shall see each other soon again!"

Bones is adding his bit by jumping high into the air and snapping at both of them. Their efforts do succeed in bringing a smile to the king's face and even to those of Princess Elina and Walter. But, they are mixed with sadness. Walter and the princess keep waving to each other as long as they can. Even after the carriage has disappeared from sight, Walter keeps standing there, looking miserable.

Bones, watching him, decides to do something about this and starts to bark. Touching Walter's leg with his wet nose also helps.

"Yes Bones," is Walter's reaction. "I know you want me to get a grip on myself, is it not? Well, my friend, so do I. So let's not linger any longer here. There is work to be done and the sooner it gets done, the better!"

"Well, I am off also then," Lorenzo cries out. "I need some rest after all this. If you are looking for me, you find me in the courtyard." With that, he flies away while Walter and Bones move back into the castle.

Thereafter, the days go by with many tasks getting completed. Never letting up, with everyone on the go, messages fly to and fro, across the river Yanta. Luckily, Lorenzo does not mind to be the carrier of all these. He happily flies from the one side to the other, resting very little in between.

Princess Elina and Walter are counting every day. Each one is bringing them nearer to each other and their wedding. And they are not the only ones who are counting. By now, the whole country is getting excited about the coming royal marriage. Much hustle and bustle goes on everywhere. Many streets are being decorated with flags and garlands. Enormous piles of wood are heaped into huge stacks for bonfires. Troubadours are singing about the coming wedding on village squares and in inns. They sing songs of praise about Princess Elina and her handsome husband-to-be. Those songs tell of Walter's courage and good deeds. About, how he defeated Queen Miranda, who was for such a long and dreadful time, queen over much of this land.

"Surely, better times are upon us now," they sing and the people are sure. This is true, for King Frederik is a good man and his daughter is beautiful and kind. Best of all, she is going to marry the man that has become the country's hero. The whole population has taken Walter into their hearts and his name is mentioned everywhere. This coming marriage unites the nation, as nothing else could have done. Everyone is looking forward to it. "Aah, what a magnificent feast it will be." That's how the rumour go.

As each day passes, Walter, meanwhile, is just working very hard, doing whatever needs to be done. The king's advisers are helping with this and together they make good progress. Among other things, they have to find time for is taking an inventory of everything the tower rooms contain. Every item has to be listed. Gold, silver, jewels. All things of value.

"There is so much," the king's advisers comment, adding. "And the good thing is that it all will be used for the country and its people."

"Yes, isn't that wonderful?" Walter responds. He goes on, "We all know, there is so much need here on this side of the river."

"Indeed, indeed," the king's wise men nod their heads in agreement,

And while all these things are taken care of, Walter also ponders about what he himself can bring or do to make this coming royal wedding extra special. His own extraordinary gift to this king that he has learned to love so much already. It should be something that Princess Elina would appreciate and admire as well. What was it again that the king told him when speaking about his father? It was his father's plan to build a bridge over the river Yanta, he then remembers.

'The material for this task was already ordered and delivered,' was King Frederik's words. Would it not be marvellous if he, Walter, could fulfil this old dream? That would be the most fantastic gift of all!

'Now, where was this building material delivered?' he ponders. The most logical answer to this would be near the river, of course. And the most logical point would be were Adrian, the boat's man, rows people over. Having come to that conclusion, Walter wonders if master Roland might know something more. After all, he was the old king's most trusted servant. So he asks him.

At first, Master Roland is not quite sure what Walter is talking about. But then, he too, remembers. "Yes," he says, "Now that you mention it. There was actually such a plan. And yes, as you say, all the material was already delivered."

"Do you know where, Master Roland?" Walter asks eagerly. "Was it at the river itself? There, where Adrian rows people over? It seems to be the most obvious place, is it not?"

"Absolutely," master Roland agrees. "I am sure that it was brought there. Yeah, it comes back to me now. It was on the farm that King Frederik gave to Adrian, because under Queen Miranda's reign, he could not do his work anymore."

"Yes, I know," Walter answers. "She put a spell over the river. Well," he goes on, "Then one of the first things I have to do is to search for this material."

"For?" Master Roland asks.

"For building a bridge over the river, of course," Walter replies. "It is of the utmost importance for the reconstruction of this land. It is a good idea, don't you think?"

"It is a fantastic idea!" Master Roland responds. His smile shows the esteem he has for this young man and this esteem grows by the day.

It does not take Walter long to find Captain Oliver Smith. Explaining his plans to him, he gets an enthusiastic reaction and support. Recruiting some soldiers and a few coaches from Master Goodman is done in the shortest time. Soon, all of them are on their way to the river.

It is as master Roland has said, the building material is on Adrian, the boat-man's farm. "Yes, he knows about the old king's plan," Adrian tells them, while leading the way to a large storage shed. "You will find all you are looking for here," he says.

And they do. Everything is very dusty, but still in a perfect condition. All that is needed and more than that, is there. Even the original drawing plan for the bridge is found on a shelf in the shed. Captain Oliver Smith has brought a few carpenters and some handy men, who know a lot about bridge building. They are all excited and eager to start with this work. Soon, the effort is underway. Tents are put up and provisions for the men arranged. Master Roland together with Master Bernard play an important part in this. They see to it that fresh food supplies are brought in regularly, while Master Goodman provides the carriage. Conrad, the groom, now often visits the site and readily lends a hand wherever he can.

Walter's great hope is to have the bridge ready before the wedding. Being able to cross the river at will is something everyone is looking forward to. It must be strong. That is of the highest importance. Masses of people shall be making use of it. They may want to go and see the wedding taking place. Or maybe they want to visit family and friends on the other side of the river. Maybe they even just want to come and see how the people in the other half of their country live. The bridge will be there for everyone to use.

Walter, on horseback, makes many trips to the side and is satisfied with the progress he sees. Bones does not mind the large distance. He always comes along. Sometimes running, but when he gets tired, Walter picks him up. Then the both of them travel on horseback, Bones sitting in front of Walter, each of them enjoying the journey immensely. As does the horse, for there are resting places now and then, beside small streams. Plenty of fresh water to drink and lots of the hay that Walter always takes with him. Enough food for Bones and himself, is never forgotten either, so all in all, they are pleasant outings.

Now and then, Adrian, the boat's man, rows over to meet with him. "How do you feel about this bridge being built?" Walter asks him on one of these occasions. "Won't you miss your work of rowing people over?"

"Well, no, actually I am very happy," Adrian answers with a broad smile; "I now much rather spend my time farming the land King Frederik gave me."

"Oh, good, I am glad to hear that." Walter laughs. Then he excuses himself. "There is still so much that needs to be done," he tells Adrian. "I really must go back to the castle." Mounting the horse who brought him and with Bones already running upfront, he waves his goodbyes to Adrian and all the others. They include Captain Olivier Smith and lieutenant Ferdinand Lopez as well as their hard working soldiers. With a warm smile, they wave back. Master Roland, who the king has left at the castle to help Walter, has big plans of his own. He decides the castle needs a big clean-up. Every room gets turned inside out. The floors, carpets, the huge paintings everywhere, they all get wiped, washed, soaked, or sponged. Not a trace of the Witch Miranda must remain. And so, the great day comes nearer.

Lorenzo brings the news that things are as good as ready on the other side of the river. Invitations have been sent out. Kings and queens from many countries will be coming. Princess Elina's wedding dress is finished and for Walter too, fine clothes have been ordered, made and delivered. "Thank you, my friend," Walter responds. "What would we do without you?"

"Ooh, it is nothing," Lorenzo answers. "I am only too glad to help. Ah and before I forget, Princess Elina sends you her love and the king his kind regards."

"Thank you, thank you," Walter utters, his face beaming with delight upon hearing these words. "And Rita and Bruno and the monkeys?" he asks. "Are they all well?"

"They couldn't be better." Lorenzo assures him.

"Right, that is so very good to hear," Walter responds, feeling happy about all the good news Lorenzo is bringing him. He can hardly wait for the wedding day anymore. Luckily, because each day is filled to the brim, they pass by quickly. He still does find time though, to visit the stables now and then, Bones as usual on his side and Lorenzo, when at the castle, mostly trails along as well. Mister Goodman, the stall master, who went to fetch the king and his convoy, from this side of the river Yanta, also, becomes a friend. This good man has instructed the grooms to start preparing Walter's carriage. "It must be totally overhauled. Fixed where fixing is needed and repainted in the colours of the king's royal household."

Conrad and the other grooms are only too happy, obeying these commands. They all like Walter and they also like his choice of horses. He has picked two beautiful dapple grey ones to run in front of the carriage. They are going to have red plumes on their heads and small silver bells as well. Those bells are going to cling softly, with every move of the horses' heads.

"Princess Elina will love it," Walter thinks out loud.

"I am sure she will," Bones replies.

"It is you, in the coach, that she will love the most, I think," Lorenzo says. This makes Walter laugh. But Lorenzo goes on, "That is, if one can drive up there. The bridge is still not ready."

"It shall be ready," Walter replies. "Captain Olivier Smith assured me of this, only yesterday."

"Yes, yes," Bones joins the discussion. "I am sure it shall. Everyone is working very hard. I saw it with my own eyes. It is nearly finished."

"Yes, fine, fine," Lorenzo responds. "I do so hope you are right."

"Well, and I do hope you have not told anyone at the palace about the bridge?" Walter inquires.

"No, no, I have not," Lorenzo shrieks. "It must be a surprise for the king and Princess Elina. Bones told me and you did too."

"Good, that is good, then. And yes, I now remember telling you so. But, with all the activity going on here, it slipped my mind for a bit. And yes, I want it to be a real surprise for both the king and the princess," Walter adds. Then he utters, "I wonder, shall w go and have a look at what Master Bernard has cooked up for dinner? I am hungry."

CHAPTER XVIII

It is a few days later, when a messenger brings the news Walter has so eagerly been waiting for. "The bridge is ready," the man tells him.

"That is marvellous," Walter exclaims. "Absolutely marvellous. And just in time, too. Now everyone who feels like it can go to the wedding. We must let everybody know about it. Let the word go out!"

And that is exactly what happens. Again, messengers are doing the rounds. Stopping at every village, house, and farm. Their words bring great joy and go from mouth to mouth. "The bridge over the river Yanta is ready!!! Now all who want to, can use it to go to the wedding celebrations."
"How wonderful, how terrific," people are saying. With the dreadful Queen Miranda gone, a great feeling of happiness has taken hold in this land. Here, where for so long, no happiness could be found, people are smiling again, talking to each other, without having to be afraid of spies. For all the spies are gone now. Rumour has it they all fled to the sea and escaped by boat to an unknown destination. But apparently, an enormous freak wave overtook them, leaving no survivors.

In village squares, the laughter and music just keep on going. The fiddlers are there with their fiddles and of course the troubadours are ever present as well. The crowds just never get tired of their music nor of the songs that are sung. Even some acrobats can be seen, who tumble and frolic about. And high above everyone, the walkers on stilts stroll around.

At the last days before the wedding, more and more people gather on the streets and markets. In the inns and taverns, speaking about little else but the wedding. Already, great crowds are on their way to take part in the festivities on the other side of the river Yanta. Cheerful groups of people who laugh and sing most of the way.

Meanwhile, Walter has finished the most urgent tasks. The not so-urgent ones just have to wait. He will deal with those later. No though, it is time to leave for the greatest day in his life. The wedding!

The day before his departure, he discusses with Master Roland what must be done after he has left. "Please lock up the castle," he says. "You, of all people, must be at the wedding."

"But what about the servants?" Master Roland asks.

"Everyone working here is invited," Walter answers. "There are enough extra carriages available. I have already organized this with Mr. Goodman. The two of you can further arrange everything. The army officers will look after their own men. They have their own transport and they are all welcome. After the wedding, my bride and I shall be travelling at our leisure as we return to the castle. This will give you time to get back here before we arrive. I depend on you to see that the whole staff gets back as well. Furthermore, the finest food should be here and the red carpet rolled out. Bring out the best silver and embroidered tablecloths of the finest linen. Fresh flowers must be everywhere. Bernard and his helpers can cook up a feast, and I want the musicians we have here to play soft music when the princess and I have our dinner. What do you think? Will you be able to deal with all this?" Walter asks, catching his breath.

"Oh yes, gladly and absolutely," Master Roland smiles. "Don't worry, everything shall be done exactly as you want it."

"Oh, great," Walter sighs with relief. "You are the best, Master Roland. Thank you so much."

"It is only a pleasure," Master Roland responds as Walter pats him on his shoulder. The two of them have much respect and understanding for each other.

When Walter walks away, he jovially waves a hand over his shoulder towards Master Roland, who is still smiling, admiring this young man for his drive and persistence. Back in the library, where he spends most of his scarce free moments, Walter sends for Conrad the groom. From him, he hears the carriages are ready. His own and those for the king's wise men who are returning to King Frederik's service.

"Good," Walter responds. "Tomorrow morning, at dawn, we will leave. Please see to it that there are some spare carriages for Master Roland and the others. You, though, must come with me. I discussed this already with Master Goodman. Your uniforms, of course, are cleaned and spotless?"

"Oh yes they are," Conrad answers, his face one big smile. "We will be there sir, spic and span and right on time!"

"Fine," Walter smiles back. "I'll keep you to that!" After Conrad has left, he and Bones go to the courtyard. Lorenzo is munching away in one of the fruit-bearing trees there. Husks are flying all around him. Without looking up, he asks, "Are we ready to go?"

"Yes, we are," Walter answers. "Tomorrow morning early. Are you flying or driving with us this time?"

"I think of taking it easy for a bit," Lorenzo replies. "I'll opt for the coach. Who else is coming with us?"

"Well, besides you, Bones and me, also, the king's advisers. We will travel in different coaches."

"Good, good, I am so glad to hear that," Lorenzo shrieks, shifting from one leg to the other, while flapping his wings. "Those people are so boring," he adds.

"They are very clever people," Walter says. "Without their help I could not have done all the work that needed to be done." His tone of voice urges Lorenzo to be more careful with his choice of words.

"Fine, fine," the big bird shouts. Then, after waiting a few moments, he adds, "And you know, I still think they are boring!"

"Oooh, and you," Walter can't help laughing; "You are impossible!"

"Fine, fine," Lorenzo utters again, not at all upset. He studies Walter's face, his head crooked to one side, while gently rocking to and fro on his low hanging tree branch. Bones, sitting just underneath him, gets an unforeseen peck on one of his ears.

"Ooh no, don't you start with me now," Bones barks.

"Stop it, you two," Walter smiles. He adds, "I suppose it is the excitement we all feel that makes you go on so, Lorenzo. Well, I am excited too and can hardly wait anymore. Tomorrow must come quickly."

Luckily, it does. At dawn, as promised, the sound of horses' hooves and carriage wheels can be heard. They clatter up the driveway, gaily and happily. Click clack, click clack, halting in front of the castle entrance. Master Roland is already there, along with a few servants, who carry trunks, valises and other baggage. The king's advisers huff and puff around them. Even here, they keep giving advice, now, of how their belongings should be stowed into their carriage. Once that is settled, the waiting is for Walter.

He soon appears with Lorenzo on his shoulder and Bones on his side. "Good morning, good morning," they greet each other, after which Walter urges the king's advisers to take their seats. He himself stands a while admiring the freshly painted carriages and, even more, the beautiful horses in front of them. The silver bells and colourful plumes on their heads, the braided manes and tails. "It is perfect," he praises Conrad. "Also, you are nicely on time as well."

"Thank you, sir and yes sir, me and Richard, the groom for the other carriage, couldn't wait to get going. The horses also. We are all looking forward to this journey."

"And so do I," Walter laughs, waving a hand at the stableman on the second carriage, who he has come to know as well. He gets a respectful greeting in return. Patting the horses in front of him, Walter says, "You are so gorgeous. I am very proud of you!"

The horses playfully tinkle their bells as they bend their heads towards Walter's now outstretched hands. When he lovingly strokes their soft faces, one of them says, "That we have been chosen as the ones driving you to your wedding makes us proud too!" The other one adds; "Yes, and very, very happy!"

"My, my," Walter smiles, "That is great. So, I say, let's be off then!" Together with Bones and Lorenzo, he takes his place in the first carriage.

Conrad is sitting up front, holding the reins. There is waving and calls of farewell, to and fro, as the horses in front of the carriages get ready to go.

"See you soon, Master Roland," Walter cries out, noticing how his old friend is moved to tears as he waves them on.

"Yes, yes, I will be following shortly," he hears him answer.

Now the whiplashes are singing over the horses' heads as they start to canter away. Slowly at first, then faster and faster until the joyfully move into a gallop, swiftly passing through the landscape of this country that already has become very close to Walter's heart. Everywhere, people shout to greet them. Many are also on their way to the wedding. Seeing Walter and his entourage pass by improves their festive mood to no end.

"Yes, yes, it is true," they tell each other. "This wedding is really going to happen, for there goes the groom! Isn't it fantastic? What a feast it is going to be!"

Walter knows these people still have a long journey ahead of them. Travelling by coach, as he does now, is much faster, of course. Still, no one seems to mind, for everyone is in a very cheerful mood. With no dilly dallying on the way, Walter and his companions in the other carriage make good progress. They overnight in an inn. Conrad sees to it that the horses are well looked after with hay and water and afterwards, a good rest.

Walter and his party are in good spirits. They enjoy a hearty meal, where Bones is not forgotten either. Lorenzo, after having eaten some seeds the inn-keeper found for him, has settled on one of the rafters high up in the dining area. From there, as he used to do in the circus of Mr. Landini, he watches what is going on underneath him.

After breakfast the following morning, they travel on. Bones and Lorenzo behave very well. Sometimes Bones runs alongside the carriages, while Lorenzo now and then flies away for a while. He then looks for and usually finds all the seeds he needs to keep him strong and healthy. Always coming back, though, to rest on Walter's shoulder. Telling him what he has seen and heard. About the excitement of the crowds that make their way towards the palace on the other side of the river Yanta. He has many stories to tell, and Walter always enjoys Lorenzo's lively banter. He admires his sharp-eyed observation of people, how they act and what they do. Even more so, because this big bird delivers his every comment on it, in his usual no-nonsense manner.

But, both Bones and also Lorenzo try to stay away from the king's advisers. They soon discover these wise men do not approve much of animals or birds. Well, not close by, anyway. Moreover, they are mostly very strict, formal and, yes, boring too sometimes. Lorenzo, although maybe not very polite, nevertheless told the truth, Walter a bit unwillingly, admits to himself.

However, nothing takes away the joy and happiness he feels by getting nearer and nearer to his beloved princess. 'Soon, very soon I will see her again,' he keeps thinking. But first, there is the bridge to be crossed. He wonders if it will be as strong and sturdy as it should be. It had to be finished in such a short time. But, when at last the bridge is reached and eventually crossed, he is satisfied. It is excellent!

Captain Olivier Smith and his men stand at attention as Walter's carriages come nearer and then halt in front of them. They are rightly proud of what they achieved.

"Well done," Walter tells them. "This is a splendid bridge. It looks solid and sturdy and just what I hoped for!" Leaving the coaches, he and the king's men are taken on an inspection tour by Captain Smith and officer Fernando Lopez. All of them are impressed with the work that has been done here and are full of praise. Taking their leave from Captain Smith and his men, sometime later, they return to their carriages. There, the soldiers start thronging around them, high spirited and cheering. It warms Walter's heart.

"Thank you," he says. "Thank you. I think you men deserve a party. Therefore, I want to invite you all to my wedding!"

"Hurray, hurray," the soldiers shout and they keep on doing so as Walter and his company drive on.

And on, they travel. Now through pleasantly green fields with well looked after farms. And everywhere there are flags flying and people waving at them. It makes for one big joy ride.

The horses hurry on, through meadows and fields, their bells happily tinkling along. They also relish this journey and know there will be warm stables and good fodder waiting for them at every stop.

For Walter, their voyage cannot go fast enough. It demands a lot of his patience, to once again, overnight in another inn. But then, the next morning, they start on the last lap of their journey. For hours, the two grooms keep the horses at a steady though fast pace. Walter and Bones lean out of the windows, most of the time, Bones now and then barking when he sees other dogs nearby. Lorenzo has moved to the front, where he sits next to Conrad. But, he is getting more and more restless. At long last, he cannot endure it anymore to just sit and wait there.

"I am off to the palace," he shouts to Walter. "We are not that far away from it now. I will tell them you are on your way and will be there soon."

"That is a good idea," Walter agrees.

"Right," Lorenzo shrieks. "See you then. Bye, bye."

"Goodbye," Walter calls after him, because Lorenzo is already gone.

"Goodbye," Bones barks. They watch him disappear into the sky.

"Ooh well," Walter sighs. "We'll get there too!" And so they do. After not much more than an hour, the hill on which the palace is situated is reached. Although half hidden behind trees, they soon see its towers rising up in front of them.

"At last, at last," Walter cries out. "We have arrived!" Through the gates they hurry, down the driveway. And then there is Rita.

"Good day, Walter and Bones," she twitters happily while settling herself on Walter's shoulder. "I am so glad you both are here!"

"Ah yes, and so are we," Walter laughs. "My, my, it is so good to see you again, Rita," he adds. "Are you well?"

"I am very well," Rita answers. "Even more so, now that you both have returned."

"Yeah, it is good to be with you again, Rita," Bones utters.

They are at the palace by now and come to a halt in front of its heavy wooden front doors. At that same instant, those doors swing open, revealing King Frederik and Princess Elina, who immediately start walking towards them.

With one big leap, Walter jumps out of the coach and they, more or less, meet halfway. Such happiness it is to see each other again. The king has his arms around Walter's shoulders and Princess Elina's arms are around both of them. They laugh and talk while Rita, now on the back of Bones, cheerfully sings along.

Then the carriage with the king's advisers arrives and now it is their turn to be welcomed back. Sometime later, they are all inside the palace. And then Lorenzo's voice is heard.

"Isn't it great to be back here again?" he shouts.

"It is marvellous," Walter calls back, noticing his big parrot friend sitting high up on a large chandelier in the hallway. Looking, watching, as always. Meanwhile, servants are darting by, smiling and greeting, to fetch the baggage.

The king leads his guests to the library. It is his preferred room, large and airy. It is here where most of his time is spent, reading and consulting about affairs of state with many men in the kingdom. Tea and light snacks are served almost immediately and a lively conversation soon follows. The king gets the latest news from the land across the river Yanta. Of the bridge that has been built over the river, no one says a word. Walter has asked the king's advisers not to mention it. He wants to keep it a surprise for a little bit longer. The king's advisers, though, do present the long lists of treasures found in the tower rooms to King Frederik.

"Good work," the king praises them all. "Thank you very much. I really appreciate what you have achieved in such a short time." His approval is received with grateful bows and words from his wise men. But Walter and Princess Elina, sitting next to each other, smiling happily, are just holding hands. They celebrate their being together again and only partially hear what is being said.

Rita and Lorenzo are also in the library now, having found a place on some book shelves, unnoticed. Since acting as Walter's spy, this almost comes naturally to them.

After a while, the king's advisers ask to be excused. They are tired and look forward to a late afternoon nap. King Frederik, who actually was hoping for some time alone with his daughter and Walter, has no objections at all. "Right," he remarks as soon as his wise men have left, "Now we can speak about other things. Two weeks from now, the two of you are getting married. Let us talk about that! Is it not like a dream come true?"

"Yes," Walter answers. "It is too wonderful for words. I can hardly wait anymore." He looks adoringly at Princess Elina, who looks back at him, with love and admiration in her eyes. Then the three of them have a long conversation,

There are so many things that still have to be taken care of before the wedding. Walter wants to know how many guests are coming and if he can invite people he befriended during his wanderings. Even workers from the castle on the other side of the river Yanta? And also the officers and some of their soldiers?

"But of course you can," the king assures him. "Let them all come. No one will be sent away from this splendid wedding feast. The only thing is, how do we get them all over here? I am afraid rowing all those people over might be getting a bit much for poor Adrian?"

This is the moment Walter has been waiting for, to spring his big surprise. "Adrian does not have to do that," he says.

"Ooh?" King Frederik responds, "But how?

"Because," Walter utters his words slowly. "Because there is a bridge over the river Yanta now!"

Both the king and Princess Elina gasp for breath upon hearing this.

"But how?" King Frederik repeats, totally overwhelmed. "How is that possible?"

"It became possible when I thought of wanting to give something special to your Majesty as well as to Princess Elina," Walter answers. "And to the whole country, for that matter," he adds. "A bridge would be ideal for that. For everyone who lives in this land, it will bring us closer together, all of us. For trade and traffic, for better communication with each other. To get this bridge built would be my way of saying thank you. Thank you for both your love and kindness to me!" Here Walter's voice wavers.

Princess Elina, overcome by emotion as well, utters. "You are very special, Walter, and you have given us all a very special gift."

King Frederik also is extremely moved. "Such a surprise and such an amazing feat. You giving us a bridge!" he says at last. "And in such a short time. How did you do it?"

"Aah," Walter replies, "I remembered that Your Majesty told me, Your Majesty's father already planned this bridge years ago. Although it never was built, the material for it was delivered. Master Roland knew about this, too. He suggested it might still be on the farm Your Majesty gave to Adrian. Well, we searched for it and indeed found it in a large shed there. We also discovered the original plan which was lying on a shelf. With the help of Captain Oliver Smith and his hand-picked, hard-working men, the bridge was built, and they succeeded in having it ready before our marriage." Walter ends his report.

King Frederik stands up, and walking over to Walter, embraces him. "It is the greatest gift you could have given us," he says. "We can never thank you enough!"

Princess Elina snuggles still closer to Walter. "Thank you," she smiles. "Thank you, my dear, soon to be husband." It is this remark, in a moment of so much emotion, that clears the air. It makes all three of them laugh and from then on, the discussion over the coming wedding is continued. Does Walter have any special wishes for this special day? Which food would he would like to have prepared, among other things? But Walter prefers to leave all such matters to Princess Elina. "You decide," he says.

"You and Master Roland, who will be here shortly, can take care of all this, please! I am sure everything you decide will be perfect!"

Wisely, Princess Elina leaves it at that. She listens with interest when Walter brings up matters which have nothing to do with the royal in-house arrangements. No, he wants to find out what can be done for the masses of ordinary people who are already streaming in from the other side of the river Yanta.

"They are coming to celebrate and I would like them to be looked after well," he says.

"Indeed, and so they shall," the king replies. He goes on, "We shall give them a real treat. We can afford it with all these riches from the tower rooms."

"Great," Walter beams.

"Yes," Princess Elina joins in. "I feel that because those riches were taken from these residents, we must do something extra for them. They have suffered for so long."

"I was thinking the same thing," Walter exclaims. "For instance, is it not possible to give out a grant? Say money for farmers to buy implements, seeds, everything they need for the next harvest. Grants to rebuild their farms, to build houses for all who have none. Schools for children, ah, there is so much we can do." Walter stops to catch his breath and King Frederik, with a chuckle, replies. "Yes, Walter, yes, we can do all that. And we sha I will get my men on to this. They can take matters further. After reporting back to me, the necessary decisions will be made. And we will do it soon!"

Princess Elina is elated by her father's response, and so is Walter. They talk for some more time about all the things that wi improve the lives of the citizens from the other side of the river. All three of them come up with then this, then that idea, but Rita and Lorenzo have heard enough. They, after a while, disappear very quietly through an open window in the library.

Bones, lying next to Walter, dozes off, but Walter enjoys every moment of this get together. Still, after some time, he finds himself listening to sounds from outside. Actually, he is expecting Bruno and Mona and Rona. Surely, Lorenzo and Rita, whose flying away, he did notice, told them about their arrival? Certainly, they will come to greet him? These thoughts flash through his mind and Princess Elina seems to become aware of it. She smiles understandingly and then looks at the window. Sounds as if a noisy party is starting to take place, can be heard right now.

"It's them," Walter cries out. "It must be them! Excuse me please, but I must go and see!" With that, he hastily leaves the room. Bones, at once wide awake, is on his heels.

The king first frowns at this unusual upheaval, but then thinks better of it. After all, Walter and his friends are a very unusual group. So he decides to follow Princess Elina as she walks over to the window. From there, they can watch everything that is going on. They see how the monkeys run up to Walter. Hugging him and getting hugged in return. Then, after all the hugging, Rona and Mona start climbing up and all over him, while babbling with excitement.

Such a happy occasion this is. Walter, overcome by his feelings, can hardly speak. "My, my," he manages to bring out at last, as he again catches and cuddles the monkeys in his arms.

"Yes, my, my," Bruno, good old Bruno, repeats after him. He has been standing there all the while, looking on with intense delight. Coming nearer, his mighty paws encircle Walter in a warm embrace. Rona and Mona shriek in mocked alarm. "You are crushing us, Bruno," they claim. But Walter nor Bruno pay much attention to their yammering. They know it is just the thrill of the moment that makes them go on so. Bruno could never ever harm them. "It is great, so great to see you again, Walter," he says in that deep voice of his. "We have missed you very much."

"Good, good," Walter laughs. "I have missed you very much too!"

Rita and Lorenzo rush above their heads. Flying low, they fully share in all the elation. "Will you be staying with us now?" Rona asks, but Walter cannot make such a promise.

"Are you happy here in the zoo?" he asks instead. "Yes, yes," both monkeys answer him.

"And you, Bruno?" is Walter's next question.

"Yes, me too," Bruno replies promptly and Walter can see all three of them are speaking the truth.

"Splendid," he responds. "I worried about that a bit."

"I told you they are fine," Lorenzo, having settled on Walter's shoulder again, shrieks into his ear.

"Yeah, I know you did and I hear you, Lorenzo," Walter react with a chuckle, while adding; "Also, you speak very loud, my friend!"

"That's what I do," Lorenzo prattles, not in the least worried, while ruffling his feathers. Bruno looks at Walter with a somewhat puzzled expression appearing on his face. "Yes, well," he utters, "As you heard, we all like it here. There is never a dull moment.

And Lorenzo, when he comes over, always tells us the latest news of all you are busy with, on the other side of the river. We are very proud of you."

"Thank you," Walter smiles while trying to calm Rona and Mona down. The one is wriggling around his legs and the other one keeps jumping up and down his chest. "Enough now, enough," he says. "I can't keep up with you anymore."

Meanwhile, Bruno calmly goes on speaking. "And now you are getting married, Walter. We all are very happy for you."

"Thanks again Bruno," Walter replies. "Of course you are invited to take part in the festivities and everyone else as well!"

"Great, great," Bruno rumbles on. "That is all very nice, but what happens afterwards? Rumour has it, you will be leaving again. Is this true? Is that why you asked us if we were happy here at the zoo?"

"We speak later," Walter stops his friend. "First thing tomorrow morning, I come over to you, I promise."

Meanwhile, Rona and Mona, totally unaware of what is being said around them, have greeted Bones too. They, just as they always liked to do before, are sitting on his back. Bones loves it and starts running in circles with them. This gives Rita the chance to take her place on Walter's shoulder again. Lorenzo flies off, after Bones and the monkeys. "We are going to the zoo," he shouts. "We are going to the zoo!"

"Is that in order?" Bones wants to know, as he runs back to Walter.

"Of course it is," Walter tells him. "I have to return to the king and Princess Elina now, but you go right ahead. We'll see each other later, I am sure."

"I find you," Bones says simply.

Although Bruno and Bones have greeted already, they have not had a chance to really speak to each other. But, after tearing himself away from Walter, Bruno tells Bones, "Ah my friend, you look well, and it is so good to see you."

"Yes Bruno, it is good to see you, too. And I feel well, especially with these two monkeys on my back," Bones grins.

"I can see that," Bruno bawls. "Well, off with you then. I am coming too, just now."

Bones, wagging his tail cheerfully, dashes away with Rona and Mona clinging on to him. They shriek with delight, totally forgetting to say goodbye to Walter. Not so Bruno. He cups Walter's hand in both his paws, careful not to hurt him. "Until tomorrow then," he utters.

"Yes, until tomorrow," Walter answers. He stares after Bruno as the large bear turns away. With shoulders hanging, he slowly totters off in the direction of the zoo. Then Walter himself, also turns around and walks back to the library where the king and Princess Elina are waiting,

"Ah, good, you are back again," King Frederik welcomes him.

"It was wonderful to watch how glad Bruno and the monkeys were to see you," Princess Elina remarks.

"It made me just as happy to be with them." Walter responds. His face still shows the sadness he felt of having to let them go again so soon.

"I know," Princess Elina whispers.

"Ahem," King Frederik says. "Well, I suggest we continue our talk." And so, many more ideas and plans are discussed. Dinner comes and goes, and it is very late before they wish each other goodnight.
Of course, Walter now is a guest in the palace. One of the finest rooms has been specially prepared for him. Upon arriving there, he finds Bones lying and waiting at the side of the bed.

Rita, who left before dinner, is sitting on one of the bedposts. "Lorenzo won't be coming," she says. "He is staying over at the zoo."

"That's fine," Walter yawns. He is tired and just wants to sleep. It does not take him long to snuggle into the luxuriously soft eiderdown, dozing off almost at once.

At daybreak, he is up again. "Are we going now?" Bones asks, after the three of them have said 'good morning' to each other.

"It is a fine day for visiting the zoo," Rita chirps.

"Right," Bones barks. "I am sure everyone there must be waiting for us already."

"Yes, yes," Walter replies. "We are going, going, going! By the way," he adds, while slipping on his shoes, "how did you and Rita manage to get into this room last night? I was so sleepy, I forgot to ask then."

"Oh, one of the servants opened the door for us," Bones answers. "I just kept go on barking a bit and that worked like magic."

"Hm, well, that is good. I suppose the servants know you by now," Walter utters. "I am certain they also received orders to go very easy on my friends."

"Very nice," Rita sings.

"Great," Bones reacts.

After freshening up in the bathroom, Walter quickly dresses and they are off! "We shall join the king and Princess Elina later for breakfast. In the dining room," Walter says to Rita and Bones as they walk over to the zoo.

"I think I'd rather stay behind with Bruno and the others," Rita declares.

"Of course, you can do that if you wish," Walter replies.

"I do not want to," Bones says. "It is no problem if I stay with you?"

"No, not at all," Walter reacts. "Why do you ask?"

"Oh, I just wondered," Bones answers.

"Don't!" Walter tells him. "All of us, we are a team. Everyone knows we belong together. Perhaps some might find this a bit odd but that does not matter."

"Right," Bones utters, happy in the understanding he will always be allowed to stay on Walter's side.

All is very still as they reach the zoo. Not for long though. The lions, whose enclosure is next to that of Gordon and Wosa, spot them first. Their mighty roar stirs up all and sunder. "Welcome, welcome," their deep voices then rumble. "How good to see you again, Walter, and you too, Bones."

"Thank you, thank you," they both answer. "It is so good to be here," Walter smiles. "How are you all doing?"

"Excellent, great, great," the lions bellow, and then the monkeys Mona and Rona are there. Climbing up and over him, as they always do, when excited.

"Good morning, Walter," they gurgle. "Good morning Bones and Rita." The greetings flow to and fro. The other animals and birds all join in calling Walter's name and welcoming him back.

Bruno has arrived too and joyfully embraces Walter, just as he did the day before. "It is marvellous, having you here," he bawls.

"It is so nice to be here," Walter smiles while gently freeing himself from Bruno's grip. Gordon and Wosa, the gorillas, are also calling out to Walter, expecting him to visit them first. And this he does. Leaving Rona and Mona under Bruno's good care, he enters the enclosure of the two huge gorillas on his own. It is a moment full of gladness for all three of them.

"We missed you," Gordon booms in that deep voice of his, as he lifts Walter up in his arms to cuddle him.

"We are so pleased to see you," Wosa says. "You look well and happy!"

"I am," Walter grins. "I am!"

Gordon, noticing Walter wavering a bit in his powerful arms, gently puts him down again. "We hear you are going to get married to Princess Elina," he remarks.

"That is what makes you happy, is it not?" Wosa utters.

"Yes, that and also because I am back here with all of you," Walter answers. He goes on, "It seems to me you are content and happy too?"

"Oh yes," Gordon declares. "Everything is so much better for us now."

"It is a blessing having all this space for ourselves," Wosa tells him.

"And the food is very good as well," Gordon adds.

"It really is great, hearing all this," Walter smiles. "It is what I was hoping for! But I also hope, you will excuse me, my dear friends. As you can see, Rona and Mona are getting a bit restless out there. Bruno can hardly hold them anymore. They want me to come back so, I better go, but you will see me shortly again, I promise."

"We keep you to that," both Gordon and Wosa tell him.

"Oh, but you can," Walter assures them as he strides back to his waiting friends.

"You want to greet everyone else here as well, I take it?" Bruno asks.

"Yes, that is what I am going to do now," Walter replies while Rona and Mona battle for a place on his shoulders. "Enough, you two," he says. "There is a place for each of you on one of my shoulders. You know that, don't you?"

"Yes," the two monkeys pout; "We know!" As at last they are settled, their small group moves on. Bruno, walking upright, is next to Walter as they go from enclosure to enclosure, greeting each and every one. It all is as joyous and happy as can be. Rita and Lorenzo are adding to the overall din, by flying than here, then there, with Lorenzo shrieking to his heart's delight.

That is when Keenan and Simon arrive to find out what is happening. By seeing Walter, their faces light up. They greet him warmly, clearly very pleased he is back.

"I am impressed with the work you have done here," Walter tells them. "I have nothing but praise for it. Everything looks clean and the animals and birds are well cared for. They are happy and content."

"Thank you sir," the wardens reply gratefully. They are happy too with the way everything has worked out.

Walter decides to keep them company, as they make their early morning rounds, to see if everything is in order. Visiting the cages for the second time, he notices how very at ease Keenan and Simon are with all the animals and birds. They, in turn, are very pleased to see them. Knowing food will arrive shortly, also helps, of course. Walter's return makes everything even more jolly and cheerful.

Coming to the enclosure where the small monkeys are kept, Walter finds one open and empty. "This is where we stay," Rona tells him. "We can come and go as we please," Mona says. "Yes, because we are not wild anymore," Rona adds.

"Oh, is that so?" Walter asks with a chuckle. He then goes on, "well, if you ask me, I think you two can be pretty wild sometimes."

"But they are just very playful," Bruno at once comes to their defence.

"I know, I know," Walter smiles. He loves the way his big old friend at once comes up for the two little monkeys. Holding each one in his arms and close to his heart, he says, "And what about you? Do you still live in your own wood cabin, Bruno?"

"Oh yes," Bruno answers, "I love having my own place. Rona and Mona can visit me whenever they like. Most nights they sleep over, which is very nice."

"Yes, and we keep it clean for him," Keenan, having overheard Walter, says.

"And see to it that there is always honey on the cabin's shelves as well," Simon joins in.

"He also gets the right food to keep him healthy," Keenan reports.

"My, my, this is all just marvellous," Walter declares. "It seems to me, you could not have found a better place than here at the zoo, Bruno. With Keenan and Simon looking after you so well. What else could a big bear like you wish for, I wonder?"

"To be with you," Bruno utters. "That would be the greatest thing I'd wish for! But that is not how it is going to be, is it?" he asks while looking straight into Walter's eyes.

"No, I am sorry, but that is indeed not how it is going to be," Walter answers his big friend. Rita and Mona have taken off on Bones back again while Rita and Lorenzo are flying overhead. Now, walking some distance behind Keenan and Simon, he decides to tell Bruno about his further plans.

"You already said there are rumours about me not coming back here," he begins. "Well, it is true. King Frederik has asked me to take care of the land across the river Yanta. How can I refuse such a great honour?"

"But," Bruno blabbers.

"No Bruno," Walter interrupts him. "Leaving you here hurts me, too. It hurts me more than I can say. And the same goes for Rona and Mona," he continues. "You must agree though, this is the best solution for all of us. I am sure you have made many friends here by now, as have Rona and Mona. To know, you three are well looked after and happy here, makes me happy too. There is so much to do on the other side of the river Yanta. The king has asked me to rebuild the country, so I won't have time to be with you much, anyway. Not as it was before. You know that, don't you?"

"Yes, I do and I understand this is the best we can do," Bruno replies. "But I will miss you terribly," he adds.

"So will I, my friend," Walter assures him. "But you shall see me now and then though," he goes on. "The new river bridge will make it much easier to visit here. And as soon as things become a bit less hectic, Princess Elina and I come over to see you all again. In fact, we will come over often. So what do you say to that? Does this make you feel better?" he asks.

"I'd say that is great," Bruno answers. "And yes, it makes me feel much better," he adds, while grabbing Walter's hand into his paw. Looking with affection into each other's eyes, the two of them slowly wander on.

Keenan and Simon, always in a bit of a hurry and walking much faster than Walter and Bruno, have already finished their inspections. "Everything is in order," Keenan reports back to

Walter. "I hope you will excuse us, but we must now start with our daily chores. The food must be dealt out."

"Yes," Simon joins in. "The enclosures and cages must be cleaned. You know how it is."

"I understand," Walter assures the two with a smile. "We'll be seeing each other again," he tells them.

"Of course, yes," the wardens answer while dashing off and Walter turns his attention to Bruno again. "I want to thank you, my friend, for looking so well after Rona and Mona. It was very good of you," he says.

"No problem," Bruno rumbles back. "It was only a pleasure, I love those two little monkeys."

"And they love you," Walter says. "One does not have to be a wizard, to see that!" He goes on; "I noticed there are some bears here from circus Landini."

"Yes," Bruno answers; "And we all get along just fine."

"I am glad," Walter smiles.

They have reached the elephant's enclosure in the meantime, where Jumbo and his friends greet them warmly. "So, what do we hear? You are getting married then?" Jumbo remarks as Walter enters their enclosure.

"Yes, indeed, isn't that marvellous?" Walter laughs.

"Yes, yes, it is," Jumbo agrees. "And you promised everyone a big party?" he asks further.

"That is true too!" Walter replies. "I want everyone here to feel part of this happy occasion. There will be extra fine food to eat for you and all the others here at the zoo."

"Nice, very nice," the elephants trumpet. Some even perform a few dance steps. Because most of them have worked in circus Landini and because elephants have a very good memory, they still know how to do this.

Walter claps his hands in approval.

Rita and Lorenzo, having flown back by now, cry; 'Bravo, bravo,' as they circle overhead.

"Splendid," Walter praises. "This was really good. But I hope you will excuse me, for I really have to go back to the palace. Farewell my friends, I come to see you, soon again, of that you can be sure." It is then, that all of a sudden, the elephants, while waving their trunks and making soothing noises, group in front of him. It is their way of showing him respect and Walter is moved beyond words. He is fully aware, it is very rare that elephants do this and a great honour indeed! "Thank you, thank you," he utters. "I will always remember this moment." Then, slowly, very slowly, while looking back over his shoulder all the time, he walks away.

"That really was something," Bruno declares, shaking his head in wonderment.

"You are so right," Walter agrees; "It really and truly was!"

Neither Rita nor Lorenzo utter any further comment on what they have observed. They are too stunned, it seems. So there is silence for some time as they walk back towards the zoo entrance. But the remarks and greetings of the many other zoo dwellers follow them everywhere they go. They are all kinds of comments, which Walter gratefully and with an all embracing warm smile receives. They see Rona and Mona again at the monkeys' cages. Bones, of course, is also there. He is sitting outside, clearly waiting for them. Upon seeing Walter, the three of them join him. "We heard what the elephants did," Bones says. "Everyone here in the zoo knows by now. How wonderful that must have been!"

"Yes, it was," Walter answers simply.

"And we missed it!" Rona cries out.

"I would so have liked to see it!" Mona whimpers.

"Well, what can I say?" Walter sighs. "It was a great honour that the elephants performed this ritual for me. And yes, I am sorry you were not there, but it can't be helped."

With Rona and Mona, each on one of his shoulders, they walk on. As they at last reach the zoo's entrance again, Walter declares; "Well, this is where we have to part."

"Can't we come with you?" Rona asks.

Bruno, reaching out, takes her and Mona from Walter's shoulder. "You stay here with me," he tells them. "Our nice food will come just now. You don't want to miss that, will you?"

"No," Mona mutters; "But …."

"No buts," Bruno says firmly. "Walter has to be at the palace. He is going to be very busy, what with the wedding and all."

"Yes," Walter adds. "That is very true, however, I promise, you will see me again soon, my dears. Yes?"

"Yes, Walter," the two little monkeys answer politely. They always feel so comforted in Bruno's arms. It even makes them forget to complain too much about Walter leaving them.

Keenan and Simon are busy doling out food in some further away enclosure, Walter notices. "Keep well," he calls, while waving to them. "I am on my way again."

"Right sir," they call back, sticking their hands into the air and waving as well. "Thank you for coming, sir."

"Right, we'll see you later then," Walter answers back. Looking anew at Bruno, with the two little monkeys in his arms, makes his heart ache. Spreading his arms around the three of them, he gives them a big hug.

"Don't worry about us," Bruno assures him. "We will be fine, Walter."

"Good," Walter replies. "That is good, then."

"I will come and play with you tomorrow," Bones promises Rona and Mona, and this makes their little faces light up at once.

"Yes, yes, we wait for you," they shout as Walter and Bones wander on.

"So, it is only us, from now on," Walter utters to Bones.

"Oh, and what about me?" Lorenzo shouts.

"Yes, and me?" Rita wants to know. Both birds have been keeping an eye on things, hovering nearby.

"Good, great, of course I meant you as well," Walter replies, cheering up a bit.

"You should not be so sad." Rita, who has flown onto his shoulder again, tells Walter. She is reading his mood, as do Bones and Lorenzo.

"No, you have no reason to," Bones barks. "You have given Bruno and the monkeys the best possible home. You should be happy about that!"

"I know, I know, and I am," Walter answers. "Only, it takes a bit of getting used to. But that aside, I am very happy. To think I am marrying my lovely Princess Elina. There is so much to look forward to. We will have such a wonderful life together."

"But naturally," Lorenzo shouts, as he settles himself on Walter's other shoulder.

"And," Bones says, looking up at him; "We are going to share this life with you."

"I would not have it otherwise," Walter smiles.

They arrive back at the palace just in time for breakfast. Rita and Lorenzo choose to fly around in the gardens, finding their food there. Bones, however, goes with Walter to the dining room. There, over a relaxed meal, with much talk and laughter, Walter tells the king and Princess Elina how he spent the early morning hours. He relates how impressed he is with the work Keenan and Simon do. It gladdens the king's heart to hear that Bruno and the two monkeys are also very happy in his zoo.

Princess Elina, though, senses that Walter, in spite of his cheerful air, is a bit upset. Upset about having to leave Bruno, together with Rona and Mona, behind. Smiling warmly at him, she says, "I know how you feel, Walter. I really do, but don't think about it too much now. Everything is turning out for the best, you will see."

Her understanding of how he feels uplifts Walter's mood no end. "I am sure you are right, my princess," he answers. He continues; "Let's focus then on the urgent matter of our coming wedding, shall we?"

"Absolutely," Princess Elina laughs.

"Definitely," King Frederik declares. He has closely listened and followed how these two talk to each other. It gives him a good insight into how well they are matched and how in tune they are with each other.

So now their attention gets focused on the wedding preparations anew. There is so much that still needs to be discussed and done. Overseeing this, ordering that. Fittings for the bride and also for Walter, as well as many other arrangements, have to be made. Retreating to the library a bit later, Princess Elina shows Walter some drawings of the clothes she has chosen for him to wear at the wedding. "I thought these might be suitable for you," she tells him. "What do you think? Do you think they are nice? Are they what you want?"

Walter can find no fault with them and indeed, they are all a man can wish for. Elegant and colourful, yet dignified.

"They look good," he chuckles. "What is your opinion on this King Fredrik?" he asks his soon to be father-in-law.

The king laughs. "If my daughter selected these, then they must be fine," is his verdict.

"Well, fine it is then," Walter tells the princess. And so it goes. Overseeing one detail after another. Luckily, not everything has to be decided in one day only. It takes far more than that, but each day, more or less fly by in this manner.

In between, Walter, mostly together with Princess Elina, visits the zoo often. Of course, Bones always goes with them, while Rita and Lorenzo, if not already there, usually come as well. It makes for a nice break from all the pressures of the wedding preparations. Bruno and the monkeys are always delighted to see them. And so are the others.

"Such a festive occasion it is, to see you all here," Bruno booms in a happy voice. Keenan and Simon are just as pleased as they are. They feel honoured and very fortunate to be around the princess and Walter. To hear how their hard work is appreciated gladdens their hearts to no end.

"Is old Leesam still coming over to help?" Walter asks the wardens one morning.

"No," Keenan answers. "It is now Leesam's grandson who prepares the animals and birds' food. He is a learner at the local animal doctor and he is very good, really."

"My, my," Walter utters. "That is perfect then."

"Yes," Princess Elina joins in. "He is a nice person who also sees to it that Bruno gets his regular supply of honey and Rona and Mona always get something extra from him as well."

"Yeah, we like him," Rona yells. "Don't we Mona?"

"Yes, I like him too. He makes good food!" Mona answers. Just at this moment, a lanky young man with a freckled face is coming their way. Carrying a large tub full of fresh vegetables and fruit, he gives a large smile upon seeing them. He also bows his head in an effort to greet respectfully as well.

Keenan puts up his hand to stop the young man in his tracks. "This is Mourice," he introduces him to Walter. "We were just talking about you," he declares. "I was saying how well you look after all the animals and birds here in the zoo. Seeing to it that they get the right food."

Mourice, at a loss for words, again bows respectfully. A bit bewildered but clearly also very pleased, he utters some words of thanks.

"I am pleased to meet you," Walter says. "Keep up the good work, Mourice. Tell me, is your grandfather still in good health?"

"Yes sir, he is and my grandfather and mother still enjoy living in the village," Mourice answers.

"Well, I am glad to hear this," Walter says. "Please give both of them my regards, will you?"

"Oh yes, sir, I shall. My grandfather often tells me how much he liked working with you here in the zoo," the young man gushes.

"Great," Walter laughs.

"Eh," it is Bruno, making this sound. Walter, seeing his bothered face, asks, "What is it Bruno? Is something the matter?"

"Yes, eh, the honey," Bruno wails. "There is no honey in my cabin anymore!"

"Oh, my, my, we can't have that," Walter reacts. Looking at Princess Elina, he says, "now can we?"

"No, indeed, we cannot!" is Princess Elina's replies sternly. There is laughter in her eyes, though. Turning to Mourice again, Walter says, "Bruno is complaining there is no honey in his cabin. Would you know why?"

"Oh, yeah, I do sir," Mourice utters. "I am very sorry, but our supplier was out of stock for a while. But it is has come in again. I'll bring the honey just now, I promise."

"Hmm, good, good," Bruno responds, looking much happier already.

"Right," Mourice says, "I think I better hurry then. I have to ge so many things done still. Can I please be excused?"

"Yes, you can," Princess Elina smiles. Bowing again, Leesam's grandson picks up the tub with fruit and vegetables and disappear from sight rather quickly.

"He seems a good sort," Walter remarks with a chuckle.

"Mourice tries his best," Simon declares. "It is not so easy for him working here and then also studying to become an animal doctor."

"He will succeed, though," Keenan adds. "He is just like his grandfather Leesam, clever and a hard worker."

"Good," Walter says. "Just the person one needs here."

"I agree," Princess Elina laughs as they resume their visits pas the zoo's enclosures. Mona and Rona who have been hanging around Walter's neck most of the time, now jump into Bruno's ever ready arms again.

"You will give us some honey also, Bruno?" they plead.

"Of course I let you have some," Bruno utters.

"I shall come tonight to see if the honey has arrived," Simon says.

"We will also come," Rona and Mona yell.

460

"Fine, fine," is Bruno's reply. He adds, "I saw the peaches in the garden are ripe, so I get some of those as well. Eating them together with the honey will make for a real feast. What do you think?"

"Yes, yes, that sounds so nice," the two monkeys yell again.

"Maybe, we might be excused as well?" Keenan asks Princess Elina and Walter, "Simon and I also have lots of work waiting for us."

"We understand and yes, of course, you are excused," Princess Elina smiles. They all watch as the two wardens walk away in the direction of the zoo's kitchen.

"Mourice is there," Bones remarks dryly.

"Yeah, and I think he will have some explaining to do," Walter chuckles.

"As long as I get my honey every day," Bruno whimpers.

"You can count on it," Princess Elina says. "I will tell Keenan and Simon to make sure you do!"

Rita and Lorenzo have been looking on from afar, but now decide to join Walter and his group as they stroll on. Settling each on one of Walter's shoulder as usual, Rita asks, "What was all that about?"

"It's the honey," Bruno says. "I did not get any for quite some time!"

"Oh, my, my, we can't have that," Lorenzo mimics Walter. "Now can we, my dear princess?" he asks her. His cheeky comments bring out a gale of laughter from both Princess Elina and Walter. Lorenzo himself snickers loudest of all. Proud to be such a show stopper.

It is back to the palace for the princess and Walter, though, after this notable outing. Leaving Bruno and the two monkeys behind is less dramatic this time around. Bruno is looking forward to his supply of honey and Rona and Mona are more than happy to just go along with him.

Chapter XIX

Overseeing the wedding preparations is a matter of tireless activity. Detail after detail has to be taken care of. A good time must be had by all the people of the land.

By order of the king, refreshments will be given out, for free. Also, bread and small cakes as well as other delicacies. Therefore, bakers are working long, long hours. Couriers have been delivering invitations everywhere. The royal kitchen is a beehive of energy. The wedding cake, in all its glory, is baked and set aside for the big day. Many meals are prepared for the royal visitors from all over the world. More and more of them are reaching the palace each day. They arrive in great style with beautiful carriages and entourage. The numerous rooms of the palace are filled one by one.

To while away the time before the marriage, music and dance evenings are held and Princess Elina even organises a masked ball. Walter, on that occasion, is dressed as a shepherd and Princess Elina as a shepherdess. They make a stunning couple. The princess looks like a porcelain doll, in the frilly dress she is wearing. Adding to this vision are her pin-upped curls, of which some playfully fall back around her delicate face. Walter, handsome as always, carries his flute with him. Much to the enchantment of the guests, he now and then plays a charming little tune. Rita is there as well. Sitting on the shoulder of Princess Elina, she is with Walter again when he starts playing the flute. As she sings along in her crystal-clear voice, the praise from the royals engulfs them,

"How delightful, this is so charming," they comment.

Bones mainly stays in some nearby corner on these evenings, keeping watch from there.

With Lorenzo, though, it is different. He also likes to be the centre of attention. After all, his performances at circus Landini were always very popular. Indeed, they were very successful. Everybody liked his act of suddenly appearing from nowhere. Flying low, while shouting, "Caramba, Caramba!" always had the audience in stitches. Surely, it will be the same here? This is what Lorenzo is thinking, totally forgetting Walter's warning not to get up to his old tricks again. Sitting on top of one of the large chandeliers, he watches the orchestra starting to play. As the king royal guests gather on the dance floor, Lorenzo decides, now is the time to act. Suddenly, and seemingly out of nowhere, he dives.

Flying low, very low over those graceful people with their lavish costumes. Expecting lots of applause, he shouts; "Caramba, Caramba!" But, the high hair-do's that adorn many of the ladies' heads are his undoing. By flying so low, he touches many of those elaborate hairstyles and causes great damage to them. This results in screams of dismay and total confusion in the ballroom.

Walter is stunned and so is Princess Elina. King Frederik is seated at the end of the room, where the floor is a few steps higher. This enables him to oversee everything that happens in front of him. Being deeply in conversation with some elderly noblemen at this moment, the king is dismayed by the uproar. Looking to see what is going on, he, like Princess Elina and Walter, is also now stunned.

"Good heavens," King Frederik exclaims. "Why all this noise? What is taking place here? Look at all these ladies with their hands in their hair. This is chaos, total chaos."

"Indeed," the elderly noblemen echo the king's words. "Total chaos it is."

As the king scans the room, he suddenly gets a glimpse of Lorenzo. The big parrot is in a state of utter panic and spurts out of sight through an open window. "Well, what we have here is a grave situation," the king remarks. "It is something very unforeseen."

"Absolutely," the elderly noblemen and their ladies sitting near the king agree. Although at first upset, King Frederik, grasping what has occurred, now also starts to see the funny side of all this. Putting his hand in front of him, he cannot help but chuckle. Being always closely watched by those surrounding the king, this does not go unnoticed. And yes, well, of course, if the king finds something funny, then so does everyone else. A second chuckle is soon heard, and then another. It is not long before the chuckles become laughs. Coming as it does, from where the king is sitting, more people feel free to start laughing as well.

Walter and Princess Elina can't help but join in either. The other guests on the ballroom floor soon take notice of the laughter coming from where King Frederik and the other elderly royals are. Some, at first, just stare in their direction. But then, as one of the ladies with a ruined hair-do herself, starts giggling, other ladies quickly follow her example. Soon, the whole ballroom is filled with laughter.

The princes and princesses start smiling at each other and joke about the hairstyles that have gone astray. The princes even compliment the princesses. They tell them the hair whirling about their faces, actually make them look even more beautiful!

King Frederik starts clapping his hands in admiration for this changed spirit engulfing the ballroom. Then everybody does the same. The young people still on the floor soon clap along. The orchestra starts playing again, and the dancing begins anew. So, the evening of the masked ball turns out to be a very memorable and special one. An evening not easy to forget and forever to be remembered.

But Lorenzo, having made such a hasty exit, does not know anything about all this. He just feels sorry for himself. He meant well. 'Why did things go wrong again?' he wonders. 'Maybe it is best to stay away from all those people at the palace for a while,' he ponders. 'I shall go to the zoo and stay with my own kind. They are all very nice parrots and no one will disturb me there.'

Of course, Walter does. Early the next morning, he is standing in front of the parrot's enclosure. "My, my, Lorenzo, you did it again. What were you thinking?" he asks.

From behind a large tree trunk comes the timid answer, "I don't know, really!"

"You thought you could re-enact your performance from circus Landini here, did you not?"

"Well, it was always very successful there," Lorenzo answers, still without showing himself.

"Yeah, my friend it was," Walter agrees. "It was at circus Landini, but one cannot say the same from last night, now can we?"

"No, we cannot," Lorenzo replies, adding, "Are King Frederik and Princess Elina and everyone else very cross with me?"

"No, not really," Walter tells his friend. "King Frederik was the one who saw how ridiculous the whole situation actually was. He started to chuckle about it and then slowly, slowly, everybody did the same. Giggles and laughter took over, so in the end, the evening was a success after all."

"Oh, I am glad about that," Lorenzo declares, emerging now from behind the tree trunk. Taking place on one of its branches, he utters. "I think I will stay here at the zoo until after the wedding. I do not want to show my face to anyone anymore. I am too embarrassed for that."

"Oh, come on," Walter smiles. "You are making it out worse than it is. But if that is how you feel, it is up to you."

"Right, right," Lorenzo replies.

"Well, I have to go now, but I do hope to see you later again," Walter tells his friend. He goes on, "King Frederik promised his guests a tour through the zoo grounds today. Princess Elina and I shall be here and everyone else as well. So prepare yourself for it, Lorenzo," Walter chuckles. Doubting that the big parrot, with his great love of being noticed, really will stay out of sight, he walks away.

Lorenzo, though, has made up his mind. When the royal guests visit the zoo that afternoon, Lorenzo is nowhere to be seen. King Frederik shows the visitors the enlarged enclosures which give the animals so much more freedom. They also see how the birds can go in and out of their coops as they choose. The king proudly tells his guests of the work he and Walter have done to improve the zoo.

Keenan and Simon and Mourice, too, make an appearance as well. Mourice gives some information about the food that the animals and birds need while Keenan and Simon demonstrate how the feeding is done. They hand out some extra portions at every enclosure. This, after receiving a message from the palace to do so. They were informed of King Frederik's plan to visit the zoo with his guests in the afternoon. All the other arrangements, including that all three of them must be there, were made beforehand. Now much praise is going around, for everyone can see how happy those who stay here are.

"This is a really excellent zoo," is the overall opinion. "And to take in all these older animals and birds. To give them a pleasant old age. How commendable."

"They have earned it," King Frederik declares. "Most of these animals have worked in a circus for years and years. Now they can rest and enjoy being pampered and with friends." At every enclosure they are cheerfully greeted. Happiness and bliss surround them.

Walter does not see Rona and Mona, though. Their space next to the other monkeys is empty. "They might be with Bruno," he says to Princess Elina.

"Yes, I think so," is her answer. "We will see them later, probably."

"I really hope so," Walter replies.

"Let me go and look for them," Rita suggests from her place on Princess Elina's shoulder.

"Then I come with you," Bones utters. Having been on Walter's side all this time and with the royal procession moving so slowly, he gets a little impatient. 'A bit of a runabout will be a nice change now,' are his thoughts.

"Right," Walter responds. "You two do that. I would think you find them at Bruno's cabin, go and have a look there first."

"Yes, yes, we will," both Rita and Bruno declare before taking off.

By now, most enclosures have been visited. The elephants on the farther side are trumpeting their approval. That King Fredrik himself is here with his daughter and Walter, along with all these other grand people, is a pleasant surprise for them. Of course, they also totally enjoy the extra tit bits, Keenan and Simon give them. "Well, well," Jumbo remarks, "Is this all because of the coming wedding?"

"Yes," Walter answers, "This festive time is not for us people only. You must also be part of it."

"Good, good," Jumbo says. "I am so glad you think about us as well."

"Yeah," Walter smiles, "how could I ever forget?"

The king's guests are looking on in wonderment. They hear Walter talking to the elephants and it seems he is getting answers too. Princess Elina, noticing some questions here, decides to tell what is happening. "Walter can understand what animals and birds say," she explains. She continues, "You must agree. This is very unusual and outstanding. It also describes exactly my future husband," she adds laughingly.

"Indeed, how very remarkable," is the reaction of the royal visitors. Everybody is highly impressed by all they have seen and heard. So much so that by walking back, there is not much conversation going on. When they land in front of Gordon and Wosa's enclosure, they notice Gordon hurrying towards them. "We had an afternoon snooze," he calls out. "We overslept and did not see you people pass by. Come, come in, won't you?"

"Yes, of course," Walter replies. He adds, "I was wondering where you were."

By this time, Wosa is also at the gate. Walter signals Keenan to open it. After that has been done, he enters and Gordon at once picks Walter up and embraces him. Princes Elina has followed Walter. She, in turn, is lifted up by Wosa and embraced as well. A hush has come over the onlookers. One of the visitors asks King Frederik, "Such enormous animals, is this not very dangerous?"

"No," King Frederik declares; "Walter knows what he is doing. He would never allow my daughter to be in any danger. One can be sure of that!"

Still, not everyone is as convinced about this as the king himself seems to be. So, a sigh of relief goes up, when after a short period, the gorillas put Princess Elina and Walter down again, whereupon they start walking back to the king and his guests. Keenan closes the gate while the gorillas start waving to everyone standing before their enclosure. It does not take long and the visitors wave back with gusto.

Then, the mighty roar of the lions can be heard. Walking over there, the royal guests look in awe as these great animals show off before them. Playing with each other, rolling over each other. Roaring as they do so. It is great entertainment and everyone is hugely impressed. Walter warmly praises the lions for their lively performance. This, they thankfully accept by once more rolling their mighty, thunderous roar over the royal party as they move on.

"Oh, and watch. Who do we have here?" Princess Elina asks after a few moments. From a distance, they see Bruno strolling over to them. Within his arms, as usual, are Mona and Rona. Rita is flying in circles above their heads, while Bones is running in front.

"My, my," Walter grins happily. "There they are then."

As soon as Rona and Mona see them, they jump out of Bruno's arms, darting towards Walter and snuggle into his embrace.

"We overslept," Mona cries.

"We so much did want to come," Rona howls.

"Well, it seems to me, a lot of sleeping is going on here," Walter utters. "I was getting worried, you know."

Bruno, coming nearer, is full of excuses. After bowing respectfully before King Frederik and his party, he addresses Walter and whines. "This should not have happened. I really am sorry, but the cabin is so warm. We had something to eat and then all three of us fell asleep. Otherwise we would have been here, truly."

"No matter," Walter assures his friend. "We are just glad to have you with us at last."

"I barked, to wake them up," Bones says.

"I nabbed them with my beak," Rita twitters.

Princess Elina starts laughing when Walter explains to her what happened. This, while King Frederik and his party, staring in more unbelief, stay a safe distance away.

"This huge bear," one of the royals stammers. "What if he comes over here? Are we not in great danger?"

"No, no," the king tells them. "Bruno is a tame bear. He does not do any harm to anyone!" This is a relief for the king's guests, who now focus on Rona and Mona. They remark to each other how cute these little monkeys are and, "what are they talking about with Walter?" they ask.

"Well," the king smiles, "Who knows, but with my daughter laughing like this, it must be something funny!"

The zoo's visitors all agree with him. The image of the happy couple, surrounded by their animal friends, lingers in their minds when they leave. Carriages are awaiting them at the zoo's entrance and soon the king and his guests are on their way back to the palace. They cannot stop talking about the great encounters on the magnificent tour. No one ever experienced anything like this before.

Keenan and Simon, as well as Mourice, having been given permission by the king to go on with their daily tasks, have left some time ago already.

Princess Elina and Walter, though, stay a bit longer with their friends. As they walk on the tree-lined lanes of the zoo, Walter asks Bruno, "Have you seen Lorenzo today?"

"Oh yes," Bruno replies, "He was in my cabin this morning. He told me he spoke to you about not coming to the palace anymore until after the wedding. What happened? Did he do something wrong again?"

"It was not all that bad," Walter answers. "He just put on another circus Landini performance, at the masked ball. It went wrong, because he flew a bit too low, thereby damaging some ladies' hairstyles."

"Hmm, that must have been a sight to see," Bruno utters.

"Indeed." Princess Elina smiles after guessing Bruno's reaction to this. "It was quite a scene. But please tell Lorenzo, I am not cross with him and neither is anyone else."

"No, need," they hear all of a sudden. From out of nowhere as usual, Lorenzo makes his appearance.

"You have been watching us!" Walter says as his feathered friend settles on one of his shoulders.

"Yes, yes, I have," Lorenzo coos. "Good day Princess," he shouts. "I am so glad to hear, no one is cross with me."

"So am I," Princess Elina smiles. "It is good to see you, Lorenzo."

"Are you coming back to the palace with us now?" Rita asks from Walter's other shoulder.

"No, no, I am fine here at the zoo," Lorenzo answers. "I stay with my friends here until the wedding is over! That is not a problem, is it, Walter?"

"No, no," Walter replies laughingly. "That is not a problem at all, my friend!"

"Right," Lorenzo yells. "We keep it like that then."

Bruno and the two monkeys are happy with his decision. They like having as many of their friends around them as possible.

Bones offers Mona and Rona another ride on his back, knowing how much they love this. The little monkeys shriek with delight when Bones runs away with them. By their return, Walter and Princess Elina decide it is time to go back to the palace. Leaving Bruno and Lorenzo behind is not easy, but leaving Mona and Rona again proves to be even more difficult. Only when Walter promises to come back soon do they stop howling.

Dinner at the palace that evening is filled with lively conversations. They all centre around the amazing tour at the royal zoo. The content smile on King Frederik's face shows how much he enjoys listening to the thrilled comments of his guests. It is late that night before anybody goes to sleep. Another special day has passed.

And there is still more to come. They are taken up with boating on the large lake behind the palace. There are also picnics in the surrounding forest. Horse riding though, proves to be the most favourite pastime.

Now, the training under the watchful eyes of the lady with the horse's act, at circus Landini, stands Walter in good stead. He easily keeps up with the royal visitors. Although his humble background is no secret, he is readily accepted amongst kings and princes alike. As for the royal ladies, they adore him!

Walter is friendly with everyone, but there is only one Princess Elina who forever holds his heart. Bones always goes where Walter goes. Be it running after the horses when the royal party goes riding, or sitting nearby, when there is a picnic taking place. And he quietly waits in the shadow of a tree, when the boats go out onto the lake, never letting Walter out of his sight.

With Rita, it is a different story altogether. She loves being with Princess Elina and the other ladies. Everyone adores her and is competing for her attention. Singing happily, she often flies from the one to the next shoulder, but after a while, always returns to Princess Elina.
In and around the palace, things are getting more hectic by the day. The king's orchestra practice their music. The king's soldiers practise their marches and servants are running in many directions. New uniforms have been given out to all of them to wear on the wedding day. The huge wedding cake has arrived and been set aside in a special room. Time marches on as well. Soon there are just three days to go. Then two, then one.

And then, the great day itself arrives. And a magnificent one at that. The best one for a royal marriage.

From early in the morning, more carriages, with more guests, present themselves. One after the other, the coach's wheels, along with the horses' hooves merrily clattering over the cobblestones. Superb surroundings welcome the guests. Seating is on the green lawns where tables and chairs have been set out. Rose coloured sunshades flutter above them. The tables with tablecloths in a darker rose, carry crystal vases with masses of red and white flowers. Further on, white and red striped tents fly the royal flag on top. This is where master Bernard and his helpers are busy. Huge amounts of food supplies have been brought out here for morning tea and cakes, just after the church service. For a light lunch, a bit later refreshments in the form of fruit juices and punch. Servants keep running here, then there, but master Bernard has everything under control. Huge tubs, overflowing with flowers have been placed at short distances from each other. Such a splendid and festive sight it all is.

The king's orchestra plays joyous music. Tempting refreshments are offered by the smiling servants in their magnificent new uniforms. The merry mood grows stronger and stronger, here and all around. In the villages, in the market square people are laughing and singing. They are happy. Nice and tasty food is handed out to one and all, for free. Fruit juices are also available for all who are thirsty. Those from the other side of the river Yanta, can't believe their luck. They do not even remember when last seeing such an incredible abundance of things to eat. And everyone tucks in happily.

At the palace, things go smoothly. The hard work is done. Now it is a matter of timing each moment. No problems have come up thus far. With master Roland's arrival and him being in command now, they usually do not.

Princess Elina and her ladies are in the bedroom chambers, busy getting Princess Elina dressed. The white wedding gown is dream in silk and organza, with pearls and glittering sequins embroidered all over it. There is the long veil to think of and the lovely, lily-of-the-valley wedding bouquet. The bridesmaids have dresses of the softest green organza, just like the six minor bridesmaids, who will join up with them later.

Walter, still in his rooms, is eager to go. He looks ravishing in his new clothes. A real prince, that is how he feels and that is what he sees in the mirror. Feeling extremely happy and pleased with his appearance, he cannot help but smile at himself.

"Yes, yes," he suddenly hears. "You really look great!" It is the voice of Rita. She, having flown in through an open window, now nestles on his shoulder.

"My, my, Rita," Walter replies. "I thought you would be with Princess Elina today."

"To busy, much too busy there now," Rita answers. "No, to be here with you and Bones is far better."

"That's what I think too," is Bones comment.

"Well, yes, but not always," Rita tells him. "Princess Elina, on other days, is great company."

"Oh, of course," Walter laughs. "But I don't mind to let you know, Princess Elina is terrific company for me at all times."

"Well said," Bones grins. "Well said!"

"Right, right," Rita agrees, "I hear you!" She continues, "Do you not have to go now? You don't want to be late for your own wedding, do you?"

"Never fear," Walter grins. "I shall not, my dear!"

"I must say, you seem very smug," Bones remarks.

"How can it be otherwise?" Walter asks. "It is my wedding day today! The best day of my life! The weather is fine, everything is perfect. What a great time all of us shall have! Old friends are coming, and then there are the new ones which are already here. By the way," he adds, "Are you both coming with me in the carriage just now?"

"No, no," Rita chirps. "I will be flying to the church on my own. I am sure there shall be trees from where I can watch what is happening."

"Oh, and what about you, Bones?" Walter wants to know.

"Don't worry about me," Bones replies. "I will find my own way as well and watch the goings on from under the same tree's, Rita is speaking of!"

"Great, great," is Walter's reply. "I'll be seeing you both then later. Maybe at the show this afternoon?"

But by now, there is a knocking at the door. "Please enter. Th door is open," Walter calls out. It is his new found royal friends, who come in to fetch him. They all look very elegant and chic, b none more so than Walter. They tell him so admiringly and while chatting and joking, escort Walter to the waiting, luxurious coach Together, they journey to the church where the wedding is going to take place. Other coaches are linking up with them, occupied royals who wave and greet Walter. The groom's coach is the first to start moving, followed by the others. The coaches of the king and Princes Elina and her ladies close the procession.

Through the village streets, lined with people, they go. Small children carrying small flags wave as they come into sight. The calls of 'hurray, hurray' fill the air and the crowd's gasp, seeing the carriages with so many beautiful people of nobility pass by. But of course, the most beautiful of all is their own princess.

The applause becomes even louder when the coach with Princess Elina and her father, the king, comes into sight. In front of the large church, the column halts. Through the open doors, organ music flows outside.

Walter and his friends are the first to enter the church. The other guests follow directly afterwards. Now they have to wait for King Frederik and his daughter. It is a sight to behold, as Princess Elina, helped by her bridesmaids, steps down from the carriage. "So lovely and sweet she is," people cheer and sigh.

Amidst much waving, the king and his daughter enter the church as well. Walking down the aisle, on her father's arm, the princess looks as if she has come straight out of a fairy tale. A dream in

At the altar, the king lifts the veil from his daughter's face before delivering her to Walter's side. That this exquisite creature next to him will become his wife is more than Walter can comprehend. 'Is it true?' he asks himself. 'Am I really getting married to this enchanting person?' He feels very proud and thankful that Princess Elina has chosen to become his bride. His smile to her says it all. The sincere and adoring look in her eyes, as she returns his smile, gives him his answer. Then the wedding ceremony engulfs them, making it all come true. All the wishes and hopes they carried for such a long, long time in their hearts.

After the service is over, they are husband and wife!

As such, the married couple drive back to the palace in their own carriage now. The others trail close behind. This time, the cheering is even more enthusiastic. The festive mood is growing by the minute. At the palace grounds, the king's orchestra merrily plays away. Walter and Princess Elina, along with the king, take their place at their special table. Now, everyone who has not already done so, can come to wish them happiness. Walter, while holding Princess Elina's hand, is looking around for some familiar faces from earlier days.

"Don't worry," Princess Elina, guessing his thoughts, says. "All of them are here. You'll see."

Just after uttering these words, amazingly and suddenly, right in front of them, stands none other than Mister Landini. Flamboyant and dashing as always. His wife, at his side, looks very elegant as well.

"Yes, it is us," Mister Landini chuckles. "We have come to congratulate and wish you both happiness forever."

"Thank you, thank you," Princess Elina and Walter respond warmly.

"We are so glad you could come," Princess Elina smiles. Shaking of hands follows and of course, King Frederik takes part in this too.

"Yes, and what about us?" Walter hears another well-known voice ask.

"Judge Martins," he cries out. "And Mrs. Martins. How wonderful to see you." Shaking hands with them as well, the happy couple receive their blessings with a warm smile.

Then they are introduced to the king, which makes them feel very special indeed. "Everybody at home is sending their best wishes," Judge Martins tells them. "Including Max, of course!"

"How is Max?" Walter asks.

"He is well and content, I am glad to say," Mrs. Martins answers.

"Good, I think of him and all of you, often," Walter responds. "Please give everyone our regards. Including Max and his family, of course," he laughs. "My bride, Princess Elina," he adds proudly, "knows all about you and Max and everyone who formed part of my life before I came to the palace. That brings me to father Tobias," he continues. "Did he not come with you?"

"Father Tobias is recovering from an ailment but not able to travel just yet," Judge Martins answers. "He begs to be excused and asked us to bring to you his wishes of joy and happiness forever."

"Thank you," Walter says again, while adding; "Please tell father Tobias he is excused and we hope his health will improve soon!" Then, he sees the others. They are all there, waiting in line, to greet and felicitate them and be greeted in return. How good it is to see these faces again.

Pico is among them and Pedro and Ingrid and her brothers. Also, Madame Emma, who makes the costumes and, 'But really, can it be?' Walter all of a sudden, notices Rosa, the gypsy girl and her husband Marik.

"Oh, my, my, how wonderful," he gushes. "Thank you, thank you all for coming. And thank you, my dear Princess Elina, for becoming my wife," he adds, overflowing with joyful emotion. Everyone is laughing and talking while getting introduced to Princess Elina and the king and the other royals at the table.

Then, afterwards, master Roland arranges for everyone to be seated at a nearby table. A bit further on, some more tables have been set apart. That is where Walter's guests from the other side of the river Yanta have been placed. They are Captain Olivier Smith and his men, the bridge builders. Lieutenant Ferdinand Lopez is with them and then there is Mister Goodman and Oscar as well. Also, the servants from the castle. So many people have come and the festivities proceed with much enthusiasm and gaiety.

The bride and bridegroom are the centre of all this, and both of them feel extremely happy and contented, along with everybody else. A joyous feeling has spread to the zoo as well. Walter and Princess Elina have seen to it that the animals and birds have very special food on this day. Keenan and Simon are not forgotten either, nor is Mourice nor any other person working at the palace or zoo. All of them also received new uniforms and extra fine provisions from the royal kitchen.

And then, on top of all this, there is the afternoon show! Princess Elina, escorted by her maidens, has made a short retreat to her chambers from where she reappears in a more practical, but dreamlike, creation. The dress has a motif of rosebuds, intertwined with soft blue flowers, on it.

"It makes you look like a rosebud yourself, my dearest," Walter tells his radiant bride as they take their place in the carriage, bringing them to the zoo.

Keenan and Simon have spent a lot of time and effort in training all the animals and birds who wanted to be part of this performance. Both wardens learned many things from Walter, and Lorenzo has been a great help. He was the one translating the commands of the wardens, making everything much easier. The result is a pleasant show. Maybe not as good as when Walter was in charge, but still, not bad, not bad at all. The royals, along with the other guests and also the staff working at the palace, appreciate every item on the program.

Then, eventually, Bruno and Bones and the monkeys come on to the stage. Bruno dances, while Bones walks behind the pram with Rona and Mona. They are dressed in the outfits of their circus Landini days. The bonnets on their heads, encircling their adorable little faces, make them look just as cute as in earlier times. A violin player from the king's orchestra plays a lively tune during their performance. Whispers from the audience about this unusual and charming act float around them. But, the viewers get another surprise when Pico suddenly joins the small group. For one last time, he wants to be with his old friends, pepping up their show by prancing and somersaulting around them. He has managed, with the help of master Roland, to whiten his face and broaden his lips with red paint. He even wears a sort of silly striped pyama. His feet look very odd and white as well. The whole display is loved by everyone. Most of all by Walter, who, hand in hand with Princess Elina, watches with admiration.

Lorenzo, although not far away, keeps his distance. Sitting as he does in a nearby big tree, he has a good oversight of what is happening on the stage. Seeing things go smoothly there makes him feel quite content, knowing he did his bit to make it all come true.

Rita has flown to the bride and bridegroom, where she has settled on Princess Elina's shoulder.

"It is a pity you two do not sing and play today," the Princess remarks. Then she goes on; "But once we are at the castle on the other side of the river, I won't let you go off so easily."

"You do not have to," Walter laughs, "As long as you will play the lute or harpsichord with us, my dear, we shall make a splendid trio!"

"Yes, yes," Rita chirps, "It will be great!"

After the show is over, Walter and Princess Elina, along with Rita, slip away to visit their artist friends. They find them all still aglow with the success of their performances. "We enjoyed ourselves so much," Princess Elina says. "You were very good, all of you!"

Rona and Mona quickly jump into Walter's arms. "You liked it too?" they ask.

"It was marvellous," Walter answers.

"Good," Mona sighs.

"We had lots of fun doing it," Rona shouts.

"Lorenzo also helped us," Mona tells Walter.

"My, my," Walter smiles. "Good old Lorenzo. I never knew he would be such a great organizer and help to make this show so successful."

Seeing Pico coming forward, he quickly introduces him. "This is my bride, Princess Elina," he declares proudly. The princess smiles brightly while looking at Walter. To Pico, who shyly bows before her, she says; "I think we have met before at Circus Landini. That was also after the show. I said then, and now say it again, you are a wonderful artist."

"Thank you so much, your Highness," Pico blushes behind his mask of white paint.

"Yes, good work, Pico," Walter also praises his circus friend. "You really pepped up the show, just as you always did," he adds.

"Thank you, thank you," Pico brings out again. Then, bowing anew, he asks, "May I please be excused now?"

"Yes, you may," Princess Elina answers, noticing how uneasy and tense he has become in her presence. With amused faces, she and Walter look on as Pico immediately sprints away.

"He is a great guy," Walter remarks.

"He must be," Princess Elina replies.

"Yes, he is very nice," Mona says.

"We like him," Rona utters.

Then it is Bruno, and Bones who get complimented over their performance. "It was such a pleasure doing this once again," Bones barks.

"It was just great to dance on this, your wedding day," Bruno brings out. He goes on; "And now Walter? We hear you are going away soon?"

"Yes, Bruno, we leave early tomorrow morning," Walter replies. "We have come to say goodbye."

"You are going to soon," Rona wails.

"Yes, well, we have to," Walter answers. "There is so much work waiting on the other side of the river. But, don't be sad," he adds. "We will be coming here often. So you see, it is not a farewell forever."

"That is good," Bruno declares. Putting a big paw around Walter's shoulder, he says, "I wish you and Princess Elina happiness forever."

Princess Elina, although not understanding what Bruno says, reads his face as he looks at her and Walter. She quickly steps closer to him and before he knows it, a royal kiss has been planted on his cheek.

"My, my," Walter laughs, "That, more than anything else, is saying 'thank you Bruno', from us both."

Bruno, totally perplexed, shuffles away in a daze, shyly rubbing his eyes while doing so.

But now, Rona and Mona want a kiss too. Smiling, Princes Elina takes them out of Walter's arms and gives the two little monkeys a cuddle and a kiss. Utterly overwhelmed, they timidly look up at her. Then both of them seek refuge in Walter's arms again. Princess Elina and Walter can't help laughing at the effect of her kisses. Soon afterwards, a round to every enclosure is undertaken. Good byes follow from all sides. From Gordon and Wosa, from the elephants, from everyone. Keenan and Simon are thanked for their efforts and all the good work they do. Then it is time to go.

Bruno waves them out. Rona and Mona, sitting on his shoulders, do the same. Back at the palace gardens, the bride and groom mingle freely amidst their guests. Bones is lying in the shadow of a nearby old tree, ever on the alert that nothing unforeseen will happen to his beloved master and mistress.

Rita, a bit weary of all the goings on today, has placed herself on a branch of this same old tree. "Now we can watch together," she informs Bones. "You from there, me from here."

"Right, good thinking," Bones tells her.

Luckily, nothing unforeseen happens on this so very special day! The hours speed by with talking and laughing and even more talking and laughing. The evening starts with a grandiose dinner in the banquet hall. The most lavish dinner one can think of. Such fine dishes. So much food. In between the flickering candles, a wealth of flowers and beaming faces.

Princess Elina is dressed in her wedding gown again, although this time without the long veil. King Frederik, at the head of the main table, is full of pride and joy. Pride in his beautiful daughter, sitting next to him and joy over her happiness of being married to Walter. This good and handsome young man next to her, who has become so dear to him as well. Later that evening, everyone proceeds to the ballroom. There, on the music performed by the king's own small orchestra, kings and queens dance with each other. The most beautiful gowns, uniforms and other elegant costumes make for a colourful scenery. Sparkling diamonds in tiaras and necklaces give even more glow to the occasion.

Walter and his bride, having opened the dance, can't get enough of whirling around in each other's arms. Their happiness is there for everyone to observe. A sea of friendly faces dance along with them. Among them are those of Judge and Mrs. Martins. Pico and his friends. Ingrid with her fiancée. Her brothers with their girlfriends, as well as many others from the circus. Mister Landini and his wife have a great time and so have the gypsies, Marik and Rosa. A bit later that evening, this couple decide to show the exclusive gathering here, how to dance the flamenco. Their illustrious audience takes it all in with gasps of excitement. The clicking of castanets and the supportive tapping of feet that go with it fill the ballroom. A few members of the orchestra provide the gypsy music and they do very well. Rosa, her deep black hair fixed tight at the back of her head and wearing a long red dress, is a striking figure. Her husband, with his intense eyes and manner, follows Rosa's every move perfectly. They dance, like only gypsies can dance, leaving everyone enraptured.

The festivities go on until the early morning hours. No one is in a hurry to leave and many of the royals will be staying on for a few more days, anyway. Some lovely cottages have been prepared for Judge Martins and Mr. Landini with their spouses. For other guests, lodging for the night is also provided. Master Roland, as always, has worked wonders. Walter and Princess Elina, though, are leaving the palace this evening. So, to all their guests, they say their farewells.

"We'll see one another again and again," is the promise made to most of them. Then bride and bridegroom have to say goodbye to the king. Princess Elina has tears in her eyes as she stands in the embrace of her father. King Frederik's eyes are not dry either.

"The castle on the other side of the river seems now so much closer," he says. "This new bridge makes all the difference. We shall visit each other often."

"Yes," Princess Elina brings out. "We shall, dear Pappa."

"Take your time, with this journey," the king tells Walter. "The two of you have earned a bit of a holiday."

"Thank you, your Majesty," Walter replies. He continues; "Yes well, we thought of making our journey a bit of a sightseeing tour. Stopping here and there, and other places," he ends with a laugh.

"Good, good," King Frederik smiles. "The castle and the woods on the other side of the river Yanta can wait for a week or two."

"That sounds perfect," Princess Elina utters.

"Right," Walter agrees, adding, "But after that, and together, the three of us will make the land on the south side prosperous again."

"Well spoken," is the king's answer. "And yes, that is precisely what we are going to do. Keep well my children. Our thoughts are with you."

"Thank you, your Majesty and farewell," Walter answers. A last kiss from Princess Elina, for her father the king, and then they quietly slip away.

Lorenzo, in the meantime, has joined Rita and Bones. As the ballroom's doors and windows are open on this warm summer evening, they have been able to watch everything that is going on in there. They have seen the newlyweds take their leave from their guests and the king and know what is going to happen next.

"We are going," Bones barks excitedly.

"I can't wait," Lorenzo cries.

"Great, great," Rita sings.

And so it is with great expectations that the three of them hasten themselves to the carriage, standing in front of the palace, ready to take them wherever the royal couple want to go.

Princess Elina, now in a charming travel outfit, is thrilled to have Rita taking place on her shoulder again. She and Walter, both so gay and happy, enter the coach with Bones and Lorenzo following suit. Conrad gives his 'whoa' commands to the horses and they are off.

"Yes, my friends," Walter laughs. "And now we are on the road again. Not walking this time, but still, travelling and wandering." It is a moonlight night and Conrad, having been told by Walter to do so, keeps the horses at an easy pace.

All of them enjoy their ride under this moonlight sky, with stars twinkling at them and being just very happy in each other's company.

After a few hours, though, the first stop is made at a charming inn, where a warm welcome awaits them.

CHAPTER XX

It is only after lunch the following day that they continue their journey. Having decided to take things very easy during this tour, they love every moment of it. They delight in the landscape of this country. The warmth of its people surrounding and greeting them wherever they stop or go. They find pleasure in staying over at the different inns, where there is much laughter and merriment. Taking part in all this and cherishing every moment.

Then, over the wooden bridge, they go into this neglected new homeland that is theirs now. But here also, they receive a friendly welcome from every person they meet, because Walter and his bride are already loved by all the residents.

The reception at the castle is just as great. The royal flag flies at the tower. The red carpet is rolled out. Master Roland has kept his promise. Along with the servants, he is there to greet them.

Flowers abound, while Bernard and his helpers have cooked up a grandiose feast. Table cloths of the finest linen are on the dinner table and exquisite silverware glows in the candlelight. Even the soft music, coming from behind a delicately carved wooden screen, is provided. Everything is exactly as Walter has discussed it with master Roland.

Princess Elina is pleasantly surprised. She praises master Roland over the wonderful service he manages to deliver wherever he goes. She compliments master Bernard on his cooking and steals everybody's heart all over again, just as she did on her first visit.

In the days that follow, Walter and his bride make themselves home in their new surroundings. The rooms, previously occupied by Queen Miranda, have been completely renovated. New painted, new furniture, everything spotless and done in great taste.

"I could not have done it any better myself," Princess Elina declares with a sigh of content.

"Yes. My, my, master Roland has really done exceedingly well," Walter agrees.

Bones even has his own luxurious basket in a small antechamber next to Walter and Princess Elina's rooms. He is more than happy to stay there. More so, because it has a hatchway that gives him the freedom to come and go as he wishes.

Rita and Lorenzo are also feeling at home again in the castle. They happily fly then here, then there, finding lovely fruit and food to eat at the courtyard again. Being with Walter and Princess Elina when these two choose a fine horse each, from the stables and ride for hours. This way, the landscape becomes more and more familiar to them all.

Bones enjoys these outings enormously too. Nose in the wind, he excitedly keeps running next to the horses. Rita and Lorenzo, when not flying around the couple, find a place either on one of the horses or on an empty shoulder. Usually, Lorenzo opts for Walter's, while Rita takes her place on Princess Elina's shoulder. They become quite settled after the first few weeks, and it is then that Walter starts thinking of going back to work. There are so many things needing urgent attention.

He Is happy with the wise men the king has sent over again. Together, they will be able to deal with each issue one by one. It will take a long time, though, before this part of the country is restored to normality. He knows this and so does the king and his wise men.

King Frederik has already visited them once. He is full of praise for the newly built bridge and also satisfied with the progress he notices. Finding his daughter, the Princess Elina and Walter so obviously happy with each other, makes him happy too. The three of them consult like in the olden days, when Walter helped to plan the new zoo enclosures. They come up with many good ideas.

Then, the king's advisers are consulted. "Is what they suggest practical and if so, what is the best way to achieve the desired results?" Together they make a fine team, working for the good of the people.

Walter and Princess Elina also visit the king every few months or so. Bones and Rita, as well as Lorenzo, always come with them. Naturally, a trip to the zoo is then one of the first things they undertake. And so much happiness this brings always. It is hard to say who is more excited then, people, animals, or birds.

Bruno and the monkeys are doing well, and yes, the whole zoo is thriving. Even Oscar the owl is here. Having found the zoo and so many new friends, he is staying for a while. Knowing what a great help he has been to Walter, Princess Elina greets him like an old friend too. They talk for some time and then go on with their tour. Gordon and Wosa, are called on next. It always is a joyful occasion to see them again.

Rona and Mona, are feeling so at home in the zoo now. Everyone is their friend. With Bruno, it is the same. That he is loved by one and all, is very clear. But, age seems to be catching up with Bruno lately and he moves much slower than before. Still, at the zoo, he is fine. After all, everyone takes it easy here.

Walter and Princess Elina are glad Bruno is content. They also understand this is where he belongs now. To take him away, even for a short time, would not be in his best interests. For Rona and Mona, it is the same. So, with confidence and peace of mind, they leave them in Keenan and Simon's good care.

After these visits, they always return with renewed energy for the tasks ahead, to the land on the other side of the river Yanta. Both Walter and Princess Elina love their new life. They love each other and yes, as in all good stories,

They live happily ever after!

494

THE END

www.ingramcontent.com/pod-product-compliance
Lightning Source LLC
Chambersburg PA
CBHW040930050726
47507CB00022B/275